LA GRANGE
PUBLIC LIBRARY

10 West Cossitt Avenue
La Grange, IL 60525
lagrangelibrary.org 708.352.0576

Woman Chased by Crows

AN ORWELL BRENNAN MYSTERY

Also by Marc Strange

Sucker Punch
Body Blows
Follow Me Down

MARC STRANGE

Woman
Chased by
Crows

AN ORWELL BRENNAN MYSTERY

ECW PRESS

Published by ECW Press
2120 Queen Street East, Suite 200, Toronto, Ontario, Canada M4E 1E2
416-694-3348 / info@ecwpress.com

LIBRARY AND ARCHIVES CANADA CATALOGUING IN PUBLICATION

Strange, Marc
Woman chased by crows / Marc Stange.

I. Title.

PS8637.T725W64 2012   C813'.6   C2011-906971-7

ISBN: 978-1-55022-969-1
also issued as:
978-1-77090-244-2 (PDF); 978-1-77090-245-9 (EPUB)

Cover and text design: Tanja Craan
Cover images: ballerina © Masterfile; crow © Shane Link/iStockphoto; gem © Andrew Reese/iStockphoto
Printing: Friesens   5   4   3   2   1

The publication of *Woman Chased by Crows* has been generously supported by the Canada Council for the Arts which last year invested $20.1 million in writing and publishing throughout Canada, and by the Ontario Arts Council, an agency of the Government of Ontario. We also acknowledge the financial support of the Government of Canada through the Canada Book Fund for our publishing activities, and the contribution of the Government of Ontario through the Ontario Book Publishing Tax Credit. The marketing of this book was made possible with the support of the Ontario Media Development Corporation.

Canada Council   Conseil des Arts
for the Arts   du Canada   Canadä   ONTARIO ARTS COUNCIL
                                                  CONSEIL DES ARTS DE L'ONTARIO

PRINTED AND BOUND IN CANADA

for Karen

Acknowledgements

For friendship, assistance and favours too numerous to list here, I offer my deepest appreciation to the following accomplices: Fred Petersen, Bob Séguin, Lisa Murray and Ian Sutherland

He had almost nothing left.

Only the sapphire and a couple of diamonds, maybe three, he didn't know how many, he hadn't opened the bag in a while. If Louie was still talking to him, maybe he could sell him one. The troll wasn't answering his phone. Probably monitoring his calls. Still pissed off. Couldn't make it over to the Danforth, anyway. No cash. What a ridiculous situation.

He had three stones worth a fortune, maybe five stones — it was time he looked — a nice diamond, not too big, easy to move. One carat, maybe. Louie would give him five for it, surely. No he wouldn't. Louie would know he was desperate. He would take advantage. He was a thief after all, what do you expect? But three hundred at least. *Something.* He needed to eat, he needed to pay for this shitty motel room, he needed to get away. Get away — what a great plan. Look where he was: back where he started, a cab ride from the very place he had jumped the fence. Except that he couldn't afford a cab ride. A fortune in stones, and he was broker than the panhandler on the corner.

It was time he checked the package to see what was left. Please Jesus, there was one small diamond that he could sell in a hurry, without attracting too much attention. He opened the closet and took down the shelf above the clothes rack, dragged over a chair and stood on it, reached up and pushed the cheap cardboard ceiling tile out of the way, felt around in the dust and mouse droppings until he found the cloth bag, climbed off the chair and spilled the contents onto the stained chenille bedspread. Good! Two diamonds. *Two* of them. One of them was small enough, one-and-a-half carats probably, maybe a bit less. Such a waste, selling it for a fraction of what it was worth, but a man has to survive. The sapphire was too big to just give away. He needed to get somewhere. Montreal. If he was careful, he could survive in Montreal. There was someone there who could afford it.

"Been waiting all night for you to come home," said the visitor who came out of the bathroom.

"Oh Christ!" he said. "You scared the shit . . ."

"Is that all of them?"

"That's all that's left."

"You're sure?"

"I swear."

"Put them back in the bag."

"Just leave me one, please, the small diamond. I need some cash so I can pay for this shitty room. I need some cash so I can eat something."

"No, you don't," said his guest, and shot him in the head.

*It is always the ruby that takes centre stage in an ornament. The rest —
pearls, sapphires, even diamonds — dance attendance upon a great ruby
like a corps de ballet.*

*It is safe to say that Newry County doesn't harbour many rubies, and
that whatever red stones are held in the jewellery cases and safety deposit
boxes of Dockerty's upper crust, they are neither large, nor legendary, nor,
in some cases, genuine. Certain of the dowagers residing on The Knoll are
known to have good pieces: Mrs. Avery Douglas is the current custodian
of a five-strand natural pearl necklace, a Douglas family heirloom worthy
of at least five burglary attempts over the years, including the recent,
unprosecuted break-in by their crack-smoking second cousin; Doris
Whiffen has a tiara once worn to a reception at Windsor Castle, but not
by her; and Edward Urquehart has thirty-odd carats in loose diamonds
along with his Krugerrands in a safety deposit box at the Bank of
Commerce. None of these are paltry, and some are truly precious, but if
all the gems held in all the private safes in Dockerty were heaped upon
a table, they would not begin to approach the value of a certain chunk of
pigeon's blood corundum. Not in dollars, not in legend, not in human life.*

*In an early year of the nineteenth century, a man whose name is now lost
in the dust of history picked up a loose stone bigger than his fist from
a scattering of detritus near a limestone cliff north of Mandalay. Even
in the rough, it glowed like a hot coal. It is estimated that it weighed at*

that time over four hundred carats. A master cutter produced three notable gems from it: an elegant twenty-three-carat cushion cut that is still part of the Iranian National Treasure, a round stone of eighteen carats once stolen by Clive of India, and a masterpiece of ninety-seven carats, one of the largest rubies ever known. Not a garnet, not a spinel like the Black Prince's legendary stone, but a true ruby, a gem of perfect colour. But size was not its most significant characteristic. In its heart there was a star. Star rubies are among the rarest gems on the planet, and most are small. The Sacred Ember, as it came to be known, was peerless, unique, priceless.

One

Monday, March 14

Orwell Brennan's parking space under the chestnut tree offered a generous mix of March's bounty — icy puddles, crunchy slush, broken twigs from last night's blow. He dunked his left foot ankle-deep in scummy water getting out of his vehicle. This made him dance awkwardly onto the dry pavement, at which point he looked heavenward. Mondays always start out bad. Laura used to say that, usually with a laugh. His first wife was killed by a drunk driver late on a Sunday night. That long ago Monday morning had started out very bad. On a scale of one to ten, a soaker didn't register.

Spring was Orwell's second-favourite time of year; a season full of the things he looked forward to all the long Ontario winter — an unselfish angle to the sunrise, spring training in Dunedin, the ospreys circling the big nest near RiverView Lodge. As with most men his age, the arrival of spring signalled a victory of sorts and he routinely breathed more deeply as the vernal equinox drew near. The sodden pant cuff slapping his ankle as he climbed the stairs to his office reminded him that he was a tad previous in his anticipation. It wasn't spring yet. Hitters might be looking for their swings and pitchers working on their stuff in the Florida sunshine, but Newry County was still salted sidewalks and distressed footwear.

"In early, Chief." Sergeant George was a tall, cadaverous man with a face like a basset hound; baggy eyes and dewlaps.

"I am a bit, aren't I?" Orwell said without elaboration. He headed for his office. "Did you leave me any shortbreads, Jidge?"

"Not following, Chief."

The office door clicked shut. Sergeant George saw the Chief's extension light up briefly and then blink out. The Chief was back again almost immediately scanning the outer office.

"Something I can help you with, Chief?"

"Paper towels? Rag? I've got a wet shoe."

"Got Kleenex."

"That'll do." Orwell accepted a wad of tissues, put his left foot on a chair and did what he could to dry his leather. "Beats me how the bag always gets so nicely folded when you work the night desk." He tossed the wet paper into a wastebasket.

"Seen the *Register* this morning, Chief?"

"Why no, Jidge, I haven't."

Sergeant George held up a fresh copy of the paper. "Didn't think you and Donna Lee were that chummy," he said.

The front page featured a shot of Mayor Bricknell and the Chief, both smiling, each holding one handle of a trophy. Dockerty High had won its first basketball tournament in ten years. The award ceremony had taken place Saturday night and evidently nothing sufficiently newsworthy had happened in the intervening thirty-six hours to knock it off page one.

"Didn't think she was going to be there," Orwell said.

"Wouldn't miss a chance like that. Not in an election year."

The flag out front snapped in the brisk and chilly wind, the trailing end of a March gale that had the house moaning all night long. He stood for a moment next to the bronze plaque bearing the likeness of his predecessor, Chief Alastair Argyle, noting that a pigeon had recently saluted the great man. To Orwell's eye, the white stripe across the former chief's cheek wasn't unattractive, rather it gave the dour face a gallant aspect, like a duelling scar, a Bismarck *schmiss*.

As was his custom, Roy Rawluck arrived marching, no other word for it, striding out of the parking lot, heels clicking, arms swinging, sharp left wheel to the entrance. "Bright and early, Chief," Roy said with a nod of approval. It was rare that Orwell arrived before his staff sergeant.

"Sharp breeze this morning, Staff," he said. "*Fresh*, as the farmers put it."

"Coming or going, Chief?" Roy was frowning, just now noticing the desecration of his late boss's memorial.

"Going, Staff. Soon to return."

From the other side of Stella Street, Georgie Rhem was waving his walking stick. Orwell could tell it was Georgie by the feathers on his Tyrolean hat and the distinctive kink in his hawthorn stick. The jockey-tall lawyer was otherwise hidden by the sooty drift lining the curb. "Soon to return," Orwell repeated, heading across the street. Roy marched inside to get his can of Brasso. Argyle's face would be shining again in no time.

"Where to, Stonewall?" Georgie wanted to know. "Timmies? Country Style? The Gypsy Tea Room isn't open yet."

Banked piles of snow followed the concrete walkways on the shaded side of the Armoury, dirty, spotted, stained and slushy, revealing as they melted a winter's worth of litter and unclaimed dog scat. Orwell detected, or thought he did, a tinge of yellow in the willow near the fountain.

"First to leaf, last to leave," he said.

"Say what?"

"It's what Erika says. That willow's yellowing up."

"Jaundice, likely," Georgie said.

"Not the prettiest time of year, I'll admit," said Orwell.

"Think she's had some work done?" Georgie was stopped at a campaign placard planted beside the walkway on spindly wire legs.

"Who? Donna Lee?"

"She looks prettier than usual, don't you think?"

The poster read: "Reelect Mayor Donna Lee Bricknell ~
Experience + Commitment = Consistency."

Orwell tilted his head. The Mayor's photograph was flattering and
he suspected some technical process had smoothed her wrinkles
a bit, but having spent an unpleasant hour with the woman
the previous Friday in her office, he was pretty sure she hadn't
undergone any facelifting. "Looks the same to me," he said.

"Don't think this reelection's going to be the simple formality
it was in years gone by," said Georgie.

"How many will this make?"

"She's got six terms under her belt." He tapped the placard
with his stick and resumed walking. "This would be number
seven."

"Think she could lose?"

"Possibility," Georgie said. He pointed at an opposing
campaign poster on the other side of the park. A handsome
young man with an expensive haircut beamed at the world in
general. "Young Mr. Lyman over there has the blood of career
politicians in his veins. Son of a sitting MP, grandson of a senator.
I smell ambition."

"Wouldn't think a small town mayor's job would be big
enough."

"Gotta start somewhere, Stonewall." They waited for the light
to change at the intersection. "Hell, he's only twenty-six. Be in
Ottawa before he's thirty-five."

"No six terms for him," said Orwell.

Anya was on the couch. "It was gone for almost a year, now it is
back." She fidgeted. The psychiatrist wouldn't let her smoke.

In her dream the man has no face and there are shadows

across his eyes. In her dream she is always ready for him, bathed and scented, wearing a white nightgown like a bride, lying on top of the covers, her feet bare, her pale gold hair across the crisp linen pillowcase, her hands tucked under her buttocks, her eyes open as he enters the dark room. When he raises the pistol to kill her, she lifts herself as if to meet her bridegroom's beautiful hands. And when he pulls the trigger she wakes up, lost, missing him.

"Every night?"

"No. Not every night. But often. Enough. Often enough."

"Once a week?"

"More than that. Just not every night. Some nights he does not come." She stood up, rolling her neck and shoulders as if waking from a fretful sleep. "I am going outside to have a cigarette now."

"You can wait a bit longer. We're almost done for today." The psychiatrist drew a square on her notepad and filled in the space with crosshatching. "And you never see his face?"

"It does not matter. It will not matter. It could be anyone. They can send anyone." Anya moved around the room, a restless cat. "They could look like anyone. Young, old, a woman even. In my dream it is a man always, but they could send a woman." She stopped at the window. "But in my dream it is a man."

"Who are *they*?"

"I cannot tell you that. It is probably dangerous for you that I talk at all."

"It's all right."

"You think it is all right because you think I am delusional. You think the assassin is in my mind."

"Isn't the assassin already dead?"

"They will send another one."

After Anya left, the psychiatrist labelled the cassette case and filed the session with the others. There were almost a hundred now. Some of them had red tags. This one didn't rate a red tag.

The case of Anya Daniel was a personal commitment for the

doctor and in a very real sense the only responsibility worthy of her talent. Were it not for Anya and her "special" situation, she wouldn't spend another day in this tiny, empty, backward little town. Some day, if things worked out, she might produce a paper, or even a book (with all the names changed, of course) detailing the bizarre elements of the case. The truly unique aspects would be fascinating, and not only to the psychiatric community.

They walked their coffees back through Armoury Park, Orwell acknowledging the occasional wave or nod of a passerby with his customary magnanimity, Georgie bouncing a few steps ahead, the scrappy flyweight of fifty years back still evident in his step. "Shouldn't be that big a deal, Stonewall," he said. "Not like you're planning a housing development."

"Thin edge of the wedge is how the township views it," Orwell said. "You'd think it'd be a simple matter to build a second house on your own property."

"I'm sure there'll be some leeway if it's for a family member."

"Claim they're merely protecting the farmland."

"Tell you what, my friend," Georgie said. "They're fighting a losing battle. New highway goes in, you're just close enough to be a bedroom community. Won't be too many years."

"That's what they're concerned about, and I sympathize, but hell's bells, a man wants to build his daughter a house on his own land, it should be a right."

"Hey, if they turn you down, we'll sue. Happy to take it to the Supreme Court. That'd be a helluva ride. But I'm not that lucky. My guess, they'll get one look at you in your brass and gold — you *will* remember to wear the dress blues when you make your pitch?"

"I'll bedazzle them."

"— and they'll rubber stamp the application forthwith."

"Forthwith."

"Even so, you're going to want all your ducks in a nice straight line. Everything they could possibly want — pictures, plans, estimates, maps, all the forms filled out."

"Hate forms."

"World's built outta forms. Beats me how you've come so far."

"It's a wonder," said Orwell.

Georgie spun around, planted his feet, grinned, threw a soft left jab at his big friend's chest. "I guess congratulations are in order."

Orwell shrugged. "Not quite. I may be jumping the gun. They haven't exactly set a firm date."

"Dragging their feet, are they?"

"Being prudent, I guess. Patty's had one bad marriage, can't blame her for thinking things through."

"Is there no escaping the man?" Georgie was pointing. Orwell looked over his shoulder to find Gregg Lyman's face smiling at him. Lyman's campaign placards were twice the size of Donna Lee's. His campaign colours were blue and silver, his slogan was "A Breath of Fresh Air," his image had a healthy glow. "There's been money spent," said Georgie.

"His?"

"Well, the family's, I guess."

Sam Abrams, the burly bearded owner and managing editor of *The Dockerty Register*, was heading their way, briefcase bulging, overcoat flapping, delicately stepping around wet spots on dainty feet. Graceful as a dancing bear, thought Orwell.

"*Register* going to endorse anyone, Sam?" Georgie asked.

"It's a one-paper town, Georgie — I can't afford to take sides. Fair and impartial, right down the line."

"Coulda fooled me with that front page this morning."

"Hey, the Kingbirds don't win a championship every year."

"Oh? Is *that* who won? Looked like Donna Lee was getting

the trophy."

"She wasn't scheduled to show up, was she, Chief?"

Orwell shook his head. "There I was, ready to hand the loving cup to the captain, and I find myself in a tug-of-war. Hope that's the last of it."

"Wouldn't count on it, Stonewall."

"I'll make sure Gregg Lyman gets a photo-op real soon," Sam said. "As soon as he does something even vaguely civic."

"Well, you and the Chief here are required to tippy-toe," said Georgie. He gave his walking stick an airy twirl. "Happily, I don't have to be circumspect. I can come right out and say I don't much care for either one of them. Tell you one thing though, young Lyman didn't get that haircut in this town."

"That'll cost him one vote, anyway," Orwell said.

"Doesn't buy his suits here, didn't get his teeth capped here. Doesn't even live here."

"I hear he's shopping for a house," Sam said with a grin. He did a dainty dance around a patch of mud and headed off to work.

"He should sublet first," Georgie called after him.

Georgie and the Chief parted company at a fork in the path; Georgie off to feed cruller crumbs to the birds and squirrels, Orwell heading back to the station. Gregg Lyman's visage confronted Orwell twice more before he reached Stella Street. He doubted the sincerity of the man's smile. He reminded himself that the coming election had nothing to do with him. He maintained as conspicuous a remove from Dockerty politics as was possible for a man in the employ of Dockerty politicians. He kept his dealings with the mayor's office businesslike and his relations with elected officials excessively polite. He refused to be drawn into conversations that might indicate which way he was leaning. In private, and to those close to him, he freely admitted that the Mayor was a thorn in his side, a stone in his shoe and an occasional gumboil, but publicly he was never less than loyal.

And while he had often entertained thoughts of a world without Donna Lee's annoying voice, the prospect of dealing with a new office holder, and one so obviously determined to climb the political ladder, gave him pause. He could do business with Donna Lee, he was accustomed to her, and their differences were clearly defined — she thought he was a sexist pig, and he knew she was a shrew.

Orwell was as convinced that he *wasn't* a misogynist as no doubt Donna Lee was that she didn't have a shrewish bone in her body. How could he be sexist? He lived and thrived in a house of women, his best investigator was a woman, he dealt with women every day — hell, half the storekeepers and waitresses in town smiled and fluttered when he walked in. He was a prince, he was certain of it: fair, respectful, non-patronizing. He had been confident enough of his gender-neutral behaviour to ask his youngest, Leda, Voice of the Oppressed, if she thought he was sexist.

"Well, Dad, you *are* a ma-an." Leda dragged the word out like a schoolyard taunt.

"Can't do anything about that," he said reasonably. He'd been driving the seventeen-year-old home from the Dockerty Little Theatre. She had auditioned, convincingly she thought, for the part of Emily in *Our Town*. Drama was her forte, although she had a tendency to declaim. Orwell worried that she might have picked it up from him.

"It's not your fault," she said kindly. When he started laughing, she gave him a critical look. "But that laugh, the one you're doing now, you don't think it's maybe a bit condescending?"

"How so?"

"Has a sort of 'oh isn't she just the cutest thing' sound to it."

"I was amused."

"In a paternalistic way."

"Right. Me. Father. Laughing."

"Okay, so maybe I can deal with it on those terms, but how

about women who aren't related by blood or marriage? You give them that indulgent chuckle, too?"

"Oh heck, that's just me. I don't patronize — how could I and survive in our house?"

"You indulge us."

"And that's a bad thing?"

"I'll let you know in a few years."

Not the ringing endorsement he'd been fishing for perhaps, but she hadn't exactly reproached him for being an indulgent father. She merely pointed out that he sometimes adopted an air of, oh well, call it *condescension* if you want to be critical. He preferred to see it as the warm and gracious outward manifestation of his need to protect and provide. There were moments of course, late at night usually, when he acknowledged that he could sometimes be a bit . . . what did Erika call it? *Herrisch.* One of those many-layered German words, the simplest definition of which was "manly," but seemed to encompass "imperious," "overbearing," "pompous," "domineering," and a few dozen other concepts that, he had to admit, were clearly implied in his daughter's pronunciation of the word "ma-an."

Anya walked from the psychiatrist's office to her studio. It was a dancer's stride: exaggerated turnout, shoulders back, head high and floating, almost motionless. She changed directions arbitrarily, side streets and lanes, dodging traffic, checking reflections in the store windows, ever watchful, never the same route twice. She was wearing what she wore most days — sweater, tights, a black and grey wraparound skirt, a plain wool coat, flat shoes to nurse her perpetually sore toes. In *Giselle* she wore flowers in her hair. In *Swan Lake* she wore egret feathers and a tiara. She had no use for fashion.

She cut across the parking lot behind Sleep Country. Two

men were loading a huge mattress into a truck. She wondered briefly if a bed like that might help her sleep, but she doubted it. Her problem couldn't be mended by pocket springs and foam padding. She turned into the narrow walkway separating Laurette's Bakery and Home Hardware — Vankleek Street at the far end — but a feathered black lump was lying on a grate, blocking the way.

Dead crow. Very bad omen in a world of bad omens. She sidestepped. For one thing, stay clear of dead birds. Some kind of virus was going around. What was it? West Nile, Avian something, Chinese chicken flu? If you paid attention to all the warnings you heard in one day you would go mad. Diseases, tornadoes, terrorists, escaped criminals — it is amazing any of us gets through a day. But a dead crow carried more than disease. It did not matter if it was killed by a mosquito or a train, it was in her path. On the roof above, other crows were looking down and making crow noises. Blaming me, she thought. Every dead crow is my fault. Go to hell. You get killed, it is your own stupidity, or bad luck, or bad planning, or bad friends. I am not responsible.

On the corner across from the Gusse Building, she lit a cigarette and lifted her eyes to the studio window on the third floor. No movement. No shadows. Three girls were waiting beside the florist shop on the other side, waiting for her to let them in. Just three. Two of them were hopeless, the third one was graceful but too tall. She should tell their parents, but she needed the money. She caught movement behind her.

"*Salut, Mademoiselle.*"

It was the Chinese girl, the one with promise, missed three classes with a sore foot. Get used to it. Anya smiled, the first smile of her day, happy to see her star pupil, the only one who might some day dance, barring the thousand hurdles and pitfalls. "*Salut Christine,*" she said. "How is your foot?"

"Much better, thank you."

"I am happy to hear it." The light turned green. Anya motioned to the crosswalk. *"Continué. J'arriverai bientot."*

"Oui, Mademoiselle," said Christine. She crossed the street to stand with the other three. They were waving at their teacher. Anya nodded graciously and then turned her back to look at the travel brochures in Dawson's window and finish her cigarette. A ship was sailing the blue Caribbean, happy golden couples danced on a beach somewhere, silver planes promised smooth flying to paradise. She blew smoke at the glass and her reflection came into focus. A petite blonde woman with pale, watchful eyes, eyes that missed nothing, took in everything, eyes that immediately saw the dark car drive by and the tall man behind the wheel. That hair: unmistakable.

Georgie said he was preparing a list of what Orwell would need to make his case: plot map, maybe even a survey, photographs, estimate of house size — now how the hell would he know that? That was Patty's decision. He didn't know what kind of house she wanted. Maybe she didn't want a house at all. Maybe he was just being Big Daddy again, throwing his not inconsiderable bulk around. Maybe he should mind his own business.

"Chief? Mayor Bricknell on line one."

"Thank you, Dorrie, just what I need to brighten my day." He knew what that was about. She was trying to wheedle him into an appearance at a conference on civic beautification. "Madam Mayor, I'm sure your presence will be more than enough to persuade the good citizens to tidy up their front yards."

"It's much more than that, Chief Brennan, I want a concerted effort at fixing up some of our more distressed areas."

"I support your vision for a prettier Dockerty and I assure you that the DPD will do what's necessary to facilitate whatever course you and the good ladies of the . . . what is it again?"

"The Dockerty Restoration Society."

"Yes, an admirable organization to be sure."

"You'd only have to put in a brief appearance."

"I know, just long enough for a photo-op."

"I'm sure I don't know what you mean."

"Donna Lee, I truly wish you well in the upcoming election, I mean that, but you already have a picture with me looking supportive. I don't like being co-opted as a tacit backer of your campaign. And I definitely don't want to be trotted out like a prize bull every time you need your picture in the paper."

After he hung up he wondered if he could have handled the exchange with more tact, but he tended to feel that way after most of his encounters with Mayor Bricknell. It was still a month until voting day. A long month.

"Chief?" Dorrie again. "There's a Detective Delisle from Metro Homicide in town. He said he was checking in."

"Well now, that might distract me for a moment from the usual travail." He opened his door and checked the big room. "He here?"

"Just missed him, Chief," Dorrie said. She was wearing a powder blue sweater set. "I didn't want to interrupt your chat with the Mayor."

"Most considerate." Orwell noted, as he often did, how very tidy his secretary looked, not a hair out of place. "Have I seen that sweater before?" he asked.

"Probably. You gave it to me for Christmas."

"Ah," he said.

"Your wife may have helped you pick it out," Dorrie said.

"Yes, as I recall I was going to get you a karaoke machine." Dorrie didn't laugh. It was one of Orwell's missions in life to make her smile. She rarely did. "This detective . . ."

"Delisle," she said. "Paul Delisle, Metro Homicide." She articulated clearly. "Said he was hungry, be back after he had some lunch."

Orwell checked his watch. "Hmm. I'm a mite hungry, too," he

said. "Know where he was planning to eat?"

"I told him to try the Hillside."

"What's he look like?"

"Can't miss him, Chief: redhead, taller than you even, looks like a basketball player."

"That colour suits you," he said.

"Thank you," she said. "And may I say that green tie suits you."

Orwell thought he detected the briefest flicker of a smile on his secretary's face, but he could have been mistaken.

Paul Delisle *had* been a helluva basketball player. Good ball-handler for all his size, decent outside shot, not afraid to stick his face in there. Went all the way through college on his rebounding and his outlet pass. He still had a floating grace in the way he moved, his head was always up, expressive wrists, wide square shoulders. He was sitting by the corner window with an angle on the bridge to his right and a long view of Vankleek for three blocks west.

"Detective? I'm Orwell Brennan, understand you were looking for me. Don't get up."

"Chief. Pleasure. Paul Delisle."

Delisle put down his hamburger, wiped his hand and extended it across the table. The two hands together were the size of a picnic ham.

"Mind if I sit down?"

"Oh yeah, please. You don't mind me eating?"

"Hell, I'm here to eat, too," Orwell said. "Doreen, sweetie, give me a small steak, tell Leo it's for me — he knows how I like it."

"Anything to drink, Chief?"

"Canada Dry, lots of ice. Thanks. Cut your hair. Looks nice."

"Thanks," Doreen said. She fluffed her new look as she headed for the kitchen.

"You know everybody in town, don't you? I watched you walking this way."

"Small town. I'm easy to spot."

"Me too," Delisle said, "but I'm more anonymous."

"That's the big city for you. So. How can I help you? You looking for somebody?"

"It's sort of complicated." He looked out the window at the Little Snipe flowing past. "There's a ballet teacher in town. Calls herself Anna Daniel these days."

"She a witness? Suspect?"

"Tell you the truth, I don't know what the hell she is." Delisle stared out at the river. "It's probably a waste of time."

"Something personal with you?" Orwell asked.

"Anna Daniel used to be with the Kirov or the Bolshoi or one of those, twenty-five, maybe thirty years ago," Delisle began.

"*Anya.*"

"Say again?"

"Her name. Not Anna, An-ya. I've met her," Orwell said. "My youngest daughter, Leda, took some classes before deciding she'd rather save the world than do pliés." Orwell's steak arrived, charred on the outside, red in the middle, salad on the side. He had foregone the excellent baked potato and sour cream he would have liked. He was trying to lose a few kilos. Again. "Where's your partner?"

"I had some vacation time coming."

"So this is personal."

"What'd you think of *Anya*?"

"Can't say we talked much. She was forthright. Said Leda was too tall, uncoordinated and had an attitude."

"Does she?"

"My daughter? Definitely. The teacher, too. I like people with attitude. She defected, right?"

"1981, did a Baryshnikov in Toronto, asked for asylum."

"She a citizen now?"

"Oh yeah, that's all square. The Russians didn't make much of a fuss. Not a *big* star."

Orwell attacked his six ounces of rare beef and, for appearance's sake, a few bites of salad. "What's the interest?"

"She confessed to a homicide."

Orwell blinked. "She did? When was this?"

"Six years ago. In the city. Before she moved up here. Somebody dead in High Park. She was questioned."

"Why?"

"Routine. She lived close to where it happened. She was seen in the park, walking in the park, no big deal, she wasn't a suspect, we were questioning people in the neighbourhood, just routine, and out of the blue she confesses."

"To you?"

"It was a follow-up interview after the uniform cops had canvassed the neighbourhood. Uniform made a note that she'd acted a bit weird and might be worth a second visit. My partner and I knocked on her door, she comes to the door with a drink in her hand, sees the badges and says, 'Ah, there you are at last.' We give her the just routine ma'am, follow up visit, in case you may have remembered something, and out of the blue she says, 'I know what you are talking about. I know the man you are talking about. I killed him.'"

"Holy cow."

"Well, ah yeah, but it didn't check out. Everything was wrong with her story. She said she shot him, the guy was strangled, big guy, strangled, she's a small woman, no way she strangles somebody that size. The body had been moved, no way she *moves* a guy that size. She took a polygraph, she lies about everything. Nothing checks out. She didn't have a gun. She had an alibi but she didn't use it, the super in her building says she was moving furniture, tying up the service elevator, he saw her five, ten times that day. She's a loon."

"I know she's seeing a psychiatrist," Orwell said. "Dr. Ruth." Delisle raised his eyebrows. "That's her *last* name. Lorna Ruth. Anyway, Lorna's in the medical building near the campus. Evangeline Street."

"She won't tell me anything, probably."

"No, she won't. I just mention it. You saying she was a loon. You want coffee?" Delisle nodded, distracted. "Doreen, couple of coffees?"

"Got Dutch apple pie, Chief."

"Temptress. But I am strong. Maybe next week. You want dessert?" Delisle shook his head, his thoughts still elsewhere. "Where's your partner in all this?"

"What? Oh, Dylan? He's retired. Six years ago. O'Grady. Black Irishman. Literally. Afro-Irish. Big guy, your size, used to play tackle for the Argos. Dylan O'Grady. Know him?"

"Vaguely. Don't think he played very long."

"Broken toe did him in. Believe that? Worked out in the end. Did his twenty as a cop, went into politics. He's a city councillor now, but I hear he's running for a vacant seat in Ottawa."

"The big time."

"Yeah, he's a go-getter." Delisle sounded dubious.

The coffees arrived as well as two bite-size portions of Dutch apple pie on saucers. "Just so's you two know what you're missing." Doreen walked away, fluffing her hair again. Orwell savoured the single bite. "The guy in the park," Orwell said, licking the corner of his mouth. "You ever find the real killer?"

"Oh sure we did, not for that one, but we found a strangler, a big gay dude, eight months later for another one, and for one more that the guy didn't finish off and the victim lived to testify. Messed up his life, but he stood up, testified, give him that."

"You should try the pie," Orwell said. Delisle shook his head. Not interested. Orwell popped Delisle's sample into his mouth. Be a shame to let it go to waste. "So you closed the first case, too," he said, wiping his lips.

"Not officially, he wouldn't cop to the guy in the park but we're pretty sure it was him."

"So if she didn't do it, what's the interest?"

"Well, we've got this other case, still open, two years previous, guy got himself shot, out in the Beaches. I was checking her out and her name pops up in this other file. She confessed to that one, too. Said she strangled him."

Orwell shook his head and stifled a laugh. "So she's on record of having confessed to two different murders, only she got the methods wrong?"

"Or backwards."

"Got anything else?"

"Oh yeah. Turns out we've got a file on this woman four inches thick. From September 13, 1987, to October 27, 1995, she called 9-1-1 fifty-four times. Prowlers, assaults, stalkers, rapists following her, assassination attempts. Fifty-four."

"How many responses?"

"Actual investigations? Maybe seven. Patrol logs, maybe another fifteen. She wasn't ignored, at least not at first, but after a couple of years she was kind of established, a crank, not to be taken too seriously, paranoid delusion, persecution complex, chronic confessor, that kind of evaluation."

"Sounds like she was going through a bad patch," said Orwell. "She seems to be functioning all right in Dockerty. Opened a dance school, teaches ballet to the kids, ballroom dancing for the grownups. Never any trouble as far as I know."

Delisle looked away from the river and the bridge and wherever his mind had travelled. "She says she did something in her homeland that will never be forgiven, they're going to send assassins after her to make her pay."

"The body in the park, guy was an assassin?"

"Not hardly. Stockbroker. Riverdale. Wife and kid. He had coke in his system. Some white collar putz taking a walk on the wild side, got himself into a dangerous situation."

"So what are you up here for?"

"Well, another guy turned up dead. Last week. On the Queensway. In a motel room."

"She didn't confess to that one, did she?"

"Far as I know, she was up here. But here's the thing, this guy was Russian, he was a defector, he was a scenic designer for a ballet company and he was carrying her picture in his wallet."

She had recognized him immediately as he drove by — not the sort of man you forget, so tall, that preposterous red hair, and there he was again, on the sidewalk across the street. He was even walking in rhythm with the music, Rimsky-Korsakov, *Schéhérazade*. The children in the room behind her were fighting the tempo, but the tall man below was floating along in perfect time. She wondered if he could hear it. The windows were closed, no traffic noise. Maybe it was a sign. A good sign. A sign that would cancel out a dead crow. It was possible, was it not? Of all the people looking for her, he was the one she always hoped would find her again. From that first time, when he came to the apartment on Quebec Avenue with that huge black man, that first look, standing in the hall, offering his badge toward her like a sandwich. Viktor had been there, getting drunk on her vodka, smoking her cigarettes, badgering her, hiding in the corner. Unlike Viktor, she had been happy to see the policemen, welcomed them into the apartment, offered them drinks. She didn't like the big black man. He was too friendly, and he crowded her with his big smile and sexy voice, acting like her uncle, the one who always stood too close. But the red-haired man, she liked him, standing by the door, not leaning, but giving the impression that he was lounging, so relaxed. He had an easy smile. He had a nice voice. She wanted to get his attention.

"Yes, the man in the park. I know who you mean," she said. "I killed him."

They hadn't believed her, they took her to the police station for questioning and that was all she really wanted, to get away from Viktor who was drunk and getting crazier every day, to ride in a car with the red-haired man, to have him pay attention to her for a while. And he drove her home as well, insisted even. She turned down a ride with the big black man, but she went home with the red-haired one. When she invited him inside, he demurred, but so charmingly, with a smile almost rueful, a smile that suggested *another time, another place, ships that pass in the night, if only we'd met last week*, and never that she was too old for him. He was a charmer. And courtly. A private part of her, the tiny part that wished for things, had prayed he would return some day.

"Mademoiselle?"

It was the tall girl, the graceful one, perhaps a model some day. But not a dancer. "Class is over now. I am tired today," Anya said. "I will not charge your parents for this class. Go home."

She heard them changing, leaving, still she watched the street, hoping for another glimpse of him. And there he was, coming out of the National Bank, talking to a pretty girl who kept fluffing her hair. Tsk. Such a flirt. Him, too. She watched him fold his cash and slip it into a pocket. He had such beautiful hands.

Her own hands were not attractive. Short fingers, the palms square and knuckles prominent. Her thumbs especially were distasteful to her, a heavy callus where she habitually bit her knuckle instead of chewing her nails. And to hurt herself. She knew how use her wrists to make her hands appear beautiful from a distance, to an audience, but offstage she held her cigarette inside a cupped palm like a convict in an exercise yard.

Maybe he will visit me tonight. That would be nice. I'll wait for him. And if he is to be my assassin, I will welcome him.

Considering that she refused to tell him anything relative to her patient, Dr. Lorna Ruth gave Detective Paul Delisle more time than she'd expected to. She enjoyed looking at him. Kind of gorgeous, she thought, in a bony sort of way. He reminded her a little of someone she knew years ago, tall, loose-limbed, except her lover back then had been dark-haired. She watched this man move his chair a foot closer to her desk and then angle it toward the window, not confrontational, giving her some of his nice profile, shaggy red hair going a bit grey at the temples, wide mouth, deep creases when he smiled, which he did easily and often. She watched the way he made himself comfortable, stretched out his legs and entwined his long fingers. He didn't fidget.

Still, she couldn't tell him anything. "You know that, Detective."

"That's okay, I don't want to be pushy anyway, it's just one of those things I have to check out, one of many, you know how it is, if you've dealt with cops before, you know how we do things." He didn't seem to be seducing her. Had he been guileless she would have been suspicious — she was alert to guileless behaviour and didn't believe in it. "I *would* like to know if you've had any other police interest in her. Asking questions. Surely that wouldn't be unethical."

"You're the first."

"When she was living in Toronto, at one point a judge ordered a psychiatric evaluation. Is this part of that?"

"She wasn't ordered to see me, and I'm not preparing a psychiatric evaluation for the police. I was recommended as someone she might feel comfortable talking to."

"Who recommended you?"

"Tsk. I can't tell you that."

He smiled. Such a charming smile. "Does she? Feel comfortable?"

"I think so. She is candid, helpful."

"Maybe I could tell you the version I know, and you could

tell me if it's way off the mark from the one you know. She confessed to a couple of murders in the city a few years back. It was determined that she was a compulsive confessor. There was no evidence that she had been involved."

"And now you're having second thoughts?"

"In a way. It's probably the same for psychiatrists. Cops don't believe a story just because it sounds convincing. We take it for granted that everybody lies. We listen as carefully as we can, try to extract the facts when we can, make sure we get the dates down, and times, and addresses, and names, the things we can verify on our own. All the rest is stories. Versions of stories. Usually self-serving versions of stories. So we hear them out, check everything we can check and reserve judgement."

They considered each other across the desk for a moment.

"You married?" he asked her.

"Yes," she said.

"Free for dinner?"

"Yes," she said.

And so she gave him more of her time than he had expected her to.

Anya smoked her first cigarette in four hours, standing in the doorway of the Gusse Building waiting for her taxi, her regular cab driver, the same man every night. His name was Ed. He let her smoke in his car. The street lights were on, there was cowboy music coming from the Irish House around the corner, a purple pickup cruised by, loud hip hop, heavy bass vibrations rattled the window of the florist shop next door. Across the street, five young people, two boys, three girls, were laughing and shoving each other. Anya watched from the shadows, watched the other shadowed doorways, the lane entrances, the parked cars, the roofline above the shops, the second-storey windows. She watched for flickering movement, for things out of place. When her cab pulled up, she dropped her cigarette to the pavement and squashed it as she stepped toward the curb, looking both ways before opening the passenger door. There was no sign of the red-haired man.

"Go the wrong way for a while," she said.

"You got it."

She looked out the back window.

"I heard about this technique they have now where they tail you from the front." Ed watched her watching him in his rear-view mirror.

"I know of that," she said. Her voice was matter-of-fact. "One in front, one far behind. Also from parallel streets they can tail you. But that requires a bigger team."

"Jeeze, how many spies are after you this month?"

"Unless they already know where I live, in which case it does not matter."

Ed thought she had great legs. Sometimes after class when she was wearing tights under her trenchcoat and she swung on the back seat to look out the rear window, once or twice the coat had opened to reveal her long flanks. She wasn't tall, but her legs seemed very long.

"I'll be taking next week off," Ed said. "I won't be driving."

"Who will take over your shift?"

"Couple of new guys; I'm not sure."

She would have to find some other way home. Ed the cab driver thinks it is a game. He likes playing spies and assassins with her, taking a different route each time while she watches for tails. She has not told him everything.

Look at her apartment. She does not live there, she perches there, on the edge of the bed, the chair, the table. Her suitcase is small and never completely emptied, always half-packed with the necessities for flight, papers and money and new clothes, a coat never worn, never photographed, a grey-brown wig, ugly and credible. Her face without makeup can be old if she wants it that way, the bones are sharp and fine, the eyes deep set. If she has to run again, she has routes picked, schedules and timetables memorized, she knows all the back doors in and out of her neighbourhood. She took this place because of the windows; the front overlooks the street, the bathroom window is two metres from the roof of the next building. An easy leap. Even with a suitcase and an unfamiliar coat. She can still fly. Ask her students, awe and reverence in their adoring child faces as she demonstrates. She can fly still. She has been flying all her life.

Tea in a glass by the window in the dark. Watching the street. Tea with a spoonful of jam, like her grandfather's tea. Her grandfather Bula, who taught her to watch. Sitting by the window as she has done so many nights. Waiting. Always waiting. Like the others who didn't watch closely enough. Waiting by windows as she waits most nights sipping sweet black tea and smoking Canadian tobacco. She loves Players cigarettes. And the jam in her tea is not Polish plum jam. She has been corrupted, she knows. Sometimes she uses sugar cubes. Sometimes she eats white bread. She deserves a few small comforts. While she waits.

Two

Detective Stacy Crean ("rhymes with brain," she informed people who got it wrong) had been working solo or as part of a task force for over a year. She revelled in it; the utility investigator, filling in when people got sick or stuck in court for days on end, a little bit of undercover work (at least until her face got plastered all over the *Register* the previous fall and pretty much wrecked that angle for her), working cases at her own pace, driving her own car. She was going to be very sorry when it came to an end, perhaps as early as the end of the week. Billy Meyer was retiring. That meant his longtime partner, Randy Vogt, would be looking for a new sidekick. It was inevitable. Lieutenant Emmett Paynter, Chief of Detectives, would call her into his office to make it official: an arranged marriage, no way out, this is your new partner, deal with it, make it work.

She didn't hate Randy Vogt, she just didn't like him very much. He had a loud voice that he exercised more than necessary, he put stuff on his spiky black hair — mousse or gel, she didn't know — plus he wore Brut, her least favourite men's scent, and then there were the plaid jackets and the flowered ties. The man was hard on her ears, nose and eyes. When Billy Meyer had his hernia operation, she'd been stuck in a car with Randy for six weeks. It wasn't an ideal pairing. He'd insisted on driving, sloppily she thought, and always took the lead even when she would have been the smarter choice.

Might as well enjoy your last few days of independence, she told herself. It was a fine, fresh March morning, the sun was shining, not too cold, and she was on her way to Dockerty High to talk to an assembly about how much marijuana was being consumed by certain elements of the student body and why that wasn't such a good thing. She didn't expect it would make much difference; the kids who were already smoking pot would continue to do so. Maybe she could convince one or two not to start in the first place. In the grand scheme of self-medication, pot didn't rank as high on the "dangerous drugs" scale as crack and crystal meth and the weird chemicals that kept cropping up. Pot was a fact of life, had been since the sixties pretty much, she'd certainly indulged a time or two, but things are always simpler before people figure out how to make tonnes of money from them. Pot was very big business these days. Some of the people involved in grow-ops were dangerous.

She was half a block from the high school when her cellphone buzzed. Her morning was being rescheduled.

"Stacy?"

"What's up?"

"Sunset Motel. Owner thinks one of the guests might be dead."

"Uniforms?"

"Dutch is there. He says he can't get in. Door's blocked or something."

"On it," she said. "Tell him to sit tight. And call the school. Tell them I can't make it." She did a smart U-turn and headed for the highway. She never liked giving lectures, anyway.

The Sunset Motel faced east and never saw a sunset, while half a klick further south on Highway 35, the windows of the Sunrise Motel faced due west. Neither operation was particularly concerned by the incongruity, nor, to anyone's knowledge, had the owners considered swapping monikers. A second patrol car was pulling into the parking lot as Stacy arrived. A uniformed officer climbed out and headed for unit fourteen. Dutch Scheider was standing by the door. Stacy recognized the new arrival, Drummond, "Drum": barrel chest, always sticking it out. The motel manager came scuttling across the lot in her direction. "You can't park there," she said. "People need to get in and out."

Stacy flashed her badge. "Who rented the room?"

"Mr. Smith," she said. "Probably not his real name."

"You think?"

"He paid cash."

"And you haven't seen him this morning?"

"Not since he checked in yesterday."

"Was he alone?"

"Far as I know."

"Okay, just wait in the office please. We'll see what's what."

"The girl can't get in to clean, I've got people coming, I don't want police all over the place all day."

"Just wait over there please, ma'am. Let us do our jobs."

"If there's a body, I don't want a big mess."

"That will depend on what's in the room, won't it?"

Dutch gave Stacy a small salute as she approached. The other uniform was leaning on the door, trying to force it. "You call for backup, Dutch?" she asked.

"Just passing by, Detective," said the newcomer. Stuck out his chest. Yeah, that was him.

"Drummond, right? Listen, don't shove on the door any more. If that's a body in there, we don't want to smear it across the rug. Dutch, any other way in?"

"There's a bathroom window 'round back. It's kind of high up. And a tight squeeze."

She pulled on a pair of gloves. "Show me."

There was a muddy path flanked by a bank of dirty snow

along the back of the cabin. The bathroom window was high and narrow, partly open. "Footprints under the window," Stacy said. "Yours?"

"I stayed back here."

"Good. Pay attention to where my feet go." She skirted the prints and edged close to the wall. "Those marks? Ladder maybe? Give me a boost."

Dutch made a stirrup of his hands and hoisted her high enough to grab the sill. She pulled herself up with arm strength and hung for a moment checking the window frame. "Some scratches under the window." She slid it all the way open and pulled herself through. She was standing in the shower stall. "Mr. Smith? Dockerty Police." There was no response. "Go around the front," she called out. "I'll open the big window."

"Right," she heard Dutch say.

She slipped off her wet boots, left them in the shower stall and checked the bathroom. The toilet seat was up. There was a towel on the floor.

The bedroom was dark, the drapes were drawn. The body of a man, naked except for boxer shorts and one red sock, was crumpled on the rug, his head and shoulders wedged against the bottom of the door. There was a lot of blood. Stacy crouched, placed two fingers against his throat. No pulse, the skin cold. She pulled back the drapes.

"Got a body in here," she said.

"Dead?"

"Oh yeah. Shot in the head, looks like. Phone it in, Dutch."

Drummond leaned in to get a look at the body. "Self-inflicted?"

"Don't see a gun yet," Stacy said. "Start knocking on doors, see if anyone heard anything, saw anything."

He stuck his chest out again. "On it," he said.

There was a red smear from the doorknob to the body, and a wad of blood in the man's hair. There was a splatter of blood and fragments of bone and tissue surrounding the bullet hole in the door jamb, higher than her head, as high as a tall man's head. She stood on her toes in front of the impact area and looked back. The line of sight went through the open bathroom door to the window above the shower stall.

Dutch reappeared. "Medical examiner on the way. Got an ID?"

A jacket and a pair of pants were draped over the back of the chair by the telephone table. She tugged a leather folder out of the jacket pocket. There was a badge and a photo ID card. "Oh craps," she said. "He's a cop, Dutch. Metro. Name's Delisle."

"Jesus H. Christ."

"Can't see his weapon." She put the ID and badge on the coffee table and stood in the middle of the room. The bedclothes were rumpled. An open leather bag was on the chair beside the bed — clean shirt, toiletries kit. There was a condom wrapper on the carpet beside the bed, a bottle of Jack Daniels on the bedside table, opened, mostly full, two glasses, both empty, one with lipstick traces. "He had female company. They had drinks. They had sex." She moved carefully around the room, talking more to herself than to Dutch. "Nothing broken. Neat and tidy. Except for the body." She slid open the closet door with her hand on her weapon, half expecting to see a cowering woman. There was a Burberry trenchcoat hanging. She patted the pockets, heard keys jangling. "Find out which car is his," she said.

"Right," Dutch said.

Still no sign of his weapon.

"Cavalry's coming," said Dutch.

She could see vehicles pulling into the parking lot, the ambulance, an OPP unit, even the Chief's big 4x4. Hi folks, she thought, good luck shoving me to the sidelines this time. I'm first on the scene.

An OPP investigative unit was in place before noon, and shortly thereafter four detectives from Metro's homicide unit had arrived and taken over the case. Orwell had been introduced to at least three of them, but hadn't bothered to commit their names to memory. The four were uniformly unpleasant, behaving as though the town was complicit in the brutal murder of one of their own. Definitely *herrisch* behaviour, Orwell decided. He gave two of them the gist of his conversation with Delisle. The other pair grilled Stacy and then as much as told her to stay the hell out of their way. She found a desk and attended to the paperwork demanded by the discovery of a murder victim inside the town limits, keeping any resentment well hidden. Orwell admired her composure.

The Metro cops split up, one team checking on Anya Daniel, the other pair calling on Dr. Ruth. The provincial police, and as much of the Dockerty force as they cared to use, were canvassing the other motel patrons, checking Delisle's credit cards, cellphone records, working to pin down his movements since hitting town.

Orwell retreated to his office. Entirely too much excitement for one day. Everything would be taking a back seat to the homicide. Overtime, shifting shifts, interlopers taking up space. Roy Rawluck would handle the details, he was good at keeping unnecessary annoyances off the Chief's back, but whenever outside police departments came to town, Orwell got the uncomfortable feeling of jabbing elbows and shoulders. It made him cranky.

"Chief. Mr. Rhem on two."

"Thank you, Dorrie. I'm taking it. Hello, Georgie."

"Yeah, Stonewall, done some checking. We have to petition for a hearing by the 'consent-granting authority.' Whoever they may be."

"Whoever?"

"I'm still not sure if we're talking about the Durham Region Land Division Committee or the Newry Township Acreage

Preservation Assembly."

"And then what?"

"Once we get a date, you show up and make your pitch. Lay on some of that irresistible Stonewall Brennan charm."

"Okay, Georgie. I'll do a dance for them."

The old lawyer chuckled. "So. How's your day?"

"You heard?"

"At least three different versions. It was a Metro detective?"

"That's right. I met him yesterday afternoon. Seemed like a nice enough guy."

"He was an asshole!"

"Say what, Stonewall?"

Orwell's head snapped up. "Unexpected visitor, Georgie. I'll get back to you." Detective Adele Moen from Metro Homicide stood in his open doorway, looking ferocious. Orwell rose, held out a hand. "Under normal circumstances I'd say this was a nice surprise, Detective, but you don't look at all happy to be here."

"You've got a homicide."

"Your guys are all over it." He watched her plunk herself down across from him. A tall, rangy woman, prominent jaw and cheekbones, big hands and chopped mannish hair. Orwell liked her a lot. They had worked a big case the previous year and had stayed in touch. This obviously wasn't a social call. "Personal connection?" he asked.

"He was my partner."

"Oh dear," said Orwell. "That's bad. I'm so sorry."

She waved a hand dismissively. "I know, I know, appreciate that, but I'm not ready for condolences and shit. I want to know what the fuck he was doing up here!"

"He said you were taking some personal time," Orwell said, "and he had some vacation coming."

"That's bullshit! I don't know what in the name of Christ he was up to, but it wasn't a vacation, and he sure as hell didn't let me in on it."

"He said there was a man found dead in a motel room on the Queensway last week, a Russian man. Were you two working that case?"

"*What* Russian man? What the hell was he talking about! Jee-zuss! You think you know somebody . . ." She stood up abruptly, paced Orwell's office looking for walls to punch, furniture to kick. "Turns out you don't know dick." She wanted to damage something.

"Don't know anything about that homicide?"

"We don't work anywhere *near* the Queensway. That's Peel Division. We were working a nightclub stabbing. I had to take a couple of days off for some medical crap that turned out to be nothing, thank Christ, and he said he'd keep working the case. We weren't getting anywhere anyway — no witnesses, too many witnesses and nobody saw . . . ah, who gives a crap!" She slumped in the chair again, long legs splayed out in front of her, rubbed her eyes, red from rage. "Anyway, that's beside the point, or that *is* the damn point. He was *supposed* to be in the city, working our case like he said he was going to." She looked directly at Orwell. "Not up here."

Orwell was at a loss. He couldn't help her. "Wish I could tell you more," he said. "I got the impression he wasn't exactly sure *what* he was doing. He mentioned a partner he had some years back, named O'Grady, you know him?"

"Dylan? Sure. Big Smoothie O'Grady. A natural politician. What about him?"

"He and O'Grady questioned a ballet teacher six years ago about a murder in High Park. The woman confessed, but it turned out she couldn't have done it."

"I know the one, I know the one. He told me about it. Said she was certifiable, always calling 9-1-1. So what? If she was the biggest nutbar roaming the city, I'd be out of a job."

"She moved up here, has a dance studio in town."

"So?"

"He thought there was some connection between her and the Russian man."

"*What* Russian man?" She was on her feet again and pacing.

"The one . . ."

"I know, I know: on the Queensway." She was impatient — with him, with puzzles, riddles, the scarcity of anything approaching rationality. "I don't know anything about any damn Russian man. What was the connection?"

"Apparently the man had Anya Daniel's picture in his wallet."

"That's the dancer?" She waited, palms up. "That's it?"

"And he was somehow connected to the ballet."

"Oh Lord Jesus on a bicycle! This is so stupid it makes me want to puke."

"I'm sorry," Orwell said. "I really am."

She rubbed her face with both hands, pushed her hair back and held it for a moment on the top of her head, staring out at Vankleek Street. "He was *such* an asshole," she said. "A charming, good-looking asshole. He kept secrets. You're not supposed to keep secrets from your partner. I mean you can have a private life, sure, but things that are going to affect the partnership, things you should know just to be able to back each other up, cover for each other, shit, shit, you have to share."

"I agree," Orwell said.

"I had a lump." She wiped a hand across her chest as if brushing away crumbs. "Turned out to be nothing, but I was a little freaked. I told him. I didn't hide it. I said I was worried, I said I was going in to have it checked out, I made sure he knew exactly what was what." She turned from the window, spread her hands wide, asking for something unavailable, something that made sense. "Okay if I hang around for a while? I'm not supposed to be working the case, but I'd like to find out what's happening. I'll stay out of people's way."

Orwell stood, spread his arms. "My house is your house," he said. "Hey, wait a sec." He motioned her toward the door, pointed to the far side of the room. "Stacy Crean. Over by the window. You met her last year."

"Right. Dating Natty Bumpo. What about her?"

"First on the scene," he said. He put his hand on Adele's shoulder and gave her a gentle shove. "She found the body."

She didn't like either of the detectives. She didn't bother to remember their names. One had a moustache like a dirty toothbrush and the other one had a pimple over his left eyebrow. Their voices matched their distinguishing characteristics — Dirty Toothbrush sounded like his yap was full of bubbles, Pimple squeezed his words and breathed through his mouth. They were both big. They wanted to intimidate her. She laughed inside her head.

"He was here to talk to you."

"He did not talk to me." She lit a Players with her brass Zippo.

"Don't smoke." Pimple.

"My studio, I pay the rent, I buy the cigarettes."

"You have children come up here for lessons." Pimple again. "You don't care about them?"

"You see any children?"

"This is a workplace, there's a law against smoking in a workplace."

"Today the place is closed. Today it is my private place. I am beside an open window, see? I blow my smoke outside with the car smoke. You going to arrest me for a cigarette?"

"I think you should put it out." This time from Toothbrush.

"You, with the ugly moustache, you smoke, too, I can smell it on your clothing. You want one but you cannot have one because your partner with the pimple in his eyebrow would not like it." She blew smoke in their direction. "You are just jealous." She smiled.

"Maybe we should take you into the station and question you there."

She smiled again. "You have badges, you have guns, you have authority. You can do what you want."

"Did you see him?"

"He was walking on the street." She looked down at Vankleek. The newspaperman, the overcoat with the black beard, was talking to a pair of OPP officers on the opposite sidewalk. "I saw him from this window."

"You recognized him?"

"Of course I recognized him. Who could forget a man like that?" She squashed her cigarette on the brick sill outside the window. The sill was black with burn marks.

"He didn't come up here? Come to your house?"

"He did not visit me. I was hoping he would."

"Why?"

"He was an attractive man. He had beautiful hands." She clenched hers.

"Where were you last night?"

"At home."

"Alone?"

"All alone," she said. "That's how I live."

"What time did you leave here?"

"Nine o'clock. Later than usual. The evening class was over at eight. I stayed for a while. I was dancing. Alone. *Giselle*. You know *Giselle*?"

"Anybody see you leave?"

"My driver."

"Who's that?"

"Ed. He drives a taxi. He picks me up every night. He took me home."

"Where would we find him?"

"I would try the taxi company," she said. "There is only one taxi company in this town."

"You know his last name?"

"Yes, it is on his license, on the back of the passenger seat. His picture and his name and his cab number. His name is Edwin Kewell. With a K and two Ls. His middle name is Arthur, it is not on his license. We talk a lot. He likes hockey. He does not like parsnips."

"Enough about Mr. Kewell," Toothbrush said. "We'll talk to him. He drove you home?"

"That is correct. He picked me up at five minutes after nine o'clock. I smoked a cigarette in the doorway while I waited for him."

"He pick you up all the time?"

"For a year now. I like to know who drives me places. Sometimes when people take you for a ride you do not know where you will wind up, you know?"

"What time did you get home?"

"About half past nine."

"You live that far away?"

"Not that far. Six or seven blocks. We took the long way."

"Why?"

"We were talking."

The Pimple liked that. "Just talking? Do you and Mr. Ed have more than a *Driving Miss Daisy* relationship?"

"Mr. Kewell has never been inappropriate."

"Depends on what you consider appropriate. Half an hour to drive six blocks? Sure you didn't park somewhere? Fool around?"

"Or plan to meet up later? Maybe go out and shoot somebody?"

"Being a policeman must be hard. Only ever thinking the worst. Poisons the heart, does it not?"

In the end they didn't take her anywhere for further questioning, but they promised her they would be back. She said she looked forward to it.

At first glance they seemed an unlikely pair — Stacy: cool, stylish, athletic; Adele: gangly, fiery, herky-jerky, no discernible fashion sense whatsoever. Adele wore basic black cop shoes, crepe soles, possibly steel-toed. Anyone getting a kick in the shins would know about it. Stacy preferred high boots and jeans with a bit of stretch. Stacy had black belts in three disciplines. She kicked higher than shins. Orwell was pleased with his matchmaking. He gave himself a reflex chastisement — *there you go again, being Big Daddy* — but it didn't diminish his pleasure in looking at the two women standing in front of him. A hawk and a heron. Both alert, fully engaged in what they did best.

"Sit down, detectives. What have you got?"

Stacy started. "Del thinks Delisle was up here seeing a woman."

"Or he found one when he got here," Adele said. "He moved pretty fast."

"There was definitely sex involved," Stacy said. "Maybe a married woman. Somebody he was careful didn't get spotted."

"We checked with the guys about the dance teacher." Adele consulted her notes. "Home alone, from 21:30 on. Her only confirmation is the cab driver who took her home, and he's taking the week off. Cab company says he went to Guelph to see his sister. They're trying to track him down."

"Anya Daniel have a car?" Orwell asked.

"No, Chief," Stacy said.

"Lives where?"

"Behind the hospital. River Street."

"His car was still in the parking lot, right?"

"Yes, sir. They checked it out. No evidence anyone else was in it."

"To get to the motel and back she'd need a ride. How'd she get back?"

"We figure he hooked up," Adele said. "Wouldn't be the first time. Someone with their own car."

"And if it was a spur-of-the-moment thing they might have had a drink somewhere," Orwell threw in.

"Dr. Ruth says he left her office around four," said Stacy. "Didn't see him again, but . . ."

A sharp knock on the door. "Come ahead," Orwell said.

Dutch Scheider half-opened the door, took brief note of the two detectives. "The Metro guys want to take me back to the motel," he said. "Walk me around back or something."

"Sounds sinister," said Orwell.

"That's how we do it downtown," said Adele.

"Well, we'll know where to start the search if you turn up missing," Orwell said. "Wait a sec. Tell me, Dutch, if you were going to have a drink and didn't want it to become public knowledge, with a married woman, say, where would you go?"

"Never given it much thought, Chief, seeing as how my loving wife would strangle me with my own shorts."

"Sure sure, I know, but think about it for a minute. Is there any place within driving distance where you'd feel reasonably safe?"

"Not in this town. Maybe Omemee. There's a nice little place just opened. Lemongrass, I think it's called. Supposed to be good. And there's that Italian place in Port Perry. Couple of places there, come to think of it."

"Thanks, Dutch. Off you go. Take your own car. Stay in touch."

"Will do, Chief." He looked back. "I'd start with the Omemee place," he said.

Orwell turned to the detectives. "Why don't you two take a drive over there and see if anyone had a discreet rendezvous late last night."

It was one thing to be cool in front of policemen, she was good at that. It was better to be resolute and unafraid with them, they were like dogs, if you cowered they bit you. Alone was different. After she locked the studio door she started to shake. Why would they kill him? Because of her? Her hand was trembling, holding the cordless phone while she paced the wooden floor. "The police were here," she said. The receiver was damp where she clutched it. "You believe me now? He found me. Sooner or later they always find me." She watched herself passing in the wall mirrors. "The police were asking about me?"

"Yes."

"What did you tell them?"

"Nothing." Dr. Ruth's voice sounded tight. "Whatever you've said to me is privileged communication, doctor/patient. I confirmed what they already knew, that you saw me regularly. Beyond that I couldn't tell them anything about you."

"They think I killed the man."

"Did you?"

"Of course not."

"You might have thought he was another assassin, coming for you."

"It was a possibility." She stood in the middle of the studio floor. From this position she could see herself from three angles. Automatically she pulled her shoulders back. "If he had come to me last night, I think . . . I would have let him do . . . whatever he had come to do." She took first position, second position, *sur les pointes;* then flat, then on her toes again. "I was ready. I was waiting. I waited all night for him to come."

"To kill you?"

"Maybe," she said. She began to dance, a practice class adagio, slow, measured steps. "Because I'm tired of waiting. It takes its toll. I have trouble sleeping. I try drinking myself to sleep: that doesn't work. I tried those pills you gave me, they make me stupid and slow and I still don't sleep. I am always looking behind me, beside me."

"I can't do anything for you, Anya, until you're ready to tell me."

"I came to this town because I had no reason to come here," she said. "It was a place on a map." She moved the phone to her right hand and stepped to the barre on *demi pointes*, began to work through the basic exercises, the foundation. "Anyone who followed me here would have done hard work to find me."

"I have to go, Anya, I can see you tomorrow. I have an hour in the morning. I think you should come in."

"And someone did. Someone found me. So I say, okay, that is enough now, I give up."

"Come and see me tomorrow morning, ten o'clock. Okay?"

"I was very good, you know," Anya said. She watched herself in the long mirrors as she lifted her leg. "I might have been a ballerina."

"You were."

"In the old sense of the word. Over here it just means a dancer, but in the Mariinsky, it is different, it is a title. It means something."

"Anya? Will you come?"

"It means something," she said.

She wouldn't come in, the doctor knew it, she could hear it in the woman's voice. She'd been spooked. The shooting of the detective would be all the proof she needed that assassins were in town, watching her, waiting for her in the shadows. It was unfortunate. So close to a breakthrough, so very close.

The road to Omemee was clear, traffic was light. Stacy drove, Adele leaned against the window staring out at acreage blotched with patches of old snow, muddy cattle pens, livestock gathered around broken bales of hay. "You like it up here?" she asked. "All this . . . scenery."

"It's okay," Stacy said. "I'd rather be down in the city, doing what you do. But I'd probably have to start all over."

"Maybe not. The Chief thinks a lot of you. He'd back you."

"He doesn't want me to leave."

"Would he stand in your way?"

"No. Hell. He thinks I'm wasted up here."

"What do you think?"

Stacy smiled. "I think that today I'm working a homicide." She looked at Adele. "Sorry. Must be really hard for you."

Adele waved off the suggestion. "So. How are things going with you and Davy Crockett?"

"Who?"

"Dan'l Boone. That Greenway guy."

"Joe?" Stacy laughed, a low chuckle deep in her throat. "Fine. Good. It works out we get to see each other maybe once every couple of weeks."

"That'll keep the romance fresh." Adele was quiet for a while. Stacy concentrated on the road. When Adele spoke again her voice was harsh, bitter. "You feel that chill in the air?" she said. "When a cop goes down. Even if it wasn't in the line of duty."

"We don't know it wasn't," Stacy said.

"Oh who knows what the Christ he was up to. Sonofabitch baffled the hell out of me. Always had something going on the side. Hard to work with a partner like that."

"Haven't had a partner yet I really got along with."

"Like a marriage," said Adele. "At least that's what the married people tell me." She snorted dismissively. "Takes some fine tuning while you work out how to deal with the fact . . ." her voice rose ". . . the fact that your partner is a lying, sneaking, selfish sack of shit who wouldn't know the truth if it bit him on the ass!"

Stacy kept her mouth shut for a full klick. "What do you figure?" she asked after a while. "Jealous husband?"

"Serve the bastard right," Adele muttered.

The potted palms and thatched canopy over the bar were an attempt to give Lemongrass a Thai motif and obscure vestiges of the pizza joint it once was. The lunch crowd had long since departed, two waitresses were setting tables and organizing flatware and linen. The bartender was watching the bar television where young men were twirling skateboards in the air. He looked up as the two women crossed his line of sight. Stacy held up her shield.

"I don't suppose you're here for the tom yum soup," said the bartender.

"No sir," Stacy said. "We're from Dockerty. You heard someone got shot over there last night?"

"Really? I just got up an hour ago. I work late."

"We're checking around to see if anybody remembers seeing the man yesterday."

"You got a picture?"

"You'd remember him," Adele said. "Six foot eight, hair like Ronald McDonald."

"The basketball player? Oh sure. He had a beer at the bar. We talked roundball . . . fuck! 'Scuse me. Was it him? Did *he* get shot?"

"Yes sir," said Stacy.

"Shot dead?"

"He's dead."

"Holy shit!" said the bartender. "Oh fuck. Sorry. Damn. He was a cool guy. We talked. March Madness, you know, the NCAA tournament. Said he played college ball in the States. Syracuse. The Orangemen. I thought that was cool 'cause of the hair and . . . Aw man, that sucks."

"We're trying to find out if there was anyone here with him," Adele said.

"What? Yeah. Somebody. Somebody came in and he moved

to a table. I didn't see who. It got busy."

"Would you know which waitress served them?"

"Couldn't tell you, but it was either Kelly or Lara and they're both here."

Kelly remembered them because they hadn't stayed. A woman had looked in and whispered to the tall man and they left right away. She didn't know where they went.

Stacy said, "Can you describe the woman?"

"Not really. She just stuck her head in for a second."

"Was she tall, short?"

"Ah . . . medium I guess."

Stacy asked, "How old would you say?"

"Maybe thirty five . . . *ish*, I guess."

"Blonde?"

"No. Not blonde. Dark hair, I think. Dark brown."

"Long hair?"

"Don't think so. Pulled back maybe? Could have been pulled back. Lara? Remember that woman who stuck her nose in for a minute and didn't stay? She left with the tall redheaded guy?"

"*I* wanted to leave with the tall redheaded guy," Lara said.

"That lets out the Russian woman," Stacy said as they headed back to the car. "She's short, her hair is blonde, almost white."

"Maybe they went somewhere else," said Adele. "Maybe she saw somebody she knew and didn't want them to see her. Can you think where else they might have gone, if they still wanted a drink?"

"Liquor store. He had a bottle of JD in the room."

"Sometimes he kept one in his suitcase."

"Well, there's the liquor store, and we're here."

After that it all happened quickly. The liquor store had surveillance cameras.

"There he is," Adele said. They were in the manager's office looking at the tape from the previous evening. "He alone?"

The manager pointed at the screen. "That woman checking out the wine? She's just stalling. She's not buying anything."

"And she follows him out," Stacy said.

"Wind it back."

"Thirties, shoulder-length brown hair, collar turned up, looking around."

"There, stop." Adele said. "She looks over at him. Clear look at her face."

"We'll have to take the tape," Stacy told the manager.

"That's what it's there for."

Staff Sergeant Roy Rawluck plugged in the VCR, fast-forwarded until they reached 20:27.

"That's Dr. Ruth," Orwell said. "Lorna Ruth. Good work, you two. Roy?"

"Yes, Chief?"

"Get those other Metro guys over here. We've solved one of their mysteries for them."

"Right away, Chief."

The Dockerty Police Department wasn't thanked and wasn't invited to participate in the Metro/OPP joint effort, but someone involved was kind enough to inform Roy Rawluck two hours later that an arrest had been made.

"They arrested the husband, Chief," Roy said.

Orwell sighed. "Well, I guess that makes sense."

Roy checked the piece of paper he was holding. "Harold Ruth. Forty-three. General contractor. When they picked him up he had a Savage lever action deer rifle in the car. Looks like he shot Delisle through the bathroom window. One shot, through the head."

"They bringing him in now?"

"Should have been here by now. I'll check."

"All right. Let's take good care of him."

"Will do. Detective Moen wants to see you."

"Oh, sure. Send her in."

Adele Moen came in. Stuck out her hand. "Wanted to say thanks, Chief."

"Hey, thank *you.*"

"For hooking me up with Detective Crean. Sorry she doesn't work in town. I'll be looking for a new partner."

"I'm glad you two hit it off. Sorry it had to be on this case, though."

"It's a bitch, but what are you gonna do?"

"You do what you did." Orwell felt an urge to put an arm over her shoulder, but resisted the impulse. Instead he walked her through the outer office to the stairs. "Locate his weapon?" he asked.

"They found a .32 short nose Smith in the bottom of his suitcase."

"Sounds like a backup piece."

"It is," she said. "He wore it in an ankle holster."

"What was his primary?"

"A .357 Smith. He was a cowboy. Liked his hog-leg."

"And no sign of that?"

"Nada," she said. "The doctor says she never saw it."

"Would he have come up here without it, do you think?"

"Possible, but I doubt it. I'll check his apartment in the city. Maybe it's there. I'll email you the particulars, in case it shows up, serial number, model number."

"Don't like the idea of a stolen handgun floating around," Orwell said.

"It's probably at his place."

"You'll let me know?"

"You bet. Just wanted to say thanks. Those other guys won't bother."

"What about Dr. Ruth? She in any trouble?"

"Maybe. She lied. Said Paul left her office that afternoon and that was the last she saw of him. I can understand her lying about it, I guess, but she could be charged with obstruction. Don't think they'll bother though, since it got wrapped up so fast."

"I'm happy with that," Orwell said. "She'll be punishing herself quite a bit, I'm sure."

"Anyway, I'm out of here. Appreciate your help."

"I'll pass it on. And I'm sorry for your loss."

"Thank you. Stupid bastard. He was a skirt chaser in the city, too. I told him his dick would get him into trouble some day."

"You will let me know if you locate his weapon," Orwell said.

"And vice versa," she said. She stuck out her hand again. "It was good seeing you again, Chief. Even though . . ."

"You too, Detective. Safe drive home."

"Thanks." She started down the stairs.

"Oh, one other thing." Orwell came out to the landing. "Just to satisfy my curiosity if you please, could you check into this Russian man business? The one your late partner mentioned? Maybe find out a few details for me?"

"Shouldn't be too hard."

"I know it's none of my business, but if it has anything to do with the dance teacher, remote as that possibility seems . . ."

"I'll be looking into it."

Orwell watched her clump down the stairs. She didn't look back.

"Chief?" Roy was at his desk, holding up his hand. "Just talked to Sergeant Turkle, headed the OPP unit. He says the Metro guys took the accused back to Toronto."

"They what?"

"Turkle says two of the Metro guys scooped up Harold Ruth and drove off before OPP could interview him."

"That's not good."

Adele took her time getting back to the city. It wasn't that far away, she could have been home in an hour and a half if she'd booted it down the 401, but she took the scenic route, a two-lane blacktop running through a forest of bare trees and mud paths. Not exactly scenic in mid-March, she allowed, but perhaps it would soothe her jangled spirit to wind through the Rouge River Valley. On the far side of the narrow single-lane underpass she parked and walked into the trees a few steps until she could see the river running high with ice melt. This was a conservation area, favoured by birders and hikers, a good place to spot wild creatures if you were quiet. Like that little brown bird with the twitchy tail sticking straight up, whatever it was — she couldn't tell a robin from a cockatoo. I swear, if he was standing beside me I'd cold-cock the sonofabitch. I'd tell him, Paulie, you are *such* an asshole! *Gawd!* So *dumb.* Worse, so *corny.* Shot by a jealous husband. I mean, how trite is that? And *pointless.* And probably overdue, considering how many dicey hookups he'd indulged in over the years, and not all of them *after* his divorce from whatever-her-name-was. Jenny, hell, *she* probably felt like taking a shot at him herself, more than once. Jealous wife, jealous husband, what's the diff? Sooner or later it was bound to catch up with him.

She had just transferred from Vice to Homicide to fill the slot vacated by the retirement of Dylan O'Grady, Paul's former partner who had expressed a desire to enter politics. There was some talk that Dylan had been encouraged to put in his papers before awkward questions could be asked about evidence that may or may not have gone missing. The general opinion was that Big Smoothie O'Grady would do well in politics. Their boss, Captain Émile Rosebart, introduced them with the words, "You two are bound to have a good influence on one another. One of you is strictly by the book, the other one can't read."

And they did get along, made a good team. They were both quick, intelligent, no private lives. Well, *he* had a private life, but nothing that compelled him to make "Honey, I'm working late" phone calls. He went through girlfriends like magazine subscriptions. Sometimes one of them would hang in there for a few months, hoping for a renewal, but sooner or later his roving eye would catch sight of someone newer and shinier and he'd shift his attention. Some girlfriends stayed enamoured even after they'd been shelved. Some of them carried a torch for years, sending him Christmas cards and birthday presents long after they'd been replaced. And some hated his guts.

In a hundred ways he was a terrible partner: he stuck her with paperwork, with interviews, left her alone on stakeout while he ran off for a brief encounter. But where it counted, where it counted to her, he was the best she could have hoped for. For one thing, he was the first partner she had who was taller than she was. She liked that. Liked not feeling like a moose all the time. He treated her as an equal, never condescended, never bullied, and yet he had a natural courtesy that let her know he was aware of her as a woman. He never made a pass at her, or suggested anything inappropriate. Well, she could hardly blame him for that, he had no shortage of women, good looking women, and she was, as her grandmother once remarked, "plain as a mud fence." She could live with it, *had* lived with it. She knew what she looked like. But Paul was always courteous, no other word for it.

There was that one time, once when they were going somewhere and she had to put on a dress, he said, "Hey Stretch, first time I noticed: you've got a great ass." Crude and offhand as the remark was, she carried it with her. Pitiful, isn't it? Some guy remarks on her butt, maybe the first time in ten years anyone's said anything remotely sexual to her about her body, and she treasures it.

She walked back to the car. A blue jay yelled at her. "Shut *up!*" She threw a stick. "I am in no mood to take shit from a goddamn woodpecker!"

And that other stuff, what the hell was *that* all about? Some dead Russian? Some *ballet* dancer? Damn! I should have at least talked to the woman. I don't even know what she looks like. He was probably up there to get *her* into the sack and settled for the psychiatrist because ... why? Who cares? Younger, prettier maybe, available, *handy*. Like Dylan used to say, "Paul would fuck a snake if somebody held its ears." Maybe he never got around to doing whatever he was in Dockerty to do. What *did* he do? Checked out the town, paid a courtesy call on the local cops, had lunch with the Chief, let them know he'd be nosing around — why bother doing that if he was just up there to get laid? Couldn't be. He was in town for *something*. He checked into a motel. Planned on spending at least part of two days in town. So? So whatever it was, he never got around to doing it. Instead he got lucky with the shrink. Paid for it.

She climbed behind the wheel and slammed the door, sat staring at nothing, muttering to herself. "Got me talking to myself, you dipshit!" She turned the key in the ignition. Turned it off. "So what's your unfinished business, Paulie?" She tugged her hair away from her scalp until it hurt, until it cleared her vision.

Checked in under the name "Smith" for Chrissake. And what's up with you and the ballet dancer? Shit, you couldn't tell a ballet dance from a bunny-hop. All the same to you, wasn't it? People jumping around, right? You wouldn't look at a dancer unless she was swinging on a pole with her clothes off. So, something about that Russian woman besides dancing. What? Not really your type, if you *had* a type, but you mostly liked them a bit younger, no? This dancer is, what, sixty? Something like that. Never into old broads, were you? Or even broads your own age. You were more into the cheerleader type, babes with boobs, or, oh who the hell knows, maybe you were branching out, maybe you were running out of cheerleaders, maybe ... She started the car again, this time put it in gear and started moving, heading for civilization.

But now she was stuck, now she was thinking like a cop again instead of like someone who'd been dumped without even a goodbye note. You were up there for something besides a quick roll in the hay, weren't you, Paulie-boy? You were snooping around that ex-Commie ballet teacher. But why? Why not just brace her? Why all the pussy-footing? Why not just pay her a visit, bang through the door? Saw you do that enough times — excuse me, ma'am, I have some questions. What questions? Were you even going to talk to her? Or were you just trying to find out what everyone *else* knew about her? If she was just a loon, a compulsive confessor, why bother? Why the secrecy?

What was it? A cold one of yours? Yours and Dylan's? Cases that don't get resolved are like bad debts. They keep eating at you, taunting, *never figured this one out, did you, loser?*

And some dead Russian in a motel room on the *Queensway*? What's all *that* about?

I don't want to know! She gave herself a mental slap. None of my business. All I want now is a long soak in my bathtub, up to my neck in bubbles, with a big glass of red wine, thinking about where I want to go for a little vacation. There's time coming. Always time off when a cop loses a partner. They'll probably make me see a counsellor, help me deal with the pain. Pain? Shit! I'd give him some goddamn pain. Somewhere warm and sunny. Maybe a week or two in Florida would help. Maybe.

And so she paid her obligatory call on the counsellor, told her she was handling it okay, a bit shaken up, still angry but getting over it, handed her notes on the nightclub stabbing case to the other team working the same incident, they weren't getting anywhere either, packed a bag and flew down to Jamaica, got some sun, drank pina coladas, even tried some local weed, listened to some local music. No one bothered her. Maybe because she was just some pale bony broad from the north, maybe because she glared at anyone who tried to start a conversation.

Three

Patty Brennan's newest horse was a three-year-old bay mare with long black stockings and a star between her bright eyes. The name in the quarter horse registry was Red Rollover's Vixen, but she was called Foxy by the woman who bred her, and Patty thought it suited her. "She's a smarty-pants," Patty said.

Orwell leaned over the top rail and watched his daughter brushing the mare's mahogany coat. Foxy had her eyes on Orwell. "She's watching me," he said.

"She sees everything. Right, gorgeous?"

"Pretty colour."

"Pretty girl. Bright as a penny." Patty moved forward to brush along the sweep of the withers and back. "And sharp as a tack."

"I talked to Georgie. He says it'll take a couple of months."

"It's sweet of you and Erika to want this. But you don't have to go through all this nonsense."

"It's the principle of the thing. When you own property you like to think it's yours to do with as you will."

"Sure you're not trying to get rid of me?" She laughed.

"Just the opposite," he said. He watched her for a moment, enjoying the sight of her. For a brief instant he saw her mother. The same generous mouth, generous bosom, generous hips. A big, good-looking woman with a hint of sadness in the tiny crease between her eyes. "I guess I'm trying to keep us all close."

She stopped brushing and turned to face him. "There's no rush, you know."

He suddenly felt awkward. "You like that spot over there by the creek, right?"

"It's a perfect spot, Dad." The mare nudged her. "Okay, okay, get back to work, got it." She resumed the long strokes. Foxy bobbed her head. "So *bossy*."

"I mean if you and . . ."

"Gary."

"I know his name," he said. "I'm just confused. Around Christmas you were sort of hinting at a June . . . you know."

"Well, we sort of hinted our way into . . . later."

"You okay, Pattycakes? You upset, or anything I could do?"

"Everything's fine. We just have a few things to work out, you know, one of them being where we're going to be. In the long run."

"And I've made things difficult, pushing you to live next door." He rubbed his face. "I'll mind my own business. One of these days."

She came to the rail to lean close to her father, head to head, almost as tall as him, one hand on top of his. "Don't go all dramatic, Daddy, I love the idea of living over there, and Gary doesn't *hate* it, he's just, you know, an independent guy, wants to make sure he has some part in things."

"Well, whatever you want, sweetie. You know." He stepped back. Smiled and shook his head in wonder. "Sometimes, in a certain light, you look so much like your mom."

"Does it make you happy, or sad?"

"Both. Mostly happy. And it's only a flash, just in a certain light, or a certain angle, I don't know. Most of the time you look just like you, which has to be one of the best looks on the planet as far as I'm concerned."

"I like your big face, too, Daddy." The mare came up behind her and bumped her again. "No, that's enough for you," Patty said.

The crows in Armoury Park were cawing as she walked by, telling the world all about her. The most unmusical birds in the world, she was sure. She hated it, that they were so unmusical. She'd been almost enjoying the morning, but now the rain was starting and the crows were complaining about it. Raspy shrieking, no doubt passing the word along that she was on her way, bringing rain with her. Gossips and liars. And thieves.

In the animal kingdom, stealing is a way of life — food, mates, territory — the fast animal from the slow, bigger from smaller, aggressive from timid, clever from dull. Animals don't consider it stealing, Anya knew that, not the way humans do. It's about staying alive — sustenance, procreation, defence. Animals are aware of risk, but right and wrong don't apply. Except for crows. Crows, she believed, were different. They were robbers at heart. They stole as humans did, because they wanted a thing. Why else would they steal shiny things, useless things? And, like humans, they *knew* they were stealing. Why else would they have warning systems? And lookouts.

She saw the man standing by the fountain right away. He was staring at a newspaper, but he was not reading it. Big man, bony skull like a concrete block. He was wearing a hat and a long coat and gloves and his newspaper was getting wet, flapping against the wind, creasing the wrong way, but still he pretended to read. Why do you not mob him? He is the interloper. You can see that. He does not belong here, he has never been here before, go and yell at him.

She wasn't surprised to see the man. And likely he wasn't alone. Are you here somewhere? Sergei? I see your boyfriend. Where are you? She could feel it. A presence. Had felt it for days. He was close. The red-haired man found her, and Nemesis followed him.

Orwell waited, patiently, he thought, at the end of the driveway
for Leda to make some last-minute decisions regarding her outfit
and to locate whatever it was that she needed so desperately for
today's activities. Why these items couldn't have been resolved
the previous evening was beyond him. His schedule was being
severely tested by outside forces — daylight saving time, March
Break, first rehearsal of *Our Town*. Leda wanted to run lines with
someone before school. Someone named Peter. Oh dear, he
thought. Well, she *is* seventeen, there was bound to be a Peter.
Sooner or later.

He beeped the horn three times, knowing full well that it
wouldn't speed up the process. On an ordinary morning, he
would be using this hour for a solitary cruise along country
roads, an indulgence he considered vital to his mental health, a
time for checking out fields and trees and taking deep breaths.
He was working himself into a mood. He could feel it. He was
beset. Bloody idiot. The wedding had been arranged. He was sure
of it. And now . . .

He beeped again, more insistently this time, three long ones.
Oh well, they'll figure it out. None of his business anyway. And
hell's bells, he couldn't be faulted for the *impulse*, the fatherly
impulse to give his daughter a piece of land to raise horses,
maybe raise children, a place on the other side of the hayfield,
the hayfield that could be turned into a big pasture with a little
work. And Erika was solidly behind the plan. *Wasn't* she?

"If she wants," his wife had said. She was grating potatoes at
the time, cold, previously baked potatoes. Orwell knew there was
rösti in the offing.

"Why wouldn't she want?"

"How should I know why wouldn't she want?"

"Well, if she doesn't want, she doesn't have to accept. I thought
it would be nice to offer."

"Offer," said his wife. "Don't push."

And he hadn't pushed. Sure, he'd looked into the red tape involved, that only made sense. Township telling him he had to have permission to give his daughter . . . *and* her husband, let's not forget *that* part, husband *to be*, he hadn't left *him* out of the equation. Damn! He was starting to feel like King Lear.

Leda climbed in beside him. "You shouldn't sit out here idling, you know," she said disapprovingly. "It's wasteful and polluting."

He put the car in gear, signalled right, even though there was no traffic and nothing behind him but a gate, and got moving. Finally. His sigh was audible. "If certain people were ready when they said they'd be, I wouldn't be forced into idleness," he said.

The dashboard clock read 6:30, but in fact it was 7:30. He just hadn't got around to resetting it. A small act of defiance. Or, he freely admitted, petulance. The Americans shoving the schedule forward arbitrarily annoyed the heck out of him, not to mention Ottawa's usual lock-step response to go along with it. You can say it's 7:30 all you want, but my internal clock knows different.

Traffic was picking up, but not yet heavy. The sky was uniformly grey and rain was beginning to spatter the windshield.

"You have to get rid of him, Oldad."

"Nonsense. He'll be twenty-five years old next year and good as new. He's a classic."

"He's antediluvian."

"He is no such thing." Leda was referring to her father's venerable and beloved (by him) 1987 Dodge Ramcharger 4x4, always referred to in the masculine. "Bozo is a loyal, hardworking . . ."

"Gas-guzzling, air-polluting . . ." Leda was an eco-warrior these days. Among other things.

"He's in complete compliance." Orwell could hear the big V8 purring sweetly. It gave him pleasure. Stan, the master mechanic at Gary's Service Centre, had Bozo tuned to perfection. "We passed our emission test with flying colours."

"Cost you nineteen hundred dollars to do it."

"How do you know all this?"

"I'm not deaf and blind to the world around me, Oldad. I see things, I hear things, such as my mother going through the receipts and yelling, 'Was it necessary to gold-plate the engine?' only she says it in German."

"The engine is *not* gold-plated." He sounded defensive, even to himself. "Certain parts might have a trace of nickel I suppose, certain areas are chrome." Orwell would have been embarrassed to admit that he'd fallen in love with the Dodge many years back while watching a Chuck Norris movie called *Lone Wolf McQuade* in which the powerful machine had performed almost as many feats of strength as the star. Despite its quirks and peculiarities, Orwell was devoted to the beast, and over the years had lavished much care and a fair amount of cash on keeping Bozo (Erika's name for him) in first-class condition. "Certain expenditures are necessary to maintain a classic."

"You're on the wrong side of the enviro-war, Daddy. Admit it. You're part of the problem."

"And you're being overly harsh. This machine has done yeoman service since I bought him. Plus, he is now officially designated as a police vehicle. Special equipment, lighting package, heavy-duty . . ."

"Everything *about* him is *heavy-duty*."

"That's why I got him. He can carry five humans, two saddles, half a ton of tack, fodder, equipment, luggage, plus haul a two-horse trailer, all in comfort and safety."

"No airbags."

"No, he doesn't have airbags, which is why you're wearing the best four-point seat harness available and sitting in a bucket seat fit for NASCAR. It's why he has a built-in roll-cage." Orwell allowed himself a glance at his daughter. She was as safe as he could make her. She was also staring forward with folded arms and furrowed brow. "Look, sweetheart," he began, gently, "save your money, take your driving test and we'll see about getting you some kind of hybrid/electric . . . *thing.*"With a ton of airbags, he added silently.

"That doesn't really solve the problem, Oldad. It adds to the problem."

"I'm not giving him up."

"Couldn't you at least save him for those rare occasions when you're actually *hauling* Patty's horse trailer and saddles and stuff?"

"You think those Crown Victorias the department drives are better? Police cars have to be big and strong. You want the DPD all driving little electrics? I don't think so."

"He's not only bad for the environment, he leaves a gigantic carbon footprint." She turned to him with her most superior expression, poised to strike a dagger into the heart of the debate. "SUVs are what went wrong with the automotive industry." She bobbed her head like Foxy. Case closed.

"Yeah, well sometimes they got it right," he said.

Orwell knew his daughter wouldn't abandon the issue, but he was prepared to beat back her arguments as they arose. He wasn't going to park Bozo any more than was necessary. He was not oblivious. The general consensus among the committed and socially aware was that machines of this type were on their way out. So be it, Orwell thought. That's how it should be. The *inevitable,* but *gradual,* evolution of machines to be less damaging to the planet. He had no argument with that. He also lived in a rural area where a large portion of the population relied heavily on pickups and other working vehicles. He somehow doubted that Fern Casteel was going to be ditching his Ford F150 for some time. And he'd like to see the Prius that could carry a load of logs and three big men with chainsaws as well as the beat-up, but still hardy, 1968 GMC pickup Rupert Kronick took into the bush five days a week.

Besides, Orwell also believed in his heart that had his first wife been at the wheel of something bigger and stronger than the little Datsun she'd been driving that rainy night, she might still be alive. Case closed.

He dropped Leda off outside the Globe Theatre, saw her run for the side entrance as the rain began to fall in earnest. There was a young man with odd-looking hair and a black leather jacket waiting for her. Oh dear. At least he was holding the door for her. Perhaps he wasn't an axe murderer, a drug dealer or a serial rapist. Maybe he was just an actor.

Her studio was undisturbed, empty. They will search it soon enough, she thought, they know where it is by now. She locked the door, both locks, checked the fire escape, the window latches, scanned the street below. When she turned from the window she caught sight of herself in the mirrored wall, a doll-sized shadow in a corner, pale face, fists clenched, shaking her head at the absurdity of it all.

All that running, and look where it got you. Nowhere, absolutely nowhere. You changed your name so many times, it is a wonder you know who you are. Can you remember? Can you remember Anya Ivanova Zubrovskaya? Can you remember how she was? How perfect? Immaculate technique, weightless as a moonbeam, tensile, like coiled steel, secure on point like a dagger. The Kirov's next prima ballerina. Remember Anya Zubrovskaya. Do not forget her. There are no pictures of her. Not one photograph of her *Giselle*. She is erased. Wiped from history. Disappeared. You will not find her name on a list of Vaganova graduates, or the company rolls of the Mariinsky. She has been expunged. Forgotten.

Damn Viktor! Damn him and his sticky fingers, his decadent love of silk shirts and 4711 Kölnisch Wasser and Colgate toothpaste. Damn Grégor for being a clumsy fool. Damn them all. Anya Zubrovskaya might have taken her place alongside Pavlova, Karsavina, she might have been one of the great ones. Instead she became a non-person. When she defected, they didn't even raise a protest, they didn't demand her return. Who cares, they said. Who will notice? She won't be missed. She gave everything for her art, for the system that honed her art, for the history and the legacy of the Mariinsky, and in the end she was discarded without comment. Forgotten.

But not by everyone. Certain people might not remember how she danced, but they know why she ran.

The night is clear in her mind. *La Sylphide*. That nice theatre in Buffalo. The orchestra had paid attention, the stage had the right spring. Her partner, Sergei, was stiff and stolid as usual, the man had the charisma of a mailbox, but it didn't matter, he was there to show her off, it was fine that he was invisible. At least he could count. And he was a strong as a tree. He didn't drop her. She deserved the standing ovation. There were curtain calls and bouquets thrown onto the stage and she was in a daze, euphoric, exhausted and starving hungry. It was a magical night; perhaps her best performance. The entire troupe was taken out for a meal. She ate wonderful roast beef and drank champagne and cognac. She wasn't drunk; she was radiant with triumph and release. She almost allowed a handsome young ballet lover into her hotel room but at the last moment decided that she wanted to savour the rest of the night in private and let him kiss her, once, before pushing him gently but firmly on his way.

She was sitting on the edge of the tub, soaking her feet when the pounding on her door started. She thought it was the young man come back to beg her to change her mind, but it was Viktor, sweating, drunk, laughing like a lunatic and terrified at the same time. Nanya, he said, look at this, you won't believe this! He had a suitcase with a false bottom and it opened very cleverly by removing the little brass feet, and inside was some cash, American dollars, and some gold coins, and, wrapped in a cloth, was a chain with links like gold coins and hanging from the chain, a crucifix, heavy, like the hilt of a Roman sword, covered with gems. Do you know what this is? he asked her. This is not real, she said. Please tell me this is a fake. But she had known right away that was not true. Look again. Look at the marks on the back, he said, look at the little diamonds around the clasp. *Little* diamonds. There was not one under two carats. Look at the sapphires. Oh my God. Look at what is in the centre. It is real? Of course it is real, he says. It is the Ember, for God's sake. Where did you steal it? I didn't steal it, he says, I just bought some shirts.

"Viktor, this is bad," she said. "This is very bad."

"Look at it, Nanya, hold it in your hands, never in your life will you hold anything as perfect as this is in your hands."

"I do not want to hold it in my hands," she said. "This is death. Take it away and do not bring it near me again."

"It's too late."

He had been right about that. It was too late. For all of them.

By the time he reached the station it was raining heavily. There was still a puddle where he parked his car (although he didn't *have* to park *exactly* in that spot) and some late night dog-walker had failed to pick up after their beast befouled the struggling grass near the flagpole. Although, Orwell noted, Alastair Argyle's bronze relief was polished to a fare-thee-well, thus encapsulating, to Orwell's thinking, the priorities of the Department.

There was an unmistakable hush as he clomped through the outer office. Heads turned away. He put it down to people recognizing that he wasn't to be trifled with this morning. "We may be exceeding the shamrock quotient, Staff Sergeant," he said loudly.

"I'll start cutting back forthwith," said Roy Rawluck. There were three shamrocks dangling on the bulletin board. Roy chided himself. One of them was supposed to be a harp. He'd missed it. Leprechauns were, of course, verboten.

Dorrie (who wasn't the least afraid of her boss no matter what his mood) handed him the morning's *Register* with more solicitude than was customary.

"No bank robberies overnight? No riots?"

"Not yet anyway," she said. "I'll wait until you've read the paper."

"Anything in particular I should be reading?

"You'll find it, Chief. It's on the front page."

Orwell located his reading glasses in the third pocket he checked. He spread the paper on his desk blotter and hung up his wet coat and hat before catching the headline: "Lyman Calls for a 'New Order,'" under a photograph of candidate Gregg Lyman, caught in dramatic mid-gesture. "Where was this?" Orwell shouted through the open door.

Dorrie appeared with her boss's morning coffee and a sheaf of the usual paperwork and messages. "A 'Lyman for Mayor' rally," she said. "The Granite Club."

"Of course. He'd be preaching to the choir up there." He accepted the coffee with a curt nod of thanks and dribbled a few spots onto Lyman's image.

"Mr. Abrams wonders if you'd care to issue a statement."

"Statement about what?"

"Second paragraph."

Orwell concentrated on the paper. His fist hit the desk. "What the *hell*?!" he bellowed.

"I'll leave you to it," she said.

"Wait a minute, wait a minute, when was this?"

"Last night."

Dorrie backed out of the room. The Chief bent over the paper, deliberately setting his cup down on Lyman's mug. He read aloud, his voice level increasing with each sentence: ". . .

growing atmosphere of *lawlessness*?? . . . general *laxity* in police performance?? . . . a new sense of *order* is demanded??" Lyman's face was disappearing in a spreading puddle of coffee. "Who the hell does he think . . . ?"

"Chief?" Dorrie's voice on the intercom was soothing. "Sam Abrams on one, Mayor Bricknell on two."

"I'll talk to the Mayor first. Tell Sam I'll get back to him."

"Yes sir."

"And I spilled my coffee."

"Yes sir."

"Mayor Bricknell. And what can I do for you on this fine sunny morning?"

"I take it you haven't seen the paper yet."

"Why of course I have. In fact I'm using it to wipe off my desk blotter as we speak." Orwell stood aside as Dorrie bustled in and attended to the ruined newspaper and the spilled coffee. "Takes a good picture, doesn't he?"

"I trust you'll have a statement for tomorrow's edition."

"I'm not at all sure a statement from me is in order."

"You can't be serious, Chief Brennan. The man as much as accused you of incompetence."

"Really? I'll have to read it more carefully." He bent over and pulled open the bottom drawer of his desk. "It sounded to me like more of a comment on the state of society as a whole. Damn!" There were only three shortbread cookies in the carefully folded bag. Orwell was certain there had been five when he left work the previous day. "I'm going to put a mousetrap in here," he muttered.

"I'm sure a statement will be much more effective," said Donna Lee.

"Will the Mayor's office be issuing one?"

"I'll be making my own campaign speeches over the next month. I'll deal with it then."

"So you agree it's a campaign issue?" Orwell sat back down.

His desk blotter was clear, a fresh coffee was waiting. "Dorrie, would you care for a shortbread?"

"No thanks, Chief. Want another newspaper?"

"I've seen it," he said. "Thank you. My apologies, Mayor. You caught me in the middle of my morning's clutter."

"I think you should seriously consider issuing a statement," Donna Lee said. "Something to the effect that Dockerty is one of the safest, most well-ordered communities of its size in the province."

"Now *that* would be a splendid fact to mention in *your* speeches, Your Honour."

Orwell bid the Mayor a polite good morning and took a deep breath. He arranged two of the three remaining shortbread beside the coffee cup and put away the bag, not as neatly folded, in a different drawer.

"Chief?"

"Dorrie?"

"Mr. Abrams?"

"Did I get a call from Detective Moen?"

"Were you expecting one, Chief?"

"I've been expecting one for a week."

"She only left town yesterday, Chief."

"Seems longer. See if you can track her down for me, would you?"

"Forthwith, Chief."

"Definitely. Forthwith. And Dorrie?"

"Still here, Chief."

"I need to talk to Detective Lackawana's . . ."

"Lacsamana."

"Lord! Why can't I remember his name?"

"You didn't like him."

"No I didn't, you're right, that's probably it. Nonetheless and even so, I need his boss, whoever he is. And find Adele Moen. *And* Lacka-whatever."

"Lacsamana," she said gently.

"Fine. Good. Find me someone to talk to."

"Right Chief."

Orwell dipped a shortbread into his coffee. A mousetrap, he thought. Must remember to bring one. "First get Sam for me would you please?"

"He's waiting on two."

"Oh. Fine. Hi, Sam? You want some response to what Mr. Lyman said last night, is that right?"

"If you'd care to make one, Chief."

"You can say that 'the Dockerty Police Department doesn't involve itself in civic elections.' Please quote me exactly, Sam. You know how I hate it when you paraphrase me."

"I trim sometimes, Chief."

"I count . . . ten words, Sam. Shouldn't require much pruning."

"That's it?"

"We are now officially *off* the record, Sam. Gregg Lyman can say any damn thing he wants while he's running for office. Should he get elected and make the same statement while wearing his mayor's hat, I would definitely have a response, but as long as he's on a soapbox he's free to speechify as he pleases."

"I like the second quote much better."

"I wasn't speaking."

"I know, I know. Wouldn't even have to trim it."

"Goodbye, Sam."

"Much."

"Goodbye, Sam."

Captain Émile Rosebart of Metro's homicide unit sounded, to Orwell, as if he was reading a prepared statement. "Detectives Warner Hong and Thomas Siffert, in a misplaced but perhaps understandable excess of zeal brought on by the death of their valued comrade, unwisely brought the accused into Toronto for questioning. He has not yet been charged."

"They bringing him back here?"

"We're making arrangements to return him to Dockerty forthwith."

"Yes of course, 'forthwith,'" said Orwell. "Was he given access to a lawyer?"

"He didn't ask for one."

"Did he get his phone call?"

"I'll copy you into everything that transpired, Chief. I'm sorry about this. It shouldn't have happened."

"*They* bringing him up? Tong and the other guy?"

"*Hong*. And Siffert. No. They've been relieved of duty until SIU has a look at what happened. There may be disciplinary action taken."

"I should think there might." Orwell was doodling jagged lines on his legal pad around the names Tong and Hong and Siffert. "So how's this going to work? He's being delivered here and then what?"

"Under the circumstances, we've decided to hand him over to the OPP and they can deal with it."

"They'd better get him a bail hearing in a hurry," said Orwell. "He's been held incommunicado for, by my watch, 37 hours without seeing a judge. Harold Ruth's lawyer, once he's given the opportunity of speaking to one, is likely to make our lives miserable over this. Who's handling the evidence? Who's got his Winchester, wait, no, it's a Savage 30-30, who's checking that?"

"All we have we'll turn over to the OPP."

"That chain of evidence better be solid."

"Chief, I am at least as pissed as you are. They screwed up. They know it, they'll have to pay for it, it'll cost them, pay, maybe grade, I don't know."

"Ship the accused home, Captain. Sooner the better."

Four

Orwell was one Irishman who disliked St. Patrick's Day and all the nonsense that went with it — green beer and ridiculous hats. He did allow for a decorous measure of emerald trim in the station, provided the place was kept leprechaun-free. All shamrocks and harps had to be promptly removed by the morning of the 18th.

"Morning, Staff. Harold Ruth show up yet?"

"No, Chief. They've still got him. He could be en route, but I have no official . . ."

"Dorrie, Captain Rosebart. Right away."

"I'll get him for you, Chief."

"They'd better be handling him with kid gloves." Orwell stormed into his office, slamming the door behind him. He was back in three seconds, jacket half off, hat still on his head. "Well?"

"Trying to locate him, Chief."

"How can that be hard, on a workday morning? This isn't the first time they've pulled this nonsense. Tramping all over my town like we don't matter, kidnapping suspects. That's right: kidnapping. Dorrie?"

"Still can't locate him, Chief."

"All I can say is Mr. Ruth better look as fresh as a newborn

70

babe when he shows up. And he'd better by God show up soon or heads will roll. Heads will roll!"

This time Orwell's office door stayed slammed.

Stacy enjoyed it when the Chief got all oratorical. From the far side of the big room she could hear the Voice booming inside his office. She couldn't tell whether he was yelling into a phone or holding court. "What, no one knows *where* she is? I find that hard to . . . yes, would you do that for me, please?" It was a phone call. She heard him hang up, heard his tone turn rhetorical, perhaps addressing the world in general. He did that sometimes. "No *problem*? Is that what passes for polite discourse these days? No *problem*?" Brennan was in a mood. No doubt about it. "Of course it's no problem. It's your *job*." She saw the Chief appear at his office door and scan the room, perhaps looking for anyone who might disagree with him about something. "Dorrie, according to Detective Laka-whatever . . ."

"Lacsamana," Dorrie corrected.

". . . who has been giving me the runaround for the past ten minutes."

Dorrie handed the Chief a piece of paper. "I wrote it down."

Orwell glanced at the paper, crumpled it and jammed it in his pocket. "With any luck I'll never be forced to speak to the man again. According to . . . *him*, Detective Moen is taking some personal time and is unavailable. *Un*-available. Nonetheless, would you keep trying her number at regular intervals?" The Chief pointed at Stacy. "Detective Crean? Are *you* available?"

The Chief wasn't alone in his office. Staff Sergeant Rawluck was at parade rest, with his hands behind his back, his shiny boots shoulder width apart. Stacy's immediate boss, Lieutenant Emmett Paynter, recently promoted from detective sergeant, was sitting by the window wearing his usual shapeless grey suit. The Owl, they called him — round glasses, feathery hair, very slow blinks. Emmett wasn't a bad boss. Stacy had no problem with him. He was organized, had a sense of humour (if you liked fart jokes), knew the town, used his small force effectively and wasn't blind to the fact that his most productive investigator was a woman.

"Grab a chair," said the Chief.

"Thank you, sir." She nodded at the other men. "Good morning, Lieutenant. Staff Sergeant." She looked around for the designated chair. It was facing the Chief, but Stacy got the impression that it was Emmett's show, at least for the moment.

"You'll be at Billy Meyer's going away bash tonight?" Emmett asked. It wasn't really a question.

"Yes, Lieutenant. I'll certainly put in an appearance."

"Good, good, glad to hear it. Irish House."

"Can I put you down as a designated driver, Detective Crean?" Roy Rawluck wanted to know.

"Yes, Staff Sergeant," she said. Stacy didn't drink. "Happy to."

"Fine. Some of the lads might overdo the auld lang syne if you take my meaning."

Stacy waited quietly. She knew Billy Meyer's retirement party wasn't the reason she'd been called into the Chief's office.

Emmett shifted in his chair, blinked slowly. "So. Randy Vogt's going to be on his own, come, oh I guess Monday morning."

Had to happen. Might as well get it over with. "You're partnering me with Detective Vogt?"

"Yes, well, that was the plan. I don't have a lot of options." She saw Emmett and the Chief exchange a look.

"Sir? *Was* the plan?"

"Still is, still is, in the long run. But Detective Vogt has some vacation time coming, couple of weeks, and I think we can wait until he gets back to finalize things. That okay with you?"

"Yes, sir, certainly."

"Right then." He looked at her. A smile might have twitched the corner of his mouth, but she couldn't be certain. "Until things get sorted out you can work solo, a while longer."

Some days you get a reprieve. "Certainly, Lieutenant."

"Chief Brennan here asked if I could free you up to look into a few things for him."

"And your boss has generously offered to lend me your services for a little while." The Chief stood, signalling that the meeting was over, for some of the participants at any rate. Emmett stood, she stood, Roy Rawluck came to attention.

"What did we wind up getting him, sir?" she asked.

"Retirement gift? I think it's a . . ."

"A Kitchen-Aid mixer," Roy said. "Has all the attachments."

". . . right," Emmett finished. "He's going to take cooking lessons, I hear." He looked dubious. "Well, leave you to it then." He nodded at the Chief, headed for the door. "Irish House. Any time after eight."

"Looking forward to it," Orwell said.

The Chief motioned Stacy to resume her seat. She heard the door close. She was on her own.

"Cooking lessons," Orwell said. He sat, rubbed his big hands together as if preparing to dine. "Well, comes to us all, I suppose."

"Cooking lessons, Chief?"

"Retirement, Detective Crean. Hobbies, diversions, avocations. Fancy chickens."

Stacy allowed the Chief a moment to contemplate the inevitable, then got back to business. "What things would I be looking into, sir?"

"Well, for starters, the late Detective Paul Delisle's service weapon, a .357 Smith & Wesson revolver, is still missing. Lorna Ruth says he *did* have a gun, but Detective Moen believes it was his backup piece, a .32. So far, the .357 hasn't turned up among the dead detective's possessions." The Chief stood, motioned to her to stay where she was. He wanted to widen his range. "Now, there's nothing to suggest that the gun is anywhere around here, and there's nothing to suggest that it isn't simply in

Delisle's apartment, or with a gunsmith for repairs, or any one
of a hundred innocent explanations, so I'm not sending up any
red flags, but can we all at least admit that there's a gun floating
around *somewhere?*"

"Yes, sir."

He turned to the window. "Really coming down out there,"
he said. The rain was steady, he could almost see Armoury
Park growing greener under the shower. His voice turned
conspiratorial. "And *while* you're nosing around, ostensibly
looking for a missing revolver — which evidently is *no problem*
to anyone else — you might have a discreet chat with the dance
instructor, Ms. Daniel, and with Dr. Ruth."

"Yes, sir. Anything specific I'd be looking for?"

"Wish I could help you there, Detective. You're the investigator.
Go investigate."

"Yes, sir," she said. "No problem."

He swung around to glare at her. She was grinning.

Discreet nosing around. That's what he wanted. I suppose I could
go back over the little Omemee junket, talk to the bartender,
waitresses, liquor store manager, whatever. Just see if anybody saw
the thing. Adele said he wore it under his jacket, right side, in a
black Jordan spring clip, maybe the jacket was open when he paid
his check, maybe somebody bumped into him.

Discreet nosing around *for,* but not limited *to,* Delisle's missing
revolver. Why discreet? No red flags fine, let's not unduly upset
the populace about a wandering handgun. But what else are we
looking for?

Adele Moen was in Jamaica. It took Stacy three phone calls
to get the information. She knew a few cops in the GTA. Even
Dorrie was impressed. But *where* in Jamaica was still up for grabs.

Wouldn't mind going over a few things with her. There it was again, "go over a few things." What *things*? All right, she had notes from the first investigation. There was a reference to the shooting of some Russian man on the Queensway. Peel Division. Worth a call.

"Staff Sergeant Hurst? Hi there, this is Detective Stacy Crean, Dockerty Police Department, trying to get some information on a case you're working down there. Russian man shot in a motel room on the Queensway last week."

"You got a date?"

"No. A detective from Metro was up here checking a few things regarding that one. He just mentioned the basic facts . . ."

"This Delisle we're talking about?"

"That's correct."

"He said the guy was shot when?"

"He didn't say exactly, he said a week ago."

"Technically, I guess. Probably late Saturday night. When did he show up in your town? Monday?"

"Monday morning."

"The Queensway vic was found DOA Sunday morning. Four a.m."

"This is the same case?"

"I know this is a tough town, Detective, but one dead Russian a week is about our quota."

"He said there was material in the man's wallet that connected him to Dockerty in some way."

"There was no wallet. We wouldn't know anything about the dude except he had his union card in his pants pocket."

"What was his name?"

"Nimchuk. Viktor."

"Nimchuk," Stacy was writing it down. "I think that's Ukrainian."

"Ukrainian, Russian, Uzbek, doesn't really matter. Guy was a Soviet citizen until he defected back in '81."

"Have you made an arrest?"

"We don't have anything yet. In fact, the most interesting thing about the guy is you saying how much interest Delisle had in him."

"Find a weapon?"

"No weapon."

"Got a slug?"

"Well, yeah, got a bullet. Pretty mashed up."

"And?"

"Looks like it might be a .357."

"Smith?"

"Far as we can tell."

"That figures," Stacy said.

The cat was on the fire escape, looking in at her. Wet. Impassive. An unneutered tomcat, tiger-striped, orange and white, built the way mature tomcats get, heavy neck and shoulders, skinny ass, big balls. He never sprayed inside the studio. The first time he showed up at her window, she told him that the minute he lifted his tail inside her workplace, he would be banished for eternity. They had an understanding. She hadn't named him. She didn't feed him. Once, a few years ago, she left a dish of canned tuna out for him. He wouldn't touch it.

She opened the window enough to let him inside. He took his time, assuring himself that she was alone before stepping across the sill and dropping to the floor. He paused for a long moment and looked to be studying himself in the wall mirror.

"What do you see?" she asked out loud.

This is how one should live, she thought. This creature has no fear. He has no allegiance. All places are the same to him. He comes here when it suits him. Who can say how many other fire escapes, laneways, back porches he knows? Sometimes he goes away for weeks. Sometimes he stays for a while. Sometimes when he's bitten and bloody and hurt, he comes here to get better. Then he stays for a while.

"I think maybe you will have to find another fire escape," she said. "I may have to find another escape myself." She lit a smoke, deliberately closed the window and locked it. The cat jumped onto the settee under the photographs of her sad career, inspected the area carefully before settling himself. "You hear me?" she asked him. "Do not get too comfortable. That is the golden rule, is it not? Do not get too comfortable. The situation will be changing pretty soon, I think." She shook the tea kettle. Good. She wouldn't have to go down the hall to fill it. She plugged it in. In the photograph above the tea canister, she was wearing black feathers. She shuddered involuntarily. "Have you ever killed a crow?" The cat didn't move an ear. "They are like elephants, you know, they never forget."

And it wasn't even her fault. She was a child.

The crows near her home in Sosnovy Bor stole constantly. They took silverware off the picnic table, they took her father's medal off his coat while it hung in the yard, and they took her tiara when she was five years old. It wasn't a real tiara, it was a thing her grandfather made for her to wear with the tutu her mother had sewn. The jewels were paste and beads and pieces of coloured glass. It was pretty and she loved it. And a crow swiped it right off her head while she was dancing in the grass, swooped down and snatched it neat as you please, the way an eagle takes a fish from the ocean, took it and flew away to a tree and laughed at her, proud of what he'd done.

As soon as her grandfather picked up his shotgun, the crow took wing and the shot missed. But the tiara was left dangling on the branch. And against all reason save greed, or willfulness, the bird turned back to reclaim his pickings. The shotgun had two barrels.

What a racket. All the crows in the neighbourhood that day had something to say about the incident. Screaming and cawing and circling overhead. It didn't sound like grieving to Anya, crows lack the ability to *sound* bereaved, it isn't in their register. Whatever they might be feeling, it sounded accusatory, they were marking her as the villain.

The tiara had drops of blood on it. Her grandfather wiped it clean, but she never wore it again.

She made a single cup of tea. Irish Breakfast, with three sugar cubes, no milk, carried it to the front window and looked down at Vankleek Street, smoking, sipping, watching the normal people hurrying by in the rain. Lucky people.

Dr. Lorna Ruth was a pretty woman, or would have been if not for the numb expression, and the distracted way she was going about her work — shifting piles of papers, opening and closing drawers without looking inside. Cardboard boxes, empty and filled, were cluttering the outer office. She stared at the crammed bookcases and her shoulders slumped. "Have they brought my husband back yet?" Her voice was frayed, her attitude distant.

Stacy said, "He's supposed to be on his way."

"Will he get bail?"

"Probably. He doesn't have prior convictions, does he?"

"For killing people?"

"For anything violent."

"No. He's a gentle person." She turned slowly to survey the disarray. "I have to move." She sounded annoyed at the inconvenience. She kicked an empty box out of her way and went into her private office.

Stacy watched her from the open doorway. "Leave this building, or leave town?"

"I gave my receptionist two weeks' severance pay. That's the best I could do. She's been with me four years. I hated to let her go." She sat heavily at her desk, almost hidden behind the stacks. "My husband is probably going to jail for a very long long time. How can I stay here? My . . . lapse of moral judgement cost a man his life."

"They'll want you here for the trial."

"Oh yes. I'll be stuck here for a while. Removing myself from this town, from this life, won't happen overnight. I have patients. Some of them have cancelled, but some rely on me."

"What about Anya Daniel? Does she rely on you?"

"I don't know. Yes. Certainly."

"She is why Detective Delisle came to see you. Can you tell me what he was asking? That wouldn't violate anything, would it?"

"We talked about jazz. He told me he played piano. I told him I once met Oscar Peterson. That was about it. We arranged to meet. After that we didn't talk all that much."

"Did he mention a Russian man who was found dead in Toronto last week?"

"No, I'm sorry. We didn't talk about his cases. Except for questions about my patient, which I couldn't answer."

"And the questions about your patient? What did he want to know?"

"He wanted to know if she was delusional."

"Why didn't you stay at the restaurant? Was there someone you knew?"

"There's always someone. I was an idiot to think we'd be invisible." She wiped her hand across her mouth as if to remove a lingering taste of something bitter. "I just wanted a little romantic interlude. The first time I'd ever done anything remotely like that."

"I was just wondering if it was someone who might have told your husband."

"No. Just some people who could have recognized me." She opened another drawer. Closed it sharply. "I was very stupid. Very stupid."

"Can you tell me anything about Mr. Delisle's weapon? Did he take it off at any point?"

"I told him I hated guns. He put it in his suitcase. Is it important?"

"Probably not." Stacy made a note. "Your patient, Anya Daniel, I know you can't tell me anything about your private communication, and I wouldn't want you to, but I'm trying to determine if there is any connection between Ms. Daniel and the dead Russian. I don't suppose there's anything you could help me with there, without breaking the doctor/patient restriction?"

"Not really. She talks about Russia in very general terms. Her years with the ballet. Evidently she was destined to be a big star back there, but for some reason she had to defect. She won't go into that."

"What year are we talking about? That she had to defect?"

"In 1981. She was touring in the United States and Canada."

"Did something bad happen at home?"

"As far as I can make out, there was some political upheaval going on. New people coming into power. I'm afraid I don't know much about Russian political history."

"That makes two of us."

"She does say that they were all thieves back there. The big shots. She seems to have a special hate for someone named Chernenko. Do you know who that is?"

"I think he's dead," Stacy said.

"Not to hear her talk about him."

"I see. I'll let you get back to your packing then."

"I feel a deep sense of responsibility for what happened. If I hadn't been so stupid that man would be alive."

Stacy couldn't argue that point. "Try not to beat yourself up too much, Doctor," she said.

No, she wouldn't be beating herself up. Not over something so completely preposterous. Harold in the role of killer, of jealous vengeful murderer, was beyond preposterous — it was inconceivable, it went against anything rational. What happened to the red-haired detective was a horrible mistake, a grotesque aberration. She had other things to beat herself up over, sloppy session work, taking too long to do what she should have done a long time ago. But not this. This was not her fault. But it was a catastrophe. This could ruin all her good work.

There was the knocking again. That woman was back.

"Ms. Daniel? Dockerty Police. I'm Detective Crean. Like to talk to you for a few minutes."

She'll go away after a while. Just sit still. There's no need to open the door. If she wants in badly enough she can kick it down the way they like to do.

"Ms. Daniel. I know you're in there, I can smell the cigarette smoke. I'm not here to arrest you. I just have a few questions. Please open the door."

"What do you think?" she asked the cat. "Should we talk to her?" She raised her voice. "What questions?"

"Please open the door."

"Why do you not kick it down?"

"I don't think that's necessary, do you?"

"Do police need a reason?" Anya found herself crossing the room to the door. "Are you alone, or do you have an armed escort?"

"It's just me."

"Because I am a dangerous fugitive, you know? Were you aware of that?"

"No, ma'am. I wasn't aware."

"Oh yes," Anya said. "Most dangerous." She opened the door.

The woman in the hall looked the way she sounded, strong, self-assured, intelligent. "You do not look like the police." She left the door open and went back to the settee where her cigarette waited in an ashtray. A big orange tomcat looked up briefly. Stacy closed the door.

"How do police look?"

"Ha!" Anya's laugh was harsh. "Ugly men with ugly ties and bad breath from too many hamburgers."

Much of the room was bare wood floor. Windows met mirrors at one corner. At the other side was a screened changing area, a small upright piano with a CD player perched on top, and the sparsely furnished corner where the woman and the cat waited.

"I can make more tea, if you like."

"No. But thank you," Stacy said.

"Sit down then. Ask your questions."

Stacy sat across from her. "I'm sure you went over all this with the Toronto detectives earlier in the week."

"Yes. The Toothbrush and the Pimple."

Stacy laughed. "That's them," she said. "I spoke to Dr. Ruth."

"I fired her."

"She didn't break any confidences."

"That is good to know. Nevertheless . . . Are you leaving?" Stacy thought for a second that the question was directed at her, but the cat was stretching, jumping to the floor. Anya butted her cigarette, then escorted the cat behind the piano. "Nice of you to visit," she said. The cat took his time. Anya waited patiently until he was on the fire escape, then relocked the window. She looked at Stacy. "The ideal houseguest," she said. "Stays for an hour, does not steal the silver."

"The policeman who was murdered Monday night, did you have a name for him?"

"Beautiful hands," she said. "That was not a name, just an observation. I did not get to know him well enough to give him a name. He was different. You saw him?"

Stacy said, "Not at his best." The woman's lips tightened for a second. "He was in town because of you."

"So I have been told," said Anya. She sat on the piano bench, ran her fingers across the black keys, too lightly to produce notes. "And yet he never came. I am sorry about that."

"Do you know why he wanted to see you?"

"I expect he would have told me, had he lived long enough."

"It seems there was another man shot, in Toronto, two nights before. This man had some connection to you as well." There was a moment of silence. Anya's hand froze in the air above the keyboard. "Your picture was in his wallet."

She played a minor triad, gave a bitter smile. "A fan perhaps?"

"His name was," Stacy consulted her notebook, "Nimchuk." She looked directly at Anya, gauging her reaction. "Viktor Nimchuk." She saw the woman's shoulders sag, her left hand flattened on the piano keys to produce a dissonant chord that hung in the air, unresolved.

Her voice, when finally she spoke, was a weary whisper. "Then that is the last of them," she said.

"The last of who?" Stacy asked.

"The little band of smugglers," Anya said. "There were four. Viktor and Sergei and Vassili and Ludmilla, who were involved with each other for a long time." She looked up. "And me," she said. "Sometimes."

"You?"

"Once in a while I brought something in, took something out. Nothing important."

"You were a smuggler?"

"No, Detective. I was a dancer." She hit the keys, both hands, fingers splayed like blunt hammers. A booming major chord echoed for a moment. "I was destined to be a dancer as soon as my mother examined my arches. My mother wanted to dance, but she had flat feet. You know when you apply to the ballet school, the Vaganova, they measure everything. My arches were perfect. In the womb I was stamped."

"The other four, the smugglers." Stacy wanted to keep her on the subject.

"In some cultures smuggling is an honourable profession, do you know?"

"What did they smuggle?"

"Out of Russia? Cheap stuff, some fakes, ikons, furs, nothing of historical importance, nothing of great value, a few hundred here, a thousand there. A little more, a little less, depending."

"And in?"

"Dollars. American dollars. Mostly. It was not uncommon."

"Then what happened?"

"Viktor got lucky, or he thought so. He stole something very big. He stole it from an even bigger thief."

"What was it?"

"A big piece, covered in gems. Worth a lot of money, too much money for little gypsy smugglers, but Viktor did not know how much it was worth when he stole it."

"What happened to it?"

"They broke it into pieces, sold it over the years. It never gave them what they hoped it would."

"How about you? Did you get any of the jewels?"

Anya spread her arms. "All I have is what you see around you. Some fading photographs, a tea kettle, a rented piano."

"It's all gone?"

"Viktor had the last of it. If they killed him, they have whatever he had left."

"If *who* killed him?"

"Who knows? He was dealing with some bad people over the years. He thought he was so clever. Bad people from Montreal, from the United States, receivers of stolen jewels."

"You have any names, any descriptions, anything you can help me with?"

"I stayed away from him, Detective. As far as I could. I did not want any part of it. I did not want to defect, I was ready to rejoin the Kirov. I was ready to take back the career that was rightfully mine. Because of Viktor I had to run."

"But why, if you had no part in it?"

"Sometimes the niceties of a situation can be lost on people. You know what I mean? The people Viktor stole from were not nice people. They would not make the distinction."

The policewoman left her card, asked if Anya had plans to leave the city. Anya thought that was funny, but she didn't laugh. "If I decide to go anywhere, Detective, I will inform you," she said. "My whereabouts are never secret for long." After locking the door, she went to the window to see if anyone was taking note of the woman's departure. Nothing. Of course he would not be seen. Being invisible was not hard. *Staying* invisible was the difficult part. Was it not, Viktor?

Ah Viktor. You should have been the first to go. It would have saved so much trouble if you had been killed. During one of your little Montreal excursions perhaps. That might have made things simpler. Or best of all, back in Moscow, the day you bought the suitcase from that junkie friend of yours. If they had caught you right away, none of this would have happened. Caught you and killed you on the spot. Pretty Ludi would still be alive, sewing costumes, fussing over feathers and sequins. And Vassi would still be alive, painting forest scenery, fussing over pretty Ludmilla. And Sergei? What about you, Sergei? Are you out there? Sitting in a parked car, pretending to drink coffee in the café across the street? You have done pretty well for yourself, haven't you?

Viktor said, "Sergei, you can't go back, you will be shot if you go back." And what did you say, Sergei? You said, "No, *you* will be shot, you little piece of shit. Your life is worth nothing any more. I will tell them what you did, and they will send someone, and they will find you, all of you."

And they did send someone. Didn't they, Sergei? They sent you.

Orwell's wife never called him at work, except for emergencies, and never simply to chastise him, that was an indulgence she reserved for suppertime, but he had just been severely castigated (unfairly, he was certain) for his part in the latest domestic drama. The wedding was off.

His first emotion had been umbrage. "How can it be *my* fault?"

"I said not to push," Erika began (he could see her shaking her finger), "but you pushed anyway, you are always pushing."

That was an exaggeration, he was certain. "I didn't push, I offered, *we* offered, a piece of land for them to build a house on." He stood, as if to address a courtroom. "Was that a crime?"

"Did you even *ask* your daughter, privately, *first*, if it was such a good idea? No. Not you. You have to stand up at the dinner table and make a big announcement like Orwell the Beneficent that you want Patty and her intended, whose name you can barely remember . . ."

"Gary. Gary. Gary."

". . . that you wish to bestow . . ."

"I never used the word *bestow*."

". . . upon them a generous parcel of ten acres for their wedding present."

"Hell's bells, it's better than a waffle iron." He was starting to get steamed. This attack was most unwarranted.

"That's not a present. That's an obligation."

"Don't you want her to have it?"

"Now you are being offensive. What *she* wants, not what *you* want."

"Of course, that goes without saying."

"The day you go anywhere without saying, I will phone the newspapers."

With that she had hung up, leaving Orwell staring with

unfocused eyes at the aerial map of Newry County on the far wall. From where he stood he was sure he could make out a pulsing red spot where his farmhouse lay.

"Chief?"

"Yes, Dorrie?" he said wearily.

"Detective Crean is here."

"Oh good." He rubbed a hand across his face and dome. "Police work. Yes, right, that's what we're here for, isn't it? Get her in here."

The door opened. "A minute, Chief?"

"I'm all ears. One of them scorched." He pointed at a chair. "Anything turn up about Delisle's missing piece?"

"Not yet. But a Sergeant Hurst, Peel Division, says the guy who was shot down on the Queensway — Saturday night, not last week — a Viktor Nimchuk, was most likely shot with a .357 Smith."

"Oh my goodness."

"But they don't have a good bullet."

Orwell shook his head. "My my."

"Yes, sir," she said, hauling out her notebook. "And that ain't the half of it."

"Enlighten me."

"Interviewed the dance teacher. She tells me that Nimchuk was mixed up in some kind of smuggling deal back in '81, when they defected. He stole some jewels in Russia, and people have been trying to get them back ever since."

"Since *1981*?"

"She says they were pretty famous jewels."

"They'd have to be, wouldn't they? Thirty years. These jewels still around?"

"According to her they're all gone now. Nimchuk had whatever was left. He was the last one standing."

"Last of how many?"

"She says four. She wasn't one of them, she said, but she was tarred with the same brush. They had a regular little thing going when they went on tour and once in a while she took part in it."

"Okay, so back in '81, four dancers . . ."

"They weren't all dancers, Chief."

". . . all right, four members of a ballet company, five if you count her, smuggled some jewels into the country . . ."

"A famous necklace or something. They broke it up and sold the individual stones."

"And Nimchuk was one of them."

"He was the main guy, the one who did the actual stealing. The others sort of got caught in the net."

"Who were the others?"

"I've got the names, Chief." She checked her notebook, pronounced the names carefully. "Ludmilla Dolgushin, Sergei Siziva, Vassili Abramov, Viktor Nimchuk." She looked up. "They'll be in my report, Chief."

"Good."

"I've started a search, see if anything pops up about the other three. She figures they're dead, but she didn't have anything definite — dates, places. They might not have even been using those names. I'll go back at her tomorrow, start pinning her down on specifics."

"You think she's hiding things?"

"Definitely. And I think she's scared. She's acting like she figures she's next."

"Why, if the jewels are all gone?"

"Couple of possibles, I guess. The whole thing is a big fairy tale. Or if there aren't any jewels left, it's just payback for whoever was involved . . ."

"Or?"

"Or they *aren't* all gone, there's still some of it lying around somewhere, and they think she has it."

"She say who *they* were, Detective?"

Stacy turned a page. "Besides the Russian assassins who've

been chasing her for thirty years? Let's see. There's a Louie Grova, a pawnbroker who used to be in Montreal, now he's in Toronto. I checked him out. Not a hundred percent clean but nothing violent. Arrested for receiving but charges stayed. His brother's a diamond merchant in Montreal, Martin Grova. No record. The brothers had a falling out some years back."

"About jewels?"

"She didn't say."

"Lot of people after her."

"Oh yeah, and let's not forget Konstantin Chernenko, president of the Soviet Union." She closed the notebook. "He's long-dead, but the dance teacher assured me that his reach extends beyond the grave." Stacy waggled her fingertips. "Booga-booga," she said.

Orwell shook his head in wonder. "How about you, Detective? You buying any of that?"

"She's persuasive. But delusional people can be very convincing."

"So which is it, Detective. Is she delusional? Or is she in danger?"

"Hard to say, sir. She has a record — paranoid about people following her, trying to kill her — file goes way back. Toronto cops had her down as a loon."

"That's what our friend Delisle said. Except we now have at least one verifiable corpse connected to this business."

"Yes, sir."

"So maybe she's not completely loony."

"Maybe not."

"Strikes me our friend wasn't entirely candid about his reasons for being in town, was he? Maybe he was hunting jewels, too." His desk phone rang. "Yes, Dorrie? Jesus Murphy, it's about goddamn time!" He hung up. "Metro just brought Harold back," he said.

"About goddamn time," said Stacy.

Estelle Macklin presided over the Dockerty Public Library like
a dowager empress, imperious and chilly until newcomers had
established their custom and assured her of their respect for
the printed word. She had nothing against properly modulated
conversation, but could not abide books put back in the wrong
place. It was a rule of the library that research material be left on
the table so that her staff could do the job properly. Once Orwell,
attempting to be helpful, had inserted a Chagall catalogue on
a shelf of photography books and had received a stern lecture
for his troubles. Estelle had been head librarian since the place
was built and fully intended to see out her days within its well-
ordered confines. By now she was used to having Chief Brennan
drop in on his lunch hour. He had begun the habit out of a
desire to learn some basic Dockerty history, but lately his visits
had become more of a diversion from the irritations of his day,
allowing him a hushed half hour or so to wander the quiet
stacks in search of nothing in particular. His foraging in scholarly
pastures also kept him from visiting the all-you-can-eat buffet at
the Szechuan Garden in the East Mall.

"Mrs. Macklin, what do you know about Russian history?"

"I know where to find it."

"Recent Russian history. Say, 1980 through 1984."

"Have a seat, Chief. I'll get you some light reading."

Orwell took his favourite chair around the corner and out of
sight.

"What you need should be in here," said Mrs. Macklin, when
she returned with enough reading matter to keep him busy for
a year.

"Thank you," he said. "I probably won't get to the bottom of
this today."

"Leave them out when you've finished."

"Of course."

Mrs. Macklin left him to his research. He had to wade through Stalin versus Trotsky to the Warsaw Pact before he got to the basic information he was looking for. In late 1982, Leonid Brezhnev died after almost thirty years at the head of a regime noted for its corruption. He was succeeded by Yuri Andropov, former head of the KGB. Andropov hadn't lasted long in office. It was said that he "ruled from his hospital bed." He died of "kidney failure," but the presence of quotation marks in a scholarly tome suggested to Orwell that there might have been another explanation. Upon Andropov's death, power fell to his former rival, Konstantin Chernenko, the last of the old guard, born before the Revolution. Chernenko hadn't lasted long, either. He died in 1985, the cause of death "unspecified" (quotation marks again), although many, if not most, believed that it was cirrhosis. According to one account, upon Chernenko's death, large bundles of money were found in his desk drawer and in his office safe. Well then.

"Did you find what you were looking for, Chief?"

"Thank you, Mrs. Macklin. I am now much better informed than I was when I arrived, but I still don't have a clue what I was looking for, or if I found it."

"It's the searching isn't it, that gives us pleasure?"

"I suppose," he said, without conviction.

"Could I lend you an umbrella, Chief?"

"No, thank you. That's why I wear a big hat."

"Yes," she said. "Perhaps you could leave it with the umbrellas when you come in. It does tend to drip."

"I was careful," he said. "Besides, the last time I left a hat like this unattended, someone made off with it."

"Can't imagine why."

Georgie Rhem was waiting outside the library, a red-and-blue striped umbrella over his head. "I hear the coconut cream is back on the menu," he said. He looked remarkably cheerful considering the steady downpour.

"Oh darn, Georgie," Orwell said. "I have to pass. I've used up my quota of personal time for the day."

"Well, there'll be fresh pies next week, I'm sure." The two men started across Armoury Park. Despite the disparity in the length of their strides, they matched pace without difficulty. They walked together often. "Got a date for your presentation, Stonewall," said Georgie. "April 25th."

"Seems a long way off."

"It's pretty speedy the way things usually go. I don't think you'll be the only petitioner."

"At least it gives me some time. Haven't even started gathering all that stuff you say I'm gonna need."

"A little bit chaotic over in the Big House?"

"An interesting couple of days to be sure."

"I hear that Harold Ruth was renditioned into the murky depths of the Metro unit's filing system."

"Lordy Lordy," Orwell said. "Don't know what they were thinking. 'Excessive zeal' is how their boss put it."

"Juicy case for a motivated legal beagle." Georgie twirled his umbrella, spraying rain in Orwell's face. "So many stumbles and bumbles to play with. My my."

Orwell stopped in the middle of the walk and fumbled for a handkerchief. Erika always supplied him with a fresh one before he left home, he just never remembered which pocket he'd put it in. His old friend looked back with a trace of a smile and gave his umbrella a twirl in the opposite direction.

"Yes, that *would* be an interesting case for a lawyer," Orwell said carefully.

"The thing is," Georgie started, "*what* case? Has he been charged? Has he been brought in front of a judge? Have you heard from him? By my watch, he was disappeared for almost seventy-two hours."

"He's here now. OPP have him in custody."

"I know. I'm on my way to see him," Georgie said. He started walking again. "He finally got his phone call."

Orwell's laugh was brief, but genuine. "And he called you."

"It's not like he's spoiled for choices up here. Barristers who've actually done a murder trial, I mean."

"When was your last one, Georgie?"

"I'd have to check my files. I believe the firm had just purchased its first electric typewriter. State of the art it was. Yessir."

"I'll bet you were a big hit with the polka-dot bow tie and the 'aw shucks' country lawyer routine."

"That I was, my friend, that I was."

They stopped near Argyle's shiny brass shrine. "You'd think with all the money they spent on this place they could have stuck a roof over the porch," said Orwell. The two men looked at each other for a moment. Georgie grinned, Orwell sighed. "Henceforth I suppose we'd best exercise extreme discretion where this subject is concerned."

"Ah hell, I don't know. I might not be up to it."

This time Orwell's laugh was full-bellied. "You might aw shucks a jury, my friend, but it won't work on me. Any minute now, you'll start breathing fire."

"I just might," Georgie said. He spun his umbrella one last time and then furled it. "If nothing else, I'll have him back on the street before five. Least I can do."

"Oh dear," Orwell said. "Gord Blumberg is in for a fight." He opened the door and waved Georgie through.

Anya dozed most of the afternoon, curled up on the little couch, listening to the rain dancing on the fire escape. Once, she got up to see if the cat was back and to check the lane between the buildings. No sign of cat or killer.

"Is this George?"

"Yep."

"This is Anya Daniel. It is true Edwin is gone for a week?"

"Yeah, says he'll be back next Tuesday. Something about his sister's in the hospital."

"Who is driving tonight?"

"We've got four working tonight, because of the rain. You'll have to wait ten, fifteen minutes."

"Is that woman driving? What is her name, Olivia?"

"She's on a run up to Fenelon Falls. She'll be back in an hour."

"I do not like her, anyway. Who else is driving?"

"The new guy."

"What new guy?"

"Name's Simon. He's filling in for Ed."

She hung up. She did not trust new guys. New guys were always suspect. She would walk home. They will not kill me. Not while they are still looking for it. And they will not do anything stupid, not while there are police poking around. You have to bide your time. Stay very quiet. You think you are close, you *must* be close, you have eliminated all the other possibilities. And as long as you think I have it, you will be careful. Oh, who knows? You might get frustrated, grab me off the street, threaten me with pain. But I do not think you are ready for that yet, are you?

What does it matter anyway? There is only so far a person can run, only so long you can keep running. After a while you give up. Or lose your mind. Or they kill you. Or you kill them.

Steady monotonous rain without electricity or thunder. Vankleek Street was bare of pedestrians. Cars went by with wipers slapping, the people inside were dry and warm and listening to music. She let the rain plaster her hair to her scalp, ruin her shoes, soak the shoulders of her coat. She did not care. She broke her prime rule and took a direct route, straight down Vankleek where at least the lights were bright.

Past the Royal Hotel. Music called to her from inside, a woman's voice, one of those black women who sing like they are on their way up to heaven. She remembered the Royal had a snug bar away from the pool tables and the big screen television in the main room. Inside it wasn't crowded, even in the big room. The smaller room was deserted except for a nuzzling couple in a corner booth, and a young man with dark, curly hair standing behind the bar. He reminded her of someone she once danced with — the curly hair, sharp nose, curved like that bird who eats pine cones. No. Not a dancer. He reminded her of Ludi. That nose.

"Vodka," she said. "Is it cold?"

"I keep one in the freezer," said the bartender. "But it's the premium stuff, Absolut."

"I will have two or three," she said. "Probably three."

"Ice, twist?"

"Do you have any caviar?"

He laughed. "No."

"Then just vodka, straight, in a small glass."

"Still coming down, eh?" he asked as he poured the shot.

"Of course," she said. "I only drink when it is raining."

The Chief arrived at the back door of the Irish House at the same time as an overloaded delivery guy from Mama Rosa's Pizza, who was wearing a poncho like a pup tent to keep rain off the six extra-larges in his arms. Orwell graciously held the door for the lad, then followed him down the hall past the *His* and *Hers*. The Pride of Erin, as the pub was bravely named, had a large back room suitable for gatherings. A hand-lettered sign reading "Reserved for Private Function" was propped on a chair by the entrance. The sign had seen much use over the years and was stained and creased from revelries past. A Guinness representative passing through town the previous month had festooned the place with harps and silly hats and there were tenacious shamrocks and bloody leprechauns everywhere. Orwell was sure remnants of St. Patrick's feast would stick around until the Halloween decorations went up.

Cheers for the arrival of food were followed almost immediately by hearty but respectful greetings as the Chief stepped in. He gave them all his most comradely handshakes, one after the other, with extra attention paid to the guest of honour, to whom he expressed the Dockerty Police Department's official appreciation for twenty-five years of service, as well as the Chief's personal good wishes and hopes for a comfortable and well-deserved retirement. He then presented the man with a medallion affixed to a small wooden plaque, and held a pose and a handshake long enough for the official and unofficial photographs. Having done his duty, Orwell accepted a cup of coffee, declined a slice of pepperoni and mushroom, and eased his way to the edge of the crowd.

As retirement parties go, the one for Billy Meyer was subdued, but it was early yet. The Chief, by no means a teetotaller, was nonetheless abstemious in public. Things would liven up after he'd gone and after the family men headed home. Dermot Grice, the publican, would be selling more drink to fewer people once the old hands settled in for war stories and lies.

Orwell's plan was to stick around for the presentation of the going-away appliance, collect Leda from rehearsal down the street and be on his way home by 9:30. Not that he was in a rush to return to the domestic fray. Erika was pointedly not speaking to him. Patty was in her bunkroom in the barn, polishing saddles and weeping. When he took her supper, he'd been told to go away. How one generous impulse could have ruined so many lives was beyond him. Let's face it, if they were really right for each other, this situation wouldn't have wrecked things. And if it did, perhaps it was good that they confronted their incompatibility now rather than later. When he made that observation to his wife, he'd been met with stony silence, although after she'd stalked out of the bedroom he was sure a stream of German invective had trailed her down the stairs. His buttons were only half-polished. He was definitely in the doghouse if she was willing to see him leave the house in that state.

He spotted Stacy checking in with Staff Sergeant Rawluck. As one of the designated drivers, she would be on call until everyone else was safely home. It was understood that while Orwell was easygoing in many areas, he was the fist of doom on the subject of alcohol and driving under the influence thereof. God might help a Dockerty cop caught behind the wheel with liquor on his breath; the Chief wouldn't.

"Evening, Detective," he said.

"Good evening, sir. Thought you'd like to know, I got a hit on one of those names."

"One of the missing smugglers?"

"Yes, sir. Female, Ludmilla Dolgushin. Montreal. Body was found inside a refrigerator at a dump site."

"When?"

"Found twenty-one years ago."

"Goodness me."

"Wasn't identified for over three years. No leads, no connections. Open case." She lowered her voice. "Montreal is suddenly *very* interested in what we're doing. I said I'd check with you about coordinating our efforts, but I didn't go into detail."

"Splendid," said Orwell. The evening was getting much more interesting. "*Two* dead bodies now connected somehow to our visitor from the big city."

"Who is also dead," said Stacy.

Orwell put down his coffee cup and led the way to a quieter corner. "Have we given any thought to a connection between his death and the other two?"

"Can't see one yet. Looks like jealousy. Not well planned. Impulsive."

"I suppose," he said, dubiously. He drummed briefly on the grimy wainscotting then grimaced as he checked his fingertips. "But you'll still be looking into that aspect."

"Of course, sir."

"'Course you will, Detective, 'course you will. I know that — just thinking out loud." He pulled a handkerchief out of his pocket. "I mean, it's a big coincidence."

"Yes, sir."

"Big." He wiped his fingers and stuffed the handkerchief back in his pocket. "Yessir. Big coincidence."

"I've been thinking, sir." She turned her back to the room, held up a fist and began laying out her thought process one finger at a time. "If it *was* a coincidence, just something that happened out of the blue, say, and if this business with missing diamonds or whatever has Montreal diamond dealers, or Toronto pawnbrokers, or maybe even a Metro cop involved, then maybe the 'coincidence' upset a lot of people's plans."

"Full report on Monday morning."

"Yes, sir."

"But maybe we should keep an eye on Ms. Daniel for a while. Don't want any more dead bodies showing up if we can help it."

"I agree, sir."

The Chief waved across the room. "Staff?"

"Chief?"

"A moment, please."

Roy Rawluck disengaged himself from a knot of uniforms at the far end of the room and marched in the Chief's direction. "I don't know who organized this shambles," he said, "but it's a bloody poor show for twenty-five years on the job."

Orwell gave a philosophical shrug. "The detective squad doesn't have a man with your organizational skills, Staff Sergeant."

"One of *my* lads reaches retirement, we do it proper. Last year ..."

"That was a fine evening, indeed, Staff. Entertainment, good food."

"And no one really liked Constable Druck," said Roy. "Still, sent him off with ceremony."

"However when I leave office, please allow me to slip out the back door," said Orwell.

Roy looked somewhat offended by the suggestion. "Something you wanted, Chief?"

"There is. Requiring some coordination. We're going to need a unit to keep tabs on someone."

"Stakeout?"

"Protection. Anya Daniel. She may be in some danger."

"We talking round-the-clock, Chief?"

"No, no. Nothing that critical." He looked around, momentarily confused. "I don't think ... at least I hope not. What *is* that?"

Stacy said, "You've got Marvin Gaye in your pocket, Chief."

Orwell looked somewhat embarrassed as he pulled out his cellphone. Leda had programmed the ringtones for him. "I'll Be Doggone" meant police business. "Hello?" He made a polite quarter-turn away. "What's up, Jidge?"

Roy, equally polite, also rotated his shoulder a quarter-turn and frowned at the sagging shamrock swags and distressed harp posters. "Could have had a proper event," he harrumphed. "The Avalon has a nice buffet."

Stacy, more familiar with cellphone etiquette in which loud one-sided conversations are the norm, stayed where she was. She heard Orwell's voice change. "Where is she now? In the ambulance? Who caught it? Danaher?"

Roy was immediately alert.

"Right, tell him to lock things down. I'm on my way." He closed the phone and looked at the two of them. "Staff, get someone over to Dockerty General Emergency."

"That Daniel woman?"

"No," he said with a look of bewilderment. "Lorna Ruth. She was attacked in her office."

After a while she got bored with love noises from the couple in the corner, cooing, coaxing and half-hearted refusals. Oh for goodness sake, find a room. With a door. She had to leave anyway: getting drunk in a bar was too expensive these days. Her budget couldn't handle her thirst.

It was still raining, but not as hard. The storm drains were keeping up. She crossed against the lights, moving lightly, dodging a solitary car and throwing the driver a wave. On the other side she crooked an arm around a signpost and swung back and forth, gathering her body, making sure it was hers. She was a little drunk. Not too drunk to walk home, or dance home if she felt like it. Or run. Her feet didn't hurt. That was a blessing. She would be on the run again soon enough. It was unavoidable, inevitable, she could feel the threats gathering. Dark clouds and darker shadows. Deep breath now, chin up, look around, four directions, up and down the streets. Where were they tonight? It does not matter, really. They will show themselves soon enough. She turned up the collar of her coat, cinched the belt, tucked the end under the buckle and started moving, paying attention to shadows.

Well now, where should I run this time? East? West? North? Maybe far north, somewhere uncomfortable, somewhere the hounds would hate visiting, somewhere very cold. Serve them right. I have made it too easy for them. Letting them follow me to places with hotels and restaurants and hot water. I will run north this time. And then what? Then I will sit on an ice floe and quietly freeze to death and they will all give up.

On the far side of Armoury Park, Kasemore Drive curved uphill above the locks. A chain-link fence ran along one side, guarding the top of a wooded slope, and through the trees she caught a glint of water. The fence was sagging and there were many holes. Transients and teens used the cover of the trees for all sorts of things. A sidewalk ran along the other side with parked cars facing downhill along the curb.

It was too bad really, I almost had a life here. Poky little town. A place to live, a place to work — for a while it was almost worth being alive. Well, nothing lasts forever. She had a limited capacity for happiness, anyway. She knew that. No doubt her mother's influence. Mama was a melancholy soul. Sad-happy at the best of times. Happy-sad. And fearful, always. It rubs off. And then there was being Russian. Yes. North. I have decided. I will escape to the ice floes and the snow.

Ahead of her, a car door opened and the man got out. The big man, the one from the park, the one pretending to read the wet newspaper. He came around the back of his car and started toward her down the sidewalk. He looked exactly like what he was.

She spoke to him in Russian. "Who do you represent? Is Sergei still hunting? Are you his big dog?" She dodged into the middle of the road, testing the footing, checking escape routes. The man was forced to squeeze between the front bumper of his car and the rear of a minivan. One of his trouser legs caught on the van's license plate and she heard him curse and stumble forward. She heard the material rip. She laughed at him. "What happened to the others? You running out of money? The last time you found me, there were three of you." The man was in the road now, moving toward her, arms wide like a farmer herding chickens. "You asking me to dance?" The man scowled. No sense of humour.

Further up the road she could make out a narrow gap in the fence. She'd have to get past him to use it. She bounced lightly on the balls of her feet, flexed her toes inside her shoes, felt the asphalt through the soles, wet but tight, thin rubber, enough traction. She waited for him to get closer. She felt the icy calm

and fierce clarity come over her, the peculiar state she entered
when she stood in the wings listening for a single note of music,
her cue to do what should be impossible, to hear an audience
stop breathing as she took flight. And this rolling tank thinks
he can catch me? Yuri was the only one who could catch me,
enfold me in mid-flight, not this ordinary human with fat legs
and clunky leather-soled shoes. Not on a wet street, in the dark.
Just a little closer, soon he will lunge, he wants me in a big bear
hug, soon, a little closer . . . and . . . my cue.

When he made a grab for her, she ducked under his arms,
spun behind him, shoved the small of his back. He stumbled,
fell to one knee. She ran for the fence, heard him cursing and
scrambling to gain his footing. The gap was narrow, a ragged
slit made with bolt cutters, mended with wire, cut again. Just
wide enough for school kids, or for a small woman. Halfway
through, her buckle caught on a wire thorn and she got hung up
as the man slammed into the chain-link making it rattle in both
directions. He reached through the gap to grab her coat and pull
her face against the fence. She could smell garlic and sweat. She
spat in his eye. He tried to hit her and cut his knuckles on the
jagged edges of the gap. She yanked the belt free of the buckle
and slipped it through the loops, left it hanging on the wire. He
lost his grip on her wet sleeve and she stepped back from the
fence. She watched him for a long delicious moment, watched
him struggle like a rhinoceros in a cargo net, his sleeve caught, his
hand bleeding. He pounded the chain-link in frustration.

"You should put a bandage on that," she said. "But the suit is
ruined, you think?"

She was laughing as she picked her way down the slope
through the dark trees. Deep delicious breaths. Survival. Nothing
like death deferred to amplify the life force, recharge the energy
reserves. There was a walkway at the bottom that ran alongside
the locks, and further along there was a footbridge she knew, and
on the other side of that, a street led to her street. She could still

hear the rattle of chain-link fencing above her. The sound elated her. She was triumphant. That is the second time you failed to hold me, she thought. I do not think you are very good assassins at all. I do not think you work for Chernenko, or whoever inherited what was under his mattress. I think you are working only for yourselves. Common thieves, that is all. Is that what you have become, Sergei? You and your thug? Just thieves? How pathetic.

She emerged from the dark trees and checked the footpath. Deserted. Sergei must be close by. Waiting for me. Expecting a delivery. He will not be pleased with you, whoever you are. The thought made her quite happy. It was an unfamiliar feeling.

There were open doors along the fourth floor corridor, curious neighbours, a uniformed policeman taking a statement from the slovenly woman down the hall, evidence of a minor earthquake inside her apartment. That goon had started out energetically, she thought, but he quit in a hurry. The bedroom was almost neat. Drawers pulled open, the mattress flipped. Silly.

"Can you tell if anything's missing, ma'am?"

A handsome young uniformed boy was standing inside her doorway. Still a child, his cheeks were pink. "Nothing missing. I do not have anything to steal."

"Ms. Daniel?"

The uniform stood aside to let someone in. It was the big man, the police chief himself, filling her doorway. Behind him was the woman from the afternoon, the detective with the stylish boots and the dark eyes. "You are too late," she said. "They have made off with my three-ply toilet paper."

"Ms. Daniel. My name is Orwell Brennan. I'm ..."

"I know who you are." She faced him. "It is Zubrovskaya."

"I'm sorry, I don't speak any Russian."

"Zubrovskaya. That is my name. Anya Ivanova Zubrovskaya."

"Very well, Ms. Zubrov . . ."

"Practice it. Zu-brov-ska-ya. Go ahead."

"Zubrovskaya."

"Bravo. You may call me Anya."

He smiled at her. She almost believed his smile. It was wicked, like a little boy who just found matches in his pocket.

"Anya. Do you know who did this?"

"What, this?" A slow pirouette amid the wreckage. "This is nothing."

"It looks like a break-in to me. Your neighbour called the police."

"How neighbourly of her."

"Otherwise they might have still been here when you got home."

"I usually arrive earlier than this, but tonight I decided to drink instead."

"Are you all right to talk?"

"I am Russian. Vodka is fuel for talk."

"Fine. Do you have any idea who did this?"

"Certainly. Chernenko did it. Konstantin Chernenko."

"He's dead, isn't he?"

"Not everyone has been informed of his demise." She turned on the little clock radio atop her refrigerator and located the all-night classical station.

"And these people are after you?"

"Not me. They do not really care about me."

"Then what?"

"Bah!" she said. "Schumann. I do not like Schumann." She lowered the volume, leaned against the refrigerator and looked at him. "You want to hear a story? Do you have time for a story?"

"Yes, I have time."

"Good. I am drunk enough to tell you a story. Let me see if they left my vodka alone." There was a small bottle in the freezer compartment. She found two glasses in the cupboard above the stove. "Okay," she said, "turn the couch back over and we will have a drink and I will tell you some things."

"Actually, I'm working now," Orwell said. "I don't drink when . . ."

"Do not be silly. If you do not drink with me, we cannot have a conversation. It is not sociable."

"All right then."

"Good. Now you are being sociable. Tell the other ones to leave us alone."

He stepped into the hall. The young cop came to attention. Roy Rawluck's influence. "Everything sorted out with the neighbours, Constable?"

"Yes, sir. No eyewitnesses. Some noise. Woman at the far end saw a man going out the fire exit, didn't get a look. Said he was big."

"Okay, see if you can get everyone back in their apartments."

"Yes, sir."

"I can go back to the doctor's office," Stacy said quietly. "Have another look around."

"And keep checking with the hospital," Orwell said. "I want to know the minute she wakes up."

"Yes, sir. I'll stay in touch."

"You do that," he said. "You'll have to drive me home. She intends to ply me with alcohol."

"Watch yourself, Chief. She looks frisky."

Orwell sighed and closed the door on Stacy's smirk.

"Turn out that overhead light," Anya said. "I found a lamp that works. I hate overhead lights. Do you?"

"It's a bit glaring," he said.

"It is punishment," she said. "Like in jail. Come over here. Take off that big coat and sit by me. Here." She handed him a small glass half filled with clear liquid. *"Nazdrovya!"* She clinked his glass with her own.

"*L'Chaim*," Orwell said.

"Yes, that is a nice one. 'To life.' Drink now, do not try to fool with me."

Orwell had a sizable bite. Raw Polish vodka, straight. He felt it all the way down to his stomach.

"There now," she said. "Now we are sociable."

"How did you come to change your name to Daniel?" he said.

"Do not get ahead," she said. "I am telling the story. Ah ... good," she said, as the music changed. "Borodin. Much better for a Russian story." She had another drink, and so did Orwell.

"Anya Ivanova Zubrovskaya," she began, "came from a family of staunch Party members. She was raised to believe without question in the nobility of the Soviet system. She learned to dance from teachers and choreographers who are legends." She refilled their glasses. "In 1977 she was a principal dancer with the Mariinsky. You know of the Mariinsky? On tour, it was called the Kirov."

"Yes, of course," he said. "Well, let's say I've heard of it."

"Believe me when I say it was the best. The finest ballet company in the world. Nureyev came from there. Baryshnikov, other ones you never heard of who were just as great, believe me, maybe greater. Sergeiev, Dudinskaya, Yuri Soloviev, he was maybe the greatest of them all."

"I've heard of Nureyev, of course," Orwell offered.

"Of course you have. But trust me, the Kirov had more than one Rudi."

"I believe you."

She drank again. Orwell pretended to.

"Anyway, I must not bore you with ancient history."

"It's your history I'm interested in," he said.

"Of course. My history with the Kirov. It ended in 1978. An asshole named Grégor dropped me during the *Swan Lake* pas de deux. Dropped me like a sack, in front of an opening night audience. The Supreme Soviet was there with all their medals. Fucking Brezhnev was there, may he rot forever in the hottest corner of hell. It was supposed to be a big night for me. And he dropped me. I ruptured my Achilles tendon. I made it worse of course. I finished the performance. Artists are so vain, so stupid."

She drank for a while in silence. Orwell sipped his drink and watched her. A commercial for a package tour to the Bahamas came on, and then one for a funeral insurance plan. Finally, music again. Orwell recognized Mozart. The string quartet seemed to pull her back from some sad place.

"I took a year and a half to recover. But I was not the same. I was good. Do not kid yourself. I was very good. Just not quite Kirov-good. Not yet. So they let me go."

"That must have been devastating."

"It happens," she said. "I would have made it back. I was almost there." She filled her glass again, topped his up. "You are pacing yourself. That is okay. Keep your wits. This is where it gets interesting."

She rose and began to move around the room as in a stately dream, no trace of intoxication, light, measured steps instinctively keeping time with Mozart's lacy figures, her head held high, her eyes almost closed.

"It was in 1981," she began, "late in the year. Brezhnev was going to die soon." At that she smiled. "And all the shitheads were trying to decide where their loyalties lay. Andropov, the king of the KGB, was moving to the head of the table. He held too many secrets to be ignored. And the one with the most to lose was Chernenko, Brezhnev's bum boy from the beginning. He was going to have to watch his back."

Anya crossed the room and picked up her coat where she had dropped it on the floor. She patted her pockets and took out a bent package of Players and a Bic lighter.

"Have a smoke with me," she said.

"I quit some years back," he said.

"Do not be unsociable," she said. "I'm giving you a great story here."

"Okay," he said. He let her light it for him and was deeply dismayed at how good it tasted. There will be hell to pay when I get home, he thought.

She looked at the glowing tip of her cigarette. Waved it in a tiny figure eight. "You see this pretty red light?" she said. "Imagine this red light as big as a pullet's egg."

Orwell, with his newfound interest in fancy chickens, had a good idea how big that would be. "Okay," he said.

"It was called the Ember," she said. "Some called it the 'Sacred Ember' but that was back when Russians believed in God."

"What was?"

"Tsarina Alexandra Feodorovna's ruby. Ninety-seven carats, mounted like a heart in the centre of a crucifix, surrounded by sapphires and diamonds and pearls. On their own, the stones around it were worth a great fortune, the four sapphires alone were worth a million. But the ruby, the ruby itself was priceless. Maybe the largest in the world. Flawless. Burmese. Blood red. And deep in its blood-red heart it had the magic thing they call a 'feather.' A star. It was very special. But a stolen treasure requires careful marketing."

She put her glass beside the sink and found a saucer for an ashtray. The radio on top of the refrigerator now gave her something that made her swoon. Tchaikovsky. "Ahhh," she sighed. "Now you are talking. I have danced to this."

She lifted her arms above her head and there, in the small disordered apartment, Orwell saw for a fleeting moment how she might have looked on a stage. The music curved her back and extended her neck. She rose on her toes, bent forward at the waist, and lifted one leg behind her, impossibly high, held the position for a full measure of the melody. And then she looked at him and raised her eyebrows. "Yes?"

"Lovely," he said. And meant it.

She returned to the couch and settled in, with glass, ashtray and freshly lit cigarette, tucked her legs under her and wiggled herself into the corner.

Orwell had another sip of vodka, another illicit puff of tobacco. "What happened to the ruby?" he said.

"Okay," she said. "Back to business." She emptied the bottle into their two glasses, in equal measures. "How Chernenko got his hands on it no one will ever know," she said. "All the big ones robbed when they could. They were looting from before the Revolution. They never stopped. But Chernenko knew if he had to run, maybe he shouldn't show up in the West with a state treasure in his pants pocket. So he called up one of his old friends, Yuli Vystovsky, who ran the Moscow black market the way De Beers runs the diamond business. Vystovsky delegated the actual smuggling and fencing to a man named Piotr Romanenko. Do not try to remember these names. They are all dead now anyway." She smiled at him as she watched him take a deep delicious drag on the cigarette. "I knew you were a sinner in your heart," she said.

"True," he said. "All too true."

"So," she went on, "this Romanenko had made many profitable trips to the West selling sable skins, caviar, even heavy artillery, but Vystovsky didn't know of Comrade Romanenko's recently acquired addiction to cocaine. It was an unfortunate craving that obliged him, from time to time, to visit a man named Fyodor Kapitsa.

"Anyway, Romanenko was about to leave for the West with certain goods in his possession, and he stopped at Kapitsa's place of business for travelling supplies. Romanenko didn't like to fly, so Kapitsa gave him something that was supposed to make his journey more bearable. Instead, it knocked him unconscious." She laughed, shook her head at the ridiculousness of the situation. "Kapista got worried. He had to carry Romanenko to bed. And while that was going on, an opportunistic little addict named

Andrei Kolmogorov made off with Romanenko's suitcase."

"With the ruby inside." Orwell butted the cigarette. He had smoked it down to the end.

"Of course, Kolmogorov did not know that. He was in a hurry to convert the suitcase into cash. All he saw inside were silk shirts and high-class toiletries, and he knew someone who liked silk shirts and was willing to receive stolen goods. Viktor Nimchuk." She drank some vodka. Her eyes were drifting away from Orwell, looking into the past. She was about to go on tour. "Viktor was to leave the Soviet Union, too, the next morning, along with the Volga ballet company." She bobbed her head as if accepting a prison sentence. "And that is where I come into the story."

The Volga company. Castoffs, also-rans, close-but-no-cigars, the nearly great and the merely good. But they had one thing in common: they were all trustworthy, loyal and untainted by 'decadent influence.' Which meant that they were allowed to travel outside the country. There were no Nureyevs, no Baryshnikovs, no incandescent stars who would fly into the welcoming arms of the West. Good solid performers capable of dancing on any stage, under the baton of any conductor. Adaptable, presentable and cheap. They toured places the Kirov did not deign to visit, tolerated marginal accommodations, second-rate orchestras, erratic tempi, borderline lighting and bad floors. And to supplement their negligible remuneration, some of them did a little smuggling on the side.

"We were already in the U.S. when Viktor found the secret compartment. By then it was too late. He had something too big to sell, too big to give back. And who could he give it back to? By then, the others were probably all dead. By then, they would know where the thing had gone. By then, they would already be after Viktor." She got off the couch. Her glass was empty. She was out of cigarettes.

They went out to buy cigarettes. The liquor store was closed, it was after one in the morning. Orwell could see Stacy's unmarked car following a discreet distance behind as they walked to the 7-Eleven on Vankleek Street. It had stopped raining. The streets glistened and the stars were out. Anya went into the store, Orwell went around the car to Stacy's window.

"How you holding up, Chief?" she asked.

"Woman tells a good story," he said. "You?"

"Dr. Ruth's had a concussion. They won't know how bad it is until they get some specialist up here to have a look. She probably won't be answering questions for a while."

"But she's going to live?"

"Hard to get a straight yes or no out of her doctor," Stacy said. "She's in a coma. Don't know how deep or when she'll wake up. She's alive, for the moment."

"Goddammit!" said Orwell, who rarely cussed. "Goddammit all!"

"Yes, sir."

"What about her office?"

"Hard to tell what's gone until she's awake enough to tell us what was in there. Place was trashed worse than that apartment."

"Two break-ins on the same night? We're way past coincidence now, Detective."

"How did Ms. Daniel react when you told her about her doctor?"

"Haven't mentioned it yet. She's nervous enough. Besides, I'm enjoying the tale too much."

"The Staff Sergeant has assigned Constable Maitland to keep an eye on her tonight. He's parked across the street."

"Good."

"Want a breath mint, Chief?"

"Give me a couple," Orwell said. "I'm probably going to have another smoke."

"You're just going to hell in a handbasket, ain'tcha?" said Stacy.

Orwell walked Anya across the street and into the park.

"You are very married, are you not?" she said.

"Yes I am," he said.

"You make her feel safe? Your wife?"

"I suppose. She's the kind of person who's always preparing for emergencies."

"Ha! Good luck to her on that."

They stopped beside a big maple. Anya ran her hand lovingly across the wet bark.

"How did Nimchuk get the necklace into Canada?"

"That was the easiest part. It was so absurd it looked right at home in a basket full of costume jewels, paste and pewter, glass beads and feathers. Once we were across the border, I defected. I had no choice."

"Then what happened?"

"Nimchuk took the gems with him and he ran. He sold a few of the diamonds, the smaller ones, and he got enough money to hide for a while. But I could not hide so easily. I was a dancer, if I did not dance, I did not eat."

She tore open the fresh package of Players, offered him one. He lit hers, and then his.

"I changed my name. I became Anna Vaganova for a while. I was engaged as a guest artist by the Winnipeg Ballet. And for a few years I was okay."

"And then?"

"And then Chernenko died. Gorbachev took over in the Soviet Union, Glasnost, Perestroika, a new age. I got ambitious again. I wanted recognition. I thought it would be safe. The National invited me to be a guest artist in Toronto. Be careful what you wish for, they say. I got my recognition. Someone saw me and told someone, who told someone, and one night they followed me home to my apartment and they broke in. They were going to kill me."

"Who?"

"What does it matter? They were hired killers working for another faceless killer. I told them, I do not have what you want, I just do not have it, Nimchuk has it, he took it all, he is selling it, in pieces, I do not know where he is, I do not know where he hid the pieces." She laughed. "So they threw me off the balcony. They killed me. Or they thought they did. From the fifth floor. They did not know I could fly."

"What happened?"

"I told you. I flew. There was a tree, a beautiful maple tree, like this one, tall and smooth, with big strong arms. When they pushed me over, I had enough time to bend my legs and propel myself away from the railing. I flew into the top of the tree like a bird, and it caught me. By the time they got down the elevator I was far away. I had cracked ribs, I was black and blue, cut and scratched, my wrist was broken, three of my fingers were hyper-extended and I tore a ligament in my elbow. But I was alive, and strong enough to climb down from my wonderful tree and run away."

"And you ran up here."

"Eventually." She started to walk again, across the wet grass, heading in the direction of the Gusse Building.

"Doesn't sound like much of a life — running, hiding, waiting for the axe to fall."

"I will tell you something, Mr. Policeman, I have *never* had a 'life.' When you are a dancer, your life is classes, rehearsals, performing, stretching, recuperating, not enough to eat, not enough sleep, and everything else, *everything*, has to fit in between. If there is a little time left over you can fall in love for a few minutes." She laughed. "I was getting to like this town," she said.

"You planning on running again?"

"I do not know," she said. "I am tired of being chased."

"I'll have my officers keep an eye on you," he said.

"Every minute?"

"This isn't a big town," Orwell said. "If the person who broke into your apartment isn't from around here, we might be able to spot him."

"To me, everybody looks like an assassin. Except you. Maybe."

"No, I'm just a poor sinner," said Orwell, popping a breath mint into his mouth.

They had reached the Gusse Building. She unlocked the front door.

"I will spend tonight in my studio," she said. "I have done it before. There is a couch, a blanket."

"I'll come up with you," he said. "Make sure it's safe."

"Your wife is a lucky woman."

"Perhaps. But she'll have questions about tonight."

"It is good for her."

"It is?" He followed her up the stairs.

"That you surprise her from time to time."

"She hates surprises."

"I know. It will remind her that you cannot prepare for everything."

The sign on her door read "Daniel Dance Academy." Orwell took the key from her, unlocked the door, reached inside and flicked a light switch. Fluorescent fixtures pulsed to life illuminating the long room, the wall of mirrors, the tall windows overlooking Vankleek.

"I will be okay now," she said. "You are a good listener."

"You tell a good story."

Orwell followed her to a corner where there was a couch and chairs and a cabinet with a kettle. On the wall were a few photographs, signed with illegible scrawls: Anya with famous partners, Anya with a famous conductor, a choreographer, Anya alone, in the costume of a black swan. Among the photographs, hanging from a nail by their fraying pink ribbons, was a pair of toe shoes, tattered, broken, scuffed, discoloured. "They take a beating, shoes like this," she said. "They do not last long." She smiled. "Like dancers."

"This is a special pair?"

"*Giselle*," she said. "For the Mariinsky. My triumph. The prima ballerina got sick and I was elevated. They are signed, you see? Soloviev. A name you would not know, but . . ." She held the shoes to her breast for an instant. "I was wonderful," she said.

"I wish I could have seen it," Orwell said.

She hung the shoes carefully on the nail, touched the signature on the toe. "He killed himself, you know, Soloviev. He was maybe the best of them all and he killed himself." She turned on a reading lamp, threw her coat across the piano bench, then opened the fire escape window to admit a large orange tomcat. The cat looked at Orwell for a long moment before coming all the way in.

"What's his name?" Orwell asked.

"Who knows? He will not tell me." She followed the cat to the couch and they both sat, side by side. "I am tired now," she said. "Finally. It was a long day."

"Yes it was," said Orwell.

"Turn out the overheads when you leave, okay? And make sure the door locks behind you. You have to turn the thing." She slumped to the couch. Looked at her hands. Orwell went to the door and turned off the fluorescent lights. She looked small in the far corner of the room, sitting in a pool of lamplight, staring at her hands. Small, and much older. Orwell closed the door behind him, made sure the lock had caught. He did the same at the bottom of the stairs and stepped onto the sidewalk.

Stacy and Constable Maitland were waiting.

"Hi, Charles."

"Morning, Chief."

"Morning. Yes. She'll be staying in her studio, top floor, on the right. There's probably a fire door or a rear entrance around back. Make sure it's secure."

"Yes, sir."

"And there's a fire escape."

"Yes, sir."

"You don't have to spend the night watching her, but make yourself conspicuous, you know, park out front for a while every hour or so, take a walk down the lane. If anyone's watching, I want them to know we're paying attention."

"Yes, sir."

"Good lad," he said.

"Take you back to your car, Chief?" asked Stacy.

"Nope. You're still designated. Drive me home and I'll tell you all about the biggest ruby in the world." He got in the back seat.

Five

Friday, March 18

Whatever the household mood, dogs are instantly cheered when boots are pulled on and a walking stick is yanked from the umbrella stand. Perhaps even more than usual on a morning when people aren't speaking and breakfast scraps haven't materialized. As it was a fine morning (and who can say that dogs don't know the difference), the romp ahead promised to be an extended one. Orwell just wanted to get away from the kitchen, where all was icy silence.

He had much to answer for, that was certain: chauffeured home well past his promised arrival time reeking of tobacco smoke and Polish vodka — "You smell like a kangaroo!" When innocently inquiring how his wife might know what a kangaroo smelled like, he'd been told to keep to his side of the bed. He had also failed to collect his daughter from rehearsal as pledged, and been compelled to pony up the twenty-three-dollar cab fare his wife had to borrow from the house funds. His quite reasonable explanation that police business forced him to alter his plans had produced a snarl, suggesting beyond doubt that any "police business" involving strong drink and cigarettes was a fabrication not worth hearing.

The rain had moved off to the north and east, leaving behind a fine fresh morning, and Orwell was determined to stretch his

legs, clear his head, fill his lungs with oxygen and rid himself of
an incipient headache and stuffed sinuses. He set out at a good
clip, leaving Borgia far behind and almost keeping pace with the
little white dog.

After marching across two rising fields over soft terrain,
Orwell was surprised to find he was puffing. He leaned against a
cedar post at one end of an ancient snake fence and took a few
deep breaths. Maybe it *was* time to drop a few pounds. More
dog walks would help. Duff was running circles again, trying to
sniff every square inch of the property. Borgia was marching past
them both, taking charge, boss-of-the-walk. Orwell straightened,
flexed his left knee a few times, gave the fence post a neighbourly
rap with his stick and set out again at a slower pace, enjoying the
air, ruminating on his many sins.

Upon reflection, he had to acknowledge that as an investigator,
he made a fine drinking companion. He could think of at least
ten questions he could have asked, *should* have asked, and at least
three he *had* asked that were never answered. Obviously there
would have to be a follow-up visit, and there he encountered
a small but knotty series of professional complications that
had to be considered. Metro Homicide, possibly Peel Division,
perhaps even Montreal, would be showing up before long, and a
murder investigation easily trumped a break and enter. While the
Dockerty police had every right, not to mention responsibility,
to investigate two burglaries and the mugging of a citizen, there
was no dismissing the connection between the murders of Viktor
Nimchuk, some woman in Montreal whose name he couldn't
quite remember, and Paul Delisle's ill-fated visit to town. Not to
mention the possibility that there was a famous Russian trinket
on the loose, as well as a police officer's missing weapon of the
same calibre that killed the aforementioned small-time smuggler,
Viktor Nimchuk. No getting away from it, the burglaries and
the mugging were probably part of something much larger and
more serious, and as such might be more effectively looked into

by detectives from the city. He should, and *would*, simply pass on what he knew to Metro Homicide, stand back and let them do what they were going to do anyway. He had important police chief duties to carry out that did *not* include late night smoking, drinking, schmoozing parties with a burglary victim who might well be an international jewel thief and/or murder suspect.

That he felt a tutelary concern for Anya Daniel's welfare was natural, given his paternalistic view of his place in the community, but his automatic response to attractive women was a solid reason for him to distance himself from further involvement. Orwell was not a philanderer, nor did he entertain reckless notions, but he did like the company of interesting women, and he had enjoyed his time with Ms. Zubrovskaya. Far too much, he cautioned himself, to make him an effective investigator. It wasn't his place, it wasn't his job, he wasn't very good at it and it was a bad idea. Definitely. An intriguing mystery to be sure. Too bad he was such an inept sleuth.

His best detective, on the other hand, deserved a chance to dig a little deeper before being shoved aside by the duly authorized heavy hitters. He didn't think it was absolutely necessary to start making phone calls before Monday morning — give her another seventy-two hours or so to poke around, see what she could stir up.

He stopped at the crest of a hill and surveyed the fields and woods, surprised that he'd come so far. A faint haze of green hovered over the land, new growth, barely showing. A cardinal at the top of a bare elm tree announced to the world that he was open for business and that this end of the hedgerow was now officially his. Orwell's lungs felt much better, his headache was receding. It was even a little warm for his leather coat. He pulled back his shoulders, lifted his face to the sun, sucked in a lungful of sweet country air. Time to head back, make some phone calls, do his job and avoid the women of his house for a while.

Not a chance. But in a good way: a gorgeous creature,

smartly turned out in clean green Wellingtons and a jacket of suede and fine tailoring was emerging from the shadows of the hedgerow, sunlight caught in her soft brown hair. She was heading up the slope to meet him. Diana had arrived. Erika's daughter, his stepdaughter, although he never thought of her as such, up from the city for one of her increasingly rare weekend visits. He stopped to enjoy the sight of her. "Now there's lovely," he called out.

"Hiya, Dad," she sang back.

"This is a lovely surprise. Wasn't expecting you this weekend."

"You were really booting it. I couldn't catch up."

They hugged. Duff ran around madly demanding a proper greeting. Borgia bumped Diana with her shoulder as she started the return trip ahead of them.

Diana hung onto his arm, matching his pace with exaggerated strides, swinging her free arm to let the breeze pass between her waggling fingers. Used to bop along exactly the same way when she was nine, he thought, going for a hike with Dad, always smartly dressed, even as a kid, great style sense. "I hear you stepped in it big time, Dad," she said.

"Oh ho!" he said proudly. "I managed to step in it at least four, possibly five times last night. I was carousing, forgetting my responsibilities, poking my nose into areas far outside my purview."

"Oh? What *I* heard was that you ruined Patty's life."

"Oh yes, forgot that part momentarily. *And* I also ruined my daughter's life, trying to 'bestow,' Erika called it."

"I think it's a great idea. Is Georgie going to handle the severance for you?"

"If it gets that far. It's a dog's breakfast of county by-laws and regulations. He's walking me through it."

"I'm seeing him this afternoon."

"Really?"

"The Harold Ruth case. He wants my advice, maybe my help."

That stopped Orwell in his tracks for a moment. "Well now," he said, for want of anything better to contribute. "That's interesting."

Diana smiled at her father's momentary consternation. "He's itching for battle," she said.

"I'll bet he is. You going to do it?"

"I don't know if my firm will let me, but I wouldn't mind a chance."

"It'll be a tough one. The man killed a cop."

"Allegedly."

"Allegedly."

She squared up to face him. "But you wouldn't mind? If I got involved. Tell me."

"My goodness, how could I mind? Meat and drink to you lawyers, isn't it?"

"Ooh yeah."

He took her hand, started walking again. "But we can't talk about it any more. You know, just to be on the safe side, legally speaking."

"We haven't talked about it at all," she said. "I have merely informed the Chief of Police that I *might* be representing, as co-counsel, the defendant in a murder trial."

"*And* while the Chief of Police, in all conscience, can't exactly wish you success in your defense of a cop-killer, excuse me, *alleged* cop-killer, he nonetheless hopes that the experience will be enlightening and fulfilling."

"That's grand of you, Dad."

"I thought so."

"And I'll make sure Georgie doesn't forget about your severance case."

"I don't think we need worry about that boondoggle for a while."

"Wouldn't be too sure, Dad." She was pointing.

A long field over, on the far side of the stream, two riders were cantering horses around the perimeter of a ten-acre section that would make a great pasture with a little work. A slight but wiry man was well seated on a buckskin mare and riding beside him was a blonde Valkyrie on a red horse.

"The red horse is called Foxy," said Orwell. "She just got her."

"She just got all there is," said Diana. After a moment she turned to him and smiled. "Looks like you're off the hook, Dad."

He hugged her arm. "I wasn't worried," he said. "They were made for each other."

After delivering her boss safely to his farm, Stacy had returned to the Irish House to collect the last of the party-goers, including, somewhat to her surprise, a moist and garrulous Staff Sergeant Rawluck, who had insisted on singing "Peg O' My Heart" all the way home. After that, she met Constable Maitland outside the Gusse Building who reported that except for a large orange tomcat observed coming down the fire escape around 12:45, and going back up the staircase at 02:30, all was quiet. Stacy took a walk around the building to reassure herself that dumpsters weren't harbouring villains, doorways were clear, doors were locked. Nothing. No crooks, no cats, nothing moving. The fire lane and back alley were still shining wet. Dockerty, most of it anyway, had washed and gone to bed.

She told Maitland to take his break, then see to his other responsibilities, and sat in her unmarked, across and down the street with a view of Anya's studio. Maitland brought her a coffee from Timmies, then drove off to check on a domestic call up on the Knoll. Stacy sipped and watched the window. Did it get any better than this? Murders, break-ins, bad guys lurking, missing jewels. She couldn't see how she'd be having more fun working in the city. This case had everything.

The last of the coffee was cold. She rolled down the window

to empty it onto the street and caught a flicker of reflected light from the studio window. There was movement, a shadow. Stacy checked her weapon, half opened the car door and then stopped. The shadow was dancing. She recognized the movement as a series of slow pirouettes. She stood in the street for a long moment watching the shadow dance. After that she got back in the car and drove away.

The three windows overlooking Vankleek Street were tall and arched at the top and light entered the studio at an upward angle and stretched across the ceiling. She danced in the dark for an audience of one; the cat's unblinking green eyes glowing in the corner. Danced in silence, hearing only the music in her head, adagios *pas seul*, linked fragments of ballet scores, passages once learned by arduous repetition and folded now into a solo piece composed by many, as arranged by Zubrovskaya.

I pity a world that never saw me dance. I feel sorry for Baryshnikov that he never got to partner me. I would have been perfect for him. He could have lifted me with a caress. Of all the truly great ones, the ones who should have held me in their hands, I had only one, only one of the great ones, but he was worthy of me. And I of him. People who were present on those nights were lucky. They saw something.

Soloviev, Yuri Vladimirovich. "Cosmic" Yuri they called him, because he could fly. Yuri Gagarin orbited the Earth; Yuri Vladimirovich Soloviev didn't need a spacecraft. His technique was flawless, far better than Rudi, the equal of Misha, with elevation like Nijinsky they said, he defied gravity, he could fly. As could she. They were as weightless as earthly creatures ever are, or can be.

After Yuri blew his brains out, after Grégor dropped her in a heap, after her years of rebuilding, strengthening, learning to be fearless again, there was her time in wilderness, with only the likes of Sergei Siziva for a partner. He was unworthy, but he didn't make mistakes. One night she chided him for dancing like a city bus, going from stop to stop. "But always on time," he said. "And not like a Moscow driver. I wait for you."

Yes, give him that. He wasn't brilliant, but he was on time. He couldn't fly, but he saw to his responsibilities: he lifted, presented, caught and held her.

And now? Still seeing to your responsibilities? Still there to catch me? It is good that you are so predictable. I will make it easy for you. There will be no more running, Sergei. I will present myself. All I have to do is fly, and you will be waiting, like a city bus.

An ambulance was pulling up to the emergency entrance. A pregnant woman was making a lot of noise as the EMT wheeled her through the sliding doors. The woman's husband stayed outside to grab a smoke. Inside it was the usual parade of pre-dawn emergencies. A big man with a bandage on his hand and an Elvis hairdo was discussing his condition with an overworked intern, two young men with bruises and bloody noses were explaining how they got that way to an OPP constable, a sad woman with an alarming cough was huddled in a chair. The pregnant woman's husband finally pulled himself together enough to come inside. His wife bellowed at him, "Where the hell did you go?" Stacy took a deep breath and headed for the elevator.

The officer posted outside Dr. Ruth's room was happy to be relieved.

Stacy settled herself on two chairs across from the hospital bed, hoping to grab a little sleep and be nearby should the patient's condition change. Good luck with that. Why the goddamn robins had to start chirping like happy idiots so early was beyond her. The sky was still dark, there wasn't any moon. Maybe they were just happy that it stopped raining. Then the patient made a small noise and Stacy went to get a nurse.

Family disputes, especially ones fuelled by alcohol, were Constable Maitland's least favourite calls. He'd rather chase a maniac down a dark alley, at least he'd have a good idea where the danger lay. With domestics you never knew. A mousy little woman, quietly sobbing in the kitchen, picks up a cleaver and tries to behead her asshole husband. A drunken man fires up a chainsaw and starts dividing the family assets down the middle, starting with that ugly fucking sofa. A wife has trouble working the slide on the pump-action shotgun, her husband laughs at her until she gets it right. At least this one didn't end with a trip to the hospital or charges laid. He should be home before his kids finish breakfast. There was time for one last check on the dancer lady.

She was standing in the doorway of the florist shop, smoking a cigarette and looking at the arrangements. Or maybe checking reflections. She spotted him the second he pulled up, turned to face him.

"You were my guardian angel all night?" She had a half smile.

"Part time, yes, ma'am."

"It was a comfort, Officer . . . ?"

"Maitland. Constable. Charles."

"Thank you, Constable Charles Maitland. I am going home now. You are relieved."

"Going straight home, ma'am?"

"Yes, I am."

"I'd be happy to drive you."

She gave him another smile, broader this time. "How thoughtful," she said. "Perhaps we could stop for just a moment. I need a cup of coffee."

"Be my pleasure."

"Pleasant young man. I would be honoured to buy you a coffee as well. Perhaps a doughnut?"

Maitland laughed. "Don't eat 'em," he said.

"I do."

Timmies was already doing good business, the parking lot was filling up, a few truckers outside slurping large double-doubles and passing around a box of a dozen assorted, unkinking stiff spines, hacking their first butts of the day.

"A medium coffee with cream and sugar," she told the woman. "And for you, Constable?"

"No thank you, ma'am. I'm hoping to get some sleep."

"Thanks to you I had a nice sleep," she said. "And three of the honey-dipped ones."

On their way to the door, she stopped, put a hand on his arm. "One moment please," she said. She headed for a man standing by the window, stared at the back of his head until he turned to her, a big man, he towered over her, but she stood her ground, her smile was tight and polite, her eyes were bright, her voice when she spoke was clear and precise.

"Good morning, Ivan, or Igor, or whatever your name is. The next time you report to your boss, tell him I am going to Grova's pawnshop. I need to raise a little cash. I have decided to take a vacation. Somewhere quiet." She gave him a little wave as she turned away. "No need to see me home. I have an escort." She took Maitland's arm.

"Is that someone I should be keeping an eye on?"

"Do not bother, Constable Maitland. He will not be in town much longer. Are you sure you would not like a pastry? They are still warm."

"Well . . ." he said.

"Go on," she said. "You deserve one after your night's work."

"Started to come to a couple of hours ago. The doctors are still with her. It looks like she's going to be all right."

"That is very good news indeed, Detective. Any idea when she might be ready to answer questions?"

"They've got a bunch of things they want to check. She's still groggy. The doctor says maybe I can talk to her in an hour or so. I'll stick around."

Orwell was in his cubbyhole office under the stairs. He could hear bright morning conversation coming from the kitchen and smell bacon and fresh coffee. "You get any sleep?"

"I'm fine, Chief. Will you be coming to the hospital?"

"It's your interview, Detective. I'll catch up with you later and you can fill me in."

"Yes, sir."

"After they let you talk to Dr. Ruth, take another run at Ms. Daniel. She can tell you all about the crown jewels of Russia."

"Just keeps getting better and better, doesn't it?"

"Enjoying yourself?"

"Having a blast, Chief."

"Good. I figure you've got until about noon Monday before we're invaded by people with bigger badges."

Orwell hung up the phone and took himself upstairs for a shower and shave and an outfit appropriate to an occasion demanding a measure of ceremony. His beloved first-born, and her fiancé ... *Gary*, right, were announcing their engagement with the entire family in attendance (a rare event in itself): Leda, the budding stage star, and Diana, the smart big-city lawyer, and of course his lovely wife, who, it appeared, had forgiven his numerous lapses and was preparing to feed him a decent breakfast. Definitely worthy of a suit and a white shirt and a tie of righteousness. Red paisley, that was the ticket.

"Change your tie," Erika said.

"Why?"

"Change your tie."

"Why?"

She met his eyes. "I don't think she's happy in the city."

"It's what she always wanted," he said. "Classy law firm, nice apartment, lots of shoes."

Erika riffled through his tie selection. "She's lonely." She chose a dark blue with a small diamond pattern. "Bend your knees." She lifted his shirt collar and deftly arranged the tie around his neck. "She doesn't have any friends. Just a bunch of lawyers. And they work her too hard. She's too thin."

"She tell you why she's up here?"

"She's consulting."

"She might wind up doing more than consult."

"Good. She can have a few decent meals for a change."

"There is that." Marvin Gaye sang out from his pocket. "Yes, Staff?"

"The Daniel woman's gone back to her apartment, Chief. We watching her all day?"

"I don't think that's necessary. Stacy will be talking to her this afternoon sometime, try to get an idea if there's any real danger."

"I'll arrange a regular drive-by."

"Anything else?"

"Looks like Constable Maitland ruffled some feathers last night."

"How so?"

"Mrs. Charles Emery has lodged a complaint. Quote, I want that officer punished, close quote."

"For what?"

"Evidently Constable Maitland was rude."

"He didn't break any furniture, did he?"

"No, Chief."

"Why I don't like single officer patrols. What was he doing

up there?"

"Domestic, Chief. Neighbour reported loud noises and screams. When he got there he was told by Mrs. Emery that nothing was amiss. He inquired how she had sustained a black eye. She told him to 'expletive off.'"

"Did he say if Mrs. Emery had been drinking?"

"Detected the smell of liquor, yes sir."

"She's probably a little embarrassed. Give her some time to cool down. See if he can drop by later. I'll have a chat with him. And if the Queen of the Knoll calls again, I'll talk to her."

"Yes, sir."

"You have a good time last night, Staff?"

"Passable, Chief. I still think the Avalon would have been a better pick. Pizza doesn't agree with my disposition."

Orwell put the phone back in his pocket. "Wouldn't admit to a hangover if he was at death's door." He checked himself in the bedroom mirror, made final adjustments to the knot in his new blue tie.

"Who is it you'll be talking to this afternoon?"

"Detective Crean will be. The ballet teacher. Her apartment was robbed."

"This is the Russian woman you were getting drunk with last night?"

"A slight exaggeration. But yes. She was upset. Understandably so."

"And you were easing her mind?" Erika sat at her dressing table brushing her hair. "For this you needed a red tie?"

"The tie was for Patty, and the occasion."

"Hmm." She was watching him in the mirror. "What's her problem?"

"She has bad dreams about Chernenko. He's chasing her. Or he sent people who are chasing her."

"Chernenko's gone to hell a long time ago. She can stop dreaming about him."

"He died in 1985."

"Yes. How do you know this?"

"I went to the library yesterday. At lunch."

"You didn't eat?"

"Sometimes I skip lunch and go to the library. You know that."

"You don't lose weight by skipping lunch. You eat a sensible lunch. You skip lunch, you sneak cookies in the afternoon."

"I don't have any cookies. My night sergeant eats them when I'm not around." He bent close to her. Kissed her cheek. "I think you tell him where I hide them." They held each other's gaze in the mirror. "Maybe I'll put a mousetrap in the drawer."

"Maybe I'll warn him."

The manager of Anya Daniel's apartment building had an enormous belly and wore his shirt outside his pants. It didn't help. There was no concealing the fact that he ate too much. Mostly fried chicken and beer, Stacy figured. His coffee table held a dozen empties and a family-size bucket of bones. "I was asleep," he mumbled. His tongue was thick and his breath was bad. Stacy took a step back. The man blinked and tried to focus on the badge she held in front of him. "Watching TV," he said. "Drifted off."

"Sorry to disturb your nap," she said. "I'm Detective Crean, Dockerty Police, this is Corporal Scheider. We need you to open 405, that's Ms. Daniel's apartment."

"What? She dead?"

"Why would you think that, sir?"

"I don't know, cops pounding. What do I know?"

"Would you come with us, open her door, please?"

"You want a key? Here's a key. Wait a minute, not that one. *Here's* a key." He lifted the correct one from a hook beside the door. "I'm not walking in on a dead body," he said.

"Did you hear any noises? Did her neighbours say anything?"

"What do I know? She got robbed last night. Cops all over the place."

"Thank you, sir. We'll bring the key back."

By the time Thursday rolled around, her nose was blistering and she'd had enough therapeutic vacationing to last her a long time. Adele booked a dog's breakfast of red-eyes and shuttles that would get her back to Toronto Friday morning. She paid a considerable surcharge for the privilege of cancelling her holiday early and flying all night. *I just hope I stayed long enough to miss Paulie's wake. Bet there weren't any bagpipes.* She crammed her carry-on and vacated the room without regret. *Shoot me a taxi driver if that frickin' plane leaves before we get there.*

"I'm sure the taxi is on his way right now, hon."

No way the Commissioner showed up. Well? Why the hell would he? It's not like he died in the line of duty, saving a pregnant mother from a roving band of crack dealers. Oh no, not my Paulie. Shot by a cuckolded spouse in a cheesy motel room. In the middle of nowhere. Wearing one red sock for Chrissake. She caught sight of herself in the lobby mirror, full length, all the better to thoroughly appreciate the benefits of her run to the sun — burnt knees, freckled shoulders, a pale mask where her sunglasses sat on her peeling nose. *No doubt about it, a raving beauty.*

"Taxi's here, hon."

There was no such thing as a smoking car on trains in this country. Not any longer. The social engineers had seen to that. The GO train between Oshawa and Toronto was strictly a commuter special, no more than a convoy of double-decker buses all hooked together. Once in a while, between the factories, malls and housing developments, she caught a brief glimpse of open water, never long enough to let her feel that this was an outing. There were no baskets of wrapped sandwiches or bottles of wine, no chattering friends and attentive suitors, and no music, no music whatsoever, unless you counted the incessant percussive hiss escaping from the earplugs of the sullen lout taking up three seats across from her. Manners have completely disappeared, she thought. No, that was not it, *conductors* have disappeared. There was no one marching down the aisle to make the young man lift his sneakers and turn down his entertainment system. And there were no purveyors of sweets or reading material. And she was not on her way to Dubrovnik for a weekend at the seashore.

Where was she going, exactly? What was she planning? Did it matter? It was time to bring them out of the shadows. All of them. No more running.

She would start with Grova. He would be easy to handle. And he could pull Sergei into the open. Sergei would be close. He was on a mission. At least, he was in the beginning. Who knows what it was now? As many years invested for him as for her. Can a man stay on the scent that long? Perhaps only someone as narrow and dogged as Sergei Siziva. He'd found his true métier as a bloodhound. Perhaps even wolf. We are all so old. By now, we all should have fallen by the wayside.

Who was first to go?

Ludmilla. Poor Ludi. Pretty girl, nimble fingers, sew fresh ribbons on your shoes in a twinkling. Sweet Ludi. She of the wicked laugh, deep, like a man's laugh, with her clapping hands and happy bouncing up and down when times were good, and the company was touring, and the hotel room was better than she expected — terrycloth robes provided, room service in the middle of the night. How that made her happy, to order a hamburger at three in the morning after she and Vassili had made love.

Gone now. Dead in Montreal so many years ago, the Chief had told her. No surprise. No shock. Just a wave of sadness. She had always known Ludi was dead. It did not matter who killed her. If Viktor did not do it personally, he was nonetheless responsible. He was responsible for everything bad that happened. He had made them all fugitives. They could not go back. What about their relatives? Ludmilla had a son in the army. What about him? Vassili had a wife. What about her? While they were on tour Ludi and Vassi were lovers, but in Russia they had families. Their lives were ruined because of him.

Viktor said it was too late for those arguments. They accomplished nothing. They must deal with what is, not with things that cannot be changed. They had stolen property, stolen from an important man who would want it back, who would kill to get it back. How many people has this man killed, or had killed? You cannot count that high. Lives are meaningless to these people. It is now necessary to decide what to do.

We can't sell it as it is, he said, it is too well known.

Viktor knew people. Of course he did. There was a man in Montreal, Grova was his name, and there was another one in Detroit named Padillo who did business across the river in Windsor sometimes. Those were the two connections he had in Canada. Viktor said he would take the stones to Montreal, to Grova. Ludmilla and Vassili said no. They didn't trust him. He could take *some* of the stones to Montreal, and if he got a good price, he could bring the money back and they would share, and he could make another run.

You were gone such a long time that first trip, Viktor. Three weeks. And when you came back you did not have the diamonds, and you did not have much money. But you had a lot of stories. You were cheated, you were robbed, swindled, mugged, someone reported you to the police and you had to run before you got paid.

Vassili called you a liar.

Ludmilla wanted to kill you. "You took forty thousand dollars in diamonds to Montreal and you come back with eight hundred dollars and a load of bullshit. Now you want another forty thousand? Go to hell!"

"It will be different this time," Viktor promised. "I know my way around now."

"I'm coming with you," Ludmilla said.

This time when he came back he had even less cash, and no Ludmilla. "She took the money and she ran off," Viktor said. "Fifty thousand dollars."

Vassili hit him. Hard. In the face. "What did you do to her?"

"Nothing! She met someone. A musician. An American. She fell in love. They're going to California. She said you can keep what's left, she just wanted enough to start a new life with her musician in California."

"You are a liar. She wouldn't do that!"

"She did it, Vassi. Don't pretend you two were crazy for each other — you were just convenient."

"That's it? She didn't write a note? She can't tell me on the phone at least?"

"She was in a hurry. The musician was leaving."

"How can she get back across the border?"

"She bought some identification. It wasn't hard. They're going first to Reno, and they'll get married, and then she'll be an American citizen. In California. Be happy for her. She found a new life."

Vassili wasn't happy for her. He was angry, and suspicious, and lonely. "I never should have let her go with you," he said.

"If you had come, maybe you would have met an American, too, and you'd be going to Reno to get married."

"I am married," Vassili said.

"They give divorces in Reno, too."

"What's the name of this musician?"

"Why torture yourself? She's gone. She's happier. We still have the best stones."

"I want to know his name."

"I don't know his name. He's a black. A big black man. I wouldn't trouble him. He looks dangerous."

"I don't care. I don't like this. I don't trust you, Viktor. I'm not giving you any more stones to sell in Montreal. I will find somebody here."

"You'll be caught. You don't know your way around."

"And *you* do? You took diamonds to Montreal and brought back nothing! You took Ludmilla to Montreal, and she's gone. What good are you?"

After the celebratory breakfast, the family went off about its divers business: Gary, the travelling veterinarian, down the road to check on cows, horses and other quadrupeds; Patty and Erika on their way to Peterborough in search of "necessary items" that they did not care to enumerate, but which were somehow vital to the upcoming nuptials; and Diana, ferrying Leda and her father into Dockerty.

"Didn't drive yourself home last night, did you, Oldad?"

"I left Bozo in the police lot. I had a designated driver."

"So did I."

"I know, sweetie. Twenty-three dollars worth. I'm sorry."

"You're forgiven. I had a good time waiting."

"What's his name?" Diana asked.

"Peter."

"This the young man with the odd hair and the black leather jacket?" Orwell asked.

"You know it," she said. "Don't get all fatherly now, Father. Perfectly innocent. We were rehearsing."

"I'll bet you were," said Diana. "He good looking?"

"He's okay."

"That good, eh?"

"He has a strange haircut," said Orwell.

"He'll be cutting it for the role, Oldad."

"If I had that much hair I'd do things with it, too," he said. "Drop me here, gorgeous. I'll walk the rest of the way."

"Sure," said Diana, with a knowing smile. They were right outside Laurette's Baked Goods, the door was open and seductive aromas were wafting.

Orwell waited until his daughters had driven off before stepping inside. He made a show of checking the selection in the glass case, but he was only there for one reason.

"Shortbread, Chief?" Laurette asked. Orwell thought she looked like a dumpling, round and warm.

"You know me too well, Mrs. Munch. Shortbread is my weakness. And pie."

"I have a very nice key lime pie, Chief."

He smiled. "Won't fit in my desk drawer," he said. In truth, Orwell considered Laurette's pies a clear notch below his exacting standard and not nearly as good as the ones at the Kawartha Kountry Kitchen. Her shortbread, on the other hand, was exemplary. "A dozen should do nicely," he said. "Just a bag, please." Laurette's white boxes with the pink and purple lettering were too identifiable to be carried discreetly into the office.

His pocket began vibrating as he was paying for his treats. He stepped onto the sidewalk before answering. "Brennan," he said.

"Stacy, Chief. Ms. Daniel's gone."

"That's it? Gone?"

"Just gone, sir. I'm standing in her apartment. Corporal Scheider and a uniform are questioning the other tenants. No one saw her leave."

"Signs of struggle?"

"No, sir. The place is tidier than it was last night. Clothes in the closets, toiletries in the bathroom. The bathroom window is wide open."

"You think she went out the bathroom *window?*"

"I guess you could make it over to the next building if you wanted to chance it." Stacy leaned out, calculating the distance, visualizing how it might be done. The gap between the buildings wasn't impossible, but the drop to the concrete below was scary. "Not a jump I'd do unless I had to."

"She can fly. That's what she told me."

"She might have done it that way. Or just walked out the front door. It's not like we had her under observation full time."

"Darn it," she heard him say. "Okay, Detective. I'm almost at the office. Get back here. We'll start tracking her down."

"Yes, sir." Stacy clicked off. She took another look at the walkway four floors down, caught a fleeting mental image of how big a splat a human body might make. She shook her head. "Have to be pretty sure of yourself," she said.

"What say, Stace?" Corporal Scheider was coming down the hall, looking into the bathroom.

"Talking to myself, Dutch," she said. She motioned him to clear the way and started prowling the apartment, opening closets, drawers, refrigerator. "Anything from the neighbours?"

"Nada. Not exactly a close-knit community. She left her studio around 08:30." He flipped open the top of an empty box, ran a fingertip across a trace of sugar. "Stopped off at Timmies on the way, came back here with coffee and a donut." He licked his finger. "Honey-glazed."

"Okay, let's pack it in here. I'm going to check her studio. Who knows? She might be back there. Giving flying lessons."

Adele landed early Friday, no luggage, a carry-on and a shoulder bag. Took a cab straight to the shop. Well where else? Home?

What am I going to do there? Might as well grind my teeth at my desk.

She checked in, made a call to her counsellor to let her know that she was feeling much better. The emotions weren't as close to the surface now, not moderated exactly, more like suppressed. The counsellor suggested she take more time off. She thanked her for the advice.

She didn't want to take time off. She sat at her desk, pawing through Paul's notes and files, they were no help. There was no mention whatsoever about dead Russians on the Queensway or compulsively confessing ballet dancers. Not even a mention of Dockerty. How the hell did he know she was up there?

"You missed a pretty good wake," said the man on the other side of the desk. He cast a shadow. He was huge, very dark skin, teeth white, smile broad, voice deep and seductive. "We drank too much Jack." He gave her one of his rumbling laughs. "Thought it was appropriate. Under the circumstances."

"Hi Dylan," she said. "Sorry I missed it."

Dylan O'Grady sat, uninvited, as though he still belonged there. "It was just a few of the old crew, and that girl from Licenses he dated for a year, you remember her?"

"Betty."

"That's her. She took it hard."

"Few more out there I bet." She leaned back in her chair. "Who's the jug-eared baldy in the pinstripes?"

On the far side of the room a tall, pale man was standing by the door, blatantly checking his watch.

"My exec assistant. Cam makes sure I get to all the bunfights on time."

"You late for one now?"

"It can wait. Just wanted to drop by, let you know how sorry I was about Paul. I know you two were close."

"You were with him longer than I was."

"We hadn't talked in a few years. But it hit me pretty hard, too.

We survived some hairy scrapes together. Always had my back."

The man by the door was fidgeting. "You'd better hit the campaign trail, Dylan. Your handler's looking twitchy."

"Twitching is what he does best. " His smile was as insincere as a campaign promise and it crossed Adele's mind that she'd never liked Dylan O'Grady very much. Even after he left the job he was always dropping by the shop, slapping shoulders, telling loud jokes, maintaining his connections, reminding people he'd been a big dog in the unit. He leaned closer and she caught a whiff of cologne. He reached for her hand, covered it, gave her a searching look. "What the hell was he doing up there, Adele?"

She pulled her hand away. "You'll have to talk to Lacsamana. He caught the case."

"You went up there."

"Wasn't any of my business. I was just so pissed off at him."

"Where'd he meet this woman?"

"How should I know?" She shrugged. "You know Paulie, always willing to travel for something strange."

"Long way to go to get laid. Or shot."

Someone placed a large paper bag on her desk. "Detective Moen?"

Adele looked up at the uniformed woman, a corporal, then at the bag. "What's this?" The bag was stapled shut and had a list of contents attached.

"Sign this please. Receipt for his personal effects."

"What?" She glanced at the list of contents. "Paulie's crap? What the hell do I want with that?"

"Got some papers for you to sign. Insurance forms, pension forms."

"What for?"

"You're down as his beneficiary."

"I'm his *what*? He has a kid. What about his kid?"

"I just do the paper, Detective. Sign here, please. His personal effects are in the bag, whatever was in his locker."

Adele scrawled her name on the lines indicated. She caught a glimpse of Dylan angling his head to read the list of contents. She reached out with her left hand and tore it off the bag and stuffed it in her jacket pocket. She smiled at Dylan insincerely, handed the clipboard back to the uniformed woman. "There you go."

The woman put the signed papers inside a file folder. "I'm sorry for your loss," she said.

"Thanks."

"If you find my wristwatch in there, you'll let me know, will you?" O'Grady said.

"Want his little black book, too?"

"Got my own," O'Grady said. He stood up. "Good to see you again, Adele. We'll see you at the funeral, right?"

"I'm not too great at sticking people in the ground," she said.

"Well, you need anything, feel like talking, you know how to get hold of me."

She nodded, distracted, happy to see him leave. His handler was happy, too.

Roy Rawluck looked none the worse for his night of revelry. Spit and polish, same as ever, automatically coming to attention. "Good day, Chief." He noted Orwell's suit and tie, nodded with approval. "What's the occasion? Lunch with the mayor?"

"My daughter's getting married."

"Today?"

"What? Oh, no. June, probably. I don't think they've decided on a date."

"Congratulations. Please convey my best wishes." He nodded at the white bag. "Wedding present?" The soul of discretion. Roy knew what was in the bag his boss was clutching.

"First of many, I expect," Orwell said. "Anything demanding my attention this fine Friday?"

"Nasty three-car over near Bobcaygeon. One dead, two injured."

"Oh Lord. From here?"

"No, sir. Two people in a van from Fenelon Falls, airlifted to Toronto. The fatality is a woman from Lindsay. Driver who caused it walked away."

"Drunk?"

"More than. Blood-alcohol was point two five."

"Christ almighty!"

"OPP says he was doing at least two-hundred klicks."

Orwell walked away, shaking his head. "Christ almighty," he said again, more quietly this time, a sad little prayer. He stood at the window staring blankly at the street below, the sunny day no longer lifting his spirits. The world was filled with horrors, he knew that, he dealt with it the way most people did, by acknowledging that there were circumstances beyond his control or understanding, and that giving them too much emotional identification was pointless. But highway fatalities cut too close to home. A drunken driver murdering an innocent woman in the middle of the night was a knife in his heart. He stepped back into the big room.

"Who was she, Staff?"

"Haven't released the name yet, Chief."

"Find out, will you?"

"Will do."

Roy looked toward the entrance where Stacy Crean was coming in, wearing last night's clothes, and looked tired and testy. "Morning, Detective," he said.

"Staff Sergeant." She walked directly past the Chief and into his office.

The Chief was about to follow her, then turned back. "Roy? See if the traffic victim has any family in town here, any help we can give."

"On it, Chief."

"Thanks, Roy." He half-closed the door, then leaned out.

"Same with the two injured. Let me know how they're doing."

"Yes, sir."

Stacy was rising from a chair. Orwell motioned her to stay where she was. "Still missing?"

"Yes, Chief. The studio's locked up. Sign on the door says, 'Classes cancelled until further notice.'"

"Anything from Dr. Ruth?"

"They wouldn't let me talk to her. Maybe later today, if she's up to it."

"You'd better get some sleep."

"I'm fine, sir. I got a couple of hours in the hospital before she started coming to." She slapped herself on the cheek. "Spent too much damn time sitting around that hospital. I should have checked on the other one."

"None of that. I have the feeling if she wanted to skip town there wouldn't be much we could do to stop her." His phone rang and he snatched it up before a second ring. "Brennan."

"Got a shitload of messages on my desk, most of them from you."

"Hello, Detective. How was Jamaica?"

"Terrific, my nose looks like bad wallpaper. Still haven't found Paul's weapon, if that's what you were calling about."

"On my mind, naturally, but other things have come up and I think you, or maybe someone looking into the Nimchuk murder, might want to come back up here."

"Nimchuk? Who's that? The Russian?"

"Sorry. Yes. The Russian. The mystery man on the Queensway. Murder weapon was quite possibly a .357 Smith." There was silence on the other end. "Doesn't mean anything, Detective. Lots of those around."

"I guess." She sounded calm, professional, dispassionate. "I don't know a lot of people who lug around a big-ass six-shooter these days, but they could be making a comeback."

"Could have been stolen from a collector. That happens.

Getting ahead of ourselves, anyway. Peel doesn't have much of the bullet."

More silence. Papers rustling. Finally, a loud hooting laugh and a sharp echo, as of a hand hitting a steel desk. Then, "Of course it's *his* gun! Who *else's* gun would it be? Why the fuck *wouldn't* it be his gun?" He heard a desk drawer slam. "Thank you, Chief. Thanks a *whole* lot. This is *perfect*." Another pause, and a sound that might have been a chuckle, or a stifled sob. "I'll get back to you. ASAP." And she hung up.

Orwell looked up at Stacy. "Didn't get to tell her about the smugglers and the jewels."

"Rocked her?"

"She thinks it'll turn out to be . . ."

"His gun," she finished for him. "Or else it's another huge coincidence."

"Entirely too many of those, wouldn't you agree? Okay, Detective Crean, what are you going to do?"

"How big do you want to go, Chief?"

"Be discreet. I don't want to put out an APB if she just went to the drugstore."

"Yes, sir."

"But I would like to know where she went."

"She said she'd let me know if she was going to leave town."

"Did she let you know?"

"I gave her my card. It's got my extension on it."

"Check your messages."

The ticket was good to Union Station but she got out one stop early, at Danforth and Main. She needed to make sure Grova hadn't moved his pawn shop, or burned it down, or lost it in a card game, or died, like everyone else. How many years was it? The last time she saw the troll? Ten? More? Had to be more. She was in Winnipeg four years. Four and a half. When she came back, she stayed away from this part of the city, avoided the old crew. They found her anyway, but that was her fault.

It was eleven years. She remembered it now — the year, the season, even the day of the week. A hot, humid Sunday night on the Danforth, sitting in the back room with Viktor and Vassili, talking about survival.

Ludmilla would have been dead by then, but they tried to believe that she was in her new life in California with her big black musician husband. It was a good thought to carry. Viktor knew better, of course, as did Grova. It was just she and poor Vassili who were still clinging to the story of Ludmilla's magical escape. Escape was much on her mind that year, that night.

Viktor and Vassili were still arguing about the stones, had been since the beginning. There were so many, but the numbers always came out uneven and they couldn't agree on the split. Vassili argued that since Viktor had already lost a small fortune in Montreal, he should give up a percentage. Viktor countered with the inescapable fact that they wouldn't have *any* jewels if he hadn't brought them into the country. That started another round of fighting about how Viktor had ruined all their lives.

In the beginning, before they had begun tearing it apart, the crucifix held forty-eight diamonds, all roughly two carats, twenty-three pearls, exceptional ones, all the same size and colour, and four extravagant sapphires, deep blue, more than five carats each. The cross and chain could be melted and sold for weight. Grova said he would handle that part of the operation. They decided not to take so drastic a step unless and until it was absolutely necessary.

The big question was what to do with the Ember. Vassili and Viktor didn't trust each other, and neither one trusted Louie enough to let him hold it. And at some point during the endless arguing they agreed that Anya should carry it until a decision was reached. And while they were arguing about diamonds and sapphires and gold, she made it disappear. "It is hidden away," she told them. "It is safe, and you cannot find it, and I will not tell you where it is. It is too well known for you to sell. It would be your death warrant. Its only value is as insurance. If someone catches up to me, if they find me, I want something to bargain for my life with. You and Vassili have all the other stones. They are worth more than the two of you put together, unless you are so stupid you lose them, or give them away like the last ones."

"Nobody gave anything away."

"Yes? How much money do you have in your pocket?"

And Grova? What were you doing that night, you troll? Sitting in your dark corner, surrounded by your mountains of junk, quietly planning how to separate Viktor and Vassili from their treasure. Wondering where I'd hidden the big prize.

She took the pearls to a jeweller in Winnipeg. Pearls are perfect; they're anonymous. She told the gem merchant a sad story of her great-grandmother. He might have believed her. It didn't matter. He brokered them for her, took twenty percent. She got enough to keep her alive for a while. She didn't tell Viktor or Vassili where she was going. They had the sapphires and all the diamonds big and small to sell. They had each other to keep an eye on. She didn't want to be near them.

Adele's apartment was as welcoming as ever: nothing edible in the refrigerator, a sink full of dishes, the new *Vanity Fair* she'd bought for the trip still sitting on the sideboard under her coffee cup and Pop Tart crumbs. Home sweet home. She put the bag full of Paulie's crap in the breakfast nook like an unwelcome guest. "Sure you don't want some coffee, Paulie? Fix you some really shitty instant. No trouble."

Sole beneficiary, was she? Well *he* damn well wasn't *her* sole frickin' beneficiary, that's for sure. Her sister's name was on *that* line of the form; a replacement for her mother's name, once there, grudgingly, because it was too much trouble to think of anyone else. Finally got around to removing it a year and a half after the bitter old woman died. But here she was, Paul Delisle's sole beneficiary, of pension, insurance . . .

Okay, enough dicking around, open it. She didn't feel like messing with the goddamn staples. She sawed the top open with her mother's breadknife, spread the contents across the table. Christ, look at this. Clothes, shoes, shampoo, tweezers, floss, combs, hair goop — "Paulie, you are such a *dude*." More beauty products than she had in her bathroom — Italian loafers, stinky Adidas, notebooks, mini-cassette recorder, pens, watch, phone book, business cards, wallet, keys, pictures of his daughter, baby pictures, birthday pictures, school pictures, "Danielle soccer" and the date, last year, what is she? Fourteen? Birthday in October. He always got her something. The only person he gives a shit about. *Gave* a shit about.

Stuffed inside a sneaker in an envelope marked "DELLA," she found a mini-cassette for the recorder. He was the only one who called her that. As far as she could remember he was the only person who'd ever given her a nickname.

"*Hey, Della. If you're listening to this . . . well, you know what happened, or maybe you don't, hell, maybe I don't, but whatever the specifics . . . I've checked out, right?*"

She swatted the machine. Made it shut up. Shit! Her knees unlocked and her back slid down the wall until she was sitting on the floor, wishing she had a drink, wishing she was still in Jamaica.

"*Well, how do you start a thing like this?*" It was the voice she remembered from nights of stakeouts and waiting: familiar, conversational, intimate. "*All the stuff, you know, pension, insurance, car and whatever, I've got to let you deal with it. Sorry. Don't have anybody else I can count on to take care of things. You'll have to handle it however you think best. If I know you, you're probably already worried about Danielle. I just never got around to organizing a fund or any of that stuff. She's still a kid, and I don't trust her mother not to make a grab at it. Anyway, when you have the time, get a lawyer to work out some system so Danielle can get some of it, for school, or leaving home, I don't care. Whatever you think makes sense."*

She heard a chair scrape. Where was he? Probably at home. She heard a siren far off. Middle of the night. Sitting in the dark, giving her his last will and testament.

"Don't do yourself in the eye, all right? Executors are entitled to a percentage. Should that be executrixes? Whatever. You're stuck with the job, Stretch (another nickname), *like who else can I trust? Right? So make sure you get the full share coming to you. And for sure keep the car, it's a great car, and any of my stuff you want, got a great TV, fantastic sound system, and my blues record collection you lust after, I know you do."*

She remembered one night after work when she was in his place for a beer, both on their way to some department nonsense, never made it, spent all night listening to his collection: Muddy Waters, Howlin' Wolf, Robert Johnson, he had them all. Sitting in the dark across from him, watching him handling his precious LPS with the same dexterity he finessed a basketball, or a set of cuffs, sliding the platters in and out of their paper sleeves, lifting the tone arm on his vintage turntable, adjusting the volume on his precious McIntosh amp. She, slightly stoned, watching his hands dancing in the lamplight, hearing the passion in his voice as he introduced her to Sonny and Brownie.

"I mean, you and Danielle are the only two people I actually give a shit about, so you figure out the split and I'll be fine with it.

"Okay, that's it for my last will and testament. Feels weird saying this into a tape recorder. There's some other stuff you need to know about, job-related, so I'll maybe put that on a different cassette. You'll need to play this one for the lawyer."

There was a long moment's pause. She could hear him breathing into the microphone. Finally, *"Sorry to dump this on*

*you, Stretch, I know you hate all this personal stuff. But hey, how do you
think I feel?"* And then his laugh, infectious, wicked. She smiled
in spite of herself.

Bastard, she thought. Thanks a heap. Get a lawyer, work out
some trust or something but make sure "ol' itchy-pants" can't
touch it. Get rid of all his stuff. Fuck! That damn apartment of
his is an antique shop. Crammed. All his crap and treasures and
who knows what? Sort it, pack it, move it, store it, sell it. Thanks
a fucking heap. You're damn lucky you're dead asshole or I'd
fucking kill you! And then she started to weep, slumped on her
kitchen floor, hiding her face in her hands and sobbing, deep
uncontrollable waves of pain and grief.

A strong west wind was in her face. She stayed on the south side of
the Danforth, walking the seven blocks from Main to Woodbine.
Grova's shop was on the north side, and she wanted to see it first
from a distance, make certain of the street number, check the
lane for fire stairs, back doors, hiding places, escape routes. The
subway station was close. If she had to run, she wanted to know
which way and how far.

"Grova's Pawn, Jewellery and collectibles, bought and sold."
Peeling paint, sputtering neon, a gigantic dusty rubber tree that
hadn't moved since the last time she saw it, and a well-used
"Closed" sign taped to the inside of the door pane. She crossed
at the Woodbine intersection, counted the store fronts to his
entrance — bank, thrift shop, smoke shop, pub and . . . five.

Grova would salivate the minute he heard the word ruby. He
wanted the Ember more than anything he'd ever lusted after, and
he'd lusted after *everything*, all his life. Greed. That's all he was.
Need. Getting, holding, owning. Through his scummy window
she could see what he valued most in the world. *Things.* The
narrow store was crammed from floor to ceiling with *things.* They

were all alike to him. Worth everything and worth nothing —
guitars and socket wrenches, cameras and ski poles, pornographic
video tapes and mismatched silver servers, some with bigger
price tags — Grova knew the difference between a Rolex and a
Timex — but the need to have them was just the same. And, as
with all those who hungered and grabbed and hoarded, he never
found the thing that would fill the hole in him. Until the Ember.
It was the ultimate prize. The one thing truly worth having. But
he only believed that because he didn't have it.

The upper floor lights were on where the troll lived, sometimes
with his wastrel stepson when the degenerate wasn't in jail or on
the run from people trying to collect money. Was there a wife
these days? She left him years ago, but she could be back, or there
could be a new one. Not likely. Likely he was up there all alone,
sitting in his crowded room, counting his things.

It now cost fifty cents to make a call from a public telephone,
if you could find a phone booth. And of course the Yellow
Pages were missing. Grova's phone number was on his window.
She retraced her steps and then read it aloud a few times to
memorize it.

In the smoke shop next door she bought a package of Players.
The price had gone up again, overnight. Someone really wanted
her to quit. At the rear of the store a fat man was methodically
tearing open a wad of tiny pull-tab lottery tickets, one after the
other, dropping them into the trash bin. Grova's stepson. What
was his name? David? Darryl. That was it. Almost didn't recognize
him; he had become a middle-aged, balding fat man, even less
appealing than when he was in his twenties. Time continues to
fly, she thought, and is not always kind. He was absorbed in losing
his money and didn't look up as she slipped out to the street.

The phone booth was on the opposite side of Danforth, with
a view of the store and the second-floor windows. She whispered
the numbers as she pressed the buttons. It rang five times before
he answered.

"Yeah, what?" Familiar voice, thick-tongued, guttural, unfriendly.

"Charming as always, Louie."

"Who is this?"

"Oh please, Louie, you know who it is. Have you heard from Viktor?"

"Viktor who?"

"Good boy. That is right. Viktor *who*. Your old business partner is not with us any longer, is he, Louie? He has gone the way of all the rest. Except you and me. And Sergei, of course. Sergei is still around, is he not? Perhaps he is upstairs with you as we speak."

"What do you want?"

"The question is, what do *you* want, Louie? What is the one thing you *really* want."

There was silence on his end except for audible breathing. She imagined him trying not to dribble. "You still have it?"

"Of course I have it. I have always had it."

More silence. She smiled to herself. His mind is racing, he is assessing his position, counting his options, trying to figure out how to turn things to his advantage. "And what?" he said. "You want to sell it?"

"That is the trouble is it not, Louie? Who could afford it?"

"There are people."

"I suppose there are, but I do not know any of them. Do you?"

Darryl was coming out of the smoke shop. "Your son is coming up," she said. "Tell him to go out for a while. Give him some money for lottery tickets and beer. I will wait until I see him leaving."

"Where are you?"

"I'm close by, but I will not be if I start feeling uncomfortable."

"I'll get rid of him."

"You do that."

People were exiting the thrift shop with huge plastic bags

filled with things. She ducked around the corner and opened her package of very expensive cigarettes, lit one and inhaled deeply. From her vantage point she could keep an eye on Grova's place. There was a dark shadow filling the upstairs window. He was trying to see where she was. Good luck. In her brown coat and brown wig she looked like any other bargain hunter.

Two cigarettes later, Darryl came outside. She was expecting him to duck into the pub next door, but he set off toward the subway station with his hands jammed deep in his pockets. She shadowed him from the opposite sidewalk until she saw him pay his fare and push his bulk through the turnstiles. Definitely going somewhere. Maybe Louie told him to get out of the neighbourhood for a while. Maybe he told him to go for help. If he was making a subway trip, he would be gone at least thirty minutes. Enough time. One way or another.

Into the lane, counting — bank, dollar store, smoke shop, pub . . . five. Grova's shaky back stairway was an obstacle course flouting any known fire code. Descending in a hurry would demand fancy footwork. As she climbed she visualized the choreography, instinctively setting it to music. It's *Giselle*, she thought, going mad and dashing through the square, only this time I'll have to avoid the boxes, plastic cartons, machine parts, cans of paint and motor oil. She smiled, a piece of cake.

The landing at the top was impregnable; a troop of Cossacks couldn't breach it, two mattresses, a wall of beer cases, a year of newspapers. The kitchen window was open. She pushed on the railing, testing it, straddling it, leaning across open space to reach the window sill. It could be done, which was good because she had reached the point where it *must* be done, there was no way back. *Flucht nach vorn*. No doubt about it, this was a day for leaping.

"*Detective Crean? This is Anya Zubrovskaya. I'm letting you know that I'm going to go away for a little. I'm not sure how long.*"

"Doesn't say where, Chief."

"Any ideas?" She had caught him with his mouth full.

"I'm not rolling in them. Hospital says I can talk to Lorna Ruth now. That's top of my list."

There were shortbread crumbs on his desk blotter. "Okay, Detective. You go talk to the good doctor, see if she has anything useful." He shifted a piece of paper to hide them. "I don't think we need to scour the town, she's obviously not here. Sure would like to know where she went, though. Wouldn't you?"

"Has she got a passport, Chief?"

"I don't know. Possibly — she's a citizen, as far as I know. It would be in her real name, Zubrovskaya." He was surprised at how quickly her name came to his lips. "Anya Ivanova Zubrovskaya. She made me practice it." There were a few stray crumbs clinging to his blue tie. Sure to be noticed. Oh what the hell, he was a grown man, if he wanted a cookie with his afternoon coffee, he was entitled. "She's travelling light?"

"Yes sir, I think so. Didn't take much."

"Well I'm not calling out the fire department. She hasn't done anything, she's not a material witness, far as we know."

"But maybe scared. Maybe running for her life."

"See, Detective? That's the part that's worrying the heck out of me. There's a lot of death and destruction connected with this thing. I'm going to have to tell someone. We could be sitting on a . . . an international *incident*, for all I know."

"Or a steaming pile, sir. Not to put too fine a point on it."

"Or, yes, Stacy, point taken, a big bunch of lies from a woman with a dubious record of sanity." He held his tie away from his shirt front and brushed it. "You've still got the weekend. Might as well stay on it. If you're so inclined."

Stay on it. Stay *on* it? Stay on *what*? What's left to stay *on*?

Lorna Ruth had a bandage on one side of her head. The right side. Hit from behind by a right-handed man, taller than her and not too particular about how badly he'd hurt her. Or if he'd killed her.

"Feeling better, Doctor?"

"Yes, somewhat."

"Do you feel up to answering a few questions? I won't stay long."

"I don't know how much I can tell you. I didn't see who did it, he hit me from behind. I *think* he hit me from behind. There could have been two of them, someone in my office and another one behind me. But I can't be sure." She touched the side of her head with her fingertips. "There was one. I know that much."

"Do you have any idea what he was after?"

"There's nothing valuable in there. Everything is in boxes, anyway. How would they even know where to . . . ?"

"Anything relating to Anya Daniel? Whose real name is . . ." she checked her notebook, ". . . Zubrovskaya." She looked up. "You knew that?"

"Yes, she told me her real name."

"She's missing."

"Kidnapped?"

"Why would you think that?"

"Just the way you said it, Detective, 'missing.'"

"I'm hoping she left town voluntarily. Do you have any idea where she might have gone?"

"None."

"Surely she talked about people, places, friends . . ."

"She didn't have any friends."

"Acquaintances then. People in the ballet world."

"I don't think she kept in touch with anyone."

"Would there be anything in your office about her? I mean

anything worthy of an assault and robbery?"

"I have notes, files, the usual records one keeps. You can't look at them, of course."

"Not without a court order. Anything special about those files? Anything worth stealing?"

"She was an interesting subject."

"Did she ever talk about smuggling?"

"I can't breach . . ."

"Yes, Doctor, I know, but your confidentiality may have already been breached if those files were stolen. And why would anyone steal them unless there was something interesting in them?"

"I don't know, Detective, I don't know."

"Did you ever discuss her case with anyone?"

"No."

"Your husband?"

"Of course not."

"Without breaching your doctor/patient responsibility, can you tell me if there's anything in those files that might have motivated someone to attack you? Or your patient? Or anyone else?"

"Could you get the nurse for me? I've got a terrible headache."

"Of course."

"Constable Maitland, thanks for coming in, I won't keep you. I bet you and your family have plans."

"Nothing too special, Chief, we were going to take the kids to a movie."

"That's special, trust me." He saw Maitland make a quick check of his watch. "Be out of here in a minute."

"It's Mrs. Emery, right? She making noises? I didn't . . ."

"Never mind her. I'll deal with Georgia Emery. You drove Anya Daniel home, right?"

"Yes, Chief. Straight home. Walked her to her door. She gave me a doughnut."

"Well sometime after that she flew the coop. We don't know where she went. Nobody saw her leave. You get any sense she was planning anything?"

"Oh cripes!"

"Oh cripes?"

"I didn't think much of it at the time. But I should have. I was thinking about getting home."

"What happened?"

"We stopped to get her a coffee and she talked to a man. Just for a second. I asked her if he was someone I should check on; she said he'd be gone soon."

"What'd he look like?"

"Heavy set, maybe six feet, wasn't smiling."

"You hear what she said?"

"I think she said she was going to Grova's pawnshop. She needed cash for her vacation."

"She told him she was going to the pawnshop?"

"Wait. She said, 'Tell your *boss* I'm going to Grova's pawnshop.'"

"Aha! Okay. Thank you, Constable. Thank you very much."

"You know what it means, Chief?"

"Haven't a clue, Charles. Haven't a clue. That's why we have detectives. Go. See a movie with your kids. Say hi to your wife. Emily, right?"

"That's right Chief." Maitland smiled. "About Mrs. Emery . . ."

Orwell waved his hand. "Don't give it another thought, Constable. I'm looking forward to speaking to the woman."

Whatever Dr. Ruth's assailant had been looking for couldn't have been found without an inventory and code key. Other than furniture and equipment, the office was a jumble of sealed boxes labelled with cryptic notations, dates and letter/number combinations. The doctor's desk drawers had been pried open, the wood was splintered. A few of the boxes had been roughly torn open and nothing but crumpled newspaper remained. The report from the detectives who investigated the attack said that a couple in the office next door heard loud noises and pounded on the wall. They then saw a large man leave in a hurry and pile into a car parked on the street. No second man, no license plate number. The car was described as "black, or dark blue, a Chevy or Ford, or maybe a big Toyota." Not much help.

Even if Stacy could locate the files relating to Anya's sessions, she was legally prohibited from opening them. It was a dead end. At least for now.

What next?

"Hey, it's Stacy. How's it going?"

"Oh, well, you know: shitty, crappy, like that. Sitting on the floor in my kitchen. Trying to decide between getting shit-faced or finding out what that crud is under my stove."

"Jeeze, I hate to drag you away."

"Oh yeah?" She ached all over. "What's up?"

"Our ballet dancer is in the wind. I'm trying to figure out where she went."

"She on the wanted list?"

"I don't know what the hell she is. You heard anything about stolen jewels mixed up in this?"

"Jewels." Paulie's crap was still scattered on her kitchen table. "Diamonds mostly."

"Diamonds." She waved her hand across the clutter as if to make it all disappear. "Mostly."

"Supposed to be a big ruby, too."

"You're kidding me, right?"

"Your partner ever say anything?"

"You know what? I don't think that shithead ever told me . . ." She picked up one of Paulie's Adidas sneakers and fired it at the wall. Bam! ". . . *anything!*"

"You okay?"

"Oh yeah. Oh yeah. I'm just great. You know any lawyers?"

"Not down there."

"The only ones I know are either court-appointed or charge a thousand bucks an hour."

"You got a problem?"

"What I got is all of my asshole partner's unfinished personal shit to take care of. He left me in charge of his . . . his fucking *legacy*!" She started to laugh. "I thought it was just his pension plan. Turns out I'll be dealing with . . . oh who the fuck knows *what* I'll be dealing with."

There was silence on the other end while Stacy waited for Adele to pull herself together.

"Okay, okay, I'm cool. All right, from the top. You're looking for the ballet dancing lady, right? You think she's down here?"

"Here's what I know: she left me a message saying she was going away for a while. And one of our constables overheard her say she was going to Grova's pawnshop. That name turns up in my notes from when I interviewed her."

"She got any Toronto connections?"

"She knew Nimchuk."

"And he's dead."

"And . . ." There was a brief pause. Adele heard notebook pages flipping. ". . . she told us Mr. Nimchuk was involved with stolen jewels."

"Really?"

"Detective Delisle never mentioned gems at all?"

"You're saying he might have been up there looking for stolen jewels?"

"It's a possibility."

"Who do these jewels belong to?"

"Near as I can figure out, they were part of the Russian state treasure, and probably belong to the Russians."

"You're shitting me, right? *Crown* fucking jewels?"

"I *know*. Not a hundred percent credible, but getting more and more interesting."

"What's your next move?"

"I was thinking I'd come down there."

"Oh yeah? You've got something, haven't you?"

"Nothing I can put my finger on, but *something's* going on. If I'm going to poke around in your town, I'd feel better if I had you backing me up."

"When?"

"Tomorrow morning."

"I'll be at Paulie's apartment. Broadview and Danforth. Call me on my cell when you get here."

"It'll be early."

"That's okay. I'm going there now. With all the crap in his joint I might as well spend the night. Saves me having to clean under my stove."

"Chief? Mrs. Emery on one."

"Thanks, Dorrie. Mrs. Emery, it's Orwell Brennan. How are you?"

"Frankly Chief Brennan, I am outraged."

"My goodness. Well, I'm certainly sorry to hear that, Mrs. Emery. Is there anything I can do?"

"Of course there is. You can fire that policeman who harassed me last night."

"Let's see now, I have his report right here. That would have been Constable Maitland."

"I don't care who it was. He was obnoxious, rude and intrusive."

"That doesn't sound like Charles Maitland. He's a very polite young man."

"I do not care to be badgered in my own home."

"Oh, was he inside your house?"

"He was on the front porch. What difference does that make?"

"Just trying to get a clear picture here. So Constable Maitland came to your door. Did he knock or ring the bell?"

"Who cares?"

"What I'm getting at is, he didn't kick in the door or anything like that, did he? You answered the door?"

"I told him to leave. He wouldn't."

"Dear me. How long did he linger?"

"Far too long. And he was impertinent."

"Do you have any idea why he was there?" Silence. "Because I have a notation here that he was responding to a call from one of your neighbours, that they heard shouts and the sounds of something being broken."

"It was none of their business."

"Perhaps not, but evidently they were concerned enough to make a phone call. Can you tell me if it was the Whiffens or the Conrads who called? Oh, I have it here. Doris Whiffen made the call."

"Meddling old busybody. I'll deal with her, too."

"I think I'd better have a chat with Mrs. Whiffen as well, find out why she was so upset."

"I think you'd be better served dealing with the riffraff in town."

"Mrs. Emery. We try to deal with all our citizens with the same level of obligation and consideration, whether they live on the Knoll or on the wrong side of the canal. Do you have any idea why Mrs. Whiffen was concerned?"

"She's always got some bee in her bonnet."

"Perhaps I could speak to Mr. Emery."

"What do you need with him?"

"I'd like to hear his side of the story."

"It isn't a *story*, Chief Brennan."

"Of course, I understand, but when a citizen demands that I fire one of my best officers, I'm going to need a bit more than a complaint. At the moment, it's your word against his."

"Naturally you'll be accepting his."

"Well, I'll certainly look into it further, if you think it'll help. Have a chat with the Whiffens, might as well talk to the Conrads, while I'm at it. And your husband, of course." The line was disconnected.

She snaked in across a kitchen sink stacked with pots and dishes and dropped soundlessly to the floor, proud of herself. Giselle never had to handle a passage like that. Conflicting sounds were coming from the front room: two television sets, different channels, both with volumes high.

On one screen was a hockey game, on the other, a crime show. She could tell it was a crime show because people were comparing fingerprints on a computer screen. She kept her hands in her pockets.

"Hello, Louie. I came in the back way."

"What is that? A wig?"

"How very perceptive of you."

"You got old."

"Not everyone was so lucky." She went to the front window, looked out. "Ludi's dead, Vassi's dead, Viktor's dead." She smiled at him. "The list keeps getting longer. And shorter, too, I suppose."

"I thought Ludmilla was in California."

"Sure you did. Where did your son go?"

"He won't be back. I gave him forty dollars. He'll buy a bottle and visit his girlfriend."

"He has a girlfriend. That's so nice. Now there's a man who

got old in a hurry." She checked the street again, a reflex.

"So? You're here. Stop sneaking around the room. Sit."

"Where?"

"I don't give a shit. Move something."

"So gracious, Louie. I had forgotten how well mannered you are."

"I don't need your bullshit, okay? All the time with the smartmouth."

She sat on top of a pile of magazines. "This is comfortable," she said. She lit a cigarette, smoothed the front of her coat, smiled at the troll.

"I think you wouldn't be here if you had anywhere else you could go. Am I right?"

"Don't be silly. I wanted to say goodbye. To you. And to Sergei, of course." She inhaled a deep puff and exhaled a thin stream through tight lips. "You still in touch with him?"

"You think he talks to me? You think we're friends all of a sudden?"

"You have a phone number?"

"Don't be stupid. He moves around. Like you."

"Then I'm wasting my time." She stood. "Goodbye."

"Wait a minute, wait a minute. Sit down, okay? Let me think a minute."

"Think hard, Louie, because I am leaving the country and I will be taking it with me."

"Where can you go?"

"I can go anywhere. I have a Canadian passport, remember? I am legal."

"You think you can sell it somewhere else?"

"Perhaps. I think it is a question of going to the right market, don't you think? Like the Sultan of Bahrain, or one of the Saudis, or some other billionaire? One of them might cough up twenty million, *thirty* million out of petty cash for one of the great treasures of the world. Don't you think?"

"What do you want?"

"I want to talk to Sergei. How do you get in touch with him?"

"You have it with you?"

"Do not drool, Louie. It is unbecoming." She dropped her cigarette butt into a handy beer can. "I will go out the front door this time."

"Can I see it?"

"I will call."

Paul Delisle's apartment in Riverdale overlooked the Don Valley and the two rivers far below. One, grey water choked with silt and abandoned shopping carts, and the other, concrete, the Don Valley Parkway, six lanes north/south, almost deserted, crews and trucks crawling in both directions, closed for the weekend for maintenance. A March wind from the west was rattling the windows. She stared across the valley at the bare trees on the far slope, unwilling to turn around and face the cluttered rooms.

All right, Della, you big stork, don't let the damn place overwhelm you. You've been here before, it's not that big — master bedroom, second bedroom with the office, kitchen, bathroom, closets, cupboards, bookshelves, desks, drawers, Christ! The man never met a space he couldn't cram. Pick a starting spot. Where? Which? First things first; find his damn gun. If he left it behind on purpose, it's in here somewhere. Please Jesus it's in here somewhere.

Where? Well, where did she keep *her* piece off duty? Desk drawer. Which desk? He had three: phone desk in the entrance hall, big rolltop near the balcony window, office desk with his computer and peripherals. Start with the little one by the door; he comes in, takes off his jacket, hangs it in this closet, opens this drawer . . . nope, nothing but takeout menus, junk mail, brass bowl filled with loose change. Okay, the office. Sit in his chair, clip-on comes off, into this drawer. Locked, but she had keys, all the keys in the world, just a matter of elimination. The phone rang. She hesitated for three rings, not wanting to talk to anyone who didn't already know he was gone. At the fourth ring she snatched up the receiver in time to hear the end of his message, "... *at home. Leave a thing. (beep)*" The other end was immediately disconnected.

The answering machine was in his top drawer along with a box of .38 Specials. Same as .357 for most applications.

"*You have seven unheard messages, three saved messages, listen to messages press one.*"

Four of them were from women. She fast-forwarded through messages from Lydia, Jasmine, Lydia again and Paula. One message from his daughter, "*Dad? You there? Pick up, Dad, if you're there. Dad? Call me, okay. It's your daughter, right? Call me.*" Oh Christ, well, Danielle knew by now, at least I didn't have to break the news. The other two messages were from a man, educated, confident. Some kind of accent. "*Delisle, you know who this is.*" Yeah, he probably knew; she didn't. And him again. "*It is Sergei. We need to talk. You should call me. Really. You need to call me.*"

"Love to, Sergei, whoever you are. Do call again." *Sergei?* Another damn Russian. How many is that?

There were three saved messages. One was from her. "*Hey, dickhead, I had a thought, I have one from time to time, you remember that big dude with the tats on his neck, the bouncer, Gregory? I think we should go back at him. What d'ya think? Get back.*" And a saved one from ex-wife Jenny, "*What am I supposed to do, hire a collection agency? It's three weeks. Your daughter needs clothes, books, call me, before the weekend, you remember the new number? Write it down.*" And the third saved one was from her old friend, Sergei, fluent English but definitely an accent, Russian, had to be. "*Don't let it happen again, Detective Delisle, I am very serious. Her name now is Daniel. That should be easy to remember, yes? Like the name of your child. Anya Daniel. You can find her. I have faith."*

Sergei, hunh? No phone number, no last name. But Sergei, whoever he was, was interested in the ballet teacher.

Might as well do the rolltop, get that over with. Where did he get this monster? Behind the sliding cover were slots and cubbyholes and tiny drawers for stamps and paperclips and who the hell would organize their lives around stamp drawers and slots jammed with empty envelopes? And in one of the stamp drawers, or maybe it was a paperclip drawer, she found the second cassette, labelled "Della #2 FYI-only-P." Oh shit. And where did I put that stupid little recorder thing?

Now she definitely needed a drink. A shot of something, it didn't matter, tequila, she hated tequila, brandy, she could stomach that, a shot of brandy to ward off the chills of a dead man's apartment filled with the dead man's things.

She knocked back two ounces of Hennessey and took a gasping breath as the heat blossomed in her belly and spread to her heart and head. "Bring it on, asshole," she muttered. Bring. It. On. She pulled the recorder out of her bag; she knew exactly where it was, had listened to the first tape more than once, more than twice too. She put in the new tape and went back to her place by the window, lit by the unexpected appearance of sunshine low in the west. She took another nip of brandy, held the recorder up like a mirror, clicked the button. Bring it on.

"Hey Della, made it to the joint, right? Being cool about all this, right? Okay, here's the deal: have a look in the freezer, way in the back, ice-cube tray. Careful when you thaw it out, okay?"

She had to chip the tray out of a thick crust of white ice. She knocked the cubes onto a dishtowel and twisted it into a sack, ran it under hot water until she felt the cubes melt away.

There were five stones on the towel. Four of them were diamonds, she didn't know much about gems but they looked to be engagement ring size, if your fiancé drove a Bentley. The other stone was bigger. It was blue. A sapphire, she thought, probably, a big one, a very big, very blue sapphire.

"*Get 'em? Nice, eh? Yeah, they're stolen, but stolen long long ago and far far away, so knowing what to do with them is a real problem. I mean, who the hell can you give them back to?*

"*What the fuck, just hand them into the department, 'recovery of stolen goods, details unspecified,' before your time anyway, well, most of it. Anyhow, at this stage, who gives a shit, right? I'll understand if you can't deal with it.*

"*Here's the thing* —" His voice was rambling — a bit drunk, maybe very drunk, he handled it well but when he drank, he drank. She could hear him, almost see him, cruising the apartment, bumping into things, settling finally into a chair that whooshed, the big leather one. She heard him take another drink, heard ice tinkle against glass, his lips sounded wet. "*It was all a big accident, the first two were anyway, the two big diamonds, that was an accident.*" He laughed, a laugh she'd heard before, his "Isn't life some weird shit?" laugh. "*I got a call, some guy dead in the Beaches, shot in the head. DOA. Had them in his pocket, well they weren't* in *his pocket, they were on the grass just* outside *his pocket, like he'd been pulling them out when he got shot. So, long story short, I palmed them. What? It was a reflex. Dylan was already there cruising the perimeter with a flashlight looking for tracks or brass, or maybe more jewellery, who knows, pitch black, the uniforms were at the car, calling in the cavalry, the damn things were under my hand when I bent down to check him out, and I palmed them, reflex, easy as pie. Shouldn't have. Know that. I'm sure Dylan would have. Maybe that was it. Save him from himself.*

"*I checked all the reports, stolen jewels, nothing like these two, these were big baby, big. I didn't even think they were real at first. I had a guy I know check one of them out, he says, oh yeah, that's the real thing, maybe fifty K worth. So there you go. My first step off the straight and narrow. Okay, maybe not the first time, but the first time I didn't get right back on. None of that matters now anyway, does it? Not if you're listening to this, not if I've got a tag on my toe, then who gives a shit how it happened, right?*

"*So anyway, I've got my hands on an easy fifty K worth of unreported,
unclaimed, anonymous ice. Nice, hunh?*"

She stopped the tape, put the recorder on the coffee table. No,
she thought, *not* nice.

Six

She slept in his bed, in her clothes, her face buried in his pillow. She could smell his hair on the pillowcase, his body on the sheets. She woke three times during the night, woke from dreams in which she was crying, woke to find his pillow damp. Three times she washed her face in his bathroom without turning on the light, sat on the commode to blow her nose and dry her face with a fresh towel that still contrived to smell of him, remind her where she was. The stars were visible and the sky was an hour from turning grey when she gave up on sleep and sat at his office desk, listening to the wind whistling across the balconies. The gems were in a brown envelope, unsealed, contents listed on the flap — "1 blue stone (possibly sapphire), 4 white stones (probably diamonds), evidence as yet unreported due to the death of the investigator." The list was signed, *"Adele Moen, Detective."* The envelope wasn't dated. Not yet. Not just yet. Not until she had an hour to think things through.

What's to think about? Turn them in.

And the tape?

Destroy it.

Well, why not? She could do what she wanted with it. Toss it, squash it. It wasn't evidence. It was a personal message, not a confession. What she did with it was up to her.

Listen to the rest of it.

"Okay, so there we are, there I am, hanging onto something I shouldn't be holding onto. But then I start wondering, who carries loose diamonds around in their pocket? And the DOA, *he's got no* ID, *nothing personal, and I'm wondering if it belonged to the vic in the first place, or if he just happened to fall down dead on fifty K worth of gemstones. Seemed unlikely . . . walking in the park, on his own, with a couple of big diamonds in his pocket? That's odd."*

She heard liquid poured, a bottle cap replaced, wet lips again. His voice thicker, slurring certain words, but still articulate, still forming clear lines of thought, his brain still operating like a cop's brain, looking for answers, searching for an explanation.

"And what was Dylan doing at the crime scene twenty minutes before I got there? Why didn't he pick up the stones? Not like Big Smoothie to overlook something like free jewellery lying around. So I went back to the park, on my own, just to have a long look around in the daytime.

"Don't know what I figured I'd find, big park, you can come at it from ten directions, weave your way toward where we found the body a hundred different ways. No way to search the park completely without a big team on foot, dogs, metal detectors, a hundred sets of eyes. On my own? Not a chance.

"The vic was found shot in the back, about a hundred and fifty metres into the park, facing the lake, a long way from the beach, so you can make some basic assumptions from where he was found, right? The way he was pointing, how he was dressed. I decided he probably came down from Queen Street, quartering in from northwest to southeast. What was he doing there? Middle of the night, jacket, pants, street shoes, not a jogger, not a dog-walker. Another assumption: maybe he was there to meet someone. And if it was a planned meeting, there'd have to be specifics. You don't go out in the night without knowing where you're going. So there's a phone call, something, where should we meet? By the big tree in the middle? Nope, a hundred big trees in the middle, something more specific.

"The park's got this big gazebo bandstand thing where they have

concerts. Kind of an obvious meeting place. And since he got shot maybe a hundred metres past there, what do we assume now? That he met whoever, and they continued walking, and then whoever shot him. In the back. It could have gone down that way.

"*So he's meeting someone in the middle of the night, he's either very sure of this person, or he's very nervous about this person. Let's jump and say whoever he's meeting scares him. What does he do? Takes some precautions, right? He's got two loose diamonds in his pocket. He's there to meet someone carrying two loose diamonds? That's not how you carry gems. Diamond merchants fold them up inside a piece of paper. That's all. They fold a piece of paper and put the stones in a little folded package. So either the guy gave them to whoever he met, or, if I was going to do it, I'd take a sample to show, but I'd stash the rest somewhere. Where, somewhere?*

"*I tell ya, Stretch, I'd'a made a helluva crook if I hadn't become a cop. I've got the devious instincts. You know it. I'm a porch-climber in my heart. Just following my nose, thinking like the crook I could be if I felt like it, and so what do I find? Well, you got them too now. Wrapped up in a piece of paper, folded into a square and stuck under the bandstand steps. The big blue one, a couple more diamonds. And the piece of paper. Even better. It's a pawn ticket. I'm on a roll . . . Damn! Battery light's blinking. I'll get back to . . .*

Paulie, Paulie, you titanic asshole. What the fuck did you get yourself into? Russian crown jewels? Are you kidding me? Tell you one thing, dummy, there is no way I am sinking my career to cover your ass. And what exactly would I be protecting? Your reputation? Hell, the time for that's long past, don't you think? Pension? Life insurance? Whatever. Your daughter loses some money coming to her, tough, sure, but not the end of the world. So why would I bother? You're already up to your neck, pal, the question is, how deep is the shit? You go under, you go under on your own.

What's the big deal? Turn it in. Some jewels were found, he didn't have time to write up a report before he was killed. I know nothing about them except they don't belong to me.

You'd think a woman her age would know how to make coffee. What kind of a person lives almost forty years without picking up that rudimentary skill? Paul had all the gear, grinder, whole beans, coffee maker, espresso machine, one of those French plunger gizmos; he prided himself on his coffee. She was okay as long as it was hot and had enough caffeine to wake her up. Not Paulie. He liked his lattes and his cappuccinos and teeny cups of bitter brew. Damn! Not one lousy little jar of Nescafé in the joint.

There was coffee dust in the grinder. She filled it with beans but couldn't find a switch to turn it on. The phone rang. She lifted the receiver before the second ring ended, held it to her ear without speaking.

"Yes. I thought someone was visiting."

She recognized the voice. "You must be Sergei. Got your messages. How you doin'?"

"I saw a face at the window."

"Really? Where were you, up a tree?"

"I was in the parking lot. Briefly. I'm not there now."

"How sweet. You've got the place staked out."

"How many of you are up there?"

"Just me, Sergei. Come on up, I'm making coffee. We should talk."

"We are talking."

He sounded relaxed, confident, perhaps a bit playful. She wanted to kick him in the scrote. "I think we should get to know each other a little," she said. "Don't you?"

"But slowly. You know my name, but I don't know yours."

"Come around, I'll show you my birth certificate."

"Will you show me your badge, too?"

"What can I do for you, *Serge*?" She deliberately mispronounced his name.

"Perhaps we can do something for each other."

"Such as?"

"Are you looking for something up there?"

"Well, you know, I kind of inherited all this stuff. It's mine now."

"I believe Mr. Delisle had something that didn't belong to him."

"Really? Paulie? Like what?"

"I believe he is also missing something that *did* belong to him."

Her voice hardened. "Such as?"

"You tell me. You're in his apartment. Is everything there that should be there?"

"Far as I know. Well I haven't looked everywhere yet. Paulie was big on storage. You ever been up here, Serge?"

"Let me just say that I might know where your partner's missing item wound up."

"You have it?"

"Not personally. I wouldn't want to be in possession of something that could be connected to a serious crime."

"Of course not. But you know where this something is?"

"Shall we say I might be able to find out."

"I see."

"How hard I look would be directly related to how hard you were looking for what belongs to me."

"Want to give me a hint?"

"Use your imagination. I'll be in touch." He hung up.

She shook the grinder, listened to the beans rattle, wondered for a moment if one could pulverize coffee beans with a hammer. The door buzzer sounded and she picked up her weapon and crossed the room. So soon, Serge? Love to get a look at you, you slimeball. Maybe pulverize *you* with a hammer. "Yes?"

"It's Stacy. Too early?"

"Not a chance. C'mon up."

She put her weapon on top of the brown envelope and took herself to the bathroom to wash the Serge off her face.

Adele looked shell-shocked, raw, her face scrubbed red, her hair wet in front. Stacy smiled anyway. Adele pulled her through the door. "Can you make coffee?" There was hope in her voice. "I mean, do you know how?"

"Sure. What have you got?"

"Oh Christ, everything. Except instant."

Stacy took off her leather jacket and folded it over the back of a club chair. "Wow, look at this place."

"I think he was going for the New Orleans whorehouse look," Adele said.

"From memory?"

"Who knows? Kitchen's over here. Need coffee. Need it bad."

It turned out you just had to push down on the grinder to get it going. Who knew?

Stacy got a pot brewing, located cups, checked the refrigerator. "We're creamless."

"Okay by me."

"Me, too," She admired the kitchen, shiny surfaces, pots and pans organized. "Kept a nice place," she said.

"Oh yeah. He was a fastidious fucker. How many single guys have a shiny toilet bowl?"

"That would impress the girlfriends."

"I don't think he ever brought one up here. I mean it. Asked him once, said he didn't like long goodbyes. Gone like a cool breeze, that was Paulie."

They watched the coffee dripping far too slowly into the carafe. Stacy broke the silence. "His piece wasn't here?"

"I wish. Nope. Found some other stuff, though."

"Such as?"

Adele waved off the question, took her time, long enough to get her first sip. "Bless you," she said. "Follow me. Sit down over there." She emptied keys and spare change out of the brass bowl and put it on the coffee table in front of Stacy. "You said jewels, right?"

"Yes."

"Big jewels." She shifted her weapon, picked up the envelope, shook it gently. "Check these out." She tilted the envelope, the brass bowl rang like a tiny gong.

"Oh yeah." Stacy looked at them for a long breath. "*Big* jewels."

"Maybe like Russian crown jewels?"

"Might as well be." She poked them with a finger. "And they're real?"

Adele sat across from her. "People going to a lot of trouble if they aren't." The stones glittered, held their eyes like crystal balls. "Do you have any fucking idea what's going on?" Adele asked.

"I know some of it."

"Yeah? Well I know squat. Except I know my dead partner stepped on his dick big time. He's involved in the theft of at least two of those diamonds — which two exactly I couldn't tell you since he got them all mixed up — but I have his recorded admission that he lifted two of them at a crime scene. Strike one. Then he went back to the crime scene and found the other ones. You could say he stole them too, but I'll withhold that charge pending further evidence." Adele began picking up the gems, one by one, sapphire first, then the diamonds, counting quietly. Stacy counted with her. "One blue, four white, right?"

"Right."

Adele sealed the envelope. "Sign it?"

"Pleasure." Stacy signed the flap. "So what are you going to do?"

"Turn them in."

"Today?"

"Yeah, well, it's fucking Saturday." She folded the envelope into a tight square and stuck it in her back pocket. "Definitely don't owe Paulie my freakin' badge!" She went to the balcony window, leaned her head against the glass, banged it three times.

Stacy waited, watching Adele. "But you don't like thinking that the guy you partnered with for . . ."

"That bastard is *not* getting me jammed up in this, whatever it is."

". . . how many years?"

"Five, almost six, who cares?" She banged her head against the glass again, gently this time.

"He had your back."

"Yeah. Mostly I had his." She picked up her weapon, checked it, holstered it and strapped it on. "Plus, I just had a conversation with a guy named Sergei who insinuated that he either has Paulie's gun, or knows where to find it." She gave Stacy a grim smile. "Strike two."

"Maybe just a foul ball," said Stacy.

"Still a strike." She emptied her cup. "Good coffee."

They had breakfast at the New York Café, a few blocks south of Paul's apartment. Adele had steak and eggs. It was her first meal in twenty-four hours and she wolfed it. To keep her company, Stacy had an English muffin with honey and a small orange juice. The power smoothie she'd sucked back before leaving Dockerty contained enough protein and nutrients to keep her going most of the day. Adele chewed and scowled at the Saturday traffic moving up and down Broadview; streetcars and taxis, a double-decker tour bus, dog-walkers, joggers and double-wide baby buggies. Stacy had her notebook open. She did most of the talking.

"Sergei Siziva. He was one of five people from a ballet company who defected back in '81. Of the five, three are dead. Ludmilla Dolgushin, murdered in Montreal twenty-five years ago, Vassili Abramov, eight years ago. And Viktor Nimchuk, barely a week ago." She looked up. "The two survivors are the ballet teacher, Anya Zubrovskaya, a.k.a. Anya Daniel, and Mr. Sergei Siziva. Ms. Daniel is convinced that Mr. Siziva, or someone connected to him, or hired by him, is out to kill her."

"Because?"

"The way she tells it, Sergei's been tracking down the jewels to return them to their rightful owners."

"The Russians? So? This guy Sergei's official? Didn't sound official. Sounded bent."

"Yeah. That sort of thing usually goes government to government. Happens all the time — works of art being identified, recovered, returned to their rightful owners. Might take a hundred years, but there are procedures."

Adele pointed at Stacy's uneaten muffin. "Gonna eat that?"

"Help yourself."

Adele had a bite, wiped honey from her bottom lip. "So, if he doesn't have some piece of paper giving him diplomatic immunity or some such bullshit, which I doubt, then my friend Sergei's just another shitheel looking for buried treasure." She had another bite. "We got a picture?"

"Of Sergei? Nope. Description from the Daniel woman — this is at least ten years old — not too tall, black hair, 'nasty eyebrows.'"

"Yeah, he sounds like the kind of prick who'd have nasty eyebrows." Adele finished the muffin. She'd run out of things to eat. She still looked hungry. "I don't think you want to get stuck in this," she said.

Stacy laughed. "Are you kidding? I mean, come *on*! Russian royal treasure. A ruby as big as a hockey puck. My boss figures I've got until maybe noon Monday before visitors start showing up: your guys, Peel Division, maybe Montreal, maybe even the Russian ambassador. After that I'll be on the sidelines. You, too." She put money on the table. "My treat. I've got an expense account."

"Forty-eight hours?"

"Give or take."

Both entrances to Grova's Pawn were taped and guarded. Patrol cars were parked at angles in front of the building, lights flashing. Traffic was crawling, uniformed officers in the street, drivers inconvenienced and unhappy about it.

"Well now," said Adele, "what have we here?"

"Something serious."

"Oh yeah, definitely."

"Can you get us in?"

"Kidding me? I own this town."

Adele parked in a no parking zone with her red four-ways flashing. Her stride across Danforth with arms spread could have parted the Red Sea. Stacy had to jog to catch up with her. Adele flashed her badge at the uniform at the entrance. "Goin' on?"

"The owner. His son found him. Body's still up there."

"Who caught it?"

"Heatley and his partner."

"Lacsamana," Stacy threw in.

The uniform looked at Stacy.

"She's with me," Adele said. "Dockerty PD. We're working a homicide that's likely connected. Door unlocked?"

The uniform opened the door next to the shop entrance. A staircase went straight up. Stacy looked back to catch the uniform watching her climb. Well, who could blame him? He blinked and closed the door.

Two more uniforms were on the landing outside the

apartment door. Adele showed her badge and they shifted sideways. The main room was crowded; medical examiner's crew, crime scene techies. The body of an old man was being bagged. Stacy saw blood on a handlebar moustache before the zipper hid his face. In the kitchen area, two detectives were talking to a man with stringy hair and a dirty shirt. The man was sitting at a cluttered kitchen table. He looked numb, or badly hung over. One of the detectives spotted them, said something to his partner and headed in their direction.

"Yo, Moen. Thought you were in the Bahamas."

"Somewhere down there."

"Missed the wake."

"That was my evil plan. You remember Detective Crean?"

"Crean the brain. Right. How's it goin'?"

"Detective Lacsamana. Nice to see you again."

He looked them over briefly. "What's up?"

Adele took it. "Vic is the owner? Louie Grova? We were on our way to talk to him."

Lacsamana nodded at Stacy. "Your interest?"

"My Chief's got a bee in his bonnet about Detective Delisle's missing revolver. Sent me down to look for it. Was this guy shot?"

"Not hardly. Lamp cord around the neck. He died hard. You find his piece?"

"No sign of it yet," said Adele. "We took a break. You ever see Paulie's apartment?"

Lacsamana made a snorting noise. "Sure, we were asshole buddies from way back. Hell, count the number of beers we had with what? One finger?"

Adele nodded. "Yeah, he wasn't much for hanging out."

He gave them both a hard searching cop look. Like most detectives, he disbelieved most of what he saw and all of what he heard. "How do you figure his piece was here?"

"All I've got is a list of names that *might* be connected to that ballet dancer he tracked to my town," said Stacy. "She's gone missing. Del and I were looking to talk to her."

"How'd this go down?" Adele wanted to know.

"Somebody was looking for something. Vic was put through some serious pain, looks like. Burned fingertips, split lip. Worse than that maybe."

"Yuck."

"Definitely. Know what they were looking for?"

Adele stood aside to let the medical examiner and the body squeeze by down the stairs. "Something worth more than Paulie's old six gun."

"You make a connection, you'll let me know."

"Oh yeah. Happy to hand it off."

The other detective, Heatley, was motioning for his partner to wind it up. Lacsamana had a last, dubious look at the two women. "Stay in touch," he said.

"Count on it," Adele said.

At the bottom of the stairs the ME's team was having some trouble squeezing the gurney through. Adele, two steps above, leaned over them to hold the top of the door, then followed them to the back of the meat wagon.

"So what's it look like to you guys?" she asked. "Strangled?"

"Won't know for a while," said one of the men. "Just a guess, I'd say he had a heart attack."

"Hate that," Adele said. She slammed the car door and fired up the engine. "Hate it. Did it all the time, but I don't like it."

"You didn't lie."

"Didn't tell the truth either." She checked her mirrors. "I was always covering Paulie's ass. He was *not* a team player." She stared across at the pawnshop. "I don't see your ballet dancer pulling a stunt like that, you?"

"Not the type, wouldn't have thought. Tough little cookie, though. Come up behind him with an electrical cord. Could happen."

"And the burning?"

"That's nasty."

"Oh yeah. Fucking jewels, hunh? Never could see it myself. You?"

"I got a diamond ring once. Gave it back."

Adele laughed. "One more than me." She put the car in gear and eased out into the traffic stream. The uniform in the street made a space for her. Horns honked. Adele thanked him with a wave.

"Next move?" Stacy asked.

"I'm open to suggestions."

"How be we park around the corner for a while? Check out the sightseers."

"Better than my plan."

"Which was?"

"Feeding my face."

"You still hungry?"

"I get like that when I go mental."

"Pizza joint over there. I'll get us a couple of slices, two birds with one stone."

"Deal. No anchovies. Coke."

"You got it."

Adele whooped her siren twice and did a one-eighty across the crawling traffic to park outside a Pizza Pizza. Stacy headed inside. Adele turned off the engine, looked back down the street. They were half a block from the cruisers. The meat wagon was departing. Spectators were being kept to the far side of the avenue.

Stacy came out of the pizza joint. She didn't get in the car, walked around to Adele's window. "The pepperoni just came out of the oven."

"All ri-ight."

"Doing good business in there."

"Street theater. Better than reality TV."

Stacy put her box on the hood of the car, wrapped her slice neatly in a paper napkin, stopped, halfway to her mouth. "That's *her*," she said. She pointed the pizza across the street.

"What? Where?"

"Bag lady. By the phone booth. Brown hair, brown coat."

"You kidding me?" Adele took a big bite of warm pizza. "The little hunchback?"

"She's hunching on purpose."

"How do you know it's her?"

"The way she's smoking." She handed Adele a cold Coke. "The way she holds her smoke. Like she's hiding it."

Adele popped open the can, took a gulp. "Looks like a . . ." she burped delicately, "ditzy old broad to me."

"It's an act. Watch her for a while. Everybody else is gawking at the store, waiting for something to happen, hoping somebody'll take their picture. She's checking faces. She's looking for somebody."

"I thought she'd be pretty."

"She's wearing a wig. Lipstick's on crooked. It's her."

"We grab her?"

"We could. But . . ."

"But?" They were both talking with their mouths full.

"Technically she hasn't done anything."

"Well, technically, maybe not, except she's definitely connected, except you came here looking for her, except she shows up at a murder scene." She laughed, shook her head. "Sounds bustable to me."

"Except."

"Except."

"Wouldn't you like to know . . ." Stacy wiped her lips, "who she's looking for?"

"I say fuckit, bust her and sweat her."

"Bust her you'll have to turn her over to Lacsamana."

"Eventually."

They thought about the situation for a long moment, different priorities, compatible objectives.

"She knows what I look like," Stacy said. "If she starts moving."

The two women finished eating, sipped their drinks, both watching the woman across the wide avenue.

Ugly is the best disguise. People look away from ugly. In the movies when a pretty woman wants to disguise her appearance she changes her hair colour. But still she is pretty. Give yourself a strawberry mark across one side of your face, people will not look at you. It is a lesson Sergei should have learned, but he was a dandy and would never let himself be less than presentable. There he was, trying to be one of the crowd, trying to blend in, and wearing a foulard and a waistcoat. I see you, Sergei. My my, but you have let yourself go. Look at you. You must weigh ninety kilos. You have a belly. What have you done to yourself? Who has been feeding you all this time? Who has been paying the bills to keep you here? Someone has to pay for all the steaks and wine. Pastries, too, by the look of it. You always were a greedy little shit. Who do you report to these days? Do you check in regularly? Do not tell me you work for somebody official. After so many years. And so many pounds. I think somewhere along the way you took a bite of the forbidden apple, did you not?

Standing beside Sergei was her assailant of last night, the clumsy ox with the torn pants. He was wearing a bandage on one hand. The two fools were lurking, no other word for it, *lurking* in a doorway down the block from Grova's pawnshop. Police all around. They might as well be wearing signs. When the body was carried out of the building, they got into a heated discussion and Sergei punched the big man on the shoulder, twice. The big man looked hurt, but not from the punches.

And poor Louie, look at you, carted away like a dirty carpet, leaving all your precious things behind. They could not let you take even one? What would it have been, Louie? Of all your things, what would you have chosen to carry to the other side? An impossible choice, I know, especially since the only thing you ever wanted, you could never have.

And look, there is that clever detective from Dockerty. She moves like a dancer and watchful as a cat. That's very convenient. And who is that with her? A tall woman, all elbows and big hands, bullying her way through knots of people and telling the uniforms what to do. The clever detective from Dockerty has a comrade. Good. Let us see just how clever they are.

When Sergei and his friend began to walk oh so casually from the scene, heading west, on foot, bypassing the Woodbine subway station, Anya followed from the other side of the street. Now we are making progress, she thought. Things were going rather well. Too bad about Louie, but it was inevitable really. And probably necessary. He had pulled the real evil out of the shadows. She had seen his face.

Adele was on foot, staying on the opposite side of the street, a block behind Anya. For a crookback little bag lady, the woman could motor when she had to. Nothing the matter with her legs. You're hard to keep track of, sweetie, tiny frame, dull clothes, disappear in a blink. Watchful, too. You've done this before, haven't you? Spot me twice it's game over. I can't vanish the way you can. But you're not checking behind you very much are you? Whatever you're after is up ahead. Where are you going, sweetheart? Who are you chasing? Who's out of place on this fine Saturday morning? Families heading out on shopping expeditions, home for lunch, off to Chinatown for dim sum, moo shu pork. I ate too fast. That damn pizza's repeating on me.

Those two men up ahead. She's matching their pace exactly. Oh yeah, got you now, boys. Mutt and Jeff. Hey, if she's tailing you two, she's got some stones. Or a weapon. Makes my job easier; the big one sticks out worse than I do. Square head, sideburns, iron grey hair, wavy, way too long. Not army, not official, some sort of muscle. And the guy he's yakking to — short, pudgy, nice jacket, fedora, silk scarf, trying to be dapper. Is that you, Serge baby? Yeah, I like you two jokers a lot. I can track you easy enough. So can she. Hasn't once looked in your direction but she's following every move, aren't you, dearie? All those reflections, yeah, you've done this before. Every time one of them turns his head you start poking around in your bag like you're looking for something real important.

At Coxwell the two men entered a parking lot. Well now, here's where it could get tricky.

"She's trailing two men. Roly-poly little guy in a fancy jacket, and a big dude, looks like a gorilla in a bad suit. Where are you?"

"A block behind you, heading west."

"The men are getting into a red Beemer, B-B-X-G, Bravo, Bravo, X-Ray, George, 227, two-two-seven."

"Got it. What's *she* doing?"

"Heading for the subway."

"Okay, I'm seeing the Beemer. How do you want to do this?"

"You stick with the car. I'm taking the subway."

"Which way is she heading?"

"West . . ."

Sound was cut off as Adele went underground. *West*. Okay by me, Stacy thought, same direction as the BMW.

Anya knew where they were headed. When the car pulled out of the lot, she watched its reflection make a right turn and head west down the Danforth, she knew. She ran into the subway, threw a handful of change into the box, more than enough she was certain, ran down the stairs to the westbound platform. They were going back to the old place. If it is still there, she thought, it has been twenty years at least since she had been inside, fifteen since she had been in the neighbourhood. But that is where they were headed. She was sure of it. Greektown. And not one Greek in the bunch.

Sergei's distant cousin — or the brother of his cousin's step-uncle, or perhaps a former lover, Sergei was never clear on the relationship, a man named Groszvili, a Georgian, son of a Stalinist, grandson of an anarchist, great-grandson of the Revolution — had a three-storey building on the Danforth with four apartments on the top two floors and a bar at street level. Bakunin was the name of the bar, a dark and sullen place as she remembered it. Groszvili liked to foster the impression that his bar was a hangout for Russian mafia and international men of mystery, but any real crooks who might have dropped by did so by accident and doubtless departed shortly. Instead it had by default become the hangout for a bunch of disaffected Bulgarians and resentful Macedonians, the inculcated offspring of unsaved Bolsheviks, Trotskyites, even a few diehard Stalinists, endlessly repeating their fathers' and grandfathers' arguments about political niceties they had never been forced to enjoy. The little band of gypsy smugglers had fetched up there when they first defected, when there were five of them, still deciding what to do, even before Sergei went home to claim his reward for being a good little boy. She had only stayed two weeks; it wasn't big enough for them all, and by then there was nothing but fighting and bad feelings. But the place itself was not bad, if it was still the same, if it was still there at all. By Moscow standards, it was a palace. The refrigerator and stove worked, there was plenty of hot water. Two bedrooms, Vassi and Ludi insisted on having one to themselves, Viktor and Sergei in the other one, arguing all night, and she in the living room, on that ugly red sofa with the coffee stains and the tape on the arms, hearing desperate love-making sounds from the end of the hall, and whining and snarling through the other wall. There was no need for her to suffer with the robber band. She deserved better. Toronto was, after all, where Baryshnikov had found rescuers and harbourers when he made his dash for artistic freedom in the West. And there were people in the city who knew of her, ballet lovers who had seen her with the Kirov. They were lining up to ease her into freedom. She was at the apartment or the bar below only as much as loyalty and shared liability demanded, but it was often enough to watch the train wreck unfold, the bickering and blaming.

And then Sergei decided to take his chances back home and Viktor started making trips to Montreal.

"West" was the last word Stacy heard as Adele disappeared into the Coxwell subway stop, but how far west was anyone's guess. Keep driving. Keep the phone handy. At least the red BMW was easy to track.

Danforth Avenue was the kind of road that kept you on your toes. An erratic traffic flow, either over the limit or crawling, drivers either racing between red lights or knotted in the middle of an intersection. It was four lanes wide but felt narrower — parking on both sides made the inside lane less than generous, and jaywalkers routinely dodged vehicles to stand on the white centre line.

"Yeah, you'll be safe there," Stacy said.

Her cell was buzzing.

"Yo, Stace, I'm out of the subway now. Hear me okay?"

"Oh yeah."

"Still got 'em?"

"Coming up on Chester. The Beemer just pulled into a lot." Stacy turned into the lot in time to see the men enter a back door. It looked to be the fourth or fifth building from the corner. "They've gone into a building. I'm parked."

It was still there. She had been certain it would be. The same flat brick façade and the red door set at an angle inside a niche just big enough to accommodate two smokers at a time on rainy days. The sign, in Cyrillic script, "Бакунин," and a notice board under a cracked plexiglass cover offering jobs, announcing meetings and entertainments and sometimes seeking companionship.

Sergei and his hulking companion went straight in, not looking around, not checking behind, oblivious to the possibility that they'd been followed. Anya however knew that *she'd* been followed, and she was quite content. The big one had been in the next coach all the way. Odd-looking woman, angular and tall, but not uncoordinated, quicker than she looked.

She found a table in the McDonald's across the street, away from the window, but with a clear view reflected in the artwork on the opposite wall. She nursed a coffee and waited. It was something she was good at.

Adele sat in the passenger seat. "You getting pepperoni repeats?"

"No."

She belched delicately behind her palm. "With maybe fried egg?"

"Need some Pepto?"

"Hell no, I need a regulated life, some order, some better habits."

"She still in McDonald's?"

"Staring at that bar across the street."

"What's she up to?"

"Sounds weird, but I get a strong feeling she was just leading the way. And now she's waiting for us." A small burp. "Too early for a beer?"

The bartender had stubble heavier than was currently fashionable. His look, lecherous when he checked out Stacy, soured when he saw her companion.

"Couple'a Coors Lite," said Adele.

"Place you're looking for is two blocks that way."

Adele was amused. "Oh yeah, what place would that be, sir?"

"You know, where the 'girls' hang out."

"This place 'boys only,' is it?" She looked around the room. "I don't know, Stace, most of the gay bars I've been in, the guys had style."

"Hard to tell sometimes," Stacy said. "Check his wrist. That's a five thousand dollar timepiece, don't you think?"

"Five easy."

"Easy. You pay retail for that?"

Bartender gave them a hard look, placed two bottles on the bar and moved to the other end. Adele put down a ten dollar bill. "No glass?" The bartender's attention was on the TV above the pinball machine. A silent soccer game was in progress.

Stacy deliberately spilled a few drops on the floor. A private ritual. The gods shouldn't have to do without just because she didn't drink. She scanned the room, taking it all in, weighing everything, locating doors and hallways, counting bodies — a dozen, all male — vodka, coffee, tea, newspapers, chess. Travel posters invited the world to visit the Black Sea and St. Petersburg, to drink Stolichnaya and fly Aeroflot. The music was the best of ABBA or something, European disco, no balalaikas. "Charming spot," she said.

Adele wet her lips. "Far side, Big Hair and Dapper Dan?"

"I think the big one was in my town," said Stacy. "Yesterday, day before."

"Oh yeah?"

"I'm pretty sure I saw him at the hospital. I recognize the hair. Who combs their hair like that?"

"And the short one has nasty eyebrows."

"You think? Yeah. Kind of objectionable."

The two men were arguing about something, in Russian, but being very controlled about it, with phony smiles and bogus laughter, sometimes audible over the inappropriate music. "Dapper Dan wants to strangle his friend but his hands aren't big enough," Adele said.

"How do you want to do this?" Stacy asked.

"Oh hell. Let's see how cool they are."

Adele walked straight across the room. Stacy left her beer on the bar and took the scenic route, crossing the room at oblique angles, checking faces, expressions, features, making an impression.

"Hi there, gents," Adele said. "Mind if we join you?"

The big one looked them over. "She can stay," he said, pointing. "You can piss off."

"And I thought this was a social club," said Adele. She sat down. Stacy remained standing, keeping an eye of the rest of the room.

"You are police?"

Stacy turned her shoulders to look the big man in the eye. "That's right, sir."

"Being police is dangerous job," the big man said.

Stacy smiled, "So's being an asshole." She resumed picket duty.

"What's your name, sir?" Adele asked him.

"Yevgeni Grenkov. I am citizen."

"Are you now? That's good to know. Pay taxes and everything? Very nice." She turned to his companion. "How about you, sir?"

"You drink on duty?"

Adele's face creased in a broad grin. "I *know* that voice. I thought that might be you. Didn't I say that, Stace?"

"You did."

"I said I'll just bet that dapper little fucker is my pal, *Serge*."

She had another sip. "And yes, *Serge*, I'm sipping a beer. I'm on compassionate leave today, *Serge*. You know, on account of my partner getting shot. You remember my partner, Paul. Paul Delisle, Mr. . . . ah, what is it?"

"Siziva," said Stacy.

"Right. Siziva. You a citizen too, Serge?"

"What do you want?"

"My friend and I were checking out pawnshops. You like pawnshops, Serge? How about you . . . ?"

"Yevgeni," said Stacy.

"That's right. Citizen Yevgeni Grenkov. You like pawnshops? How do you feel about pawnbrokers?"

"He's never met any."

"Let the big guy talk," Adele said.

"I talk for myself."

"You didn't just kick him under the table, did you, Serge?"

"It's *Sergei*."

"I *know* that, *Serge*, but you know what, I'm going to call you whatever the fuck I feel like calling you because I think you are seriously bent and I'm looking forward to substantiating that. Where were you two guys, say, last night, early this morning? Around eight, when you called Paulie's apartment?"

"You are confused."

"Well, we can check that, phone logs, you know. You weren't stupid enough to call from Grova's place, were you? That would have been dumb, even for you smart guys."

By now Stacy had made eye contact with each man in the room, establishing to everyone's satisfaction that she was badged, armed and authorized to make their lives miserable. She turned her attention to the two men. "If we were to check you guys out, would we find any weapons? Guns, knives, electrical cords?"

"We are not armed," said Sergei. He spread his fine wool jacket revealing a bright silk lining. "You are welcome to look."

"How about you, big fella? You packing?"

"No."

"Care to stand up for a sec, open your coat, turn around. Hurt your hand, huh?" She was brisk, efficient. "Been in Dockerty recently? Like yesterday? I think you were noticed. Reason I'm asking, had a serious mugging and a couple of break and enters up there. Not the sort of thuggery our citizens are known for." To Adele. "He's clean. Nasty bandage on those knuckles."

"Ripped his pants, too, looks like. What happened? Grova put up a fight?"

The big man sat down. "We weren't there."

"You were definitely in the neighbourhood. Shopping no good this end of town?"

Sergei shrugged. "Very well. We were going to pay Mr. Grova a visit, but when we arrived we saw all the police cars so we decided to leave."

"Why were you paying Mr. Grova a visit?"

"He was keeping his ears open for us. About certain items."

"Right. So what happened? Did he call? 'Hey Serge, guess what I found?'"

"We did not go upstairs."

"Not what I asked, Serge old boy, stay on topic here, what happened? Did the pawnbroker give you a call? What?"

"It was just a friendly visit."

"I see, out of the blue, hey, let's go see our old pal the pawnbroker and strangle him for a while?"

"We weren't there!"

"Calm down, Serge," Adele said. "We should be able to clear it up, a little forensics, you know, fingerprints, blood work, footprints, fibres."

"Go ahead. Police were all around his place. Why would we stay if we had done a crime?"

"Because you're stupid?"

"What do you want?"

"Oh, shit, Serge, what everyone wants, you know, world

peace, stiffer sentences for parole violators, that kind of thing. Where were you last night?"

"I was home."

"And where's home, Serge?"

"I have an apartment. Upstairs."

"You live here too, Citizen?"

"He is staying with me."

"Visiting? From where?"

"I live in Montreal."

"Aha. You ever run into a diamond merchant, also named Grova, in Montreal?"

"I don't know him."

"Really? I got the impression you guys all knew each other." She was still for a moment, looking at both men, a smile on her face. "Stace? How these guys doing so far?"

"Don't seem very well informed about anything."

"May have to invite them down for separate interviews. I have a feeling Citizen Grenkov is a bit intimidated by his friend Serge."

"You arresting us?"

"I'm considering it."

"On what charge?"

"Torture, strangulation and there's that business with some guy named Nimchuk who got himself dead in a sleazy motel room last week."

"I don't know any Nimchuk."

"Oh sure you do, Mr. Siziva," Stacy said. "You two were in the ballet together, weren't you? Along with Ludmilla and Vassili."

"And one more, isn't there, Detective Crean?"

"Zubrovskaya. Anya Ivanova Zubrovskaya."

"I hear you two used to dance together," Adele said. "Back in the day. Before you all became international smugglers."

"I was never part of that."

"Not at the end, maybe. You got scared and ran home." She

leaned forward. "Question is, why did you come back?" She
turned to Stacy. "You be okay if Mr., ah, Siziva and I have a
private chat?"

"Oh sure, Yevgeni and I will stay put." She looked at the big
man. "Won't we?" Grenkov made a noise something like a low
growl.

Adele said, "You have an office, *Sergei?*" This time she pronounced
it correctly. "Maybe the ladies room? It's probably vacant."

Sergei didn't blink. "There is a place in the lane." He
straightened his jacket as he rose. "They don't allow smoking
indoors these days," he said.

Adele followed him to the exit. She looked back to see Stacy
taking a chair across from Grenkov.

Adele gave the narrow lane a thorough inspection, checked the
fire escape above, looked behind the lone dumpster, then walked
to the street entrance and back again, stood close to him, forcing
him to lean back. She smiled. "You wearing a wire, Sergei?"

"What?"

"Me neither," she said, patting him on the chest. "You can
check if you have to, but don't get familiar."

He took a step back. "What do you want?"

"I just want us to be comfortable during these negotiations."
She returned to the lane entrance, watched a car or two go by.
"It's cards on the table time, Sergei," she said. She took one more
look at the sidewalk. "You feel exposed here? I guess it's okay."
She shook her head and walked back. "When Paulie got his head
blown off, you picked up a new partner." Sergei was staring at
her. "Didn't tell you about me?"

"Not much."

"That's Paulie all right, so cool, but also dead, which sorta
leaves things up in the air, right?"

Sergei's manner changed. He relaxed a few notches, settled his jacket more comfortably on his shoulders, adjusted his scarf. "I'm not sure I know what you are talking about," he said. "What is it you think you know?"

"See? That's the deal. Paulie was one cagey dude. He just gave me a paper bag and told me that if something should happen, which, go figure, something *did*, I'd be dealing with his friend Sergei. He said there was some big money in it for me. It's you and me, pal." She looked around again, lowered her voice. "And the jewels, of course."

"You have them?"

"Oh yeah. Coulda knocked me over."

"How many do you have?"

"How many are there supposed to be?"

"More than you have. What colour are they?"

"What? Let's see . . . I've got a bunch of white ones and a big blue one. What colours did you get?"

"The policewoman inside? She knows about this?"

"Her? Fuck no. She's a hick down from Hooterville. I'm not telling her shit. Let's face it, Serge, I'm kind of on shaky ground here. I've got an envelope full of stones connected to who knows how many fucking murders. You think I'm *talking* to people? Look, if we're going to be partners you'll have to open up. What was your deal with Paulie? Finder's fee, piece of the action?"

"I guess he didn't tell you everything."

"Dammit, Serge! All right, fuck it. I don't need this shit. I'll just turn the frickin' jewels in to my captain, get a slap on the wrist for turning in some evidence a few days late. So what?"

"But you would prefer not to do that?"

"Well sure, shit, I could use some extra dough. And I don't want to drag my partner's name through the mud if I don't have to. But I won't deal with amateurs. I'm not putting my tit in a wringer because you guys don't know what you're doing. Put a price on what I'm holding. If we can do this quietly, we can make a deal."

"Did you like your partner, Detective?"

"Hell no. Giant pain in the ass. Do you like *your* partner?"

"A necessary inconvenience. That man who was murdered in a motel room, two weeks ago, he was shot through the head, I believe."

"This would be that Commie smuggler, Nimchuk, right?"

"You have recovered the murder weapon?"

"Not yet."

"This would be an important piece of evidence, would it not?"

"Describe the weapon."

"I believe we are talking about a large calibre revolver. A Smith & Wesson."

"All right. Sure. I'd like to get my hands on it. Don't want murder weapons hanging around, do we?"

"Of course not. Especially evidence that your partner had been a very bad boy?"

"Right. Tell me something I *don't* know."

"And in exchange I'm going to need what you have."

"What? Straight swap? Where's my end?"

"That could be negotiated. *After* I get the gems."

"Tell you what, Serge, how be we trade for, say, a couple of the white ones. The big blue one I think maybe I'll hang on to until I see some cash on the table."

"I'm sorry. The item in question is the only card in my hand. If I turn it over I have no leverage whatsoever."

"Money works. Those sparklers are no fucking good to me. What am I, a broker? No. I'll trade *some* for the gun. But only for Paulie's personal weapon. Understand? I'm not swapping the mint for some Saturday night special you picked up on eBay."

"It is what I say it is."

"Good then. You give me the piece, I give you, say, a portion of what I've got, and the rest I'll trade for cash money. Makes sense to me."

"It takes time to convert items like that into cash."

"Think about it Serge, you're not in the strongest position here. You're in possession of a murder weapon. Never a good plan. What are you going to do with it? Sooner or later you have to get rid of it."

"I could mail it to the police."

"Sure. Fine by me. Go right ahead."

"Even if it proves your partner is a killer?"

"Even if it proves my partner had improper relations with a hamster. I don't give a shit. You want to hang him with that killing, be my guest."

"I could involve you."

"In what? Talking by the dumpster? However this goes down, I'm in the clear. My partner died, I inherited his case, I tracked down some jewels and I found his confidential informant. And then you'll have lots of time to explain yourself. Face it Serge, this is the last chance you're gonna have to talk to somebody who might listen. Once you're in custody, it's out of my hands."

"How do we make the exchange?"

"Just you and me, pal, what d'ya say? Only thing, it happens *now*, today, no dicking around — hell, bring your big ass bodyguard if it makes you feel safe. I'll bring the stones."

"Are they close?"

"In my pocket."

"Let me see them."

"I don't think so. You can squeeze the envelope. See? Nice big stones inside. That's enough. Let's go get the gun."

"No, I go by myself."

"Oh don't be stupid, Sergei. You think I'm going to let you run off to collect a weapon and then show up armed and greedy? That'll be the day. No, we'll go there together, and we'll do an exchange like civilized people, and you'll be very careful because

I'm not as trusting as my partner was."

"So then, Citizen Grenkov, how'd you mess up your hand?"

"I tripped."

"Really? Over someone's face?"

"The sidewalk."

"That where you ripped your trousers? Which sidewalk? Local, or a hundred kilometres north of here?"

"I fell down. That's not a crime."

"Also not an answer. *Where* did you fall down?"

"I don't remember."

"Okay, let's work it out. *When* did you fall down? Last night?"

"No."

"Can't be much before Friday night, Saturday morning. Sound about right?"

"Yes."

"Yes. Good. So where were you Friday night, Saturday morning?" No answer. "You forget?" Sullen. "Okay, I'll tell you where you were, you were in Dockerty, breaking into a doctor's office and putting her in the hospital, then you broke into someone else's apartment. Didn't find what you were looking for, did you? That's why you're still looking."

"You have no proof of this." Something caught his attention and he leaned sideways in his chair to see past her shoulder. Anya Zubrovskaya was standing at the table. She had approached so quietly, Stacy hadn't heard a thing. The Citizen gave a low, involuntary moan as he registered yet another inconvenience in a long, unsatisfying weekend.

Anya smiled at Stacy. "Hello, Detective. I am pleased with you. You are good at your job. May I join you?"

"Please do."

"Your partner is in the laneway talking to that little peacock.

I was hoping she was going to shoot him, but no luck, so I came inside. She is very tall, is she not? Like a flagpole. But she did not lose me. I am happy about that." She smiled at the man across the table. "You can arrest this one for assault. He tried to kill me two nights ago."

The chair didn't scrape and the table hadn't budged, but Stacy was standing. "That true, Citizen?" She had her cuffs in her left hand. "You might as well turn around. I have to take you in."

"Because she says so?"

"Because I say so." As before, when she frisked him, Stacy's tone was calm, polite and unequivocal. "Turn around please, hands behind your neck, fingers interlaced, I'm sure you've done it before."

"I demand a lawyer."

"Supreme Court says this week you don't rate one. Last time, turn around, hands behind your neck. Don't make it worse than it is."

"Go to hell." Yev kicked over the table and threw a bottle followed by a roundhouse punch at Stacy. She avoided all three without appearing to do more than twist her shoulders and arch her back. She chopped down on his right kneecap with the heel of her boot, dislocating it immediately and rendering that leg unusable. As he lost balance, she hacked his throat with the axe edge of her hand, stabbed him in the solar plexus with a dagger made of stiffened fingertips and swept his one serviceable leg out from under him. He dropped to the barroom floor, retching and gasping. She was on him like a leopard; a hard knee dropped onto the small of his back, an arm twisted between his shoulder blades, and then handcuffs. Citizen Yev was under arrest.

Stacy looked up to see a dozen men, most of them standing, all looking at her. "Please stay back, gentlemen," she said. "This doesn't concern you."

Anya was applauding. "Bravo," she said.

"Do me a favour? Fetch my partner."

"Of course, Detective."

The laneway was deserted. Not a crow in sight. A few gulls, the small ones with the black wingtips, she liked them, they reminded her of somewhere else. She caught a glimpse of Sergei and the tall woman going into the parking lot at the far end.

In the parking lot, Sergei was opening the passenger door on the red BMW. He bent over and rummaged under the seat. Anya saw the tall policewoman unsnap her holster and put her hand on the butt of her pistol. "Now, Sergei," she said, "I want you to be *very* careful lifting it out of there."

"It's wrapped in a plastic bag."

"I've seen weapons go off inside a cardboard box. Now hand me the bag with your left hand. Good."

"Detective. Your partner wanted me to fetch you."

Adele swung around. "You. Get over here where I can see you. Stand there."

"Sergei Gregorovich, you got fat."

"You got old."

Anya pulled off the dull brown wig and didn't look nearly as old. "But not fat," she said. "Did you hear what happened to poor Louie?"

"You two can catch up on old times later."

"We had a bargain."

"Oh, you can forget about that, Serge. You're under arrest."

"For what?"

"Start with possession of stolen property. That's my partner's service revolver. It could be the murder weapon in an unsolved homicide. That will do for now."

"My prints are not on that gun."

"Couldn't care less."

"I have done nothing wrong."

"That's good. You can explain it all to the three or four police outfits on your case. Plus the Canadian government will likely get involved, probably the Russian government. You guys are ass-deep in all kinds of bad shit. At least that's how it looks to me. Turn around, hands on your head. Don't fuss, I'm good at this."

"Detective? Your partner . . . ?"

"Right. You walk ahead of me, dancer lady."

"Anya."

"Whatever."

Most of Captain Émile Rosebart's homicides were either domestic or gang-related; a case involving crown jewels, Russian thugs and ballet dancers would have been an interesting way to end the work week were it not for the .357 Smith & Wesson revolver with special grips in a clip-on holster on his desk, along with the brown envelope (now unsealed) holding a sapphire and four diamonds and the mini-cassette labelled "Della #2 FYI-only-P." He shook his head and looked up at Adele, pacing the room, then at Stacy, sitting up straight and perfectly composed. "Brennan sent you down here? Jeeze, he's a persistent bugger. This woman? She wanted for something?"

"The Chief was worried about her," Stacy said. "Her place was robbed, there was a mugging and she was also assaulted."

"By the big Russian. The one with the dislocated kneecap."

"He resisted arrest."

"In my town."

Adele spoke up. "I was otherwise engaged, Captain. Otherwise I would have made the arrest."

"Of course. You had other Russians to bust." He looked again from one to the other. "So how'd this go down again?"

"Detective Crean's a friend. I had a day off, she had a day off, you know what cops are like, let's have a coffee, why don't we swing by this Grova's place . . ."

"Yeah, that's what I generally do after breakfast. You ever hear of this Grova before this?"

"No."

"But the ballet woman knew him?"

Stacy spoke up. "His was one of the names she gave the
Dockerty police when she told them about the jewels. I had him
on my list of people to check out."

"So you two swung by there as a, what, just a natural
progression after breakfast?"

"That's right, sir."

"Unh hunh. Right. And out of the blue you walk in on a
crime scene and a murder victim and the missing woman and
you decide to trail two strange men you see in the crowd."

"We were trailing her; *she* was trailing the two men," Adele said.

"One of whom turns out to be the very man who was calling
you at Delisle's place and hinting that he had Paul's gun."

"Worked out that way."

"A natural progression. This guy Sergei some kind of secret
agent? Or just a hood dealing in stolen goods?" He picked up the
brown envelope. "Goods which belong to . . . ?"

"Most likely the Russian government, sir," said Stacy.

"Better and better. Governments. Mounties. Frickin' CSIS
maybe. 'Cause if they want 'em, they can have them."

"Except there's the dead pawnbroker."

"Maybe I'll get lucky. Maybe the pawnbroker was a foreign
agent, too, and they can take all of 'em off our hands." He spread
his arms across the inventory on his blotter. "It's a clusterfuck. No
doubt about it." He gave Adele a searching look. "And you knew
dick about this? Nothing? Your partner."

"Whatever it was, he was doing it on his own."

"Where'd he get his hands on these things?"

She sighed. "It's on this cassette, how he picked up two
diamonds at a crime scene."

"More than two diamonds in here."

"Yes, sir. It's on the tape. He went back the next day and

found them. Wrapped in a pawn ticket."

"Pawn ticket in here?"

"Haven't found it yet. Probably somewhere in Paulie's apartment."

"Right. So. One blue, four white, five stones. Your friend signed, too."

"I figured I should have a witness."

"Okay. And it's his gun? Definitely?"

"Yes, Captain, definitely."

"Shit!"

"Yes, sir."

"Match?"

"Peel's got the bullet. It's pretty mashed up. They're trying to match it. Should get back to us today."

"Who's the guy I talk to? Speed it up?"

"A Staff Sergeant Hurst," Stacy threw in. "He's heading up the investigation into the other . . ."

"Right. The Nimchuk." Rosebart poked the plastic bag and the revolver spun a lazy quarter turn to point across the desk in Adele's direction. "Where this weapon was used. Maybe. By one of my detectives. Maybe." He shook the brown envelope. "While stealing a sack of jewels. Maybe. Jesus H. Christ. And it goes on. The two jokers you brought in, what do they have to say? He tell you how he got his hands on Delisle's piece?"

"I didn't question them. Turned them over to Lacsamana and Heatley forthwith. I'm staying arm's length. Keeping my distance."

"Except you're already in it."

"I didn't ask for it. I just picked up Paulie's phone. This guy Sergei said he'd trade the weapon for the jewels. I convinced him I was willing to do that. When he turned over the gun I arrested him. That's as far as I went."

"Well, shit, I don't know what we've got here. Those Russians, they look good for the pawnbroker?"

"Not my call, sir. They were nearby, they knew the deceased."

"Right. And the dancer lady? She look good for it?"

"I wouldn't say so. But not my place to say."

"Right. Not your call. That prick partner of yours is lucky he's dead the way this thing's shaping up."

"I read those jewels as evidence that Detective Delisle didn't get a chance to turn in before he was killed. If it turns out different, I won't be the one who makes the call."

"Evidence of *something*, that's for goddamn sure. With extras. Don't suppose this cassette says how he came to lose his service piece?"

"No, sir."

"Or why he didn't report it missing?"

"No, sir."

"Kee-rist!" Rosebart pulled a Kleenex out of the box on his desk and blew his nose. "Snow mould," he said. "My wife says when the snow melts off it lets out crap that's been trapped all winter." He wiped his eyes, gave his nose another rub. "All right. So *you*," looking at Stacy, "come down here looking for the dancer, who just happens to show up at a murder scene, along with two Russian hoods, who all seem to know each other from the last movie." He shook his head slowly and began collecting the pieces of evidence. "I give up. Hand this stuff to Lacsamana and Heatley, they can log it in. Give them what you've got for facts but don't go speculating. Let them do their jobs and we'll deal with it."

Stacy stood up. "It was nice meeting you, Captain Rosebart."

"Sure, sure. Tell that big busybody you work for I don't need any more of his business."

"I will."

Rosebart motioned for Adele to stop before she went out the door. "Moen? You all right? I thought you were taking some more time."

"Soon as I hand things over."

"Slug got mashed up on the bed rail. They might not get a clean match. It was likely a Smith revolver, that's as far as they'll go. Doesn't mean it wasn't his gun. Probably not crucial. It's not like he'll be on trial."

"He may be dead, but he's still on trial," Adele said. "There's going to be an inquest. If the coroner pins it on Paulie, that costs him his pension, his reputation, screws up his kid's life."

"Well I can't bury it. It's got to play out. You stay away from it. You're too good a detective. I don't want you smeared with this." He waved his hand vaguely, either dismissing her or dispersing a bad smell. "You got any other thoughts about this?"

"I hope to Christ Paulie's clean."

"Yeah. You can hope."

The Pimple and the Toothbrush had been very happy to see her again, very happy to take away her cigarettes and make her wait two hours before they allowed her to pee. It was disappointing that her favourite policewoman was not allowed to question her, or even the tall one with the sad eyes, but she took her medicine, sat quietly and answered patiently.

It is hard sometimes not to think police are stupid, the way they go over and over a thing, but that would be a mistake. They plod because it is the surest way of getting somewhere. They write things down so they can reexamine the facts at a later date, catch you in a lie, confuse you with your own details. You cannot gloss over things. You cannot assume they will connect the dots on their own. And so she plodded with them and after a while they got bored with her story. They were much more interested in Sergei and his thick-necked partner, with stolen property and suspicion of assaults and robberies.

They provided accommodations in a holding cell and said they'd get back to her.

The bed was hard, but she'd slept on worse. With any luck she'd get a few hours rest, uninterrupted by dreams of killers. She might be locked up, but for now she was safe.

Pete Lacsamana's moustache wasn't exactly like a toothbrush, but it did have a squared-off bottom edge and clipped sides. Dale Heatley was taller, and likely to develop a dowager's hump if he wasn't careful, the way he nosed around like a vacuum cleaner. They both stood, both leaning on the front of her desk, bending over, pinning her down. Fuck 'em.

Adele sighed. "Shit, and I was almost out of the building." Stacy was waiting for her on the other side of the room.

"We haven't got enough to do with this Grova business," Heatley started, "now you dump a bunch of Russians on us?"

"Spread the action around."

"Yeah, well, Hong and Siffert are taking a few days off."

"If they fucked up and Paulie's shooter walks, they'll lose more than a few days."

"No big deal. He just got misplaced."

"Fucking idiots."

Lacsamana wasn't about to lose the advantage. "What was all that shit you laid on at the crime scene?" His tone was accusatory. She wasn't offended. That's how cops start most conversations.

"No shit. My friend was looking for the ballet woman; she found her. I was looking for Paulie's gun; I found it. Now you've got the whole bag. Where's the problem?"

"What about this shooting in the Beaches?"

"It's on the tape," Heatley said. "Where he says about the diamonds. What, eight years ago?"

"Before my time, Dale. Check Paulie's files."

"I'm checking the files. Can't find a report."

"Still an open case, right? I don't think they made an arrest. Paulie might have copied me in after O'Grady left. Have you checked with him?"

"Yeah. Sort of," said Dale. "Talked to his campaign manager. He'll come in 'as soon as he can make room in his schedule.' Frickin' politicians."

"Maybe I can track down Paulie's paperwork."

"Yeah, well, we need to get into Paul's place."

"Knock yourselves out. Give you the spare key."

"To have a look around."

"Do what you have to do," she said. She pulled the spare off her keychain and fished around in her drawer. "You've got everything I found so far, but there's still a lot of shit to go through." She found a piece of string. "Fair warning."

"It's his gun," Dale said.

"Yeah, I know." She hung the key on the string and tied a big bow.

"I mean in the Nimchuk thing," Pete said.

"You got a match?"

"Nothing that'll hold up. Slugs all bent to shit. All they know is it was a Smith, Magnum, .357.

"Dead end."

"Except this is his weapon. And he showed up in Dockerty without it."

"Far as I know."

"Next thing, this Russian dude has it."

"Look guys. I don't want to know. It's all yours. If Paulie comes up dirty, it'll be because he was. And if there's a different way it went down, I know you guys will keep an open mind as much as you can. I'm taking some time off." She handed Dale the key.

Not Jamaica this time. Maybe just check into a nice hotel for a week. Room service, spa, swimming pool, good bartender, did she mention room service? Forget about packing up Paulie's stuff. Let Lacsamana and Heatley have a week to go through the place with sniffer dogs if they wanted. They had everything she'd found and if there was any more, they could find it for themselves. And she'd stay away from her place as well, except to pack a bag. Wouldn't need much, credit cards, maybe she'd do some shopping, buy *something*, just to be buying something. Mostly just sleep a lot and get massages and watch movies. Sounding better and better.

"You want to come out and get drunk?"

"I don't drink," Stacy said.

"You want to come out and watch me get drunk?"

"Sure."

"You can have the couch — it folds out if you want, but it works okay as is. I'd offer you the bed, but I don't think I've made it up for a month and there may be socks hidden under the blankets. Or worse."

"This will do fine," Stacy said.

"I'd apologize for the mess except that it usually looks like this and I'd really be apologizing for what I am. Which is a slob."

"It's not dirty, just disorganized."

"Right. Exact opposite of Paulie. His house, organized; his life, a mess."

"*Your* house *dis*organized, your life . . ."

"Okay, not the *exact* opposite. But when it comes to the job. Notes, reports, details. I've got that shit covered." She checked the refrigerator. "There's a Red Bull, a Yoplait and a bottle of water." She yanked the cork out of a mostly full bottle of Spanish red. "I'll be drinking wine. *Lots* of wine."

"I'm okay for now." Stacy shifted a stack of newspapers and magazines and sat on the couch.

Adele grabbed a tall water glass decorated with flowers,

filled it, had a big slurp and topped it up. She sat across from Stacy and the two women stared at opposite walls for a long moment. "I have a couple of pictures I should probably hang. Spruce up the place."

"Pictures of what?" Stacy had trouble with the words.

"Oh shit, I don't know. Scenery." She had another drink. "They came with the last joint." They were both laughing. "Getting there," she said. "You don't drink at all?"

"My parents were boozers. Both of them. It was a cautionary childhood."

"My parents were Christers. Probably why I say fuck so much. But I still pray. Sometimes I do both at the same time." She drained the glass, studied the flowers for a moment. "Grova died of a heart attack, possibly brought on by 'enhanced interrogation,' but no direct connection. No prints, no weapon."

"So no murder charge."

"ME says he died around 03:30, give or take. The Russians have an alibi."

"What about the dancer?"

"She has an alibi, too, not quite so solid, but it hasn't fallen apart yet."

"They turning her loose?"

"Tomorrow. If they don't charge her. Why? You want her?"

"I figured I'd give her a lift home."

"Why not?" She stood up. "Sure you don't want something? We could send out. There's a Chinese place a block away."

"Maybe later."

Adele came back from the kitchen with the bottle and refilled her glass. There were wine-red brackets beside her upper lip. "Stupid motherfucking bastard. I couldn't count the number of times I told him to shape up. Fat lot of good that was, save my fucking breath."

"He must have had some good qualities."

"Oh yeah. He was a prince." She slumped in her chair. "Never met a rule he couldn't bend. Or break." She sat with the glass at her mouth for a while. "Got my brother off a drug charge a couple of years back. Claimed he was a confidential informant. He didn't have to do that. Could've got his ass in a sling for it."

"Did it for you."

"He brought Jamie here and gave him the lecture. Yada yada, you're going to wind up dead or doing time and the only person on the planet who gives a shit whether you live or die gave up on your sorry ass a long time ago, yada yada."

"Did it work?"

"Oh yeah. For a while. Jamie was clean for a year, more than a year. He wound up dead anyway." Her glass was empty. The bottle was empty. "I'm over it now. You have to get past things like that." She was holding the empty glass in one hand and the empty bottle in the other. "Paulie didn't have to do it. But he did it. I can't hate him." She put the empties on the coffee table. "Question is . . ."

"Is?"

"Do we go out, or do I try to sleep?"

"Long day."

"Yep. Long day."

The bar was dimly lit and sparsely populated and within walking distance. The bartender recognized Adele. "Hey, Del. Where's the big guy?"

"Oh, you know, probably chasing something blonde. Give me a half of the house red and a Perrier for my driver." She led the way to a table in a quiet corner. "I don't want to get into it tonight," she said. "I'll tell him some other time."

Stacy had a careful look around. "This a cop bar?"

"Shit no, hookers and dart players. Hate cop bars. Nothing but cops."

"Don't like cops tonight?"

"I like working with cops, most cops; don't like drinking with them. Cop talk. Tonight they'll be cop-talking about you-know-who and how he fucked up and maybe shot somebody and stole some jewels, got his head blown off, and I'd wind up getting into a fight with some asshole."

The server put the wine and water on the table and Stacy handed her a twenty. Adele couldn't locate her wallet. "This is mine," Stacy said.

"Okey dokey," said Adele. She lifted the carafe and slopped some on the table. Stacy took it from her, filled her glass neatly and wiped the table with a napkin. "I'm getting there," Adele said.

"You've probably worked it out for yourself, you don't need me rubbing it in."

"Go ahead."

"If I was building a case, if I wasn't teamed up with you and getting involved in your version, if I was coming into this cold, I'd be looking at Paul."

"Yeah. Me, too."

"He had the gems, his gun might be the murder weapon, he was at the Beaches crime scene. He took diamonds from there."

"All that. I see all that. Only thing in his favour, he wasn't in Montreal in 1982 because in 1982 he was playing college basketball in Syracuse."

"Right. Good place to start. When did Paul and Dylan team up?"

"Dylan quit football in 1982, broken toe I think. Went to the police academy. Got his shield twelve years later. '94. His first partner retired in '96. In January '97, Dylan is teamed up with Paulie in the homicide unit.

"They called them the 'Jock Squad.' Basketball star, six eight, two hundred pounds; Argos defensive tackle, six five, two seventy. I saw them in action a few times when I was in uniform. Impressive team. The kind of dicks you really don't want going through your laundry and bothering your customers. And you definitely didn't want to piss them off."

"Scarier than you and me?"

"Not as polite. Nobody fucked with them."

"They got along?"

"Closed a lot of cases. Paul didn't talk too much about it. I know he had to cover for Dylan a few times. Par for the course, right? I was always covering Paulie's ass. But I got the impression it was more than that. Paulie wouldn't rat out his partner, but there were plenty of rumours around the division. Things went missing, defence witnesses didn't show up when they were supposed to, not everything got turned in. Once in a while Paulie would let something slip, like some guy we busted who had a suitcase full of cash. Paulie said, 'Put Dil's twenty percent in a separate bag.' It was a joke, but later he said, 'Forget I said that.'"

"How about when you were with Paul? Was he straight arrow?"

"See, that's the weird part. We were together five years and seven months, and he never once made a sleazy move. He was always bending the rules in his favour, and he got raked over the coals plenty for how he got results, but I never saw him take a bribe, or a free lunch, or even hint that we could get something extra if we wanted to." Adele picked up the carafe and swished it back and forth a couple of times. She put it down without refilling her glass. "Possession of stolen jewels? Out of character."

Stacy leaned closer. "So I'm thinking, if the Russians didn't mess up the pawnbroker and likely cause his heart to explode, and if his son didn't do it, and if the dancer lady didn't do it . . ."

Adele took a moment to work her way through what Stacy was talking about. "There's somebody else out there. Who we missing?"

"There's the brother. The other Grova."

"Montreal Grova? Nope. They called him at home. He's pushing eighty. He'll be here tomorrow to collect the ashes."

"Releasing the body already?"

"They hurried it up. The Grovas are Jews. They don't leave

dead bodies around if they can help it."

"That's nice. You should talk to him anyway."

"Not my case. I'm staying clear." She looked at the empty glass. "What's he going to tell us?"

"Who knows? Maybe who else might be involved. They were doing stolen jewels in Montreal, too."

"That they were. But what, twenty-five years ago?"

"Which is when the first smuggler got herself killed." Stacy pulled out her notebook. "Ludmilla Dolgushin. That's one dead body your partner *didn't* have anything to do with. Then there's the second dead smuggler."

"Nimchuk. The jury's still out on that one."

"Not him." She turned a page. "That would be . . . Vassili Abramov. He's the dead guy in the Beaches with the diamonds in his pocket. Eight years ago. Another one your partner didn't kill."

"Probably."

"I'd say pretty sure. So add it up, *somebody* has been knocking off the smugglers one by one, and you can't stick it all at your partner's door. Because if he didn't do the other two, if he just did Nimchuk, then that's a really big coincidence."

"Seriously."

Seven

Orwell was a late-night house roamer. He often fell asleep in his little office under the stairs and woke with a crick in his neck and a need for a small bite of something sweet. After an hour of foraging, checking the weather, looking for the *Fancy Fowl* magazine he'd misplaced, making certain that the house was secure and all who should be home were home, he would take himself to bed. Only to be up again long before dawn, fussing with paperwork and fretting about inconsequentials just to have something to occupy his mind. Erika was by now accustomed to her husband's odd routines. She had tried on many occasions to ease him into a "normal" schedule of sleep, plying him with hot milk, Ovaltine and cocoa. But while he was happy to have a warm drink in the evening, especially if a couple of sugar cookies were on the saucer, he tended to fall asleep in a chair as easily as in a bed, and rarely spent more than three hours in any one location.

Saturday night and pre-dawn Sunday were even more unstructured than usual. Detective Stacy Crean's lengthy phone report had dragged him from the dinner table just as dessert was being served and had lasted until dishes were being put away. By the time Stacy had finished giving him the high points of her excursion, his family was scattered to who knows where and he was reduced to eating dessert alone at the kitchen table, a not entirely unhappy occasion (an ample slice of Erika's mixed berry crumble, an unfinished Saturday crossword to wrestle with) but not as agreeable as it might have been with all family members present for the weekend recap and projections. He never did get to hear how close Patty and Gary were to pinning down a date (sometime in June if possible), or how brilliant Leda was in rehearsal that afternoon, or how Diana's meeting with Georgie went, if in fact she was inclined tell him.

04:30 Sunday morning found him back under the stairs checking his murky aquarium for signs of fish and replaying Stacy's verbal report in his mind. Sounded like an exciting trip, even though Stacy was prone to gloss over the bits where she beat people up. The retrieval of the missing handgun was satisfying. The possibility that it had been used in a homicide was unfortunate. The unspoken awareness that the murder might very well have been committed by a member of the Toronto police force was troubling. But however you looked at it, the excursion had been a success. Stolen gems were recovered, suspects were arrested, a missing woman was located. All parties had been processed, interviewed, and their overnight accommodations arranged. Stacy had done everything expected of her and more. She really was too good to be stuck in Dockerty for an entire career. As much as he would hate to lose her, if he could help her move on, he would.

"Anybody alive in there?" It was Diana, in the doorway, pointing at the aquarium.

"Oh. Well. Oscar's fat and sullen, as usual, but I thought I saw a fishlet lurking in the weeds at the bottom."

"A fishlet?"

"A little Molly or Platy or some kind of hybrid minnow critter. Oscar ate all the grown-up live-bearers but mayhap there's a tiny survivor in there."

"Stay out of sight if he knows what's good for him."

"You're up early."

"Beat some of the traffic back to Toronto. You want coffee, Dad?"

"Oh sure, I'll make some."

"It's already made."

He followed her into the kitchen. "I didn't hear a thing," he said. "When I make coffee in the morning it wakes up the whole house." He sat at his end of the table and watched her fix him a cup. "You and Georgie come to any arrangement?"

"Oh yeah," she said. "He's all raring to go." There was amusement in her eyes as she watched him struggle to appear disinterested. "It's okay, Dad. I haven't even spoken to our client yet."

"*Our* client."

"That's assuming Carey-Michelson & Carey will turn me loose to work with Georgie."

"Is there a possibility they won't?"

"They're touchy about image. They might not think it's in the firm's best interests."

"And if they say you can't?"

"*Then* I'll have a tough decision to make. I'd be walking away from a good spot with a very classy outfit."

"You'd *do* that?"

"As I said, tough decision."

The stars were still out when they walked to her car. A first-quarter moon was falling in the west. Horse noises from the barn, clomping and blowing.

"What's today? The twentieth?"

"Sunday."

"Tomorrow's the equinox," he said. "Start of spring."

"Damn cold for spring," she said.

"Nevertheless," said Orwell. "Your mother's snowdrops are up. They know what time of year it is."

She got behind the wheel, cinched up, checked her mirrors, aware that he was making sure everything was done properly.

"Listen up, Dad, if my getting involved in this is going to cause you any grief, I won't even consider it."

"Somebody has to defend the poor bugger."

"Doesn't have to be the police chief's daughter."

"Ha! That does make it more . . ."

"Complicated."

"I don't mind complicated," he said. "As long as we observe the rules we'll be okay."

"Who knows if I'll even be involved?" she said. "They could tell me to forget it."

"Anything you decide is okay by me, sweetheart." He patted the roof of the car. "Drive safe."

She had red hair like her father, and the fair freckled skin and bright blue eyes that went with it. She was locking her bike in the rack at the condo entrance. Adele felt a melancholy flutter — the wide mouth, tiny creases at the corners, so much like Paulie's. "Danielle. Hi. How are you doing?"

"I'm okay, you know."

"How's your mom holding up?"

"She's okay, too. She's sorry it happened, you know, she cried, a little bit."

"How about you? You cried?"

"Sure. Of course I did. We were supposed to go away for March break. He said we'd do something special. He was always saying stuff and then it never happened. I was used to it. I figured he forgot."

Adele collected Paulie's mail and jammed it into her coat pocket. "I'll deal with it. I'll deal with it," she muttered. "Just not. Right. Now." The elevator doors opened. Danielle took a step back. "We don't have to go up," Adele said. "This can wait."

"It's okay."

It didn't look like Lacsamana and Heatley had even been in the place. The cups from Sunday morning were still on the coffee table, the rolltop desk was shut up tight, the room hadn't been searched.

Danielle went first to look at the framed photographs covering most of one wall. Many of the pictures were of her. "I've only been up here two times," she said. "Mostly we'd go to a movie."

"He loved you a lot."

"Oh sure, I know."

"He wants you to have his pension and insurance and whatever else there is. He wanted to make sure your . . . that it went to you. Only you. So he asked me to set up some kind of trust or something, I don't know shit about stuff like that. I'll get a lawyer to work out something. He figured you could use the money to go to school, university. You planning on going to university?"

"I guess. Yes."

"Any ideas?"

"Not really. Maybe art school. I like fashion."

"I can see that."

"You don't."

"Never saw the point.

"You'd be surprised. You should let me do a makeover sometime." She lifted a photograph of her and her father from the wall and held it like a book. "You going to sell all his stuff?"

"Nope. He said you should have whatever you want."

"Didn't he give you anything?"

"Oh sure. He left me his music, his blues collection. But if you want it you can . . ."

"No. You should have it. I'm not into that old-timey stuff anyway."

"You don't have to cart things away, we can maybe stick Post-it notes on whatever you want, with a 'D' on them. I'll have it delivered."

"I'm not into furniture. Maybe I could have his leather jacket.

The college one."

"Sure."

"Not to wear, well, maybe sometimes, but to have."

"He liked that jacket." Adele had absolutely no idea where to start. "So. You want to look around? Pick stuff out?"

"I'd like this picture. From when we went to a baseball game. He almost caught a foul ball. Bounced right off his hands. He was so mad."

"That would have pissed him off."

"I *know*."

"He was such a jock."

"I've got a picture of him playing basketball. He looks totally dorky. His shorts were really short. I mean *really* short."

Adele felt suddenly overwhelmed. Her legs felt soft and she plopped onto the couch. "Suffering Christ, it's going to take forfuckingever to go through all this."

"I can help."

"Would you? Shit. I'd appreciate."

"We should start collecting boxes."

"Right. A plan. A place to start. Boxes."

"You're bad at this, aren't you?"

"Very. I'm hopeless when it comes to personal shit. I moved into my place five years ago and I still haven't unpacked everything. Thing is, I don't miss any of the stuff I haven't unpacked. Probably means I should just get rid of it."

"At least my dad's stuff is organized. So, did he have a storage locker?"

"Oh fuck." The thought hadn't occurred to her.

"Our building has lockers."

"Is it going to rain?"

"I don't think so, clouds are too high. Maybe tomorrow."

"I am in your custody?"

"I'm just giving you a lift home."

"I suppose I may not smoke in your car."

"Police vehicle. Sorry. I can stop for a while, if you like."

"You would do that?"

"Sure. I need some gas. Up the highway."

They were on 35, heading north, Dockerty was a half hour away. Weather coming in, gusty March weather from the northwest, always from the northwest it seemed, grey clouds moving and climbing. Anya leaned against the passenger door, her hands inside her coat sleeves. She wasn't wearing the brown wig and she had scrubbed off the crooked lipstick. "The detectives wanted to keep me one more night," she said.

"Your alibi checked out," said Stacy.

"The best alibis are simple, do you not agree, Detective? I was asleep. Refute it if you can. I had the receipt for a nice little motel on Kingston Road. Silver Lake Motel. Sixty-three dollars. Not cheap. But it had a colour television. I had a long bath and went to sleep." They passed a dark stand of trees and she caught a brief reflection of her face, a flicker of white. She smiled at herself. "I *could* have had a long bath and a short nap and gone out after midnight. A receipt is not much of an alibi. Is it, Detective?"

"Not much."

"But you would need a witness who saw me leave, or return, and a witness to put me at another location."

"That would be helpful."

"Otherwise there is no point holding me."

"It takes time to build a case. Just because you aren't in jail doesn't mean you're eliminated as a suspect."

Anya turned to face her. "Yes. That is good."

"Why is it good?"

"So you do not stop looking."

Delisle's locker was crammed. Adele banged her head softly on the wall. "Oh Jesus fucking Christ."

Danielle marched inside, taking over, checking boxes, shifting piles. "I bet he hated it when you talked like that."

"Fucking right he did. He was always giving me shit about my language."

"I never heard him swear. Not once."

"A real choirboy."

"Not really. He screwed around a lot, didn't he? That's what my mom says. A skirt-chaser."

"Women liked him." There wasn't room for two people to rummage. Adele stood in the doorway and watched Danielle being busy.

"Did you?"

"Hell, yeah, sure. We were partners for six years."

"I mean like that."

"What? No. He never made a pass at me. I wasn't his type. We worked together."

"Would you have?"

"The subject never came up."

"Did you want it to?"

"This is a fucking weird conversation to be having with Paulie's daughter."

"I'm just asking because you're crying."

"It's the dust and shit."

"It's not that dusty."

"Oh man, he was my partner, six years, he saved my ass more than once, and I saved his, too. We were tight, the way partners get tight. Hard to explain."

"No. I get it."

"So you wind up . . . loving the person. In a way."

"You're still crying."

"I miss him."

"I'm glad. I'm glad he had somebody who cares that much."

"Okay, enough emotion. We've got work to do." She took a deep breath. "How do we do it?"

"Three piles, right, no, say four piles. Stuff to sell, stuff to give away — Sally Ann, Goodwill, whatever — stuff to keep, and stuff to toss. Call up Clear My Junk or one of those places, have them come around and haul it away. Okay?"

"Bless you."

"Here's more records. Like five more boxes. You're keeping them, right?"

"Good Christ Paulie, what did you do, corner the LP market? I don't know if I've got room. I'll take them home, sort through them. If I wind up selling any, I'll put it into your school fund."

"Don't worry so much about that. Another box of pictures. Hey. Here's one of you. Wearing your uniform."

"I know, I look like a geek."

"There are models out there who'd kill for your frame."

"Yeah right."

"I'm serious. What are you, six feet?"

"Six one."

"Right, square shoulders, long neck. I'm telling you."

"Face like a horse."

"No way. But you don't wear makeup and you cut your own hair. That doesn't help. You could look way better."

"Maybe next lifetime."

"See, here's one of my mom all dolled up. She's not perfect, but she knows how to pull it together." She handed the picture to Adele. "It's about making the most of what you've got."

The photograph had marks that suggested it had been framed at one time. Paul and Dylan O'Grady and their wives were at a party. There was a Christmas tree in the background and shadows and shapes of other partygoers. Many were in uniform. She might have even been one of them, somewhere in the crowd, on her own. Filling the frame were Paul and Dylan, both wearing tuxes, and their wives, wearing gowns. Jenny Delisle's dress was low cut and the photographer had caught Dylan O'Grady's eyes looking at her cleavage. Paul was oblivious, his attention elsewhere, but Dylan's wife knew where her husband's eyes were straying.

"Dylan O'Grady," said Adele. "You remember what his wife's name is?"

"I don't like him," Danielle said. "Mom said he made a pass at her after she and Dad split up."

"Like an African name or something. Keyasha?"

"No." Danielle stood beside her, having another look. "Keasha."

"Keasha, right. Now *she* looks like a model."

"*She* looks pissed. *He's* staring at my mom's boobs and *she's* staring at the back of his head. She totally wants to brain him."

"Men and women," Adele said. "It never stops."

"You a lesbian?"

"Nope. Not that either."

"I was thinking about being a lesbian."

"Don't know that it's any easier for them."

"Except you wouldn't have to deal with men."

"There is that." She looked at the photograph. "Holy fuck," she said. "Will you look at the size of the rock on that woman's finger."

Anya sat at a picnic table on the far side of the parking lot, wrapped in her brown coat, facing out, watching the traffic roll up and down the highway. Stacy finished gassing up, then pulled away from the pumps. She parked close by, but didn't get out of the car. Anya still had half a cigarette. She wasn't going to throw it away. At these prices? She turned her shoulder and resumed counting cars. After a while Stacy got out and leaned against the driver's side door. Anya knew she was there and spoke without turning. "It really is too bad about Louie. He was a loathsome creature, but still, it is too bad."

"Why did you go there?"

"I do not take much joy from life, Detective. It is the way I am. A small measure of pride I have, small pieces, pride in what I was, long ago, but not much joy. Small pleasures. I live on small pleasures." She lit a second smoke from the ember of the first. "I wanted to bring the thing to a head and end it. End it and have some peace. So I could enjoy my small pleasures."

"Did it work?"

She shook her head. "Not yet." She swung around to face Stacy, lifting her legs neatly over the bench, knees together, toes pointed, stretching them out in front of her, placing them gently side by side on the dirt. "Sergei Siziva is a nasty little man, but too fastidious to kill anyone with his own hands. And his big dog is too clumsy not to leave enough evidence behind to hang himself. Those two didn't kill Louie. You know that. And neither did I. I think it would be good if you kept looking"

"What happened to the big ruby?"

"Ha! That thing! I hope Louie swallowed it. I hope they find it when they cut him open." She butted the second smoke and stood up, brushing ashes off the front of her coat. She faced Stacy, straight and proud. "That would be fitting."

They had made progress. It was difficult to see much change but progress had been made. She was sure of it. Clothes had been sorted and boxed, Danielle was headed home with a full suitcase holding two of her father's leather jackets, an Ironhead watch cap, his gold Bulova and a baseball glove signed "Paul Molitor." A tentative date for the following Saturday was agreed to. Danielle was sure they could finish the job next weekend. Adele didn't think it was possible given the stacks of boxes now crowding Paul Delisle's living room. Five more boxes labelled "Records" were lined up by the bookcases where the other thousand-plus recordings stood upright in their proper paper sleeves, along with the thick ledger holding a complete inventory of the "Blues, Jazz and Roots Music Collection of Paul Alfred Delisle."

Alfred? No wonder you never mentioned your middle name.

The collection was organized alphabetically, cross-referenced by artist, label, recording date, sidemen . . .

. . . and on and fucking on. Jesus Paulie, if I'd known you were this meticulous, you could've handled all the paperwork. Saved me hours of crapola. How'd you manage to convince me you couldn't handle forms? What a bastard. Why lift a finger when you can charm your way out of it?

Okay, so I've got the records. I'm taking the bookcases too, I'm not having these things lying around my place. Plus those boxes are looking a little mouldy on the bottoms. That's not like you, Paulie. What if Big Bill Broonzy's face is getting slimy?

Adele tore open the first box and carefully lifted the albums to the floor. Most of them were RCA Victor classical collections in heavy bound covers, like picture books. Complete operas, Beethoven's nine symphonies . . .

Oh great. Just what I need. These I'll be selling. Nothing against the classics, Paulie, but I've got a classics channel on my cable package pumps out this shit 24/7. Very soothing when I can't sleep.

And another box full of geniuses, and another one, and . . . a box filled with records. The side split and the contents spilled out. Records. Not recordings: file folders, notebooks, case files, Paul's entire career as a cop.

Adele lowered herself to the floor. Oh fuck, Paulie. Now what?

July 24, Responded to a call from my partner, Detective Dylan O'Grady at the scene of a homicide near the Beaches boardwalk. When I arrived Det. O'Grady was present, searching the area with four uniformed officers from 52 Division. Victim was a white male, approximately 50 years

*old, wearing work clothes. Initial examination revealed what appeared
to be two bullet holes an inch apart in the victim's back. Wallet and
identification were missing. Medical Examiner rolled the victim. Both
exit wounds visible, slugs not recovered. No brass found at the scene.*

*August 19, Detective Dylan O'Grady informed me that the July 24
victim has been identified as V.A. Abramov, age 54, a Russian émigré, self-
employed. A search of Abramov's residence, suite 305, Hollis Apartment
Hotel, was unproductive. Apartment was empty, contained few personal
effects and produced no useful leads. No suspects, no evidence.*

*September 11, Detective O'Grady received a phone tip that Abramov
was carrying a large amount of cash from a housepainting job. Canvassed
the Beaches area, but couldn't find his employer. Robbery is the likely
motive. Possible random assailant. Case to remain open.*

But you didn't you leave it there, did you, Paulie? You poked
around a bit more. Went back and found some other stuff, right.
Why isn't that in here? Getting suspicious about Dylan? About
how he got to the scene way before you, got the identification,
found the residence, heard about a "large amount of cash"?
Who'd he hear that from, Paulie? Or fucking 'whom' if you
want to be your usual pain-in-the-ass self, whom are we talking
about? Who's giving all this good information to Dylan? Why
not to you? What's gnawing on your cop mind, pal? You worried
you're walking around with diamonds you took off the dead
man? Is that it? Or something else? Were you building a case
against your partner?

Oh this makes so much sense, haven't been in Union Station in
months. Even if he's not there it'll get me out of the house for an
hour, away from mouldy cardboard boxes and piles of paper I am

not going to read if I can fucking help it. And who said the man was even going to be there? What are the chances? It's not even your case anymore. It never was your case, or at least it shouldn't have become your case. The minute you found the diamonds in Paulie's apartment you should have washed your hands of the whole frickin' business.

That was Pete Lacsamana's reaction a half hour back. "Del, dammit, it's Sunday, I'm watching basketball. Bugger off, get off the phone, you're tying up my phone."

"You finished with Paul's place?" It was the only excuse for calling him at home she'd been able to come up with. "I needed to get back in there. To take care of his stuff. You know, for his daughter." The longer she talked the weaker it sounded.

"It's all yours. We never got in there. We've been pulled off that end of it. Whatever your shithead partner was up to, that's a whole 'nother bag of crapola. It's all gone Internal. Pretty soon they'll be sucking your brains out your nose, too. Smartest move for you is get your ass back wherever the fuck you got your sunburn and lie low, get drunk, get laid and *stay out of it.*"

"Right, sure, that's cool." She hated begging. She tried to keep it conversational. "So, come on, cop to cop, how's the Grova thing going?"

"It's going, it's going. Hell, we're just getting started. Not like it's the only case we're working. Best candidates were the two Russian dudes. We like 'em, can't connect 'em."

"You looking at anybody else?"

"Oh yeah, got a list of at least twenty-five dipshits who wanted to break this Grova dude's face. So far they all have alibis."

"Including his kid."

"That one can barely tie his own shoes, but his alibi is solid. He was passed out at his girlfriend's place. She wasn't a hundred percent pleased about it."

"So nothing."

"Well, he croaked at least an hour *after* somebody beat the shit out of him, so even if we track the perp down, they likely walk on murder one."

And this would be the tricky part. "You finished with the body?"

"Oh yeah, his kid didn't waste any time. Straight to the furnace. Didn't even want the ashes. His brother had to come in from Montreal to collect them."

"His brother? This is Martin Grova?"

"That's the guy. Eighty-two years old. Taking the ashes back to Montreal this afternoon. The kid couldn't care less."

"He flying back?"

"Took the train."

She would have pushed for more details, but that was just about all the slack Pete was going to give her. That was how she came to be wandering through Union Station on Sunday afternoon, looking for a man she probably wouldn't recognize, who probably wasn't there, anyway. What the hell, take a shot, right? If the brother came in from Montreal that morning he probably took the express. Okay, not "probably" but "likely." It would have been the best way. And if that's what he did, and if he had a round trip ticket, then he'd be catching the express home. Maybe. That train left at 5 p.m. It was 3:47. That gave her, hell, a whole hour to track down Louie Grova's brother.

Sunday shoppers were streaming in from the subway laden with booty, racing for the GO trains, making the lower concourse a stampede. He wouldn't be down here, anyway: Via Rail loaded upstairs.

For all its size, the main concourse bore the unmistakable stamp of Toronto's ungenerous nature. The limestone columns were thick, perpendicular, half Greek, partly Roman, not quite certain of anything except their structural integrity. It wasn't pretty, but it wouldn't fall down. That was Toronto.

The man sitting in the corner of the cafeteria was the right age. He had on a black suit and a black wool topcoat with velvet lapels. He wore a yarmulke. On the tray in front of him was a small metal teapot with a teabag string hanging down the side. A rectangular package sat on the seat beside him. It was about the right size for a container of ashes.

"Mr. Grova?"

The old man blinked before he looked up as if she had awakened him from a sad dream. "Yes? Who? Do I know you?"

"No. My name is Adele Moen, I'm a detective." He rubbed his eyes, replaced his thick glasses and then appraised her badge as if it was collateral for a loan. "I'm looking into the circumstances surrounding your brother's death," she said.

"Circumstances? Someone beat him up."

"Yes. Would you mind if I talked to you for a minute?"

"A minute only. I'm waiting for my train."

"Your train doesn't start loading for half an hour. If I could just ask you a few questions."

"Sit, sit." He shifted the tray to one side, wiped the tabletop with a paper napkin. "You like some coffee?"

"No. Thank you." She sat across from him. "Did your brother have a bad heart?"

"Louis? He had bad everything — heart, pancreas, veins, name it. It's a wonder he lasted as long as he did."

"Were you close?"

"He was my brother. Hate, love, what's the difference? Blood is blood." He shifted the package on the seat beside him. "Cremation isn't what we do," he said. "Cremation is when you want a person to disappear. I would have given him a place, a stone." He studied her face. After a while he nodded. She felt as if she'd passed some test. "You're investigating his death?"

"Yes. Peripherally. I'm investigating a murder that may be connected."

"A murder. I see. And who else was killed?"

"A man named Nimchuk."

At the name his eyes looked heavenward. "Of course." His

laugh was short and bitter. "Why not? 'Someday,' I told him," he waggled a finger, "it took nearly thirty years but I knew. Someday, this will all come back and bite you on the tuchus. Excuse my language."

"All what?"

"His life, his connections, his involvements." His lips pursed for a moment as though he wanted to spit. "Viktor Nimchuk." He lifted the lid on the little tin pot, but let it fall without looking inside. "The first time Louis brought that man around, I knew. 'Stay far away from this man. He brings trouble.'"

"Why did he bring Nimchuk to see you?"

"I need more tea," he said. "Would you watch this package for just a moment?"

"You stay put. I'd like some, too." The line was mercifully short. She slid a tray along the steel track and got tea for two. The cashier took her money without looking up. When she returned Grova was checking his ticket. He looked up. "How much time do we have?"

"You have lots of time. I'll make sure you don't miss your train."

"Good. Thank you. I don't walk so fast these days. I have to start early."

"So, this happened some time ago, right?"

"Twenty-eight years, I think. Yes."

"In Montreal."

"That's right. I've been in Montreal all my life. Louis, too, until he moved here."

"When was that?"

"Fifteen years, no, eighteen years."

"Okay. Can you go back to the beginning? Your brother came to see you with Viktor Nimchuk."

"This Nimchuk, he's Russian, yes? He did some business with my brother once before, a fur coat, sable, none of my business, I stayed away from what he was doing. This time he had some diamonds he wanted to sell. Fine, good. That's what I do, estate jewellery is my area of expertise, so, let's have a look. Very nice. He has six stones. Old European cut. Maybe 1890. Something like that. Probably Vienna. Nice enough, two carats, two and a half. So I ask, where do they come from? That, too, is part of my job. This Nimchuk doesn't have his story straight. Maybe he doesn't think it's important. They belonged to my grandmother, he says. Really? She must have been a wealthy woman."

"Did you buy them?"

"I have a good business, Detective, legitimate, pay taxes, keep records, I'm very careful. *Very* careful. When it comes to diamonds, it's good to be careful. Make sure the person who's selling the diamonds has the right to sell. Some putz comes in off the street with a handful of stones wrapped up in a dirty handkerchief. These are *not* his grandmother's diamonds. These are probably stolen. So I said no. But Louis, he had his own business, and not so . . . fastidious."

"Do you know what Louie did with them?"

"He sold them. One by one. Sold them for less than they were worth."

"Any idea who he was selling to?"

"I stayed far away from those transactions. I know he sold some to professional athletes."

"But you don't know their names."

"I don't know from sports. Players from here, players from there, Toronto team, Montreal team. Football players. I never met any."

"That was the only time you met Nimchuk?"

"Once more. A year later, maybe. This time he brought a woman, I don't know from names. They wanted an appraisal on a blue stone."

"A sapphire."

"Yes. A sapphire. Louis had a buyer, he said. He wanted me to look at it, make sure it was the real thing, tell him how much I thought it was worth."

"How much was it worth?"

"Back then, maybe five thousand dollars a carat to start with. But it isn't like adding up pounds of coffee, the price multiplies, a two-carat stone is worth more than two *one*-carat stones. This one was over five carats." He dipped his tea bag up and down three times and then used the back of his spoon to press the goodness out. "A lovely Kashmiri sapphire. Perfect, round, deep blue fire. I recognized it right away."

"You knew this one jewel?"

"I not only knew it, I knew where it came from. Russia. And if I knew that, I knew what else they had. You just had to add it up, by now they were trying to sell another eight diamonds, all cut before 1890, plus the sapphire. Not too hard to put things together — old diamonds, sapphire, Russians. I said, 'Where are the other three?'"

"What did he say?"

"He said that's all he had. Who knows if he was telling the truth? He was a good liar. I said to him, if this is what I think it is you have a big problem, my friend. This is one of the Sisters."

"The Sisters."

"The Seven Sisters. They were stolen over a hundred and fifty years ago. Pakistan would like them back. India would like them back. India and Pakistan have a disagreement over who should get them. Who knows? The Taliban would probably like them as well."

"You said four."

"Yes. Well. There *used* to be seven. Four in the pendant, plus two earrings, somewhat smaller. And a finger ring. But the four in the pendant were the real prizes."

"Who has the earrings and the ring?"

"They're in England. They aren't leaving soon."

"You never saw them?"

"Not in person."

"Is there any way you could tell from a photograph, and a black and white photograph at that, if *this* . . ." She took the carefully folded picture from an envelope and spread it out in front of him. ". . . is a sapphire?"

His eyes lit up and his face creased in a hundred wrinkles. "Oh sure. That's it. That's the stone."

"How can you be sure?"

"You just know, Detective. It's like recognizing a face. Stones like this one have names, personalities, even fan clubs. Stones like this don't disappear. They live forever. And sooner or later," he smiled, "someone wants to wear them to the ball."

"If I could show you the real thing, in your hand, would you be able to swear under oath that it was one of those sisters?"

"Under oath, you say? Would this in any way help to convict whoever killed my brother?"

"If I can get enough evidence to arrest him. It would certainly help."

"You know, it's been a hundred years since those jewels were worn in public. There is a photograph of the Dowager Empress Feodorovna wearing them. Part of a crucifix. An ugly piece, really, all those stones clumped together like that. Not really beautiful. Excessive. The four blue stones at the points of the cross don't really go with the big red stone in the middle."

"The big red stone in the middle. You're talking about a ruby, right?"

"Of course, very famous. The one they called the Ember. But it was a fake."

"Oh."

"That size, usually fake. Or maybe a spinel, garnet, hard to tell them apart if you don't know the difference. But that size? I've seen pieces of glass that would fool a lot of people." Smiles. "Somebody says they've got a ruby as big as a doorknob you can bet money it's a fake."

"They don't make rubies that big?"

"A few. But the Ember hasn't been seen since the Revolution. It belonged to the Tsar's mother. Maybe once it was real, but most of the royal jewels were sold by the Party. For cash. Stalin didn't care for jewels, he liked cash. He was a bank robber at heart."

"If you saw the Ember you could tell if it was real or not?"

"Of course. But I've always had my doubts about that one. Too perfect, if you know what I mean. But the sapphire in your picture, it's definitely real."

"So why didn't you buy it when you had the chance?"

"And do what? I have no personal use for gems. I don't wear them, I don't have them in my house. My wife doesn't care for jewels, she likes china. We have lots of nice china. What I do is *sell* stones, for a decent profit, not too much, I'm not a greedy man, just a fair deal for all concerned. So, here's a beautiful stone that I *can't* sell. So why would I buy it? The person selling it to me has committed a crime. If I sell it, *I'm* committing a crime, whoever *buys* it is committing a crime. Legitimate merchants wouldn't touch it. They'd recognize it. The best of them have a photographic memory for stones, believe me. Start mentioning Russians, and Russia, and old diamonds, that starts to narrow it down. Then show the blue stone? They'd all know." He checked his watch. "Please? I have to start now."

"All right."

He walked like a man with faulty hips and fragile knees, and halfway up the long climb to Track 16 he relented and allowed her to carry the package. When they reached the loading platform he needed to rest, but they had arrived with time to spare.

"Thank you," he said. "That's some climb for old legs."

"Will you be able to sleep on the trip home?"

"Oh yes. No stops, clickety-clack, puts me right out."

"Good. You've had a long day."

"I don't mind. There are things you need to attend to for

family. I don't count that boy. He's not a blood relative. Louis' wife's child. No connection at all. He'll sell what he can, probably drink himself to death. None of my business." He took the package from her. "My car is down there somewhere."

They started walking again. She kept a hand under his elbow in case he lost his balance.

"Why did your brother move to Toronto?"

"Something scared him."

"Do you know what it was?"

"He wouldn't talk about it. By that time Louis had some kind of partner. Or something. Someone else was involved. A man. I never met him, but I got the feeling he was dangerous."

"Was he a musician? I heard something about a musician."

"I never heard about that. I only heard about football players. Okay, this is me," he said. He held out his hand. "Thank you for your help, Detective."

"Thank you for talking to me."

"You know, some people just like to have something that no one else can have. People like that would buy the Mona Lisa and keep her locked in a closet, visit her in the dark once a year. I'm not one of those people. If I can't sell it, it's no good to me. Louis wasn't like that. He would keep Mona in a closet."

"Some people thought Louie had the big ruby in his closet."

"If he did, he gave it to them. Louis didn't like pain."

Eight

The Vernal Equinox. It was official. First day of "Muck Season," according to Orwell. The previous week's heavy rains had melted any exposed snow, mud was everywhere, impossible to avoid. And even though it was much too early for plowing, Dean Halliwell, who leased three of Orwell's fields for hay, had already been up and down the lane in his tractor at least twice, leaving sloppy ravines in his wake and making a good case for Bozo's ability to handle boggy terrain. The mud-room was at peak capacity: wellingtons, gumboots and galoshes were crowded under the long bench and every coat hook bore at least two muddy outer garments. A pan of water and a grubby towel were on hand for sluicing paws. The concrete floor was slick. Slippers waited on the mat by the kitchen door if you could make the jump.

Erika was in her element. Seed catalogues covered the dining table, and Dermot Dell, her partner in horticulture, showed up twice a week to discuss garden expansion.

"If you call him 'Dingly' while he is here I will brain you with a trowel."

"I never do."

"You want to, I can tell. You think it's cute."

"I think you're both kind of cute, huddling over that plan. What's going in this year, an olive grove?"

234

"Don't be ridiculous." Orwell wouldn't have been surprised. Last year it was a nuttery. "This year we will have a pond."

"With fish?"

"Of course with fish."

"Fish we can eat, or fancy Japanese goldfish?"

"Not an ornamental pond, a real one, big enough so you can row a boat across, with frogs, turtles, ducks . . ."

"If you dig it, they will come."

Three days without her morning run and she could feel it. Doesn't take long, she thought. Only on her third klick and her thighs were already complaining about the pace. The rhythm of her breathing was breaking up, ragged around the edges. Not good. Don't let it happen again. She thudded across the wooden bridge at the east end of the locks and turned for home. The familiar black Labradoodle chased her enthusiastically for the usual hundred metres before acknowledging a sharp whistle. She had never seen the owner. Don't you even think about slowing down, Stacy told herself, work through it, there's serenity on the other side of the pain.

Three days. Fun while it lasted, no doubt about it, it was a rush, but the job was complicated down there, easy to blow your routines, she'd have to fight for her alone time if she ever got to work in Metro.

Yeah, like that was going to happen. Maybe it's better to be the top investigator in a six-investigator town. After all, things had been pretty interesting in Dockerty lately. Not that a person could count on that much excitement every month, but no doubt about it, this case had been . . . *stimulating*.

But not finished. Well, maybe *her* end was finished, there wasn't much more she could contribute from up here — talk to Dr. Ruth again maybe, push the Zubrovskaya woman a little harder — but what good would that do? And what would she be looking for? What part of the case was still unresolved? The murder of Viktor Nimchuk in a motel on the Queensway in Toronto. The *Queensway*. In *Toronto*. Definitely *not* up here, and most definitely *not* her case. Not any more.

Almost home. Quick shower, a protein shake, find something to wear, verbal report to Lieutenant Paynter, another one to the Chief, then write it up, wait for orders.

She stopped running at her front gate, but kept moving, pacing the perimeter of the little front lawn, cooling down, around and around the three rowan trees Joe Greenway had given her last year. One male and two female. Hope those babies made it through the winter. Their trunks were wrapped in burlap and chicken wire. At least the wild things hadn't wounded them. If Joe said they'd be happy there, they'd probably be happy. Trees, he knew about. Staying in touch? Not so much.

"Chief? Captain Rosebart on line one."

"I'm picking up, Dorrie, thanks. Brennan here."

"Chief? Émile Rosebart."

"How do you do, Captain? What can I do for you?"

"Giving you a heads-up, Chief."

Orwell was alert. "Appreciate it," he said.

"We let those two Russians go."

"Really? "

"Right, we've got nothing to charge them with."

"Stolen handgun?"

"No evidence he stole it. Says he bought it from the pawnbroker. Plus he turned it over to a police officer."

"In exchange for stolen property."

"Which was offered by the officer. In any case, he didn't actually receive the stolen property."

"Well then, thanks for letting me know."

"Something else. There's likely to be some fallout over the arrest. The Russian who was taken into custody by your detective got a dislocated kneecap in the process. Says he's going to sue her for assault. Claims she crippled him for life. Police Services is going to have to look into it."

"I understood that he was resisting arrest."

"His lawyer's going to claim she didn't have jurisdiction to *make* an arrest."

"She was helping out a fellow cop."

"I know. I know. We'll sort it out. Right now Detective Moen's . . . taking some time off."

"*She's* not suspended, is she?"

"Lord no. She lost her partner. Hit her pretty hard. She's grieving."

"Plus you're investigating the man."

"Plus. And yeah, she's staying clear of that."

"Anything you can tell me about how it's going?"

"Nope."

"Fair enough, Captain. This Grenkov still in the city?"

"Far as I know."

"Good. Detective Crean can come down there and arrest him again."

"Say what?"

"Well, he's wanted for assault and breaking and entering up here. Wait a minute, make that *two* assaults, and *two* B&Es. I don't see why he can't pursue his lawsuit at the same time he's being tried in Dockerty. If you folks are done with him, I think we should get him up here to answer the charges."

Rosebart had the good grace to laugh at that. "Say the word, we'll pick him up for you."

"Thanks. I'll let you know."

"Might save his other kneecap." Still chuckling.

"Might at that. Crean's a good one, Captain. For future reference."

"I take your meaning, Chief. Big difference, working down here. A lot to learn."

"Steep curve, I'm sure, but if anyone could handle it, she'd be the one."

"Wouldn't happen overnight, Chief."

"I hope not."

A familiar shape was visible behind an open car door on the far side of the police parking lot and even from the back Stacy recognized the square shoulders and sharp elbows. She pulled into an open spot. "Just can't stay away, can you?" she said as she got out.

Adele Moen turned. "I am definitely putting in for gas and mileage," she said.

"Something come up?"

"Oh yeah. Did you know you can tell how old a diamond is by how it was cut?" She pulled a brown envelope out of her jacket pocket. "You can tell where it came from, too."

"You've been talking to an expert."

"In this case, I've been talking to *the* expert." She pulled the photograph out of the envelope and handed it to Stacy. "Recognize anything?"

"That's not a diamond."

"No, *that* is one of the Seven Sisters. Except now there are only four sisters, the other three are somewhere in England, probably hanging around some duchess's neck."

"And whose finger is it on?"

"Exactly."

Orwell was happy to see the pair of them. The sight appealed to him, although he couldn't say why exactly except that they seemed to complement each other. "Detective Moen, welcome back. Your captain tells me you're on compassionate leave. And grieving."

"Yeah, well I grieve better when I stay busy." She put the photograph on his desk.

"What am I looking at?" he asked.

"Christmas party, maybe ten, twelve years ago. Paul and his wife at the time, Jenny, and his partner at the time, Dylan O'Grady. That's Dylan's wife, Keasha."

"Very attractive," said Orwell.

"Check out the rock on her third finger, left hand."

"I see it."

"We recovered one just like it on Saturday," said Stacy.

"You think this gem is stolen."

"Not sure enough to walk in and bust the happy couple just yet," Adele said, "but I have it on good authority that we're looking at a five-and-a-half carat Kashmiri sapphire worth at least forty-thousand dollars, maybe a lot more, part of the missing trinket behind a shitload of dead bodies."

"How good an authority?"

"The best."

"You'd put this person on the stand?"

"In a second. And he says that the sapphire she's wearing is part of what they've all been chasing. I think it's a reasonable assumption that she got it from her husband. Probably a guilt gift. Caught him with his dick someplace it wasn't supposed to be."

"This man is a cop?"

"*Was* a cop. Paulie's ex-partner. Now a city councillor running for a vacant federal seat."

"Curiouser and curiouser."

"And before he was a cop, he played football for the Argonauts and — here I'm making an educated guess — had business dealings in Montreal with both Viktor Nimchuk, deceased, and Louie Grova, likewise deceased, and possibly Ludmilla Dolgushin, also deceased, and, in a bizarre twist of fate or a fucking *huge* coincidence, some years later was one half of the team investigating the freshly deceased Vassili Abramov, also one of the smugglers."

"Mercy! Up to his neck, isn't he?" Orwell said.

"Circumstantially," said Stacy.

"And only if we can prove it," said Adele.

"Prove what?" Orwell wondered.

"Who the fuck knows?"

The three cops were silent for a short while, each one focused in a different direction — Adele looking at the creased photograph in her hand, Stacy at the window watching the traffic go by, Orwell, as was his habit when looking for answers to tough questions, scanning the aerial map on the far side of his office. "By the way, they're letting the two Russians walk."

"What kind of bullshit is *that*?" Adele was livid. "What do they want, signed confessions?"

"Your boss is under some scrutiny, given recent events. He's treading lightly." He swung around to face Stacy. "Rosebart tells me that Grenkov character is going to sue you for crippling him."

"Fuck, I wish I'd seen that," said Adele.

"I told him I might send you down there to arrest him again."

"Dibs on the other kneecap," Adele said.

Orwell stood up and rubbed his big hands together briskly as if preparing to do physical labour. "Dang! I expected us to be swamped with outside troops by now," he said. "These people are awfully slow off the mark, don't you think? So far, nothing from Montreal, nothing from Ottawa, nothing from the Russian embassy. We should have officials from all over hell's half acre showing up, don't you think? We've got jewel thieves, murders going back twenty-five years, what does it take to get their attention?"

"I'm sure they'll saddle up any day now, Chief," Stacy said.

"I mean, this is . . . *international*."

"They've got a lot to sort out."

"Yes. Yes. And no doubt a joint Russo-Canadian task force is massing on our borders." He stopped pacing and made a few minute adjustments to the piles of forms, files and printouts on a side table. Stacy and Adele waited for him. "But it seems we're to be on our own a little while longer," he said at last. "Now, what we *could* do, probably *should* do, is wait until the duly authorized get their acts together and come in here to take over."

"Is that what we're doing, Chief?" Stacy asked.

Orwell went back to his desk, rubbed his hand across his dome, picked up the photograph. "Okay, just for the hell of it, let's say your man O'Grady got his hands on this particular stone back when he was playing football."

"Louie Grova's brother says Louie was selling stones to football players," Adele started. "Argos are playing in Montreal. Somehow Louie Grova meets Dylan, or knows him from before, offers him a deal on a rock. Dylan buys it. Okay, not a hundred percent kosher, but, long time ago, doesn't tie him to anything."

"Players," said Stacy.

"What?"

"Your friend the diamond merchant said *players*, plural, right? Maybe Louie sold jewels to other players. Maybe there's someone from that Argo team still around that we can talk to without tipping O'Grady off."

"Jee-zuss," Adele muttered. "Good luck tracking one down."

"What are we talking about here?" Orwell asked his map. "The 1982 Argos?"

"Yeah, '82, somewhere around there," said Adele.

"Because it just so happens there's a resident Canadian Football League expert right here in town. Knows the name of every man on every Grey Cup winner for the past fifty years. And we don't have to look back nearly that far. Hell, 1982. That'd be recent history to him." Orwell picked up his phone, punched in a number from memory. "Georgie? How about a slice of pie?"

"You're buying, right?"

"Need to pick your brain."

"You're buying."

Georgie was waiting in their usual booth. It was after three, the lunch crowd had moved on, allowing the pie fanciers to check out the selection and indulge their choices in peace. "Easiest decision of the day," Georgie said. "Coconut cream's been missing for weeks."

"I was thinking of putting together a petition," said Orwell.

"Woman who makes them had a baby," said Ethel. She waited patiently. The choosing process was important she knew, at least on the Chief's part. "And there's pecan," she said. "Really good."

"Can't justify it, Ethel, calorically speaking. I think a slice of the apple, with maybe a piece of that nice cheddar cheese."

"Not sure about the calorie count," Georgie said, "but it *sounds* nutritious."

"Exactly," Orwell said, with a virtuous air. "Wholesome to a fault."

Ethel lifted her eyebrows. The apple pie was as thick as a dictionary. "And you'll be wanting the sharp cheddar, Chief?"

"If you would be so kind, Ethel, my dear," he said. "And coffee, of course."

The Chief began his ritual unfolding of the napkin and polishing of the fork and spoon. To Georgie, it looked as formal as a tea ceremony.

"Gregg Lyman getting on your nerves yet?"

"What? Pah. Politics is politics. He can blather all he wants."

"Taking shots at you and yours."

"Consider the source, Georgie. Lyman's base is on the Knoll. That's where the money is, and those are the people who would love to have me out. If he gets elected, I wouldn't bet on me getting a contract extension."

"Doesn't piss you off?"

"Ever hear of a Jersey Giant? Or a Bearded Wyandotte? How

about a Buff Orpington?"

"These are chickens, right?"

"Fowl. Fancy fowl," Orwell said. He beamed as Ethel set his massive wedge of pie before him. "That looks scrumptious, Ethel dear," he said.

"Wouldn't know," Ethel said. "Screws up my blood sugar." She put an equally large slice of coconut cream in front of Georgie. "Coffee's on the way."

"Just black for me," Orwell said.

Ethel shook her head. "Sure," she said. "Mustn't overdo."

"What about the Ruffled Hottentot?"

"When I retire, or get canned, I'm going to raise chickens."

"Sure you are."

"I am, Georgie. Patty says horses and chickens get along just fine."

They concentrated on pie for a few moments. For all his size and gusto, the Chief was a very neat eater, feeding himself cheddar chunks with the fingers of his left hand while wielding his fork like a scalpel. "Diana phoned this morning," he said. "She's coming up. The two of you will make a formidable team."

"We've got the pre-trial hearing set for tomorrow. You want to watch her in action? I tell you, Stonewall, she's a dynamo when you turn her loose."

"I'd better stay away, Georgie." He carved a neat section of pie, topped it with a nugget of sharp cheddar and made the arrangement disappear.

"Any fallout from that outfit she works for?"

"She was a little evasive on the subject. I expect we'll get the full story come suppertime."

"Must be the Pie Club for Men," said Sam Abrams.

"Grab a seat, you ink-stained wretch," Georgie said. "Coconut cream has returned in time for spring." Georgie slid sideways to accommodate Sam. The Chief's side of the booth couldn't handle both bulks at the same time.

"Oh dear," said Sam. He was aware of his girth as he squeezed into position. "I don't think I'd better."

"Then you have to leave," Georgie said.

"All right. A small slice of, I don't know, any of that strawberry rhubarb left, Ethel?"

"You bet. Ice cream?"

"No. But thank you."

"Warmed?"

"Please." Sam beamed at the two men. "So? Discussing the Harold Ruth case?"

"Off limits for the duration," said Georgie. "We're talking fancy fowl."

Sam looked confused. "Chickens," Orwell said helpfully.

"Okay. Chief, I've got a quote from Mr. Lyman's camp that you might have to deal with."

The Chief put down his fork. "Really? What's he saying now?"

"He says you used police funds to pay for customizing your personal vehicle."

"He did?" Orwell started laughing. "And how much did I bilk the people of this fine community for?"

"He wasn't specific. More than twenty thousand dollars."

The laugh exploded into a huge barking roar so genuine that Georgie and Ethel joined in without a clue what they were laughing at. "Lordy me, will my wife be delighted! She thinks we paid for all that stuff *ourselves*!"

"So it isn't true?"

"Do I really have to bother with this while I'm having my pie?"

"Pretty much taken care of that pie," Georgie said.

"He said it in public," said Sam. "There was an audience."

"Let me guess."

"Wouldn't be the worst thing they've tried to pin on you," said Georgie. "You have an actual quote?"

Sam had it scrawled on a piece of paper. "'Chief Brennan's

misuse of the police budget in order to customize his personal transportation . . .'"

"He *said* that?" Georgie was outraged. "*Misuse*? Not *alleged* misuse, or *reported* misuse?"

"Just misuse."

"That fits the definition of slander, Stonewall."

"Oh who gives a flying fig what Mr. Lyman says?"

"You plan on printing this, Sam?"

"I was hoping to get a response." He looked up. "Thanks Ethel. This is a *small* slice?"

"I can give you a doggy bag."

"Oh I think he can handle it," Georgie said.

"You care to comment, Chief?"

"Why the hell is Lyman poking *me* with a stick? I thought he was running for mayor, not police chief."

"He needs an issue. He's picked law and order, hearkening back to the good old days of Chief Argyle."

"I'll stack the current record of the DPD up against Argyle's any day."

"You want me to say that?"

"No, I don't want you to say that. I refuse to dignify campaign horse-pucky and I sure as heck don't have to defend myself against a professional haircut who hasn't lived here long enough to pay tax."

"Doesn't finish his pie, either," said Ethel. "Was in here last week, left most of his blueberry."

"Afraid of staining his caps," Georgie said. "You don't have to print his nonsense, do you Sam?"

"It's not going to stop, Chief. He's picked his hobby horse and now he has to ride it. Last week's murder, the recent increase in muggings and break-ins, complaints against one of your constables for harassment, plus egregious misuse of public money. He's saying the police department's a disaster. He even wondered how much the DPD might have contributed to the refurbishing and renovating of the Brennan Estate."

"Jesus, Stonewall, he's throwing everything at you but your taste in neckwear, which, in my opinion, would be an inviting target."

"Said the man wearing daisies and bluebirds."

"Spring, dammit, get with the season."

"And there's a rumour, as yet unattributable, to the effect that you were seen carousing at all hours with a woman who was clearly not your wife."

"Well now that's going a bit far," Orwell said. "I was hardly carousing."

"Rumours spread, Chief. They're worse than outright lies. You can't refute a rumour, all you do is keep it alive."

"Take this down, Sam. Word for word. Chief Orwell Brennan's vehicle carries the necessary modifications required for its use as an official police car — lights, siren, communication. All of which are now, and will remain, the property of the DPD. Any *other* modifications to my old Ramcharger were paid for out of *my* pocket and I have, or rather my wife has, all receipts and cancelled checks dating back seven years." He picked up his fork and pushed the last crumbs of pie around the plate. "She'd be very happy to show everyone exactly how much money I've lavished on my personal transportation." He tossed his fork onto the empty plate and stood up. "That last sentence is off the record."

"What about the rumour?"

"As you say, anything I say just helps to keep it alive." Orwell went to retrieve his hat and coat and leave money beside the cash register. Ethel was talking to someone at the other end of the counter. Orwell raised his hand in farewell.

"What was it you wanted to pick my brain for, Stonewall?"

"Oh Lordy," Orwell said. "Almost forgot, what with defending myself against scurrilous attacks. Argos. 1982. You remember anything about them?"

"Of course."

"Anyone from those years in the vicinity?"

"Surely you jest."

"I do not jest."

"We're talking history here."

"Georgie, I'm a baseball fan. And I watch junior hockey when I can get to a game. I don't know much about the CFL. It's a failing, I admit."

"I'm shocked. Sam? Aren't you shocked?" Sam was otherwise occupied wiping rhubarb juice off Orwell's statement. "Well *I'm* shocked."

"When you're through being shocked maybe you can help me out. I need to speak to someone who was part of that team."

Georgie savoured the last morsels of his favourite treat. "And aren't you just the luckiest police chief in the country?"

"How so?"

"Touchdown Toyota. The dealership on 35? Just south of Bethany? You know who owns it?"

"Remind me."

"The name Nate Grabowski strike a familiar note?"

"Not even a glimmer."

"I fear for your soul, my friend."

Nate Grabowski had the unmistakable look of a former athlete. Rich living had added a substantial layer of lard since his football days, but he still moved like a gladiator. When he saw their badges, his shoulders hunched and he put up meaty hands as if to ward off a linebacker. "What is it this time? Somebody's claiming his brakes quit? Worse? Accelerator pedal stuck? Tell him there's a lineup."

"Nothing like that, sir," Stacy said. "We want to talk about football."

"Oh yeah? Okay. Good. Police starting a kids' team or something? You want some coffee?"

Stacy took the lead. "No, thank you, we don't want to take too much of your time. Need some information, if you can provide it, about the 1982 Argonauts team you played on. Do you remember any trips you made to Montreal to play the Alouettes that year?"

"Nope."

"Oh."

"Trick question. They weren't the Alouettes in '82. Montreal Concordes. They went two and fourteen. Don't know how they won two games. Terrible team. They didn't last long."

"Whatever," Adele said. "But you *were* with the Argos '82?"

"You know it."

"You remember that season?"

"Well, hell yeah! We went to the Grey Cup. Played the Eskimos. Exhibition Stadium."

"Congratulations."

"We lost. Scored two touchdowns in the first quarter and after that we couldn't do dick."

"Montreal."

"What about it?"

"You remember a teammate, Dylan O'Grady?"

"Dilly? Sure. What is this, a background check? You don't think there's a snowball's chance of him getting elected, do you?"

"I wouldn't know, sir."

"Some diamonds have turned up that Mr. O'Grady may have been involved with," said Stacy.

"In 1982," Adele added.

"Oho! Oh yeah, I remember that one. 'Dilly's Deluxe Diamond Deal.' They were hot, right? I figured. I didn't go in on that one." He looked from one to the other and shook his head. "Listen, I've only had one bite out of my sandwich, mind if we sit in my office?"

"After you, sir."

The sandwich waiting on his desk was a foot-long Subway creation. He picked it up and looked at it without affection.

"Supposed to be slimming," he said. "I don't know. Sit, sit." He put it down without taking a bite and had a sip of Diet Coke instead. "He always had *something* going on the side. Leather jackets, big name handbags for the wives, and every time there'd be a story to go with it."

"What was the story that went with the diamonds?"

"Wait a minute, wait a minute, it'll come to me. It was a beaut." This time he had a bite and chewed for a moment. "Now I've got it. Dilly had this pawnbroker. Fat little creep. Always checking out your stuff."

"Your stuff?" Adele distinctly heard her stomach rumble.

"Yeah, like your watch, like 'How much you pay for that? I can get you a Rolex,' and then he has like three watches up his arm. That kind of guy."

"Remember his name?"

"Louie something. I wouldn't buy a newspaper off him."

"So what was the story they gave out about the diamonds?"

"It's coming to me." He swallowed. "Right, they belonged to a woman who was *maybe* the great granddaughter of Anastasia or something."

"You didn't believe it?"

"I never believed his bullshit, excuse my language."

"No fucking problem," Adele said.

He laughed. "Right. He even had a couple of real live Russians to back it up."

"Remember their names?"

"Boris and Natasha. I don't know. Man and a woman. Only met them once. They could speak Russian anyway."

"You remember what they looked like?" Stacy asked.

"The woman was kinda pretty as I recall. I checked her out. Had a beaky nose. Not ugly beaky, sorta like Barbra Streisand. Dilly was all over her."

"You think they were involved?"

"Him? Like I say, he always had something going on. I was

never into that stuff. I was saving myself."

"For marriage?" Adele was amused.

"No, shit, saving my *strength*. Wife and I were trying to have a baby. She was taking her temperature every five minutes. I'm telling you, I was on call day and night, and I'd better have the necessary inclinations."

"Did it work?"

"Four kids. Two of each. Then she packed it in. That's plenty, she said. Get your tubes snipped, I'm retired."

"What about the Russian man?" Stacy again.

"Him I don't remember. Just a guy. Dylan and the Russian woman were leaning on him pretty hard."

"In what way?"

"I got the feeling Dilly was taking over the deal."

"You recall anything about the deal?"

"Dilly wanted to get a bunch of players to kick in a thousand dollars apiece and they'd each get a diamond worth like five times that much."

"Did he pull it off?"

"Couldn't tell you. I was just having a beer when all this was being discussed. I said no thanks, move your head, there's hockey on or whatever. I figured the diamonds were hot, anyway. I think a couple of the guys bought one, but not as many as Dilly was hoping for."

"You ever see any of those people again?"

"Not the other two, but I'm pretty sure Dilly snuck the woman into the hotel later that night. Pretty sure."

"Do you remember anything else Dylan was involved in?"

"Nah, he broke his big toe right around that time. Didn't make the Grey Cup game. Coach was pissed. I heard Dilly joined the cops. Is that right?"

"That's right, sir. He joined the force in 1985."

"Last guy I would've figured to go legit. He's a smooth operator. Probably why he went into politics, right?"

"Chief? You've got the crown prosecutor on line one."

"Hello. Mr. Blumberg?"

"Chief. I just found out your daughter is Harold Ruth's lawyer."

"One of my daughters is one of his lawyers, yes."

"Is this likely to compromise my case in any way?"

"I shouldn't think so. And for the record, beyond informing me that she'd been asked to work with Georgie Rhem, we have been scrupulous to avoid discussing the matter, even casually."

"She won't be calling you as a witness?"

"She might, I suppose. I can't see why she would."

"You were involved in the arrest."

"I helped identify Dr. Lorna Ruth as the woman who was with Detective Delisle on the night he was killed. After that, it was Metro and OPP all the way."

"Detectives Lacsamana, Heatley, Siffert and Hong. You weren't present at the arrest?"

"No."

"You didn't see the accused that day."

"No. They never brought him to the station. Took him straight back to the city."

"Which they shouldn't have done."

"Definitely not. He was returned to Dockerty on Wednesday."

"You realize this makes at least forty-eight hours that the defendant was held incommunicado, unable to speak to a lawyer, not charged, nowhere near where the charge should have been laid."

"I put it at closer to seventy-two hours."

"Jesus Lord. Bloody idiots."

"I understand they've been reprimanded. To what extent I don't know. You'll have to check with Captain Rosebart."

"We've spoken."

"For what it's worth, Gord, there were no procedural irregularities at the Dockerty PD end."

"Cold comfort, I'm afraid, Chief. SIU is investigating. Police Services are involved. The accused may have grounds for a suit. Toronto hasn't exactly been covering itself in glory lately."

"I'm sure they'll straighten things out."

"This isn't about protesters being penned up; this is a murder trial. Which may be seriously compromised."

"Gordon, if there's any way I can make your lot in life easier you'll let me know, won't you?"

"The only thing I can think of at the moment is your reassurance that the case won't be further embarrassed by the involvement of your daughter."

"I'd say you have bigger problems than Diana's participation."

They drove north toward Dockerty, Stacy behind the wheel, Adele working on a Wendy's Double Baconator. "Beaky," she said with her mouth full. "But not ugly-beaky."

"Barbra Streisand beaky."

"You figure the dancer lady ever saw them together?"

"Wouldn't that be nice?"

Adele peeked under the bun, wished she'd gone for a Triple instead, had another chomp. "So what exactly are we doing? What do we know now that we didn't know last week? Not suspect, *know* for fucking fact?"

Stacy was dealing with crawling traffic ahead of her and a huge Kenworth semi climbing up her tailpipe. "We *know* Dylan O'Grady was in Montreal when the first diamonds started to hit the market." Her words were carefully measured. She was occupied with checking her rear-view mirror and looking up front for the cause of the problem. "We *know* Dylan had dealings with Louie Grova in Montreal." She spotted it, a pickup with busted shocks and a poorly secured load of hay bales leading the parade. "We *know* he was one of the investigating detectives when the body of Vassili Abramov was discovered in the Beaches." The Kenworth was filling all the mirrors. "We *know* Abramov was carrying jewels . . ." She suddenly signalled, hit the siren, flashed her reds and passed six cars and the weaving pickup in one long swoop. She continued without any change in tone, ". . . because your partner picked two of them off the grass."

"That's it?"

Stacy checked the rear-view and smiled as the entire line of traffic behind them came to a lurching stop while the pickup made a wobbly left turn onto a side road. "I can tell you what we *don't* know for a fact. "

"A *fucking* fact."

"We *don't* know for a fact if the two Russians, Boris and Natasha, were really Viktor Nimchuk and Ludmilla Dolgushin. We don't know if O'Grady and Ludmilla Dolgushin had sex that night in the hotel. We don't know if she was carrying the big sapphire at the time."

Adele joined in. "We *don't* know if, after fucking her beaky brains out, Dylan stole the rock and turned her lights off. We *don't* know if he strangled her in the hotel, or waited until they were in a more convenient spot, or if he was back in time for the fucking kickoff."

"That's a long list of ignorance."

"We know shit."

"Except that Dylan's wife has a sapphire as big as a bottle cap on her ring finger."

"I'll grant you that much."

"No witnesses."

"None alive." Adele crammed the last bite of burger into her mouth. "Feel like coming back to the Big Smoke with me again?"

"You want to arrest O'Grady?"

"Not yet. No way. With what we've got he could still wiggle.

I don't want him to have any wiggle room."

"What then?"

"I think we need to take another run at Serge and Citizen Grenkov. I don't like them roaming around. They might fuck off. Serge still has some 'splainin' to do." She wiped her mouth. "You got a couch?"

"Better," Stacy said. "I've got a guest room."

"You're kidding."

"Clean sheets and cable."

"You're spoiling me, partner," she said. She wadded the hamburger wrapper and looked around for the bag it came in.

"By your foot," Stacy said, "partner."

Nine

It was a morning for carefully worded greetings, polite avoidances, nods and smiles and conversations that went nowhere. Diana was going to court and Orwell wasn't sure how he felt about it except that he was unusually fidgety for a man so calm. He had to admit that his daughter looked entirely competent: bright, brisk, smartly turned out in a dark jacket and a crisp blue shirt. He watched closely (but discreetly) for signs of nerves and couldn't spot any. What he saw was eagerness. Diana was standing at the kitchen window looking out at an eastern horizon barely tinged with pink, and one foot was tapping. She was champing at the bit.

"No!" Erika was emphatic. "You will not begin your day on a cup of coffee. Sit."

"I'm in a hurry," Diana said.

"You are in a hurry to get out of the house. You aren't late for anything. Sit."

"All right, but nothing heavy."

"You will eat what I feed you."

Diana resigned herself to getting nourished and sat. She glanced at her father. He was offering her some toast. She took a half slice. He took the other half. There was a moment's silence. "Watch your shoes getting to the car," he offered. "It's a quagmire out there. One of these days we should pave the lane."

He slathered on a layer of Erika's sour cherry jam. "Maybe after we dig the lagoon."

"It is not a lagoon." Erika served Diana a measured portion of scrambled eggs. "Eat that and have some juice so you don't fade away before lunch."

"Georgie says we'll be done in ten minutes."

Everything stopped for a moment. Diana looked up, aware that alluding to the forbidden topic might have been a breach of protocol. Orwell came to her rescue. "Pretrial hearings are usually just in and out," he said.

"You will still need your strength," said Erika. "And you, not so much jam. Have some eggs."

"As soon as I receive eggs, I will devour them," he said. He had a defiant chomp of toast. He was particularly fond of Erika's sour cherry. "That Lyman fellow has taken to calling this place the Brennan Estate," he said happily.

"That is nonsense," said Erika.

"It is, isn't it? The place deserves something grander. Xanadu, maybe."

"Xanadu." Erika was offended. "If you ask around the neighbourhood, it is still called the old Robicheau place and will be for another hundred years. Then, maybe, they'll start calling it the old Brennan place." She put a plate in front of her husband, then sat at the other end of the table and looked from one to the other. "Go on," she said. "Eat before it's cold."

Orwell surveyed his breakfast plate, knife and fork at the ready. If he was upset at the absence of sausages he didn't mention it. From Leda's third floor atelier they could hear lines being declaimed. Leda was rehearsing Emily's goodbye speech from *Our Town*.

"She's going to be great," Diana said.

"You too," Erika told her daughter. She looked at Orwell. "Well, she will be."

"I have no doubt of that," he said.

It was Adele's first good sleep in more than a week. The bed in Stacy's guest room wasn't large, but it was a hell of a lot more comfortable than the one she had in her apartment. I should break down and get a new bed. One of these days. And the shower had a massage nozzle to beat the tension from her neck and shoulders. She wasn't a hundred percent convinced that a "power protein smoothie" would ever take the place of bacon and eggs, but had to admit that the woman did make a good cup of coffee.

Nice little house, too. If I had this setup, I wouldn't be in a hurry to ditch it. "I don't see any moose heads on the wall. No bearskin rugs."

"Joe's pretty much a fishing guide these days."

"No fish, either. What's wrong with the guy?"

"He planted three Rowan trees in my front yard. A male and two females. That was kind of romantic."

"A threesome is romantic?"

Stacy laughed. "Never thought of it that way."

"Wait a minute, boy and girl *trees*?"

"Otherwise you don't get the red berries, he says."

"Yeah, I guess it's romantic."

"Technically I think they're mountain ash but I like calling them rowans."

"Because?"

"Rowans are magic."

"Oh. Would that be practical magic? I mean, anything we can use?"

"Good for wands, I hear. You want more protein shake?"

"No. Thanks. It was good. With the banana and the soy milk and the whatever else you tossed in there. I feel energized. So, what's it gonna be? Think your boss was serious about you going to town to bust Citizen Grenkov?"

"One way to find out."

Orwell was amused. "You realize I was blowing smoke when I suggested that, right?" he said. "We don't have a case. They processed Lorna Ruth's office. No prints, no eyewitness, no evidence that Grenkov hit the doctor or trashed her office. Likewise with the assault on Ms. Zubrovskaya. No eyewitness, her word against his. Have a hard time making it stick anyway, since she wasn't touched."

"She says he cut himself chasing her through a chain-link fence," Adele said. "Might be blood, DNA."

"This isn't New York, Detective. Who's going to pay for that? *We* can't afford it. Takes months the way the system works these days. And then he might wind up making a countercharge since he obviously got the worst of it."

"Lost my head."

Stacy said, "Chief, we just want a chance to question them again. If we wind up charging either one, it's a bonus."

"Do it all by the book. But let them know they're going to be very inconvenienced by the process." Adele was enjoying herself. "Mention Immigration and the extradition process, ask them if they'd like to contact the Russian embassy."

"And what do you figure to get out of this production?"

"We need bait," said Stacy. "We're after a bigger fish than those two. We think they might give us something we can dangle."

"And what do you think your big fish might do?"

Adele was honest. "Who knows? I don't have a fucking clue what he'll do. But I sure would like a chance to rattle his cage, make him mess his laundry. This man is a killer. I know it the way I know it's lunch time."

"Chief?"

"Yes, Dorrie?"

"Sam Abrams on one."

"Thank you." He snatched up the receiver. "Hi, Sam. No comment."

"No comment about what?"

"Whatever it is you wanted me to comment on."

"All right, Chief. I just thought you might have some fatherly reaction, aside from your position as chief."

"Why fatherly?"

"I just came from the courthouse. Harold Ruth's pretrial hearing. I guess you haven't heard. I suppose no one's in a hurry to report."

"Report on *what*? Jeeze, Sam, don't get all coy. What is it with you this morning? You're almost giggling."

"Your daughter and Georgie. Formidable team. Formidable. A dazzling display."

"When's the trial date?"

"Won't be one. Gord Blumberg's declined to prosecute."

"Declined? Why?"

"It was the smartest move. The judge would have tossed it."

"How do you know this?"

"I have a source. Someone who overheard a somewhat contentious exchange between the Crown and the defence counsels. Some of which I myself heard while, ah, passing by."

"And which you are just about to share."

"Georgie and Diana ambushed Gord Blumberg in the hall. Diana had a gun expert lined up who claimed that the bullet they dug out of the door jamb came from a Winchester 94, 30-30 lever action and *not* a Savage, model 1899 of the same calibre. The footprints at the crime scene would show that whoever was back there had big feet, probably eleven and a half or twelve. Harold Ruth wears a nine and a half. Harold was arrested with a recently fired rifle in his hand. Members of his gun club confirmed, or *would* confirm, that he'd been sighting it in at a shooting range and that he was there when he said he was."

"Georgie got all that in the hallway?"

"Diana did. Like a machine gun. To top it off, she knew the two Toronto detectives had been suspended for seriously bad conduct and exceeding their authority, holding the accused in isolation, denying him any right to counsel, and on and on. She told Gord his whole case was a collection of useless evidence and poor police work and he should hold off or the judge would toss the whole thing."

"They had no case."

"May I quote you?"

"No, you may not. You can say that 'Under the circumstances, the DPD will consider the case still open and assumes that the OPP and Metro's homicide unit will be doing the same.'" Orwell hung up and sat for a moment staring at his map with unfocused eyes.

"You forget we were here, Chief?" Stacy asked.

"Did I hear right?" Adele asked. "They're cutting Paulie's killer loose?"

"Harold didn't do it."

"The fuck he didn't!"

"Settle down. Take a deep breath. Harold Ruth didn't do it. There's a killer out there. Been walking around for two weeks."

Adele paced the room. She looked ready to punch a wall, she just hadn't decided which one. Stacy sat quietly near Orwell's desk, waiting for the smell of sulfur to die down.

"So all right! Who did it?"

"I don't know, but until we find out I can't spare Stacy for any road trips." He spread his hands apologetically. "Sorry."

Stacy didn't look sad at all. She leaned forward, her eyes bright and her head lifted, a hunting animal, testing the wind. "Any chance Del and I can take another run at that one?"

Adele liked the sound of that.

Orwell looked at the two of them. "I don't suppose you two have ever heard of a Buff Orpington?" He held open his most recent copy of *Fancy Fowl* to a colour photograph. "Handsome creature, don't you think?"

"Is that supper, Chief?" Stacy asked.

"Retirement. Something to look forward to after I'm kicked out of this office by a new administration. I figure it'll be around the same time Captain Rosebart chains *you* to your desk for a year, and around the time Emmett Paynter teams *you* up with Randy Vogt for the duration of your career."

Stacy smiled. "We're either doomed, or bound for glory."

He shook his head. "Tell you what. I'll give you twenty-four hours. Twenty-four hours that you can use any way you like." He held up an admonishing finger. "But *without* going anywhere *near* Lorna Ruth, *or* her newly released husband, Harold. Got me?"

Stacy grinned. "Twenty-four hours."

"Unless you want to wait for Lacsamana and Heatley to get back up here and do their jobs properly."

"And if we pull it off?"

"Well then, I guess I'd have to let you take another run at Yevgeni Grenkov and Sergei Siziva."

Adele picked up the magazine and looked at the cover. "Seriously, you gonna be *eating* these chickens, Chief?"

The landscape had changed since their first drive to Omemee; the snow was gone, green was starting to show in fields and hedgerows, winter wheat waking up, grasses springing, branches budding. Adele wasn't soothed by the change. "Do those cows ever get washed?"

"They will. Next time it rains, I think."

Adele shook her head at a mob of muddy Herefords. "Need a power-washer on some of them." She was glum and edgy at the same time. "We might as well eat," she said.

"Where? Lemongrass?"

"While we're there. Did you check out the menu last time?"

"I know they have tom yum soup."

"Whateverthefuck that is."

Reading the bill of fare didn't lighten Adele's mood. What she craved was something bad for her. A burger, or a medium pizza with too many toppings. The bartender was the same young man as last time and one of the servers had a familiar face. Stacy had them neatly gathered at the end of the bar under a flatscreen TV showing a glimpse of Florida and someone in a batting cage sending long flies toward a bright centerfield. Adele was trying to find something recognizable on the menu while listening with one ear to Stacy work her way through the preliminaries.

". . . week ago," Stacy said, "asking about the tall red-headed man."

"The basketball player. The one who got killed."

Adele turned a page. The menu totalled six pages and absolutely nothing decent to eat.

"You're Lara, right?" Stacy said. "You remember anyone else who was here or left around the same time?"

"I don't know. It got pretty busy."

"How about you, sir? You said you were watching basketball. Was there anyone else at the bar watching the game at the same time?"

"Yeah, couple of guys."

"Names?"

"The only one I know is Ed."

"Last name?"

"Ed Kewell. He drives a cab. Sometimes he comes in after his shift. Or maybe during his shift. Only ever has one."

Adele lifted her head to look at Stacy. "He's in the notes."

"He is?"

"Yep. Dancer lady's cabbie. Drove her home. Went off to look after his dying mother . . ."

"Sick sister," Stacy said.

"That's the guy."

"He's a regular?"

"Not really. Drops in once in a while," said the bartender.

"Doesn't eat," Lara said.

"At these prices, I'm not surprised," said Adele.

"Would you know where we could find him?" asked Stacy.

"Lives just up the road."

Adele closed the menu. "Any chance we pass a McDonald's getting there?"

A phone call and the onboard computer gave them the necessary details. Edwin Kewell lived with his father, Lucian Simon Kewell, in a trailer park. The sign at the gate said "Rosteen's Haven ~ water, power, cable, gas, garbage, security." The park manager directed them to pad 23 where two mismatched units faced each other across a concrete patio. A Kropf double-wide with awnings and a barren flower bed, stood opposite a distressed twenty-eight-foot Prowler Travel Trailer sitting on cinder blocks, but still wearing tires and a towing hitch. A gas barbecue, Muskoka chairs, planters and other necessities for summer living were parked under a roofed walkway that ran between the two units.

"You figure Edwin bunks in the guest house?" The Prowler had a rack of antlers hanging over the door. "See?" Adele pointed. "Now that's romantic."

"Joe has a cowbell over his door."

"He shoots cows?"

That got a laugh from Stacy. "Swap meet." She knocked. "Mr. Kewell? Edwin?" She tried the latch and the door swung open. "It's Detective Crean, Dockerty PD." She stuck her head inside. "Edwin? Dockerty PD. Like to talk to you for a minute."

A small dog started yapping inside the double-wide followed by a man's voice. "Hugo! Shut it! He's not home."

"Then could we talk to you for a moment, sir?"

The door opened and a man looked them over. He was in

his sixties, dressed for an afternoon of nothing much. A Yorkshire terrier bristled between the man's feet, growling and yapping. "Hugo. Shut it. Shut it." The dog refused to shut it and the man shoved him back into the room with his slippered foot and stepped outside, closing the door behind him. The dog continued yapping, but with less enthusiasm.

"You looking for Ed?"

"We are," said Adele. "He's your son?"

"He's working." He leaned to one side to check on what Stacy was up to. "Should she be doing that? Going inside without a warrant?"

"Oh, it's okay. The door was open. She's just making sure he isn't dead or something."

"He's not dead, his car's gone."

"See? Someone could have harmed him and stolen his car. Any bodies in there, Detective Crean?"

"I'll just look in the bathroom."

"Bathroom, right," said the man. "That'll take about two seconds." He frowned as Stacy disappeared inside. "He done something?"

"We have no reason to suspect him of anything. Do you?" She crossed the pad to stand in front of the man. "We wanted to ask him about a trip he took recently. To look after his sister. That would be your daughter?"

"Lorraine. Yeah. What happened to her?"

"I wouldn't know. We heard that Edwin left town to look after her for a while."

"Woulda been a neat trick. She lives in El Paso."

"You're saying Edwin wasn't visiting his sister last week?"

"Don't know what he did last week. We don't spend a lot of time together. Sure as heck wasn't flying to El Paso. Unless he's got a whack of frequent flier miles."

"All right then, thank you for your time, sir. We'll try him at work. Dockerty Cab, right?"

"Visiting his sister. That's a hoot. They haven't spoken a civil word in ten years." He opened his door and yapping Hugo reappeared immediately. "Shut it. Hugo. Shut the hell up." He scuffed the little dog backward and the door closed.

Adele turned back to the trailer. "Anything interesting going on?"

"Might want to have a look," Stacy said.

Adele stepped inside. The unit had the dark cramped feel of a fishboat below decks. "What's up?"

Stacy was standing at the table near the messy kitchen area. An unmade bed, partially hidden behind a sliding accordion door, occupied the other end. "What do you make of this?" she asked. Spread across the table were week-old newspapers, *Star, Sun, Globe, Lindsay Post, Dockerty Register*, all of them were open to articles dealing with Delisle's murder — "Metro Detective Shot in Motel Room," "Cop's Love Nest Homicide" and variations on the theme. "One of these clippings is from last Thursday's *Globe.*"

"When he was supposed to be visiting his sick sister," Adele riffled through the clippings, "in El Paso."

"I thought she lived in Hamilton."

"He sure was following the case."

"Has a girlfriend." Stacy picked a framed picture off the floor. The glass was shattered. "Or *had* a girlfriend."

"Don't cut yourself. This place is probably crawling with cooties."

"Wasn't an accident, this getting smashed. Bounced it off the wall."

"Anything on the back?"

Stacy turned the picture over. The frame was falling apart, the photograph slipped out easily. "Just says 'D.'"

Hugo started yapping again the instant Stacy knocked on the door. "Mr. Kewell? Could we ask you something?"

"What? Hugo, shut it, you barked at these people already."

The door opened halfway. "What?"

"Just wondering if you know who this is?"

"Doreen something."

"She's his girlfriend?"

"I guess. She only came around once. I don't think she liked the *ambience* if you get my drift."

"You know her last name?"

"Couldn't tell you. Lives up around your neck of the woods."

"Thank you," Stacy said. "Here's my card. If you see your son before we do, tell him to give me a call, okay?"

"Everything okay in there?"

"Cozy place."

Adele hadn't found a fast food outlet to her liking on the way out of town and was making do with a bag of Cheetos Puffs. "These things are better when they get a bit stale," she said. Her mouth was full.

"Stale."

"Not *really* stale, just chewy. Leave them out for a day or two with the bag open. Makes all the difference."

"Obviously I'm missing out on a whack of culinary adventures."

"You're a health nut. This stuff would be poison to you. You need to build up an immune system before you can handle ...," she lifted the bag to read from the list of ingredients, "hydrogenated vegetable oil, maltodextrin, artificial flavours, monosodium glutamate. Bag of these would probably kill you."

Stacy reached over and helped herself to a cheese stick. She chewed for a moment. "And they're *better* when they get stale?"

"It's an acquired taste."

They drove in silence; Adele munching, staring out the window at muddy cows passing, Stacy dealing with the maltodextrin on her lips and the orange colouring on her fingertips. "What do you think?" she asked after a while.

"Oh I think we've got *something*, partner. Oh yeah."

"Those antlers over his door, you think he shot that deer himself?"

"Oh we've got *something*." She munched a bit more. "Should've picked up a Coke when I had the chance," she said.

The dispatcher pointed out Edwin Kewell vacuuming the back seat of his cab on the other side of the lot. "That's him over there. He needs to clean out his unit. I had a complaint, yesterday."

"Is that a regular thing for him?" Stacy asked.

"No. Just lately. Since he got back."

"From visiting his sister?"

"Said he was going away for a week. He was back in two days. I guess she got better."

Stacy had to raise her voice to be heard over the vacuum. "Mr. Kewell? Hi. Mind turning that off a minute?"

Edwin switched off the Dirt Devil and looked from one to the other. "What?" he said.

"Hi. Detective Stacy Crean, Dockerty PD. This is my partner, Detective Moen, Metro Homicide Unit."

"Yeah?"

"So. How's your sister?"

"My sister? What about her?"

"We heard you left town to look after your sister."

"Oh. She's okay."

"Did you visit her?"

"For a couple of days."

"In El Paso," Adele said.

"What?"

"We were just talking to your father. He said your sister lives in El Paso."

"Yeah, okay. That was just something I told people. It was a secret."

"What was?"

"I was, my girlfriend and me, we were eloping."

"Oh, hey, congratulations."

"Yeah. Only it didn't happen."

"That's too bad. Was it Doreen you were eloping with?"

"Yeah. What's it to you?"

"Just interested." Adele moved away, began looking at cars parked along the fence.

"Why didn't you get married?" Stacy asked.

"We changed our minds. These things happen."

"Mutual decision?"

"I guess. It's personal."

"Okay, we can leave that for now. I'm just wondering, did any detectives talk to you about events on the night of Monday, March 14?"

"Why?"

"That was the night a man was shot at the Sunset Motel on 35. When they questioned one of your regular fares, Anya Daniel, she offered your name to corroborate her whereabouts that night."

"I drove her home, if that's what she says."

"That's what she said."

"Fine then."

"Would you mind telling me where you went after that?"

"Me? Lots of places. Have to check my sheet."

"Did you stop in Omemee on your way home?"

"Probably."

"Stop in anywhere for a beer after your shift?"

"What? Yeah. Probably."

"Remember where that would have been?"

"Probably the pizza place."

"What pizza place?"

"It's not a pizza place any more. Lemon-something."

"Mmm hmm. Right, Lemon-something. Yes. You were there. We've got two people who identified you, the bartender and one of the servers. You were watching a basketball game. The other man there, you'd remember him, tall, red hair? He's the man who was shot later that night."

"So?"

"Do you by any chance know Dr. Ruth? Lorna Ruth. She may have spotted you at the bar when she came in. She had a date with the man at the bar. You might be the reason they didn't stick around."

"None of my business what she does."

"According to the bartender, you left immediately after they did. Didn't finish your beer."

"I was late, I had to get home."

"So what time did you get home?"

"I don't remember exactly."

"How did you know you were late?"

"I don't know, might've checked my watch, checked the clock over the bar . . ."

Stacy lowered her voice, stepped closer and spoke as to a child. "And what did the clock say?"

"8:30, more or less."

"And how long does it take to drive from Lemon-something to your house?"

"Ten minutes. Sometimes fifteen. Usually."

"So if we talk to your father he'll confirm that you got home by around 8:45?"

"I don't think he heard me come in. He was watching TV."

"So what were you late for? Was there a show you were going to watch?"

"It was just getting late."

"Bartender says you left in a big hurry. What was so important?"

"What's going on? Person's not allowed to live their life? I wanted to check my emails. What's the difference?"

Adele stepped in. "You own any firearms, Edwin?"

"What? Yeah. Sure. Still legal, isn't it? Owning a hunting rifle?"

"Depends. What sort of hunting rifle do you own, Edwin?"

"30-30."

"What kind of 30-30?"

"Winchester."

"Mind if we take a look at it?"

"I don't know where it is right now."

"Well, I'm sure we can figure it out. Is it in your trailer?"

"I don't know."

"We can call your father and have him check."

"I don't think it's there."

"Well?"

"I remember now, it's in the trunk."

"Trunk of your car? This Chevy over here? Would you mind popping the lid, sir?"

"Don't you need a search warrant or something?"

"You want us to get a search warrant? Fine, we can do that. Stace, why don't you drive over to the courthouse and get us a search warrant and I'll keep Mr. Kewell company until you get back."

"Oh what the fuck. I'll open it." Edwin pulled keys out of his pocket and opened the trunk. A tartan blanket was draped over most of the contents.

Adele grabbed the corner of the blanket and pulled it back. "There we are," she said. "Winchester Model 94, 30-30 lever-action saddle gun. Just like John Wayne."

Stacy began taking pictures of the trunk's interior with her digital camera.

"It's not loaded," Edwin said.

"Don't touch it, sir. We'll have to take it with us."

"What for?"

"Ballistics. Turns out my partner was shot with a carbine just like this one. Might have even been this one. What do you think of that?"

"What are you talking about? They arrested the guy, didn't they?"

"You getting pix of those gumboots, Detective? Got some bootprints we can match up."

"But you got the guy already!"

"Oh fuck, Stace, we might as well take the whole car in for a thorough examination. You a housepainter, Edwin? Notice you have a nice little folding ladder in there too."

"In fact," Stacy said, "there's everything you need in there to shoot someone through the bathroom window of a motel room." She took another series of pictures, boot treads, the ladder's feet. "Were you aware of that, Edwin? Were you aware that you had a complete murder kit right in your trunk?"

Edwin leaned against the side of his car and slowly slumped to the concrete. He buried his face in his hands. "I don't know how she . . . she just met the guy. How could she do that?"

"I'm out of my jurisdiction, Stace. You better do the honours."

"Edwin Kewell, I'm placing you under arrest for the murder of Detective Paul Delisle. You have the right to keep your mouth shut."

"Doreen? From the Hillside?" Orwell shook his head with something like admiration. "He just met her at lunch. That day."

"Fast worker, my Paulie."

"And you have statements?"

"From all concerned," said Stacy. "Once we brought him in he was happy to tell his story."

"Couldn't shut the fucker up."

"Made him feel better. He seems to think his actions were entirely justified."

"Maybe two hundred years ago. In Spain."

"Or last week, in Tehran," Stacy said.

"I told you it was his dick that got him killed," Adele said.

"My my." Orwell allowed himself a rueful laugh. "Ha! Vain

old coot that I am, I thought Doreen was flirting with me."

"They all flirt with you, don't they, Chief?"

"This was more than flirtation. What's her story?"

Stacy consulted her notes. "Doreen McCallister. Told her boss she had a headache and needed to see her doctor. Left work at 2:30 p.m., met Paul Delisle in the parking lot of the Hillside Chef, drove with him to the Sunset Motel. He drove her back to the Hillside parking lot at approximately 4:15. She went back to work."

"Bet her headache was all better," Adele said.

"Unfortunately for all concerned, Edwin Kewell was delivering a fare to the Jiffy Lube across the highway just when Doreen and Delisle were exiting the motel. He followed them back to the Hillside Chef and saw her go back to work, then he followed Delisle to Dr. Ruth's office where he waited for a while, but had to leave because calls were piling up."

"How'd he happen to be at Lemongrass?"

Stacy turned a page. "Drove Ms. Zubrovskaya to her building at 8:30, then went back to the Sunset and parked. He says he just wanted to talk to Delisle. He saw Delisle drive off and followed him to Lemongrass. Followed him in but didn't confront him, sat at the bar and watched him. Said Delisle was coming on to both servers, Kelly and Lara. Then Dr. Ruth showed up and they left. He followed their two cars to the motel. Went around to the back."

"With a ladder."

"And his Winchester."

"Tsk tsk," Orwell clucked. "That's looking premeditated."

"What really pissed him off?" Adele was baffled. "He said Paulie was being unfaithful to Doreen by chasing someone else the same day. In some weird way he thinks he was defending her honour."

"Everything was by the book? Phone call? Read him his rights?"

"All recorded, Chief, and a stenographer."

"All right. I'll let you two inform the OPP. Hand it off. Tell them to tread carefully. You never know, Mr. Kewell might hire Georgie and my daughter."

"Sam, time to blow the DPD's horn. You ready?"

"Shoot."

"Detective Stacy Crean of the Dockerty Police Department, in cooperation with an investigator from Metro's homicide unit, have made an arrest in the murder of Detective Paul Delisle. The man's name is Edwin Kewell. K-e-w-e-l-l. Resident of Omemee, drives taxi for Dockerty Cab Co."

"That's it?"

"You'll have to check with OPP for anything else. It belongs to them now."

"Will Diana be defending him?"

"Ha! Very funny. I have no idea what her plans are."

"Just wouldn't mind seeing her in action again."

"I wouldn't mind seeing that myself, Sam."

In Orwell's world, the taking of whiskey had a ceremonial character; there was form to be observed, a level of appreciation that went beyond the mere enjoyment of triple-distilled Irish spirits. It was (for the most part) reserved for those occasions worthy of a toast — a victory, a momentous development, the resolution of a complex problem — and since he considered the lifting of a glass an intimacy not to be wasted on people with whom he had no connection, most of the time he savoured such moments alone in his little cubbyhole office under the stairs. Tonight was different. He had company. A beautiful woman was touching her glass to his, looking deep into his eyes as she raised it to her lips, smiling broadly as she swallowed.

"I wish I'd been there," said Orwell. He knew that he too was grinning.

"I started talking, and something took over," said Diana.

"You were in the zone."

"Even Georgie was impressed."

"I'll bet that was the most fun he's had in a while." Orwell lifted his glass again. "Proud of you," he said.

"Thanks, Dad." She knocked back the rest of her whiskey. "How's your fishlet?"

"Keeping a low profile, just as you suggested." Orwell poured them each a second tot, added a like amount of water to his, contemplated for a moment the light from his desk lamp dancing in the amber. "Must be hard going back," he said. "Tax law won't feel nearly as exciting."

"I won't be going back."

That turned his head. "This is news."

"Well, I'll be going back for a while. Work out the separation agreement, as it were. Probably cost me a few bucks." She had a sip, cocked her head to match her father's quizzical expression. "This feels right," she said.

"What feels right?"

"Georgie says Rhem, Treganza and Swain need some fresh blood in the firm."

"Since both Treganza and Swain are long gone to their rewards, it's probably time," said Patty. Orwell's eldest filled the doorway. There wasn't room enough for three bodies inside the room. Nor was there a third chair.

"Hey, sweetie," Orwell said. "Just in time. May I pour you a dram?"

"Would, but can't. Driving to Uxbridge later. Gary and I are looking at a new stud just arrived in the neighbourhood. Great bloodlines. Might be a good mix with Foxy. If the stud fee isn't too steep."

He raised his glass again. "So, what do we drink to this time? New horizons?"

"How about the Dockerty Police Department's arrest of the *real* shooter?" Diana had a cheeky smirk on her face.

"Forgot to say 'alleged' shooter," said Leda. Patty had to turn sideways to let Leda squeeze into the doorway beside her.

For one perfect moment Orwell felt complete. His three daughters in front of him, all healthy and happy and fully engaged in their lives, a productive day behind him and, judging by the rich scents coming from the kitchen, a fine supper ahead of him. He lifted his glass a few inches higher. "I believe I'll thank a benign universe for this day, this moment, these three beautiful faces before me," he said. He drained his glass.

"Amen," Diana said.

"Very nice, Oldad," said Leda. "I bring an invitation from the kitchen. Either come now or be banished to the outer darkness where there will be much weeping and gnashing of teeth."

Ten

"There you are," Anya said. "I thought you had moved on to greener pastures." The cat was sitting on the fire escape, facing away from her, watching the pigeons on the roof of the Irish House. "Will you come in, or are you thinking about your breakfast?" One ear twitched. "Well, if you want to come in, knock like a gentleman." And, on cue, there was a knock, but not on the window. "I am closed for the week," she called out. "Until next Monday. Or maybe forever."

"Anya. It's Dr. Ruth. It's Lorna."

"I am all healed now. I do not need a doctor."

"May I come in?"

Anya took her time opening the door. When she saw her visitor's face she stepped back. "Should you be out of the hospital?" Lorna was pulling off dark glasses and a headscarf revealing a bruise on the left side of her face and a bandage over her right ear.

"I apologize for just dropping by."

Anya stepped back. "Please. Welcome to my studio. As you can see, I have no students."

"That makes two of us. I've cancelled all my patients. May I sit? Please?"

"Yes, of course. I can make some tea."

"No, I'm fine, maybe later." She slumped onto the straight-backed chair and took a deep breath. "The stairs," she said.

Anya sat on the couch opposite her. "That one looks fresh."

Lorna touched her left cheek with a fingertip. "Yes. It is. After my husband, after they let him go . . . He didn't kill that detective. He had nothing to do with it. They locked him up for three days and he had nothing. . . . When he came back from the courthouse he . . . had a few things to say about what happened. About what I did. What trouble I got him into, what I did to us, to our marriage. Then he hit me."

"Did you report it? No, of course you did not, you thought he was justified."

"Something like that."

"And now you cannot go home."

"Later today. I stayed in my office last night. He's packing. Packing his things. Someone's coming with a truck. A friend. He's going to stay with a friend for a while, until he finds someplace. . . ." She pulled a wad of tissues out of her coat pocket. "I didn't know where to wait."

"I am going to make some tea. And I am going to have a cigarette. Here I smoke when I feel like it. You take off your coat. Sit on the couch, it is marginally more comfortable. And I will not spill hot water on you if you are over there."

She began to bustle efficiently around the studio, finding some relief in the movement, the small chores. She opened the window to admit the cat, turned on the CD player — *Ancient Airs and Dances* — took the kettle and the teapot down the hall to the washroom, filled the kettle with cold water, warmed the teapot from the hot water tap. When she returned she saw her guest huddled in the corner of the couch. The orange cat was sitting in her lap and she was gingerly stroking his head.

"What's his name?"

"I have no idea." She plugged in the kettle. "Is he making you nervous?"

"A little. His ears are very chewed up."

"Yes, it is the life of a back alley tomcat."

"Scars on his head."

"Just like the rest of us. They heal." She put three Irish Breakfast tea bags in the pot.

They sat without speaking while the tea brewed and the music played and under it Anya distinctly heard the rasping purr of the big orange cat. She lit a cigarette. "I have never heard him purr before this."

"That man, the tall detective, I keep thinking I got him killed."

"When you have regained your equilibrium, you will of course realize that is nonsense. He was in this town to see me. So *I* got him killed. He was chasing a bad man, so perhaps that got him killed. There were two other nasty creatures from my past in town, so perhaps they killed him. And in all probability, once you deconstruct the elements of his life, probably he got himself killed. You know that as well as I do. It is hardly ever one thing, is it?"

"I didn't need much coaxing, to run off with him."

"He was a charmer. Blue eyes, laugh lines and just the right number of freckles to be attractive, but not so many that it looked like an affliction."

Lorna laughed. Not a big laugh, but a small note of amusement nonetheless. "Yes. Charmed the ... socks off me in a hurry. Furthest thing from my mind when he walked in."

The cat jumped to the floor and Lorna emitted a small sad sigh. "Aaw."

"He never stays very long. He heard you laugh so he knows you'll be all right. But you may have some cat hair on your scarf."

"Oh. Oh well, I don't mind. I felt ... honoured by his attention."

"Yes, cats have that power, do they not?" Anya reached over to touch the material, a cashmere/silk blend in autumn tones, rust and orange and deep red. "Hermés," she said. "Very lovely. Is it new?"

"No. It isn't mine. I . . . I think my assistant left it in the office. I'll return it to her. I needed something to hide my head. I have this awful feeling that anyone who looks at me knows everything about me. All my sins, all my failings."

"All the more reason to hold your head up and look them in the eye."

"Interesting example of role reversal, don't you think? You helping me confront things? I suppose I'd better get used to dealing with it all."

Anya opened the window for the cat. The sun was above the Irish House now. In the distance she heard a crow cawing like a maniac. "I have declared war on all crows!" she called out. "Be advised, I am sending my personal assassin after you. All of you. It is time to pay up."

"Dockerty Police Arrest Murder Suspect."

Sam Abrams had given them as laudatory a review as possible without losing all objectivity. Stacy's name was prominent. Adele (as per her request) wasn't identified. Further down the page, mention was made of the dismissal of charges related to Harold Ruth. Orwell was somewhat amused to note that Sam had mentioned Diana by name and even added an adjective, something his writing style rarely allowed: "capable"; not overly effusive, but telling nonetheless. Orwell's daughter had a fan. And for once, Gregg Lyman wasn't quoted.

"Chief? Mayor Bricknell on one."

"Thank you, Dorrie. Madam Mayor, good morning."

"Chief Brennan. You're sure you got the right one this time?"

"I might remind you that *we* didn't arrest Mr. Ruth. Something the newspaper article makes quite clear."

"But this Kewell did it?"

"That will be for the court to decide, of course. However, we have the motive, the murder weapon and a signed statement from the accused, so I think we're on solid ground."

"I'm pleased to hear it. Now, about your daughter defending criminals . . ."

"Once again, Mr. Ruth is decidedly *not* a criminal, nor is he under any suspicion. My daughter and Mr. Rhem saved the Crown a lot of time and embarrassment by getting the charges withdrawn."

"Still, if she plans on doing any more of this, it could get sticky, don't you think?"

"Madam Mayor, my family is composed of staunch individualists who do pretty much what they feel like when it suits them. They won't stifle themselves because I have a public function, nor would I want them to."

"There is that other matter," she said. "Georgia Emery is threatening to file a civil suit against one of your constables."

Orwell's bark scattered a few crumbs across Sam's byline. "Oho! I sincerely doubt the woman is that daft no matter how early in the day she starts imbibing, but I hope she does. I really do. Constable Maitland will be only too happy to give detailed testimony of his encounter with Mrs. Emery on her front porch at 3 a.m., responding to a call from Doris Whiffen, the Emerys' next door neighbour, who was awakened by loud voices and the smashing of glass and furniture. We will also need the testimony of Mr. and Mrs. Darley Conrad, her neighbours on the other side, who, and I have the reports before me . . ." He had no such reports. He brushed a few crumbs off his newspaper for sound effects. ". . . have complained on no fewer than five separate occasions about what they were sure was a homicide in progress."

"That probably won't be necessary, Chief Brennan."

"I'm sure it won't, Mayor Bricknell. I mention it only so you will have ammunition the next time one of the Anointed ruins your morning. You might also remind those folks that Constable Maitland was one of the officers who apprehended the young man who stole Mrs. Avery Douglas's pearl necklace last year. The fact that the thief's name was also Douglas was treated with great discretion at the time, you may recall, which I'm sure Mrs. Douglas appreciated, although it might come out at any hearing I'm forced to convene regarding the conduct of one of my constables."

"Why do you think Lyman is coming after you?"

"Your administration doesn't have many weak spots. You run a tight ship and the people in town know it. But if he can smear the DPD, some of it's bound to get on you. Do yourself a favour. Don't stand beside me when you have your picture taken."

"Don't you think we're letting him get the upper hand?"

"I don't have to run for reelection, Mayor. I just get hired and fired."

"*I* hired you."

"I wasn't your first choice."

"Nevertheless."

"You could fire me. Show the town you're the woman in charge."

"I *am* the woman in charge. And despite our differences, Orwell, despite the fact that you can be insufferably smug and rude, on the whole I think you have been an asset to Dockerty."

"Thank you, Donna Lee. And while we're being so civil and supportive, may I say that you are a fine mayor."

"Might I suggest then, that until the election is over, and without overdoing it, we present a somewhat . . . *united* front?"

Anya was locking her studio door when she saw the two detectives coming down the hall. They looked fierce.

"I was just about to go home," she said.

"We won't keep you more than a minute. Detective Moen has something she'd like you to look at."

"Of course." She unlocked the door and swung it open. "I suppose you had better come inside."

"Have you ever seen this man before?" Adele handed her the picture.

She had a quick look, handed it back. "You know I have."

Adele forced her to take it again. "Not him, the *other* man."

Anya studied the photograph. A sad little smile tugged at the corners of her mouth. "He gave Ludi's sapphire to his wife? How sweet."

"The man," Adele reminded her.

"A dangerous man, yes?"

"What makes you think that?"

Anya shook her head. "Because my dears, you are being so very careful. You tippy-toe like sugar-plum fairies. You are both police, and this man too is police, but you do not want to ask him to his face."

"He *was* a policeman. Now he's a politician."

"Now he is a politician. How fitting." She crossed the room and turned to face them, looking from one to the other. "And you are *still* being circumspect." She sat without taking off her coat. "Sit, if you like."

"We're fine."

"All right." She rummaged in her pocket for cigarettes and her lighter. "Remember when I said there was someone else?"

"You didn't say who," said Stacy.

She lit a smoke and took a deep drag. "Once, many years ago," she began, "an uncle of mine complained to the chief of police in our town, that one of his men was abusing his position, helping himself to food, extracting protection money, forcing his attentions on certain women. My uncle Boris went to the police station to make his complaint and we did not see him again for five years. It is a lengthy process, I think, accusing someone with power."

"We aren't in the Soviet Union."

"Of course. But what would happen if I accused that man of being a criminal? Put it a different way, what if I had accused the *other* man, the red-haired man of being a criminal?"

"*Are* you accusing him?"

"You just proved my point."

"I did?"

"Of course. You were ready to tell me to go to hell. This man was your partner, yes? And because of that, you would defend him to the death."

"Wouldn't bet money on it."

"Now say some deranged Russian dancer told you your partner was a crook. You would say, who is this crazy woman? She is the one with assassins in all her closets. She is the one who makes false confessions, and reports stalkers twice a week, and changes her name all the time. You would say the woman is certifiable."

"*Did* you tell Paul that his partner was a bad man?"

"My uncle never spoke of the five years he was gone. He went back to being a woodcutter. And he never complained about anything ever again."

"Ma'am, just answer the fucking questions, okay? Did you say anything to Paul about his partner?"

Anya smiled slowly, blew smoke at the ceiling. "Oh yes. We had a long talk. Just the two of us."

"What did you tell him?"

She had another drag on the cigarette, taking her time, not caring that Adele was shifting from foot to foot. "They came to my apartment one night to question me about a body they found in the park. Viktor Nimchuk was there. I thought Viktor was going to have a heart attack when he saw the black man. I wanted to get them out of there so I told them a lie. I said I did it. They took me in for questioning. The red-haired man was very nice. He drove me home. He said it was very bad to confess to things you had not done, that it wasted their time and made it difficult for them to take anything I said seriously. He gave me his private number and said if I ever felt the urge to confess again I should call him first."

"Did you call him again?"

"Do not run ahead. When I got home, Viktor was gone, but he phoned right away — he was in a bar down the street. He wanted to know if I was alone. He was very drunk. He was very scared. He did not want to come back up; he asked me to meet him, to make very sure I was not followed.

"He said he would have to run away, that I should run away, too. He said the black man was the man who killed Ludi."

"He said that? How would he know that? Did he witness it?"

"No. But he knew. He knew because he helped them hide the body. They used Louie's van. They put poor Ludi inside a refrigerator and took her to the dump. On the way they dropped the refrigerator on the black man's toe. They made up a story to tell Vassili, about a musician who took her to California. After that they had to stay away from each other for a while. That is why Louie moved to Toronto, to get far away from whatever happened. When Ludi went to Montreal she was carrying a sapphire." She pointed to the photograph. "*That* sapphire." She butted the smoke, made certain it was out and tossed it into a wastebasket. "What should I do?" she asked them "Should I accuse one policeman to another policeman? In the world I come from that would never be a good plan."

"Let's say that right now it's the only plan," Adele said.

"You are really after this man, yes? That is good. I am pleased with both of you."

"What can you tell us?"

"I can tell you that this man paid a visit to Louie on the night he died."

"How do you know that?"

"I know that because I saw him leave. I did not see him arrive, but I did not get there until 3 a.m. or so."

"You were there?"

"Across the street. I was watching. I am good at that, the way you two are. I saw him leave. Then I called Louie from the phone booth, but he did not answer."

Dockerty's police chief proudly, somewhat ostentatiously and most deliberately, arrived at the Dockerty Restoration Society's luncheon driving his freshly washed and waxed 1987 Dodge RamCharger with chrome accessories gleaming. His blue dress uniform was pressed, his brass and gold trim bright. And Erika had provided him with *two* snow-white handkerchiefs: one for propriety and one in case he got a spot of mud on his shiny shoes. Orwell Brennan wasn't exempt from the occasional surge of vanity, but concern for his appearance was in this case a pardonable offence, a mental girding (and guarding) of his loins before entering potentially hostile territory. Women made up a substantial percentage of the society's membership, and many lived on the Knoll, thus it was reasonable for him to speculate that not all were fans. As he dismounted, he caught sight of himself in Bozo's big side mirror and allowed that he did look rather impressive in full regalia.

The Restoration Society reception was being held in the newly refurbished greenhouse/conservatory complex at Borden College, a bright and airy (if somewhat humid) space filled with flora from far and wide. Some of those attending had flowers on their hats, which seemed a tad superfluous to Orwell, but then women's hats had always baffled him.

Unlike the Chief, Gregg Lyman never needed reassurance that his shoes were shined or that his tie was knotted properly. He was at all times prepared for a photo opportunity. Today he was dressed in a suit of sincerest grey wool matched with a plum tie over a pale lavender shirt. His lapel held a discreet gold maple leaf pin. His hair was impeccable. When he spotted the Chief entering the room, he excused himself from an attentive circle and strode across the floor with his hand out. "Chief Brennan, this *is* a pleasant surprise. I've been looking forward to meeting you for some time. I'm Gregg Lyman." He gave Orwell the full sparkle of his expensive smile.

Lyman's grip was firm, but not too firm, eye contact was maintained without blinking, and to emphasize his sincerity, he added the overlay of his left hand to the top of the squeeze. Orwell was tempted (but only for a flicker) to top off the hand sandwich with his own massive paw but resisted the impulse as unnecessarily *herrisch*.

"Mr. Lyman, a pleasure. How goes the campaign? This is your first one, isn't it?"

"At this level, yes. I did run for class president in high school. Lost in a landslide." This prompted a ripple of sympathetic laughter from an obviously smitten gathering. "How about you, Chief? Ever throw your hat in the ring?"

"Never had the impulse," Orwell said. "I have a hard enough time getting a consensus at the dinner table." The ripple of laughter had a somewhat different character this time, a note of relief — the boys were going to play nice, and the Chief wasn't going to be mean to the charming Mr. Lyman.

"Chief, allow me to introduce the chairperson of this year's fundraising committee, my lovely wife, Cheryl."

"A pleasure to meet you, Mrs. Lyman," Orwell said.

"Chief Brennan," she said. Her press was cool, brief and single-handed. "Mrs. Brennan not with you today?"

"Alas, no. My wife is up to her chin in plans for the beautification of the Brennan Estate. I believe this year we're digging a lagoon."

"How nice. I'm so sorry we won't get to meet her." Cheryl Lyman had the lacquered look of a woman who had spent all morning preparing for a public appearance. She was, if anything, even more carefully put together than her husband. Her ash blonde hair was perfect, her designer frock was appropriate and her single string of pearls tasteful in the extreme. She was the picture of the rising candidate's wife. Her smile, however, couldn't quite hide the stainless steel at her core. Orwell knew instantly that if Gregg Lyman was the public face of the campaign, Cheryl was its motivating force. "Chief, we're hoping your officers will be able to help our campaign this year."

"Which campaign are we talking about, Mrs. Lyman?"

She didn't bite. "We're trying to raise funds to clean up that awful stretch on the north side of the locks. It is quite unfortunate, don't you think?"

"A worthy cause, I'm sure," said Orwell. "Have you checked with the owners?"

"I understood it was township property."

"Some of it is, I think. But quite a bit of it belongs to the brickworks and the wrecking yard."

"Those are the very places we're targeting. They're both terrible eyesores."

"Well, the brickworks has been abandoned for many years, although I couldn't tell you who owns the property right now. The wrecking yard, I'm afraid, is a going concern and unlikely to relocate."

"Businesses like that should be kept to the outskirts of a community, don't you think?"

"When they were established, those *were* the outskirts," said Orwell. This brought forth a murmur of recognition from some of the senior members of the congregation. "How long have you lived in Dockerty, Mrs. Lyman?"

"I've been away for a while, but my family has been here for many generations."

"Then I'm sure they'd remember the Bannock Brickworks. It was a thriving enterprise in the twenties and thirties." This prompted one or two nods of confirmation.

"Have your people been here that long, Chief?" Lyman asked.

"Me? No, no. I get all my local history from the library."

"Ah, there you are, Chief." Mayor Bricknell was making her entrance, timed to the second, neither late nor early, a working executive with a tight schedule. Donna Lee was the anti–Cheryl Lyman. Her outfits tended toward the frumpy and discordant. Today she was mixing narrow stripes and big dots. Her glasses were hanging sideways on a chain, and, as was often the case, her hair had strayed from its assigned order. She looked just fine to Orwell. Donna Lee clasped his hand in both of hers. "I'm so happy you could spare us a little of your valuable time." Her smile was genuine.

"My pleasure, Mayor Bricknell. Always happy to support one of your causes."

She nodded graciously at the Lymans. "Gregg, Cheryl — how nice to see you together. Given any thought to a date for our debate?"

Lyman gave a vigorous noncommittal nod. "My staff is looking at our schedule for a possible time."

"Great. Have your people get in touch with Mr. Frith here." She turned her shoulder just enough to exclude the Lymans from any position other than audience. "Chief, you haven't met my new press secretary, Cullum Frith. Chief Orwell Brennan, the man who keeps our streets safe."

"A pleasure, Chief." Mr. Frith was lean, dark and had an assassin's eye. It crossed Orwell's mind that Donna Lee was taking the election seriously. The Lymans were in for a scrap.

"Mr. Frith, nice to meet you."

"Chief, I'm hoping we can get a shot of you and the Mayor together." In a series of smooth moves he steered both Orwell and Donna Lee away from the Lymans while giving a discreet signal to a young woman with two cameras slung around her neck. Orwell recognized Sam Abrams' eager young reporter, Kathy somebody. "Maybe over by these flowering bushes."

"*Chaenomeles japonica,*" Orwell said, "flowering quince." He heard the distinct intake of a half dozen breaths from the flower ladies. "Lovely, aren't they?" A dozen women in flowered hats were nodding approvingly. The man knows his plants.

"Nice touch," whispered Mr. Frith.

"My wife has Vita Sackville-West's ghost on speed-dial."

"Oh my yes," said Donna Lee, loud enough to be overheard, "Erika's garden is becoming quite famous."

Orwell knew for a fact that Donna Lee Bricknell had never set eyes on his wife's garden, nor had she to his knowledge ever called Erika by her first name, but as a public relations move it was on target. The lines had been clearly drawn. Donna Lee Bricknell and Orwell Brennan were united.

As Orwell took his place beside the Mayor, bending his knees a bit to reduce the height differential, he spotted the Lymans on the far side of the room, near a large yucca, having a whispered conversation. "I think you won that round," he muttered through his smile.

"That was just batting practice," she whispered. "Game hasn't even started yet." She lifted her chin as the flashes went off.

The two women stood by their respective cars in the police lot, having a last word before taking off.

"Gas and mileage, I'm telling you," said Adele. "Need a bank loan to fill my tank these days." She was in a great mood.

"You got a spot at your place I can stick my car?"

"Sure. Don't waste any time getting to the big city, partner. I'll be booting it." She climbed behind the wheel. "You eat meat, Stace?"

"From time to time."

"So you're not a total fucking vegan, right?"

"Nutritional facts. Red meat is the most efficient protein delivery system."

"Definitely. Later. After we brace Serge and his pal. And they better not make us come looking for them. My blood's up." She slammed her door and peeled out of the lot.

Stacy took her time getting settled. She had no intention of trying to beat Del into the city. Not the way she'd taken off. What they had was thin, no getting around it: no witnesses, no evidence except a sapphire ring that might or might not still be in the possession of someone entirely innocent of anything other than being married to someone who's committed . . . how many murders? And still she was smiling. She buckled up and put the car in gear. Multiple murders. I *mean*!

Adele pounded on the door of apartment 304. "Open up, Citizen, it's the police."

There was a distinct snarl from inside, followed by loud Russian phrases that sounded unwelcoming. Yevgeni Grenkov yanked the door open. He was wearing last week's shirt. The collar was dog-eared and grubby. He pointed at Stacy. "If that woman kicks me again I will sue her for a million dollars. *Ten* million dollars." He limped over to the kitchen table and sat sideways. There was a bottle of vodka open. "I have brace on my knee, you know that? I have pain, I can't sleep. I'm going to sue. I have lawyer now."

"Keep yelling like that I'll fucking kick you myself," said Adele.

Stacy had a quick look around the apartment. "Where's your partner?"

"He has moved out. Good riddance. He gives me nothing but troubles." He rubbed his knee and glared at them. "What do you want?"

"We're here to arrest you and take you back up to Dockerty," said Stacy.

"For what?

"You've been identified as the man who assaulted Anya Zubrovskaya Thursday night. She's sworn a formal complaint against you."

"She is a crazy person."

"Yeah, she is kindá daffy, isn't she?" Adele agreed. She sat across from him. "But she *was* attacked, and she says *you're* the asshole who did it. So what choice do we have?"

"I know nothing about that crazy woman." He poured himself a shot and knocked it back in one gulp.

Stacy kept moving, checking the bedroom, opening the bathroom door, talking as she moved. "Also, Dr. Lorna Ruth has sworn out a complaint. She says you attacked her in her office. You were a busy boy last Thursday."

"Who is she, she's so important I should rob her? You know this woman? She's rich maybe?"

"You tell me."

"Better you should ask Sergei, maybe he knows who she is. I never heard of her before."

"It looked like you were trying to find something. Did you find it?"

"How could I find it if I wasn't there?"

"The two people in the other office saw you run out. They say you and your friend jumped into that little red BMW."

"Hoo ha! This is a big laugh. We don't drive red car on Thursday."

Adele smiled. "Oh. What colour *was* the car you drove?"

"She did not see anything."

"Really? Why? Because you blindsided her? You should have checked for mirrors. Anyway, a judge can decide how credible she is."

"Never mind. I don't say anything."

"Well, that's okay. When we get our hands on Serge, he'll probably be happy to pin it all on you."

"I don't think he has very high regard for you," Stacy said.

Grenkov poured another shot. "He has no regard for anybody except Sergei." He drank. "He owes me money. He treats me like shit. I was hired to bodyguard, but he makes me do things I was not hired to do. And still he doesn't pay. When you catch him, do the world a big favour. Send him back to Mother Russia."

Citizen Grenkov was only too happy to direct the two women to the Distingue Lounge, where he was certain they would find his employer. The handsome young man Sergei had been chatting with skittered away when he saw their badges. Stacy and Adele sat across from Sergei and let him fume for a moment.

"You'd better not make us come looking for you again, Serge, or I'll fucking tie you to a tree until I'm done with you."

"I refuse to spend any more time in the company of that animal."

"He's your animal."

"He has not changed his shirt in a week."

"Yeah, yeah, he's a brute. Not our problem."

"You've got a few problems though, haven't you, Mr. Siziva?" said Stacy.

"I have no problems. I have been released. No charges against me."

"That's in Toronto. We have other priorities in my town. Two breaking and entering charges, plus two assaults, both committed in Dockerty last Thursday."

"I assault no one!"

"Your partner may have actually done the assaulting but you were working together, and that makes you equally culpable."

"You can't prove any of these."

"Truth, Mr. Siziva?" Stacy leaned across the table, her face close to his, her expression hostile. "I don't really care. You'll be charged. You'll be given an appearance date. And while that's happening, Immigration Canada will send someone to look into your situation. After that, you'll be their problem."

"What situation?"

"You tell me. The story *I* heard was that you returned home to what was then the Soviet Union in 1982." She checked her notebook. "Do I have that right? And then you came back some years later." She closed the notebook and gave him a chilly smile. "Problem is, we can't find any record of you going back to Moscow, and no record of you reentering Canada. As far as we can figure out, you never left. Can you explain that?"

He held his face with in both hands and took a deep breath. "What is it you're looking for?" he asked. "Really. Because it isn't any silly burglary attempt. And it isn't my status as a refugee."

"Refugee? Is that what you're calling yourself?"

"I think maybe you want something else."

"Tell you what, Serge," Adele took over. "Why don't you try to figure out what that might be."

"I think I have things you need to know."

"Good. Let's start with this: you had my partner's gun in your possession. I need to know how you got your hands on it. You told them downtown you bought it from some street kid, didn't know his name, never saw him before."

"I would need protection. And some guarantees."

"Who will you need protection from, Serge?" She took the photograph out of the envelope and smoothed it out on the table in front of him. "Depends on who scares you the most, I guess."

They ate steak. Stacy had a six-ounce New York strip, rare, and enough salad to stock a manger. Adele opted for the twelve-ounce bone-in rib-eye, medium, baked potato with sour cream and chives, stuffed portobello mushroom, a basket of rolls (extra butter was required), a big glass of Chianti, coffee (cream and sugar) and something called "Chocolate Intemperance." When she had cleaned her plate she sat back, wiped her lips and emitted a ladylike burp. Stacy was looking at her with awe.

"What? First thing I've eaten since that protein thingy you made this morning."

"I'm impressed is all. You don't look like you have any body fat."

"Metabolism," Adele said. "Nervous energy. Plus I need fuel, we've got stuff to do." She checked her watch — 9:30 — and signalled for a coffee refill.

"I'm good," Stacy told the server.

Adele helped herself to cream and sugar, stirred and then leaned back as plates were cleared. "Okay. Got your notes handy?"

"Always."

"So what have we got?"

Stacy turned to the appropriate pages. "Not enough to make an arrest. Not yet anyway. Let's see — questionable witnesses supplying hearsay evidence from mostly dead sources, a weapon and a sack of stolen jewels neither of which we can connect in any way to the man we're after."

"Christ! We're doing great, ain't we? Thieves, thugs, illegal immigrants and registered crazies. And those are the ones on our side."

"On the bright side, it's looking less and less like your partner committed murder." Stacy leaned back and shook her head with something like admiration. "So she was there after all. Cool customer our little dancer. Give her that."

"I get the feeling she's been jerking us around all the time. You?"

"I think she's been playing a dangerous game. See it from her side: who can she trust?"

"Better not be playing *me*."

"Feeding us information in neat little pieces."

"Yeah, well one of these days maybe I'll sit her down and sweat the whole story out of her."

"I'd buy a ticket to that."

Adele finished her coffee and signalled for the check. "This one's on me," she said.

"I should hope so."

"So. What's the drill when you visit a drunk?"

"You bring a bottle."

"Any idea what he drinks these days?"

"I don't think it matters," Stacy said.

"We'll get him a bottle of Canadian Club. He'll think he's died and gone to fucking heaven."

"A small one," Stacy said. "We want his tongue lubricated, not numb."

It was dark. Lights on inside the store. Sign on the door: "Close until firther notice." Figure moving around inside. Knock. Loud voice, crabby. "Closed!" More knocking, less polite this time, brought forth a shambling figure. Darryl looked shaky, rheumy-eyed, unkempt. Stacy and Adele held their badges against the window. He opened the door partway. "Now what?"

"Mr. Grova?"

"Louie's dead. Didn't you get the news?"

"Yes, your father," Stacy said.

"Stepfather. My name's Kamen."

"Oh, fine. Sorry. Mr. Kamen. Would it be all right if we talked to you for a few minutes? Just clearing up some things."

Darryl left the door open and shuffled back to the counter. "He married my mother. That's the connection. That's the *only* fuckin' connection." He slumped in his chair behind the glass-front case. On top were an empty paper coffee cup and a torn bag of ripple chips.

Stacy looked at the display; watches, cameras, pens, cigarette cases, rings, all of it dusty, jumbled. "So you were his stepson. But you've lived here quite a few years, haven't you?"

"So?" His eyes were on Adele, who was checking out the shelves up and down the narrow aisles, lifting things up and putting them down. "Listen, don't mess with that stuff, okay? It's all in the right order."

"I can see that," Adele said. She continued poking and shifting. "Power tools, electronics, very nice."

"Gotta do a complete fucking inventory."

"Tell me about it," Adele said. "I'm doing the same thing myself."

"Pain in the ass."

"Got that right." Adele moved out of sight.

"Thirsty work," Stacy said. She picked up the empty coffee cup. "You deserve a drink, don't you think?"

"My girlfriend's trying to get me to cut back," he said.

"Yeah, that's probably a good idea." She put the brown paper LCBO sack on the countertop. "Your mother died eleven years ago? Is that right?"

"So?" His eyes were on the paper bag.

"So I'm wondering, if her marriage to Louie Grova was the only connection, why'd you stick around all these years?"

"Hey, I work here, I earn my keep. I drive the van, I pick up the furniture and tools and heavy shit and hump it in. I clean and repair and make sure things work. He didn't do shit except count his money. Sit behind here like a fat slug all day screwing people out of their nickels and dimes. Get a few bucks out of him like getting the last pickle out of the jar."

"But it's all yours now. You're his only relative."

"Sure it's mine. Can I open the store? No. Can I sell anything? No. Can I start unloading all this crap? No fucking way. Gotta wait for the courts and the cops and the tax man and everybody else who wants to fuck me over so they can come here and stick in their noses and count up how much they want."

Adele's voice had an echo now, she was at the far end. "Should be a nice profit though, once the legal bullshit gets straightened out."

"I'll try and live that long."

"Y'know Mr. Kamen, it's possible we can speed up the process for you." Stacy took a small bottle of rye and a can of ginger ale out of the paper bag. "Got any glasses?"

He waved at a shelf of crockery and crystal. "Take your pick."

Stacy chose a glass then pulled a Kleenex from the box on the counter and wiped the rim. "This is probably a difficult time for you. We're not after you for anything." He watched her unscrew the cap. She deliberately took her time. "We're just trying to figure out a few things that your father may have had knowledge of." She poured a double and handed him the glass. "Ginger ale?"

He drank it straight down, one gulp, took a deep breath through his nose. "Next round," he said.

She poured again. This time she added mixer. "And we've pretty much run out of people who were involved, or who knew any of the people who were."

He snorted. "That's because they're all dead, right?" This time he drank more slowly, enjoying the taste and the glow.

"Many of them are, yes."

"I'm not stupid. I stayed far the fuck away from those deals."

"What deals?"

"Whatever illegal shit he had going." He had another swallow, waved a hand. "He was into."

"You lived with him for how long?"

"Altogether, I don't know, twenty years."

"Twenty-two," said Stacy.

"Whatever. Working my ass off. In the store, picking up consignments, organizing. Keeping books."

"Seems to me in all that time you probably overheard a few things," Stacy said, "maybe met some people, casually, people who dropped by to see your stepfather."

"Yeah. Tell me to get lost. Wanted me out of the way for a

while maybe, slip me a few bucks and say, 'Go to the movies.' Cheap bastard."

"Even so, smart guy like you, over twenty-two years you probably saw and heard a lot. Maybe some stuff you don't remember. Maybe some stuff you didn't one hundred percent understand."

"Oh I fucking understood all right. I understood Louie was a sneaky piece of shit."

"And you probably saw him with some people." Stacy located the right image on her digital camera and handed it to him. "Like this man, Sergei Siziva."

Darryl looked at the face. "Sir Gay Sissyboy. Sure. Showed up once in a while. Wouldn't sit down in case he got his fancy coat messed up. Usually with some fat prick to watch his back."

"Oho! What *have* we here?" Adele sounded triumphant. She emerged from the darkness holding something by the tips of her thumb and finger. "Hey there Darryl, know what this is?"

"I haven't sorted that end yet."

"That's good news," Adele said. "Your fingerprints might not be all over it."

"Is it . . . ?" Stacy started.

"Oh yeah. It's a Jordan spring clip holster."

"I thought we already had his." Stacy opened the top of the LCBO bag.

"Beats me. Got an initial on the back. 'D.'" She dropped it in the bag. "Any idea where this came from, Darryl?"

"Christ, who knows? Louie the pack rat. Stuff in here from before Jesus."

"Maybe it came from one of these guys." Adele pulled out her brown envelope. It was getting ragged around the edges.

Darryl had a brief glance, pushed it away. "What about them?"

"You know either one of them?"

"Not especially."

"Not 'especially.' What does that mean, exactly?"

This time he helped himself to a drink. "Because this is like the *main* guy I stayed away from, know what I'm sayin'? Whenever he showed up, I made myself scarce."

"Which one?"

"That big black fucker."

Stacy folded the brown bag and put it in her pocket. "I guess they had private business to discuss," she said.

Darryl leaned across the counter and drummed his finger on Dylan O'Grady's image. "You know this guy, right?" His tongue was already thick. "Used to be one of you guys. Carried a badge. His fucking passport to whatever the fuck he wanted to do. Wave it under my nose. Making jokes about people he'd 'disappeared.' Not funny jokes. Got this loud voice. 'Hey Darryl, how'd you like free room and board for about seven years at the Crown's expense? I can arrange it anytime you say. Heh heh heh,' and then he flips his coat open so I can see his gun again like I haven't seen it fifty times already. A real asshole."

"Was he here a lot?"

"Couple times he wasn't around for a year, then he'd be showing up once a week, middle of the night, private meeting, here's ten bucks, fuck off. Two o'clock in the fucking morning. In fucking December. Where the fuck am I supposed to fuck off to?"

"Right. And where *did* you fuck off to?"

"Depends. Not too late I'd go next door. Have a few beers. Wait for him to leave."

"If it was too late?"

"I'd let myself into the store. Stay down here."

"Sure," Adele said. "Have a look, Stace. In here. Doesn't look too bad."

Stacy joined her at the open door. The back room had a saggy couch with a blanket thrown over the back. There was a coffee maker and a small refrigerator, two chairs and a table covered with magazines and comic books. The magazines featured huge-breasted women, the comic books had superheroes on the covers. "Looks comfortable," Stacy said. "And listen to that. I can hear the TV upstairs."

Darryl pushed his way between them and flopped on the couch. He didn't spill a drop. "My girlfriend. She's cleaning up, moving in. Probably."

"That's nice," said Stacy. She pulled up a chair and sat close to him. "So you'd be sitting down here, reading your magazines, drinking coffee, or beer maybe, waiting for the big man to leave."

"Yeah, so?"

"So. So come on, Darryl. You can tell us." She poked him teasingly. "Come on. You were listening, weren't you? You could hear what they were talking about."

Adele pulled up the other chair. "I bet you could sure as shit hear what the big asshole was saying, couldn't you?"

He looked at the two women, from one face to the other. They were hemming him in, but they were also listening to him. "Think they're so fuckin' smart."

"Who does?"

"All do. Louie and his secret meetings. Big frickin' deals."

"So you were eavesdropping."

"Don't give a fuck. Looking out for my interests. That black prick threatens me one more time he'll get a big fuckin' surprise."

"Oh yeah? That's great. Because we'd like to surprise him too."

"Like to surprise his ass into the gas chamber. Strap him to a fuckin' gurney and shove some serious shit up his arm."

"We don't have the death penalty."

"Yeah. That's a crying fucking shame. People like that. Prick bastard. Deserve to fucking die."

"Why?"

"You wanna know what really makes me laugh? I just fuckin' crack up?"

"What's that, sir?"

"They send me outta the room like I'm some kid gets on their nerve. Ah, he doesn't know shit. Fuck off for a while, Darryl, let the big men do some business. Fuck 'em. Whatta they think I do? Disa-fucking-ppear?"

"Of course not. You come down here and listen in. What is it, an air vent or something? Lets the sound come down?"

"Better."

"Better?"

"Oh, way better."

"Come on Darryl, we're on your side here. If you can provide us with any ammunition . . ."

"Ammunition. Fuck. I've got a nuke-ular frickin' missile. I've got a weapon of fucking mass de-fucking-struction."

Adele touched Stacy on the shoulder. Pointed to the cassette deck sitting on the shelf above the coffee machine. "Holy shit, Darryl. You've got them on tape."

They went to Paul Delisle's apartment. They had six cassettes — JVC, Sony and 3M. None were dated. "He's got a cassette deck somewhere," Adele said. "Maybe two. He always liked having a backup." She stood in the middle of the living room looking lost. The place was still a jumble of half-packed boxes, half-read report files. "Plus there's coffee. We'll probably be up late."

Stacy saw it. "Right up there. Top shelf. The silver thing. Can you reach it?"

"One thing I'm good for."

It was a Sony unit, CD/cassette/AM-FM, with speakers. Stacy cleared a space on a side table and found a place to plug it in. "Hated doing that," she said.

"Doing what? Taking his property? We gave him a receipt."

"Enabling. Getting him drunk. Al-Anon would not approve."

"Give me a break. You figure we blew his last chance at sobriety?"

"Not the point."

"No. I get it. Too close to home, right?"

"They used to send my brother out to buy for them. Fake ID. He wasn't old enough."

"Yeah. That sucks."

"In the end he got just as messed up as they were."

"It bother you when I have a drink?"

"Nope. It just scares the hell out of me that I might have a genetic predisposition to go down the same road. I'd like to avoid that if possible."

"Well, give yourself a pass on this one, partner. Did it for the greater good. We nail Dylan O'Grady's ass to the wall, it'll wash away all sins." She gave Stacy a rough one-arm hug and pushed her toward the kitchen. "Make coffee."

"Place stinks."

"That's Dylan," said Adele.

(unintelligible)

"You know that? Stinks? Like rotten marmalade."

"Kid won't wash up."

"What kid? He's over forty! Jesus! Your legs broken? You can't turn on the hot water tap? Have a little respect for yourself."

"Make an appointment; I'll get a Molly Maid."

"That's Louie?" Stacy asked.

"Probably."

"Never any place to sit around here."

"Move some stuff."

"No place to sit, nothing to eat or drink. You run a class operation."

"You want food, look in the fridge."

"Have you looked in your fridge, Louie?"

"There we go. It's him."

"You know what's in there? You've got creatures living in the pork fried rice."

(long break in conversation, sounds of things being moved, dropped

to the floor, television turned on, Jeopardy *audible in the background)*

"*Jeopardy*. 7:30 to 8," Stacy said. "We might get the date from the episode."

"Yeah right: when did they ask the two-hundred-dollar question about Nairobi?"

"No. Seriously. That's the College Championship. You could track it down."

"You watch that show? Probably get all the answers, don't you?"

"Mostly."

(long silence)

"What the hell are they doing?"

"Watching Alex Trebek."

"Fuck, how many hours of this we have to wade through?"

"You had a visitor, last week."

"Here we go."

"Yeah, it's a store. People come in."

"You had a visitor up here." (chair being moved) *"My partner dropped by for a chat, didn't he?"*

"Whoa. This is at least seven years ago," Adele said. "Dylan's still a cop."

"You got this place under surveillance now?"

"No. He told me. We're partners. We share information."

"Sure you do."

"Says he came by to ask about a pawn ticket from a crime scene. Pawn ticket for gold badge or something."

"Oh yeah."

"Well?"

"What about it? I didn't have it. I said I didn't know what he was talking about. I said check my records."

"Did he?"

"He looked. What's he gonna find?"

"Listen close. He had a pawn ticket. It had your name on it. It had a date on it. You lent that Abramov shit twenty bucks for a piece of jewellery."

"Vassili." Stacy was making notes.

"That thing. Wasn't jewellery, a little badge or something."

"What happened to it?"

"He came around later, said he wanted to sell it outright. I gave him another twenty."

"So where is it?"

"It's nothing to do with your thing."

"Where is it?"

"It's safe. It's put away."

"One more time. Where. Is. It?"

"All right. I'll get it. You don't have to start acting like King Kong."

"Say what?"

"Just wait a minute, take it easy, wait a minute."

(more silence, more Jeopardy)

"He didn't like the King Kong reference."

"Sounds like a dangerous man."

Adele stopped the tape. "So this is at least seven years back." She was working it out. "After the DOA in the park. After Paulie picked up the diamonds, went back the next day and got the blue one and the pawn ticket."

"Which led him to Louie Grova."

"And didn't tell his partner about it until after."

"And Dylan isn't happy about it."

"Why tell him at all?"

"Get him thinking, maybe?"

"Paulie's suspecting Dylan already. Of what? Killing Abramov?" She started the tape again.

"What are you doing out there, Louie? Fighting with the garbage. You're gonna lose."

"I'll be there. Gimme a minute."

(more noises, aspect change, Dylan has moved away from the mic.)

"Is that it?"

"What'd I tell you? It's nothing."

"You dumb shit."

"What? Couple of grams."

"Eighteen carat?"

"Fourteen."

"Probably eighteen. And what's this? Little crest. See that? You know what you got here. Sure you do. This is part of the chain. Any more pieces?"

"Vassi needed some cash."

"Vassi, is it? Old pals by now. Worked out a secret handshake yet?"

"He wanted to go away."

"Yeah, we'll that's too bad. He never made it out of town."

(long silence)

"What do you care about a little pin? You got the biggest share."

"Oho!" Adele liked that one.

"What's the matter with you? I don't care about this piece of crap. My partner smells misconduct. He's on the trail, asshole. He's a hound dog."

"What's to find out?"

"There's nothing to find out unless you do something dumb, like get caught with any of this stuff around. Where's the rest of it?"

"I don't have any more." (sound of slap, yelp) "I don't have any more. I wish I'd never seen any of it. From the start. What did I ever get out of it?"

"You did all right. You got your share."

"Fucked my life is what it did."

"I'm taking this."

"Aw Jesus, Dylan . . ."

"Okay, O'Grady's identified, for the record." Stacy made another note.

". . . give me a break. At least give me the forty dollars."

"Give you a couple of broken thumbs you get me jammed up. My partner comes around to see you again, you keep your mouth shut."

"Don't you guys work together any more?"

"Mind your own business. He shows up again, you let me know. Don't wait for me to find —" (tape ends)

"Damn. Nothing substantive," Stacy said.

"Maybe not, but interesting shit. Paulie was playing Dylan seven years ago. He tracked down Louie. Connected him to Abramov. Dylan had it right: Paulie was a hound dog. If he smelled something, he wouldn't let it go."

Stacy printed "#1–seven years ago?–O'Grady/Grova" on the label and set it aside. "Ready for another one?"

"Maybe we should send out for a pizza."

Eleven

Around 3:30 a.m., Adele went into the bedroom, took off her cop shoes and crashed. Stacy stayed awake for another hour, cataloging and labelling, making notes and approximate timings, fast-forwarding and rewinding her way through the four ninety-minute cassettes. Six hours of random sounds, half-audible hockey games, reality shows, laugh tracks, long stretches of relative silence punctuated by bodily noises, tires squealing, sirens passing. The actual conversations (banal, vulgar and at least sixty percent unintelligible) totalled eighteen minutes and twenty-three seconds. Several of the main players were clearly identifiable: Louie Grova, on all tapes; Dylan O'Grady (all except 6); Sergei Siziva (tapes 3 and 5) and Yevgeny Grenkov (briefly, in the background on tape 3). The problem was that, in addition to being an inept audio engineer who had evidently hidden his microphone under a couch cushion wrapped in a sock, Darryl had neglected to number or date the recordings. Stacy had no way of pinning down whether the reference to Viktor Nimchuk on tape 3 took place before or after the reference to what might have been Paul Delisle's handgun on tape 4, or *when* the meeting between Dylan and Sergei Siziva on tape 6 happened. Evidently Darryl hadn't been on the job the night his stepfather had died, or for that matter, the day Sergei Siziva took possession of Paul's

.357 Smith & Wesson revolver. Those tapes might have tipped the balance. Sadly, either they didn't exist, or Darryl was saving them for dessert. With what they had so far they could allege motive, indicate opportunity, deal with denials and interpretations, but without physical evidence, without a murder weapon, a blood trail, fingerprints, or something they could hold up for a jury to gaze upon, they'd have a hard time getting a conviction.

"You up all night?" Adele helped herself to a slice of cold pizza.

"I got a few hours on the couch. There's coffee."

"What d'you think? Anything we can use?"

"What we have is a steaming pile of circumstantial, conjectural and conditional, and not one shred of irrefutable." Stacy poured a cup of coffee for Adele, turning her head to avoid the whiff of pepperoni and cold tomato sauce. "Hard to build a murder case when all the prime witnesses are either dead, or have guilty knowledge."

"Not quite the 'nuke-ular weapon of mass de-fucking-struction,' is it?" Adele went to the window, sipped coffee and chewed leftovers, watched the southbound traffic building on the Don Valley Parkway below. A cruiser with lights flashing was weaving through the traffic flow, chasing someone. Adele watched until it disappeared from view. She snorted. "Darryl's gonna need a month at Betty Ford before we can put him on the witness stand."

"I don't think we'd make it that far," said Stacy. "We've got recordings, illegally obtained, from a questionable source, and who knows *what's* been done to them? Any half-decent lawyer gets them tossed pretrial."

"Well fuck! Just for my own pathetic amusement, partner, give me the highlights."

Stacy checked her notes, plugged in a cassette, reset the counter to zero and hit fast-forward. "This would have been good but the television's on in the room so some of it you can't hear." She hit stop. "Dylan and Louie. I get the feeling it's in the stairwell because of the echo."

"Is it loaded?"

"Keep it wrapped . . . want . . . your fingerprints on it."

". . . it yours?"

"Do what . . . all right? Hide it . . . your shithole." (sound of feet clumping down the stairs to the street) "Shut your fucking mouth, forget all . . . when I want it back."

"Like when?"

"Mind your own fucking . . ." (traffic noise, door closes)

"Okay, okay, I'm just saying . . . Motherfucker, Jesus, fuck fuck fuck."

Stacy stopped the tape. "Sounded like Dylan was handing over Paul's gun."

"Yeah, well *we* know it sounded like that, but like you say, worthless."

Stacy popped in a new tape. Found the spot she was looking for. "This is Dylan and Louie again. Talking about where Nimchuk was staying. Maybe."

"Where on the Queensway?"

"It's a motel. All he gave me was a number."

"Give it to me."

"He just wants to talk."

"I'll call him."

(aspect changes, another room, unintelligible exchange, door opening, voices faint but clear)

"He's afraid of you."

"Nothing to be afraid of. What's he holding? He say?"

"He just wants enough to get away from here."

"No problem."

(outside door slams)

"So that happened *before* he stashed the gun with Louie, right?"

Adele asked. "He had the phone number. No trick for an ex-cop to find out where it came from. He pays Nimchuk a visit at the motel, maybe picks up some jewellery, pops him, then comes back here to hide Paulie's piece. Does that add up?"

"Sort of. I'm playing them in the order they were in the box." She cued up the next cassette. "Here's a good one except it sounds like Darryl recorded the first part on toilet paper. We've got O'Grady, Grova, Siziva and, somewhere in the background, Citizen Grenkov."

(unintelligible, possibly in the kitchen)

"*. . . going on?*" *(Dylan)*

"*This . . . to meet you.*" *(Louie)*

"*Yes, good ev . . . is Siz . . . , . . . gei . . . ziva.*"

"*. . . the moose?*"

"*. . . my protection.*"

"*. . . is?*" *(chuckles)* "*(unintelligible) to stay out . . . worth shit . . . tear him a new asshole.*"

"*. . . civilized, okay? Neutral ground. Mutual interests . . . in . . . differences.*" *(Louie)*

"*. . . listening. . . . a cold beer at least? . . . Fuck no, I've seen how you wash your glasses. You? Siz . . . what?*"

(Random noises, a short exchange in Russian. Yevgeni's voice is recognizable. Sound of beer cans being popped open. Swallowing, burping.)

"*Okay . . . called this . . . on your mind?*"

"*We . . . mutual interest. . . . tor Nim . . .*"

"*Who he?*"

"*. . . should. . . . not play games. I . . . he . . . happened in Montreal.*"

"*. . . Nimchuk . . . ything? . . . who gives a . . . anyway? Nothing to do with me.*"

(Three minutes thirty seconds unintelligible. Possible move outside.)

"Wait a bit," Stacy said, "it gets better."

(Closer to mic. Entering living room?)

"... *a big man, and that makes you untouchable, you think.Yes?*"

"*That's not a threat, is it?*"

"*But, you admit, currently you have much to lose.*"

"*Careful Ivan.You don't want to piss me off.*"

"*When you were a policeman you had much more control over a situation, yes? You had a gun, a badge, a code I suppose. Now you are a public figure.You seek elected office.Your image is important.*"

"*Cut the crap. What do you want?*"

"*I believe we have mutual interests and can help each other get what we seek.*"

"*Get me another beer, Louie. And you, tell your big friend to sit down. He's not making me nervous, he's making me angry.*"

(Brief exchange in Russian.Yev is heard grumbling.)

"*I'm sure you don't want an altercation in this place, my friend, with all the secrets it might contain. We wouldn't want to attract the attention of the police, would we?*"

(sound of a beer can releasing gas, chair sliding)

"*All right, whatever your name is, I'm listening.*"

"*Viktor is worried about what might happen.*"

"*Happen?*"

"*To him. What might happen to him.*"

"*Why should anything happen to him?*"

"*Because of what happened to Vassili. That you will do the same to him.*"

"*I didn't do anything to this whoever.*"

"*Vassili.*"

"*Never heard of him.*"

"*Viktor told me about Montreal.*"

"*Un hunh.What happened in Montreal?*"

"*You and Viktor and Louie here. The woman.*"

"*Okay. I've heard enough of this. I don't know what you think you know but if it comes from Viktor Nimchuk it doesn't mean shit. So why am I listening?*"

"*He would like to make an arrangement. He has another of the blue stones you are interested in."*

"Yeah? What about you? What are you interested in?"

"Mine is a different colour."

"You want the diamonds? Fine. More trouble than they're worth. What else?"

"That's all. Viktor and I will arrange for you to acquire another of the blue stones. You already have one, am I correct? Viktor and I will deal with the remaining diamonds and whatever remains of the neckpiece."

"What do I get out of it?"

"Much peace of mind, I'm sure. Viktor and I will both depart the vicinity, albeit in different directions, and you can sleep well at night knowing all is clear."

"Right. And what's to stop you coming back next year and getting another bite."

"Do not forget that both Viktor and I will have engaged in numerous illegal acts as well. It would be in our best interests to get as far away from you as we can."

(long silence, sound of beer can being crushed)

"You tell him to give me a call."

"I'm certain we . . ."

(tape runs out)

"Darryl's never getting that job with the CIA," Adele said.

"Seems like they're in reverse order, doesn't it?" Stacy said. "Sergei sounds like he's trying to broker a deal between Nimchuk and Dilly. Then after that we've got Louie coughing up the phone number of the motel. And then we've got Dilly handing over Paulie's .357 to Louie Grova and telling him to stash it."

"If that's what was happening on that tape, because nowhere is the actual fucking weapon mentioned."

"Right. So, you'd figure he hands the weapon to Louie *after* he shoots the Russian in the motel. Right?"

"Sounds reasonable."

"Nimchuk was killed sometime between Saturday night,

March 12th, and Sunday the 13th. Which means that O'Grady has to show up here with Paulie's piece sometime Sunday, at the latest, Monday, because he's on the campaign trail and he can't be running around stashing guns when he's supposed to be cutting ribbons and kissing babies. But here's the thing." She needed to change the cassette and find the right spot. "Wait a sec. Here. Listen to what's on the television."

In the foreground of the section where Dylan O'Grady is clumping down the stairs and Louie is cursing, they can hear audience laughter and cheering and women's voices.

Adele spread her hands. "So?"

Stacy spread her hands as well. "So? That's *Ellen*."

"And that means . . . ?"

"Ellen Degeneres? She isn't on Sunday. It's a weekday show."

"You watch *Ellen*?"

"No, I don't watch *Ellen*, but I know who she is, and I know when she's on television. How come *you* don't know?"

"All right, so he shows up here on Monday and gives the gun to Louie. While fucking *Ellen's* on? What's the diff?"

"Listen again." She rewound the tape a few seconds and played it again. "Hear it?"

"Hear *what*? What am I missing?"

"Ellen is talking to . . ." Stacy looked embarrassed. ". . . *Denzel*."

"Denzel? Denzel who?"

"Oh Jesus," Stacy hid her face briefly with both hands, as if about to reveal a shameful little secret. "Denzel *Washington*. The . . . actor?"

"So?" Adele suddenly hooted. "Ha! Wait a minute. You've got the hots for a movie star?!"

"All right. I admit it. A little crush. You happy?"

"Old Daniel Boone's leaving you alone too much."

"Okay, okay, can we get past that part and concentrate?" She wiped her hands across her face to erase the blush in her cheeks. "The thing is, I *saw* that show. It was on Friday. I didn't see the whole thing, I just checked it out for a minute after my workout."

"Ri-ight."

"Nimchuk was killed March 12th, okay? Sometime that night. That show was on the week *before*. Friday the 11th."

"You sure?"

Stacy sighed. "Yes, I'm *sure*."

"Holy shit! "

"If Dylan's showing up with the gun on the 11th, then he, or for that matter, your partner, couldn't have been using it to shoot Viktor Nimchuk on the 12th."

"Motherfucker! Murderer fingered by Ellen."

The two women took a moment to enjoy the absurdity of the situation, then Stacy became businesslike again. "When Dylan was a cop, what did he carry?"

"Same as Paulie. Smith .357 Magnum."

"A .357 fires .38 Specials, too. Interchangeable. The slug they recovered from the Queensway scene was a magnum, right? Paul's revolver was loaded with .38 Specials. Did he ever switch? Any Magnum slugs around?"

"No. Not in his locker, not in the apartment. His ammo in the desk, box of .38 Specials."

"So unless he loaded a Magnum bullet exclusively and *specifically* for shooting Nimchuk, Paul's piece isn't the murder weapon."

Georgie Rhem carefully removed the white tin letters that spelled "Treganza & Swain" from the lobby directory board and dropped them into a brown envelope. "Oh darn," he said, "I'm going to need that ampersand. Find it for me would you, Stonewall?" He handed the envelope to his friend and began inserting the D-A-I-L-E-Y of his new partner.

"I guess this makes it official," Orwell said.

"Soon as you find that thingy."

"End of an era," said Sam Abrams.

"Or the beginning of one," Georgie said.

"Here's your thingy."

Georgie inserted it between the two names and the three men took a step back to admire the new listing.

RHEM & DAILEY
Barristers and Solicitors
3rd floor

"Calls for a ceremonial slice of pie, don't you think?" Georgie said.

"Well, a cup of coffee, at least," said Orwell.

When the three men reached the opposite sidewalk, they turned back to look up at the third floor windows where "Rhem, Treganza & Swain" still glowed in fine gold leaf.

"It'll take a while to get that scraped off," Georgie said, "let alone find someone who does that kind of gold leaf lettering in this town. I think the guy who did that died in '64."

"I'd leave it up there, Georgie," said Orwell. "It's worth preserving."

"A heritage site," said Sam.

"I suppose. They were middling lawyers, but they taught me a lot." He clapped the two big men on their backs. "Come on then, I'm buying."

Ethel smiled when she saw her three favourite regulars come through the door. "You make a lovely couple," she said.

"There are three of us," said Georgie.

"I meant the Chief and Donna Lee." She held up a copy of the *Dockerty Register*, where the Chief and the Mayor were on the front page. Again. "Was she standing on a flowerpot, Chief?"

"He was bending his knees," said Sam. "Kathy told me. Most considerate."

"Hard to get them both in the frame otherwise," said Georgie.

"Glad to see you're taking the election seriously, Chief," said Sam. "Not in a rush to start raising chickens?"

"Not just yet. If Donna Lee gets reelected maybe I can hang in for another five years. After that, who knows?"

Ethel brought coffee and three menus. "We all having pie, gentlemen?"

"I'll hold off until next week," said Orwell. "I made the mistake of stepping on the scales this morn. Not a pretty sight."

"I broke mine," said Sam. "Just coffee, thanks."

"That leaves you, Georgie," she said.

"In that case I'll have French toast and maple syrup. And sausages."

"Atta boy."

The two big men shook their heads sadly.

"So Georgie," Sam started, "you handling the Edwin Kewell case perchance?"

"No one's called," he said. "Two murder cases in two weeks? A bit much to hope for."

"Too bad. When does your new partner get here?"

"Well, she has to take care of a few hundred things in the city."

"She won't dawdle," said Orwell. "Once she's made her mind up, she moves pretty fast. I'll drive down when she's ready, get her stuff packed up."

"You need any help, let me know," said Sam.

Orwell smiled to himself. His pocket started singing. "Brennan," he said. "Okay, on my way." He stuffed the phone back in his pocket and levered himself out of the booth. "Duty calls, gents. Visiting dignitary." As he was heading out the door, he heard Sam's voice.

"Oh what the heck, Ethel. Give me a small slice of the rum raisin."

It is good to have friends, even if you never see them, people you can call upon without worrying whether they will remember you. Gita Crystal (born Brigitta Schneiderschnitz) was one of those. Twenty years ago at the National Ballet she had attended to Anya's fine golden hair on a nightly basis. These days she owned and operated a salon and day spa in Yorkville. Arabesque, an intimate oasis, neither trendy nor excessively posh, was, like its owner, elegant and devoid of affectation save for (in Gita's case) a fondness for rose-tinted glasses. She loved Anya Zubrovskaya.

"Nanya! My goodness. How wonderful! To *see* you! My darling! Come in here! Give me kisses! *More* kisses. Let me look at you. Ach! You are as lovely as ever. *But.* Of course, your hair . . . *Something* must be done! You agree?"

"That is why I am here. Perhaps you can work a little magic on this wreckage."

"A new man?"

"In a way."

"Oooh. Lovely. You must tell me all about him."

"He is quite dangerous."

"Wonderful. We will make you irresistible."

When Anya left Arabesque three hours later, she did look, if not irresistible, certainly acceptable. Her skin was glowing, her hair was a chic tousle of platinum feathers and even her forlorn hands and aggrieved feet had been pampered and soothed.

Gita sent her on her way with an admonition never to stay away so long again, and gave her an address just three blocks distant where another old friend would be sure to greet her just as warmly.

"Anushka! My goodness! How long has it been. Good Christ don't tell me, I don't want to know." Alain Abaire's establishment, Redemption, dealt in high-end fashion and vintage couturier consignments. Even the super-rich, it seemed, ran out of closet space from time to time. "And you have kept your figure. Bless your heart. So many of us have not. I myself, as you see, have become a blini. It's happiness, does it. My lover cooks. He is killing me with kindness."

"An outfit, Alain. Daytime, in public. Something tailored, perhaps, not frivolous."

"Secretary of State?"

"Satan's emissary, come to collect an overdue soul."

"Oh, well then, you'll want Chanel."

The hotel wasn't four-star, but it was pleasant enough. Her crusade was after all being financed (posthumously) by Louie Grova, and she considered it only fair that she keep her expenses within limits. Honour also demanded that she spend every penny on the assault. Her own resources were limited, and the battle ahead might go on for some time. She hadn't taken Louie's cash box because she wanted his money; wars require financing.

Poor Louie. What a sad way to go, tied to a chair, surrounded by his things, and not one of them of any use. He could not even lift his head to see who was climbing in through the window. She stood in the kitchen doorway and heard his last rattling breath. There was no way for her to help him. Louie was a goner.

She left no trace of her visit. The scene must not be disturbed. Louie's killer might have made a mistake before he departed, slipped up somehow, left a fingerprint or dropped a glove. Probably not. He was a careful and clever man. But you never know, it is often the little things that cause the most damage.

And Louie, you should have changed your hiding place once in a while. Ten years ago, while Vassi and Viktor were in the living room arguing about God knows what and she was on the back porch smoking and breathing in the humid summer air, dreaming of Dubrovnik, she caught sight of him through the filthy kitchen window. Saw him pull back a tile from above the sink and cram in a wad of bills. The tile was greasy and grimy and stuck in place with rotting grout and glazier's putty. Behind it was a black tin box and rolls of cash clenched in rubber bands. She loaded her pockets, replaced the box and the tile and went back out the window. "Goodbye, Louie," she said.

In the motel room she counted out the money on the bedspread. It came to $8,400. She was expecting a fatter nest egg, but who knows: Louie might have had more than one hidey-hole.

Concealing the cash wasn't difficult for an experienced smuggler. Her brown coat had secret pockets that had served her well on many trips and across many borders. Ludi had sewn it for her many years ago. Clever, sweet Ludi. This is for you as much as for me.

A hundred dollar donation to the campaign fund gave her an O'Grady button and a complete schedule for the coming week. She could mix and match elements of the two Chanel suits and the three blouses in the new wardrobe to furnish her with several outfits for the crusade. It was important that she always look her best. If necessary, she could make a quick trip to Redemption for something fresh to wear. She intended to be there until the victory party on election night. And perhaps beyond. Perhaps she would follow Dylan O'Grady all the way to Ottawa and sit in the visitor's gallery during question period. The money would be enough, if she spent it wisely. Louie would get a good return on his investment.

The man waiting for Orwell was a little person, less than a metre tall, with long arms, short, bent legs and a rolling gait. Orwell felt a fleeting twinge of embarrassment as he bowed to shake the man's hand.

"Police Chief Brennan, how do you do? My name is Mikhael Tomashevsky." His hand wasn't small: his grip was strong, and he was unruffled by the size of his host. He had dealt with taller men.

"Mr. Tomashevsky, hello."

"Mikhael, please, Chief. Thank you for seeing me." His accent was under control, his English was precise and formal. "Would you care to see my credentials?"

"Maybe you could just tell me who you represent."

"The Russian Ministry of Culture."

"Right. Yes, well that makes sense. I've been expecting someone to show up. Come on in." He led the way into the office and pointed to a chair. "Please, sit down. You're here looking for a missing treasure?"

"In one way or another, we have been looking for it for many years. I myself have made seven trips to Canada." He lifted himself neatly into a chair and hooked the toe of one shoe behind the opposite ankle. One pant cuff slid up, giving Orwell a glimpse of a metal brace. "Before me there were three other individuals assigned to the case."

"Really?"

"Not permanently. I myself have not looked into this particular matter for several years."

"This particular matter being the Ember."

"That's right. That gem and the cross were part of our national treasures."

"I was told that the crucifix was broken up and sold piecemeal over the years."

"Yes. That is unfortunate, but not uncommon. People on the run, needing money."

"But some of the gems have been returned."

"*Located*, not returned. That will take a while. Provenance, identification. It is necessary to be certain."

"Of course. Can I offer you some coffee?"

"I am floating already today, but thank you. You have a very pretty town."

"You think? I guess. This isn't its most beautiful time of year. In another few weeks though it will start looking very nice."

"It is the same where I come from. In April, things . . . improve."

"So. How can I help you?" Orwell said.

Tomashevsky opened a small, leather-bound notebook. "Let me see, I would like to talk to one of your officers, a Detective Creen."

"Crean."

"Yes, thank you. Would she be available?"

"She's on assignment in Toronto right now."

"Oh dear. And I just came from there. When will she be back?"

"I'm not exactly sure. Later today. Tomorrow, certainly."

"Good. Good. I'll see her then. And I would also like to talk to Anya Ivanova Zubrovskaya."

"You don't need my permission for that."

"I find it's best to be as clear about my intentions as I can be."

"I appreciate that."

"Of course, but it is really for *my* benefit, Chief. If I'm not precise I can get confused. Two days ago I was in Washington, D.C., looking for a Rembrandt. Next I fly to Berlin."

"I hadn't considered that aspect. I guess you're chasing after a lot of things."

"Half the treasures in the world are in the hands of people who don't really own them."

A sigh was heard to pass Captain Rosebart's lips as Stacy and Adele walked into his office. A sigh or a barely audible moan, Stacy couldn't be sure. "Am I going to love this, or am I going to hate this?" he asked.

"You'll definitely love it," Adele said, "and maybe hate it a *little*, but mostly love it."

"Why?"

"Because *I* fucking love it."

He looked at Stacy. "You love it too, Crean?"

"I have enjoyed being part of it, Captain."

"Your boss send you down here again?"

"I have his blessing."

"Keeps throwing you at me, like I'm supposed to do something about it." He turned to Adele. "All right, let's hear it, and keep the F-bombs to a minimum, if you please."

"Certainly, sir. Paulie's off the hook for the Nimchuk murder."

"Okay, I don't hate that part. How'd you pull that off?"

"It wasn't his gun."

"You can prove that?"

"Yes, sir."

"Lay it on me."

"We've got tapes you need to hear, things to look at, we've got statements, interviews." She nodded in Stacy's direction. "We're building a case."

"A case against anybody in particular?"

"This is the part you might hate a *little*."

"Because . . ."

"Because we think that a former detective with this squad, who is now running real hard for a vacant federal seat, is responsible for three, make that four, deaths."

"Oh fuck," said Rosebart.

Rosebart wasn't a man easy to convince. Their case was built mostly on hearsay and speculation and riddled with holes, and while he had to admit they told a great story, it was his job to point out exactly how flimsy it was.

"You're not rousting some pickpocket here, Detective. You'd be dragging in a very high profile local politician about ten days away from getting himself elected to Parliament. He's polling about forty-seven percent, which is pretty damn high. The next candidate is at nineteen."

"What's the big deal? Dilly's always dropping in here. He showed up at Paulie's wake. He was here last week nosing around. He still thinks he's got privileges."

"That's a five-minute drop-by. You're going to want his butt in a chair a bit longer than that. He brings his campaign manager who let's say turns out to be a hotshot lawyer and Dylan says I'm outta here, what are you planning on holding him with?"

"We've got Sergei. He'll testify that he brokered a meeting between Dylan and Viktor."

"Was he *at* the meeting? No. Is he credible? Let's see, he's been arrested twice in the past week, he's an illegal immigrant, he's been hiding out in this country for thirty years doing who knows what. This guy is your big weapon?"

"Dylan's wife is in possession of a sapphire that was previously in the possession of a murder victim."

"What we have is a ten-year-old *picture* of her wearing what *could* be a sapphire, that *maybe* was once in the possession of some Russian woman thirty years ago, although we only have your loony dancer lady's word for that."

"I don't think she's loony, Captain," said Stacy.

"Given her past history, any defence lawyer makes her look like a raving lunatic inside ten minutes. Anyway, she wasn't in Montreal when it happened. And the two other men allegedly involved are both conveniently dead."

"Both of them can be connected to Dylan," said Adele.

"Says who? The dancer who wasn't there? The illegal Russian who's trying to stay in the country? The dead pawnbroker? His drunken son?"

"You're not buying any of this?"

He looked at them both, one to the other, smiled. "I'm buying it, Detective Moen, Detective Crean, I'm buying it. *But.* I'm buying it on the installment plan. You haven't got enough. Not yet. Go back to work."

Stacy munched toast and honey. Adele wasn't hungry. She was sitting in front of a perfectly respectable BLT with mayo, on whole grain toast (Stacy's suggestion), and had yet to take a bite. The diner was on Queen Street, east of Yonge, the sketchier part, not far from the Sally Ann and within sight of the Sherbourne intersection where men with nothing to do but wait waited.

"We fuck this up, that's where I'll be next week: busting assholes on that corner."

"The murder weapon's still out there," Stacy said.

"Who knows? Maybe Dylan 'liberated' his old service piece. He was always 'visiting,' showing up, slapping hands. Dropping in on Paulie at his desk. Being extra smooth to me, like he wanted us to be real good pals." She picked up half the sandwich and examined it carefully.

Stacy stuck with it. "It's somewhere to start. Check storage to see if any weapons are missing, check on what happened to Dylan's piece after he retired."

"That oughta be a load of laughs." Adele dropped the sandwich, still intact. "What's the difference? The slug's so fucked up we couldn't get a match anyway." She pushed the BLT away from her. "I'm cool with that. We got Paulie off the hook."

"Your blood sugar's low. Eat the sandwich before you curl up and die on me." Stacy's cellphone began buzzing. "That's probably the Chief letting me know Mounties just showed up and it's time to come home. Hello?"

The voice on the other end was familiar. "Detective Crean. I think you are in the city, yes?" She sounded pleased with herself. "You spent the night as well, did you?"

"Anya? Where are you?"

"I am following a politician on his daily campaign rounds. Right now he is kissing babies and shaking hands and having his picture taken as many times as he can."

"Where?"

"Many places. I have his itinerary right here. I believe next we are going to plant a tree. A bit early in the year, no?"

"Plant a tree *where*?"

"You should pick up a copy of his schedule at his campaign office. He has a full afternoon and evening planned."

"What are you doing?"

"I am smiling every time he looks in my direction, I am adding my voice to the general cheers, I am waving from the crowd when he makes his little speech. Now and then I ask a question but so far he has not acknowledged my presence."

"What sort of questions?"

"When we stopped at the deli, I asked him how the pastrami compared to Montreal smoked meat. By the library steps, I asked him if his broken toe hurt him on chilly mornings. I know my toes hurt when it is cold."

"Has he said anything?"

"There was a vigil at a public school where a young girl was run down last week by a delivery truck. Candles were lighted and flowers were laid at the intersection where it happened. There was a moment of silence. I looked at him the whole time."

"Did he look back?"

"Finally. He had to. He stared right at me. And, after a decent interval, I lifted my voice and said, 'Is it not tragic when a beautiful young life is snuffed out by a heartless monster?' People said 'Amen' all around me. They agreed. It *was* tragic. Even *he* was forced to agree. He had to nod and say something."

"What did he say?"

"Something suitably unctuous, about bad things happening to good people, and making our streets safer for our children. I did not pay much attention. I was looking at him and smiling."

"That's a dangerous game."

"I am breaking no laws. I am not even heckling him. I am being supportive and engaged and committed to his campaign. I donated a hundred dollars to his election coffers, I am wearing an O'Grady button. I want him to know I will be there all the time, right up to election day. And after that if necessary. You don't have to do a thing. Consider me your cat's paw."

"Tell me where you are and we'll come and pick you up."

"Oh we have several stops to make. He is going to talk to a group of concerned citizens who think our health care system is broken, and then he is going to put in an appearance at a garden show to have his picture taken with some tulip bulbs. This evening there is to be a fundraiser. A seventy-five dollar buffet. I'm sure the food will not be worth the investment."

"I don't think this is a good idea."

"Good ideas, bad ideas, I do not much care. I have been running from dangerous men for a very long time and I have grown tired of it. Now I am the one who chases."

The line went dead.

"What?" Adele asked.

Stacy whispered. "Fuck."

"Good Christ, you swore." Adele grinned. "I'm so proud of you."

"Wrap the sandwich. Our little ballerina's started poking the bear with a sharp stick. Let's at least be there when he wakes up."

Cam Gidrick was Dylan O'Grady's special assistant. It was his responsibility to make sure that the Candidate got where he was supposed to get, arrived on time, departed on time, knew the names he needed to know, shook the hands he needed to shake, thanked the donors he needed to thank and otherwise cruised through the campaign smoothly and without stumbles. Cam's job required tact, organization and the ability to deal with unforeseen developments.

Cam was a bachelor, and not by choice, for while his

skills as a facilitator were valuable to campaign operations, they tended to showcase what many women viewed as a humourless and punctilious personality, lacking spontaneity, romance and sexual attractiveness. This wasn't helped by the fact that he had an annoying sinus condition, was rapidly balding and possessed ears that his father once likened to a pair of "open car doors."

Nonetheless, he was very good at his job, and prided himself on having shepherded the successful campaigns of three city councillors, two MPPs and the mayor of a medium-size city. O'Grady's run for a federal seat was Cam's first shot at the big leagues and he was determined to pull it off with style and grace. Granted, the recently vacated seat was in a riding whose voting pattern hadn't changed in fifty years and was considered "safe" by the party. However, the fact that the previous office holder had been forced to resign when found in the company of someone other than his wife made it vital that the candidate picked to replace him appear stable, trustworthy and a good family man. In this respect, the choice of Dylan O'Grady seemed to be preordained. His former career as a decorated police officer, his earlier days as the member of a beloved local football team and his most recent position on Toronto City Council cast him as a man for all seasons. Add to that the fact that he had been happily married for twenty-four years to a woman who might easily be mistaken for a fashion model, and Dylan O'Grady looked like the complete package. As a man of colour, he appealed to the multicultural nature of the nation's largest city, not to mention the diverse ethnic makeup of the riding in which he was running. As a retired law enforcement professional, he wore the mantle of moral strength. And as a former athlete, he was considered by the party's strategists as likely to be attractive to both men and women.

It would seem, then, that Cam's job was already half done. His candidate was polling close to fifty percent in a three-man race, the coffers were full and the crowds were responsive. What could go wrong? By any applicable measure, the race was already won. So why should Cam be sweating like a cold beer bottle on a hot day?

Well, to start with, there was the fact that his candidate was telling him lies, and they weren't just the effortless misinformation that goes with being in politics, nor the sloppy fibs about what a hotshot cop he'd been, or how many opposing players he'd put in the hospital in his football career.

No, these were the tiny, troubling lies that tended to gnaw at the back of Cam's mind and make him queasy. Small lies about why the man's cellphone had been turned off (dead battery? — one of Cam's duties was to make sure that didn't happen) or where he'd been when Cam tried to reach him in his hotel room late at night (an old friend needed a ride home? — surely he could have come up with something better than that). Worse, he'd been asked to lie, *twice*, to the candidate's wife: once to say he was in a meeting with some union officials when no such meeting was scheduled, and later to tell Mrs. O'Grady that they couldn't meet for a late supper because an emergency had come up when there was no emergency. It wasn't that Cam was unwilling to cover for his candidate, lying to people was part of his job; it was the fact that Dylan was lying to *him*. It's much harder to tell convincing lies if you don't know the truth.

Most troubling was the matter of the package he was holding on the candidate's behalf. Dylan had assured him that what was in the package was quite legal and that he had every right to own such a thing, but *why* was there a package at all? And why was it necessary to keep it wrapped up and hidden under the passenger seat in Cam's campaign car?

Finally, there was the matter of the small blonde woman who had spent all day following the campaign from stop to stop. She was clearly getting on the candidate's nerves, to the point where he'd whispered instructions to Cam — "Keep an eye on that one, she may be trouble," and "If she moves too close, get in her way." He refused to explain why the woman was bothering him, but there was no doubt that Dylan O'Grady was rattled by her constant presence. All of this was causing Cam's palms to sweat and his sinuses to act up.

Orwell, convinced that he could be unobtrusive if he wanted, slipped into the back row of the Globe Theatre and slumped as low in the seat as his dimensions would allow. Onstage, the Dockerty Players were having a technical run-through of *Our Town*. Leda Brennan was bathed in a pool of blue light and looking ethereal, which was entirely appropriate since at this point in the story she was the ghostly presence at her own funeral. Orwell wasn't entirely comfortable with the thought of his daughter as deceased, but since the play was being repeatedly stopped for adjustments to the lights and the position of other actors, he wasn't forced to dwell on the implications. Besides, his daughter sounded extremely healthy, so lively in fact that at one point the director was moved to remind her of her otherworldly condition and ask her to tone it down a peg.

She did look lovely. All in white, with flowers in her hair, moving about the stage in a dreamlike state, saying goodbye to her butternut tree, among other things.

As Orwell was unobtrusively dipping his hand into his jacket pocket hoping to locate a stray hard candy, he noticed another figure sitting in the back of the theatre. Unobtrusiveness was probably a bit easier for Mikhael Tomashevsky, whose head was barely visible. Orwell moved down a row. "Mind if I join you?" he whispered.

"Could we keep it quiet back there?" the director yelled.

Mikhael motioned Orwell to slide in beside him. "The tall girl in white is very good," he said. It wasn't audible to the director.

Orwell made a conscious effort to lower his voice. "My daughter," he said.

"We can still hear you," the director bellowed. "We're working here!"

"Quite lovely," Mikhael said. "Perhaps we should step outside."

As Orwell was squishing himself sideways into the aisle he saw his daughter shade her eyes to see who was there and then look heavenward directly into the blue light. She had recognized her father's distinctive shape. He hoped she wasn't too embarrassed.

"And Ms. Brennan," the director yelled, "please try to remember that you are a dead person. Dead people don't declaim."

The Globe Theatre was on Lock Road, dead centre in the cross of a T intersection that marked the eastern terminus of Vankleek Street. To the right and slightly downhill were the locks alongside the Little Snipe, to the left, the road curved past St. Barnabus and joined a meandering series of tree-lined avenues climbing to the Knoll. The two men stood under the portico looking down Vankleek.

"My daughter too is an actor," said Mikhael. "In Moscow. She was in *Uncle Vanya* just last month."

"Really. You must be quite proud."

"I didn't get to see it. I was far away."

"That's too bad."

"We all give up things for our jobs, do we not?"

Orwell, who had to admit that currently his life was rather full, was at a loss for adequate words of commiseration. "This front door has been smashed at least six times since place was built. In 1923," he said, "someone comes speeding down Vankleek, can't make the turn, kaboom."

"Are we safe, standing here?" Mikhael wondered.

"Usually happens late at night." He hesitated, not sure if the man was up to strolling. "We can walk down to the locks . . . if you'd care to."

"Lovely," Mikhael said. He smiled to put the big man at ease, "I walk all the time. It is therapeutic."

"I feel the same way," Orwell said. He patted his torso. "Move it or lose it, they say. Although in my case, losing it is the point of the exercise." The two men started down the sloping sidewalk and onto the first bridge. Tomashevsky's rolling gait was surprisingly nimble and Orwell didn't have to slow his usual pace very much at all. "How'd you wind up here?" he asked.

"A Captain Rosebart in Toronto pointed me . . ."

"I mean at the theatre, this afternoon."

"Oh. Ha. Curiosity. I ran out of things to do. I couldn't find Zubrovskaya, your detective is out of town and the only other person on my list could be almost anywhere."

"You'll be staying in town another night then?"

"Yes. More if necessary." The little man smiled. "What I would like is a month in one place; the same bed, the same view, the same newspaper every morning."

"I could never do it," Orwell said. "Travel all the time."

"I don't mind. Most of the time. But I've been away for eight months now and I miss my wife. On this trip I have been in a dozen cities, interviewing hundreds of people about a thousand missing artworks, artifacts and relics. These are approximate numbers, Chief Brennan, it could be more."

"Well, any help I can give. Who else is on your list?"

"It was always a long shot. Have you had a visit from any other representative of my ministry?"

"You mean recently?"

"It could have been any time in the past few years I suppose."

"You're the first."

"In the years before me there were three perhaps four other people assigned to this case. Two of them have since retired and are home." He sighed. "Well, they did their duty, they earned their rest. As some day so will I."

"And the others?"

"One married and is living in Saskatchewan, I believe. And the other, well, we are not certain."

They stopped in the middle of the bridge and watched the water moving by underneath. Mikhael took a deep breath. "It is good to see another spring, is it not?"

Orwell nodded with enthusiasm. "Oh yes."

"It is the same in all northern countries, I'm sure. The winters are long. To see green things returning gives hope to people who have been cold for so many months."

The two men enjoyed the fresh air for a few moments, their eyes scanning the open land of the far side of the bridge for signs of green things emerging. At the same instant both men looked up at the sounds of honking and watched a ragged V of Canada Geese heading northwest.

"That must be one of the signs," said Mikhael. "We have them too, in Russia. Perhaps a different kind, but high-flying geese. It always cheers me."

Orwell gave a delighted laugh. "Me too," he said. "Brightens my whole day to hear those honkers heading north."

They shared the moment of connection with eyes lifted to the sky and simple smiles on their faces. After a while, Orwell broke the silence. "I haven't been chief here all that long. I could check our records. About who you're looking for."

"That won't be necessary, Chief. It would have been in the last three years or so. She wouldn't have come by until after Ms. Zubrovskaya arrived."

"She?"

There was a time when Anya would have attended an event such as this in the company of a suitable escort, someone who would perhaps have given her a flower, opened a door, taken her arm as she climbed the steps, held her chair, leaned close to tell her how lovely she was, how brilliant she had been. Tonight was a *pas seul*, a solo turn. Not that there was dancing, or a dance floor. The music was recorded chamberbabble, schmaltzy fiddlepop, the room was too bright, the flowers inappropriate, the conversation was gossip about bureaucrats she was unlikely to meet. She had attended anarchist gatherings in basement flats boasting more hospitality. And better wine.

She reminded herself that this was about Ludi. And Vassili. Yes, and even Viktor. Our little gypsy band paid a big price. Someone must be held accountable. It falls to me. I am the lucky one. I am alive. I survived. Three of my friends did not. Someone must collect what is owed.

And there he was, entering the room with the texting woman and the vigilant man. He looked refreshed, showered, shaved, fresh shirt, power tie, moving through the gathering, shaking hands, kissing cheeks, very smooth, every inch the rising political star. But no matter how tough he is, or was once, no matter how ruthless, surely he knew this day must come, that someday, someone would call on him for a reckoning.

"I'm afraid I'll have to ask you to leave." It was the watchful man with the jug ears, her dance partner of the afternoon. His nametag read, "Cam Gidrick." He took her arm. "Please don't make a scene," he said.

"I am registered," Anya said. "I paid seventy-five dollars for my ticket."

"I'll get you a refund," he said.

"But why must I leave?"

"The candidate believes that you are here to disrupt the reception."

"Nonsense," she said. "I have been most supportive, all afternoon. This is quite outrageous. When exactly did this become a fascist state?"

"Just leave quietly and I won't have to call for a police escort."

That made her laugh. "Oh, I do not think you want that

just now, do you?" This last comment caused the man to sneeze violently for some reason.

Odd how things work out. Here she was getting thrown out of the reception mere moments after walking in, when who should be entering but her new best friend, Mrs. Andrew Lytton, in the company of none other than the candidate's wife, Keasha Asange-O'Grady, looking tall and lovely in a silk dress the same shade of blue as the ring on her finger. Where are you going? asked Mrs. Lytton. Why, I have been denied admission, Anya answered. Whatever for? No reason was given. Who asked you to leave? Mrs. O'Grady wanted to know. This man. Nonsense, said the candidate's wife. I've been looking forward to hearing all about the Bolshoi. It was the Kirov, actually, said Mrs. Lytton. Oh, of course, said Mrs. O'Grady, that's even better, isn't it? Many would agree, Anya said. And the three of them walked inside together, much to the discomfiture of the candidate's assistant, who was forced to stand aside and endure Anya's entirely smug smile as she passed.

"I swear," said the candidate's wife, "these campaigns get more paranoid every year. Last week Cam evicted someone who was wearing a 'Save the Whales' button. Come on, I'll introduce you to my husband. He's not as fierce as he likes to think." She led the way straight toward the man himself, who watched their approach with a wary grin. "We have a celebrity with us tonight," she told her husband.

"Really? I hope you vote in this riding," said the candidate.

"No, I will not be able to vote for you, but I am sure you will do well. They tell me this is a safe seat."

"That's what they told me, too. I should have got it in writing."

"Yes. Nothing is certain, is it? Except perhaps Judgement Day."

His laugh was hollow. "Ha ha, yes, oh, and taxes, of course."

"Still, it is brave of you to seek such a public verdict. I myself have kept a low profile for many years."

"But that's soon to change," offered Mrs. Lytton.

He was already looking for a way to disengage. "It is?"

"Your lovely wife and I are determined to involve Anya in the arts centre." Mrs. Lytton had decided this would be a good moment to press her case. "She is, after all, one of the ballet world's great artists."

"Perhaps Mrs. Lytton exaggerates my reputation," Anya said. "My career was somewhat brief."

"But incandescent, my dear. Besides, you represent what is great about the Russian ballet tradition, training, technique."

"Pain, loss." Anya smiled to take the sting out of the words.

"We won't lose you this time," Mrs. Lytton said. She turned to the candidate. "I do hope you'll find the time to look over the plans I sent you," she said. "Our list of supporters is growing every day."

"I'll have to get back to you on that. After election day." He was already tugging his wife's elbow and stepping back. "Nice to have met you, Ms. Daniel," he said as he turned away.

"Zubrovskaya," she said to his retreating back. She turned to Mrs. Lytton. "Daniel was my alias, for a time. I wonder where he might have heard that."

This night was becoming a trial for Cam Gidrick. Not only was the annoying little blonde woman still hanging around, schmoozing with the old doll in the flowered hat and making nice-nice with his candidate's wife, the man himself was getting increasingly nervous about something, snapping at him about nothing. Barb was no help; she was thumbing her damn iPhone off in a corner somewhere, probably blogging or tweeting — that's all she did these days. And now these people? Three new arrivals who obviously didn't belong: some gawky beanpole in a trenchcoat for Christ's sake, another one who looked like a biker chick in a leather jacket and paratrooper boots and an obvious pansy filling his face at the buffet table. Whoever they were, they had to leave, even if it meant calling out the storm troopers.

The tall one was heading his way. Where the hell were the rent-a-cops when you needed them? He took a deep breath. "Something I can do for you?"

"For a start, how about getting out of my face?"

"I'm sorry, you'll have to leave. Mr. O'Grady has a speech to give in about three minutes."

Adele flashed her badge. "This won't take long."

"Look here, Officer . . ."

"*Detective.*"

"Detective. This is hardly the appropriate time."

"I *know.* If it isn't one damn thing it's another, right?" She leaned closer to read his nametag. "But I promise, *Cam,* not to get all *official,* and *loud,* if your boss meets me over by the punchbowl in about thirty seconds. Okay?"

"I'll see what I can do."

"You do that."

Cam made his way back to where the candidate was pretending to laugh at some idiot's lame jokes. He wiped his brow. Police? *Detectives?* An immediate sinus headache unfocused his eyes and made him stumble. *What* in God's name was going *on*? He felt overwhelmed by guilty knowledge, but knowledge about *what*? His ability to do his job depended on knowing the details, and there were details he didn't know, and for the first time in the campaign there were things he didn't *want* to know.

Adele was tempted to load a plate with goodies from the dessert table but restrained herself when she saw Dylan coming toward her, trying to look like he wasn't ready to blow up. "Hey, Dilly, how's it going?" she asked sweetly.

"Del. Didn't read the invitation? Formal, you notice?"

"My prom dress has barf stains on it. I just need a minute. Lacsamana's been trying to track you down. Wants you to come in for a sit down about that DOA in the Beaches."

"The *what?*"

"Case you and Paulie worked eight years ago. Something about jewels. Guy named Vassili Abramov. Shot in the back. Twice."

"Doesn't ring a bell."

"Sure it does."

"Lissen, why don't you go down to campaign headquarters and talk to my guys and we'll work something out, all right?"

"All these people all kicking in to your war chest, Dilly?"

"It's a real bad idea sticking your nose into the political snakepit, Del, know what I mean? You don't want somebody calling up Rosebart, telling him you're being a pain in the ass."

"Trust me, he knows I'm a pain in the ass."

His smile was brief, insincere and dismissive. "Gotta go." He started walking away.

She raised her voice, just a notch. "Hey, we found Paulie's gun. Was that what you were looking for last Friday night at Louie Grova's? The one he didn't have any more."

He stopped in his tracks. His whisper was deadly. "Get your ass out of here."

"How do you figure a guy looks like you flies under the radar? You aren't exactly hard to spot." She grinned. She was having a great time. "We've got a witness."

"Witness to what?"

"You at the scene, coming out of Grova's around three in the morning, about the time the ME says the poor shmuck left for that big pawnshop in the sky. Not very smart for a high-profile political wannabe. I don't think Lacsamana has that information yet."

"Are we done?"

"*Hell* no. Got a whole lot of shit we need to straighten out. We're still talking to some people." She pointed. "Way at the back there? Chomping on chicken parts? You know Sergei, don't you? Turns out Louie's sneaky stepson was taping all your meetings upstairs. Got the two of you on record talking about another

DOA. Guy named Nimchuk. Also shot. Remember him? Motel room on the Queensway?"

"You've got nothing."

"But fuck, have I got a lot of it. All sorts of interesting shit. There's Louie's brother in Montreal. Remembers you and Nimchuk doing a deal with some diamonds. Back when you were playing football. Ring a bell?"

"We're not doing this here."

"And the woman. Her name was Ludmilla. Remember her? Russian? Friend of Nimchuk's? Turned up in a dump site inside a fridge. Your old linemate Nate Grabowski says he saw you sneaking her into the hotel that night."

"None of this sticks."

"Sure gonna fuck up your trip to Ottawa though, ain't it?" She watched him consider his next move. He didn't seem to have one. "You should have got rid of the sapphire, Dilly. That wasn't smart. I bet your wife'll be really pissed when I have to pull it off her finger."

She could tell by the way his mouth started to open that he wanted to yell at her but he remembered where he was and instead snarled. "You go near my wife . . ."

"And what?" She pulled her jacket back far enough to expose the butt of her weapon. "You'll stuff me in a freezer?"

Cam was coming to get him. He had a worried look on his face. "Getting ready to introduce you. Everything okay?"

Adele smiled. "What do you say, Dilly? Everything okay? Might as well go make your speech. I'll stick around. We're not quite done yet."

Keasha glanced in Adele's direction as she rose to meet her hubby. She straightened his tie and dabbed his forehead, whispered a question. He waved it off curtly. She stepped back as if slapped.

Cam stepped close to Adele. "Is there something I should be concerned about?"

"Depends. You haven't been aiding and abetting have you, Cam?"

"What are you talking about?"

"Oh, you know, covering things up. You're not involved in anything illegal, are you?"

Cam blew his nose noisily and winced. "Excuse me," he said. "The air in here is bone dry. Gives me a headache."

"Oh you've got a headache all right. Big headache. You might have to start beating the bushes for a new candidate."

It was odd, she thought, that Sergei Siziva had been dragooned into joining the campaign as an ally. It should have been difficult, if not unthinkable, that an arch enemy of almost thirty years could be this close without her fearing him, or loathing him, or at the very least wanting to push his fat head into the platter of shrimp on ice. And yet there she was, standing beside him, as she had done for so many years, and feeling a certain . . . *kinship* was the only word that came to mind. After all, in his way Sergei had been as much a victim in the initial affair as the other gypsy smugglers. His response had been understandable, if not wholly admirable, and the tragic aftermath, as it turned out, had not been his responsibility. And he too, as he made quite clear in a whispered aside, was there to "see justice done." Besides, his presence allowed her a certain latitude, since he was more than willing to assume responsibility for keeping Mrs. Lytton entertained.

"This man partnered me for six years with the Volga company," Anya announced as she introduced them.

"I believe my husband and I once saw the two of you dance *Giselle*. I remember you as very . . . stalwart."

"You are too complimentary, Madame Lytton. I was never of the first rank, I admit that, but not once did I drop a ballerina on her derrière."

"Bless you, Sergei, that is true," Anya said. "Always strong."

"Well, this is a pleasure," said Mrs. Lytton. "One doesn't expect to find genuine artistes at these affairs. What brings you here tonight?"

"It is more a question of *who*, Madame Lytton. I am the reluctant guest of the local gendarmerie. I am, as they say, helping them with their inquiries."

"How exciting. Is it top secret?"

"Hardly, Madame, they believe the gentleman at the microphone may be guilty of a crime. More than one, actually."

"Really? My goodness. This evening is turning out to be much more fun than I anticipated. I think I'll have a small glass of wine."

Sergei was full of juicy gossip about Rudolph Nureyev and Erik Bruhn and other stars of the ballet world, and Mrs. Lytton was hanging on every word. Anya decided it was time for her to visit the man again. The candidate was about to make a speech. Anya wasn't interested in the substance, she'd heard it before, only in the manner of its delivery.

He's developed a twitch, she thought. He's started wiping his palms on his jacket, he has to refer to his notes in order to locate the next talking point in a speech he's given many times before. Each time she applauded he lost his place. Or perhaps it was what was happening on the other side of the room that was bothering him. The campaign overseers appeared to be having a heated discussion about something. Anya could only guess what was so important, but the sight had a cheering effect.

"We don't pull this off we're in *so* much trouble," Stacy said.

"*We're* in trouble?" It appeared that Adele had regained her appetite: her mouth was full of macaroon. "Ha! Check it out. There's a gaggle of party hacks in the corner working on damage control already." Three men were huddled at the rear of the reception hall. "I think the big boys are wondering if they bet on the wrong horse."

"Kinda late in the game to find a replacement."

"Maybe, but better than having your man busted on the floor

of the House of Commons. The woman with the phone growing out of her ear is probably calling party HQ. His ass'll be off the ticket in a fartbeat."

"Wish we had more to hit him with."

Adele helped herself to a few more cookies. "That guy Cam's looking shaky. I asked him if he was aiding and abetting and he nearly pissed himself." Cam was standing apart from the meeting in the corner, wiping his nose and squeezing the crease between his eyebrows. Adele had another bite of macaroon. "Why don't you take a run at him? You might handle him better than I would. I think he scares easy."

"I'll be gentle."

"Not *too* gentle."

"Hi there. It's Cam, is that right?"

"Yes."

"I'm Detective Crean, Dockerty PD. And you are Mr. O'Grady's right-hand man, is that right?"

"I'm his special assistant. For the duration of the campaign."

"You don't get to go to Ottawa?"

"What? Oh, no, this isn't full-time with me. I sell real estate."

"So this is a sideline?"

"Well, it's a bit more than that."

"Have you known Mr. O'Grady long?"

"No, not long."

"Like back when he was on the police force?"

"Oh, no."

"How about when he ran for city council? Did you work on that campaign?"

"No. This campaign is actually the first time I've been involved . . . with him . . . in his political career."

"And how involved are you? Special assistant sounds like an important job. You, what, look after all the details, right?"

"Yes. Details. I'm the detail person."

"So you pretty much know everything about his day-to-day activities. For the duration of the campaign, I mean. What? Five weeks? Something like that? Where he goes, what he does. You have his entire schedule, don't you?"

"Yes. I'm supposed to."

"Supposed to."

"Well, I can't account for every . . . it's not like I'm *with* him every minute . . . of every day . . . for the entire campaign."

"Of course not. The man needs some privacy, after all."

"Yes."

"But he would have to be on call, wouldn't he? You have to be able to get hold of him. If something should come up."

"Yes."

"What sort of things might come up, do you think?"

"Oh, I don't know, changes in schedule perhaps, reporters wanting a comment about something . . . things like that."

"And he's always available?"

"Well . . . yes. Usually."

"Usually. Is he ever *un*available?"

"Well, once or twice there's been miscommunication."

"I see."

"Nothing that had a serious impact. He missed a meeting once. His cellphone was off and I couldn't reach him."

"You remember when that was?"

"I'd have to check."

"But you could pin it down? If you had to?"

"Excuse me." He sneezed violently. "I'm sorry. My sinuses. I think it's the air in here."

"That can be very annoying."

"It gives me awful headaches. Right between my eyes."

"Ouch. And stress can bring on a headache as well."

"I'm pretty sure it's allergies."

"So there's nothing else eating at you? Things going the way they should? All smooth sailing on the campaign trail?"

"It's been pretty smooth, yes."

"That's good. Not many more days until the election, is it?"

"Not many."

"This would be a bad time for something unforeseen to come along and mess up all your good detail work, wouldn't it?"

"Like what?"

"You would know better than I would, Cam. Thing is, I'd hate to see a nice guy like you, with a what, wife and kids?"

Cam shook his head. "I'm not married."

"Really? Even so, you want a regular life, don't you? You wouldn't want to get caught up in something that could wreck all your chances. Know what I mean? If the man you're working for turned out to have secrets, things he was keeping from you, or even worse, things he was asking *you* to keep secret, well, that could make you an accessory to something bad, you know? And maybe you wouldn't even know what it was you were covering up, but when it started to come out, it might not be clear to people that you were entirely innocent. Know what I mean? People might think, hey, he must have known things weren't right, otherwise why would he be covering things up. You see where I'm going with this?"

"Yes."

"So let's do this very quietly, confidentially, while there's still time to get your side of the story."

"What is it you want to know?"

"Well, for starters, I'll want you to pin down those times when you couldn't reach him, when he wasn't available say, or when his reasons for not being available didn't quite add up. Because you being a detail guy, you probably keep a close watch on things, don't you?"

"Yes I do."

"So. For a start, I'm going to need a list of those dates and times. That would be helpful. Now, think carefully, Cam. Is there something else you want to tell me?"

"I don't, I mean I don't know if it's important."

"You'll have to let me decide that."

"I guess I do. Well . . . there is a package."

The candidate's wife in heels was the same height as Adele in cop shoes. The two women were nose to nose. Neither was blinking nor backing down, but where Keasha O'Grady had fire in her eyes, Adele was unruffled.

"I want to know what's going on here."

"It's Keasha, isn't it? I'm Detective Moen. You probably don't remember but we met years ago."

"I know who you are. You were Paul Delisle's partner after my husband retired."

"That's right."

"This is about Paul? Have you caught the person responsible?"

"We did."

"Then do you mind if I ask what it is you're doing here?"

"Just asking your husband a few things."

"And it couldn't wait?"

"That's a beautiful ring, Mrs. O'Grady. Gift from your husband, wasn't it?"

"A great many years ago."

"He tell you where he got it?"

"He won it, in a poker game."

"Must have been a pretty high stakes game. It's worth a lot of money."

"This is about a ring?"

"We tried to arrange a less intrusive interview but . . ."

"It's a campaign. Our schedule is unforgiving."

"I'm investigating multiple homicides. And *I'm* unforgiving."

"Multiple . . . ? What on earth is going on?"

"I think there are some serious questions that need to be answered. By your husband. When he can make himself available."

But the candidate's wife was no longer listening, she was

looking across the room at the empty speaker's platform. The audience was murmuring in confusion. Dylan O'Grady was gone.

Damn! Well what did you think was going to happen, you big stork? Keep poking him like that he was bound to do *something*. Confess? Grab a hostage? Pull out an AK-47 and blast his way to freedom? *Something.* So he picked the simplest one, he ran. Great. Now all we have to do is find him.

"Anybody see which way he went?"

The general consensus among the pointing fingers suggested that Dylan O'Grady had taken off through the side door to his right, although there was a contradictory view that he'd left by the front door, and a few people thought he'd gone up the stairs. Obviously not everyone in the room had been paying attention. Adele ran for the first choice.

The hall led in two directions. Stacy and Cam Gidrick were coming from one of them.

"Did you see him?"

"See who?"

"Dilly. He booked, Stace. Just took off. Where were you?"

"Went to the parking lot, to check out Cam's car."

"Okay, so he didn't go that way."

"Car wasn't there."

Captain Rosebart was not happy to be called away from his favourite television show at 9:23 p.m. on a Thursday night. He refused to tell Adele what show it was, but she suspected there were Kardashians involved.

"Oh Lordy Jesus, Moen, what did you do now?"

"I talked to him. I told him we wanted to bring him in for questioning."

"So why didn't you bring him in?"

"He was making a speech. We're waiting for him to finish. Hell, there was a room full of heavy political types. We were trying to keep it quiet."

"Yeah, that worked out great."

"What would you have done?"

"Well, for starters, I probably wouldn't have started hassling him in public."

"We didn't have a lot of choice, Captain. Our dancer lady was on his case all day long. She wanted to rattle him."

"Well you all did a great job. He got rattled. We've got newspapers and TV reporters up the wazoo, the goddamn political party's accusing us of screwing with their election . . ."

"Tell them, better it happened now than *after*."

"I don't need you to tell me how to handle those assholes."

"Of course, sir. What *do* you want me to do?"

"For starters I want a *huge* fricking report laying out exactly how you got to the point where you spooked this guy so bad he ran off in the middle of his campaign."

"I think you should get somebody over to that pawnshop. He may have gone after Louie's kid."

"Yeah, yeah, all right, I'll cover that. You stay the hell away from it. Got me?"

"Yes, Captain."

"Do your goddamn paperwork and have it on my desk in the morning."

"Yessir. What about the dancer?"

"What about her?"

"Should I bring her in?"

"What for? She do something?"

"No, but . . ."

"We've got enough problems without nursemaiding that crazy woman. Tell her to get her ass back up to Dockerville. If we need her, let your pal Crean round her up."

"Yessir. What about the other one, Sergei?"

"Jeezuss! It's never going to end with these frickin' Russkies, is it? Tell him to keep himself available. Tell them all to keep themselves available."

"And Dilly's wife? His assistants?"

"Stay the hell away from *everybody*. We'll handle it from here. You've caused enough goddamn wreckage for one night."

"She's still got the ring. And the assistant was holding some package for O'Grady. Might have been a gun."

"Christ! We're *on* it. Hear me? *We're* on it. Not you. You do some paperwork and stay the hell out of my hair for a while! Full report. On my desk. 09:00. Got it?"

"Yes, Captain."

After that it was a long night.

A very long night.

First on the scene were two uniformed cops Adele didn't know well and didn't like much, who didn't know what the hell they were doing there anyway. Dylan O'Grady wasn't a fugitive, wasn't charged with anything and the only element worthy of police attention was an unsubstantiated claim by one of his assistants that he "maybe" had a handgun in his possession, although Cam Gidrick hadn't actually seen the weapon, only inferred it from the weight and shape of the "package" he'd been asked to keep in the campaign car. Said car was "possibly" being driven by the missing candidate, although no one had actually seen him drive away in it.

More troubling to the campaign was the sudden swarm of reporters who smelled blood in the water and were hungry for information. Neither Adele nor Stacy had any intention of helping them out. The campaign organizers and aides weren't any more forthcoming and Cam Gidrick had been admonished by Stacy early in the proceedings to keep his mouth shut.

The cobbled together semi-official statement issued by the campaign manager was a cryptically worded paragraph suggesting that the candidate had suffered a "sudden attack of indigestion." This prompted many in the gathering to experience sympathetic stomach cramps. Most blamed them on the shrimp platter.

Sergei Siziva immediately demanded around-the-clock police protection. Adele told him to move to a hotel, and no, she wasn't going to pay for it. Anya told them she'd be catching the morning train back to Dockerty and would spend the night in her hotel room, and no, Sergei wasn't invited to share it, although she offered to lend him money to get a room of his own.

And after an hour of what seemed an interminable inconclusive explanation, Stacy and Adele were allowed to depart the room, leaving behind a crowd abuzz with conflicting opinions of what exactly had transpired. The only consensus seemed to be that a formerly secure federal seat was now very much in play.

Stacy decided to spend another night on Adele's couch. She not only wanted to help her friend craft the necessary report for the morning, she also had a few ideas she wanted to talk out.

"Okay, I'm just spitballing here."

"Spit away, partner." Adele was pulling the cork on a bottle of her favourite Spanish wine.

"Paul was a pretty good cop, right? I mean he bent the rules, but he didn't mess around."

"Okay, that's how I'd like to remember it."

"So what happens if a cop loses his weapon? What does he do? He reports it, right?"

Adele stopped with the cork half out. "Oh yeah. Immediately."

"From the start we've been stuck on the idea that Paul's gun was used to shoot Nimchuk. Then we sort of proved, at least to our satisfaction, that it wasn't the gun, that it just as easily could have been Dylan's gun."

Adele finally got the cork out but didn't pour herself a drink. She was still mulling the implications. "Keep going."

"So if it wasn't his gun, what reason could he have for not reporting it missing?"

Adele finally poured her flowered water glass half full of Spanish wine and had a long drink. She lowered the glass. "No reason I can think of."

"The first time we hear that his weapon's gone is up in Dockerty. And the only person's word we have is the woman he was having his little fling with. She claims she never saw it."

"So?"

"So who could have got their hands on it? The waitress he boinked after lunch? Edwin Kewell who shot him through the window?"

"Or the shrink."

"So what would she want with a gun? She planning on offing her hubby?"

"Hold that thought." The phone was ringing. Adele had another gulp of wine before she picked up. "Moen," she burped. "Wha? When? Where? Oh shit. Yessir. Yessir. In the morning." She hung up and looked at Stacy. "They found him," she said.

"He in custody?"

"Nope. He's in the morgue. Spotted his car out at the Leslie Street Spit, parked on the grass. Looks like he blew his brains out."

"Oh cripes."

Twelve

It was a fine and fresh Friday morning. Almost April. Less than a week until opening day of the baseball season. That was something good.

Far less good was the news of Dylan O'Grady's suicide the previous night. It had yet to hit the newspapers, but the early television broadcasts had been filled with speculation as to why the man had done such a thing.

Orwell needed a walk, a good brisk walk across the fields to clear his mind. The dogs *always* needed a walk; across the fields, through the woods, over the footbridge across the stream, back along the side road, down the gully, up the other side, as much as they could get, and certainly more of a walk than Orwell was prepared to lavish upon them, that was certain. But they would happily walk to the ends of the earth if he had a mind to hike that far, and this morning Orwell was prepared to walk at least as far as the footbridge. It would do him good he was certain. He was getting fat. Well, not exactly *fat*, not *obese*, definitely *not* obese, but, face it, he hadn't lost any of his "winter weight," that's what he was calling it, *winter* weight, as opposed to *summer* weight, which, for the past few years had been roughly the same as what he carried during the cold months.

Yes, it was a nice morning and he was out of the house and

moving in plenty of time to see the sun come up from the top of the second rise. A bright clear morning: birds, breeze, the air rich with the smells of things starting to grow, things beginning to come back from the cold and dark. And to kill yourself on such a morning. To miss even one more sunrise. Orwell couldn't begin to grasp such a thing. He knew, even without referring to the crumpled faith of his childhood, that such a thing was a terrible sin. Despair. One of the great sins, albeit not listed among the Seven Deadlies, but perhaps the *worst* sin, giving up entirely, ceasing to believe in even the possibility of salvation. Or if not salvation of the soul, at least in the value of life, the worth of one more breath, one more sunrise, one more walk with the dogs, one more conversation, meal, idea.

And dammitall, he wasn't about to waste a fine morning such as this one letting it drag his spirits down. The dogs were enjoying it; even Borgia had been inspired to break into a trot from time to time, and Duff had battered himself ragged charging through brambles and hedgerows, splashing across the stream, digging furious holes in the muddy earth. His paws would definitely need sluicing when they got back.

Something else was nibbling at the back of Orwell's mind, something vague and unresolved. Tomashevsky, that was it, Tomashevsky and the missing investigator on his list. Her name, according to Tomashevsky, was Lorena Wisneski. *Doctor* Lorena Wisneski, an art historian and retrievals expert. He wished Stacy was back. Like to set her loose on that one. He wished he'd had the presence of mind to mention it to her during last night's phone report. That would have prompted her return forthwith he was certain. Forthwith, indeed. Just the sort of thing she could sink her teeth into. He supposed he could give it to Emmett Paynter, let him pass it on to one of the other investigators, but Orwell didn't like that idea. This was Stacy's case. And his. Lengthy explanations wouldn't be required. Hell's bells, she had a cellphone, she wasn't *that* far away.

"Come on beasties! Let's ramble. Breakfast is waiting. At least I have high hopes it's waiting. God knows I've worked up a hell of an appetite."

"Front-Runner Bolts Fundraiser."

The early television news programs were already full of conjecture as to why Dylan O'Grady had shot himself, but that news had come too late for the morning papers and they only had the first part of the story. Still, Anya read them all on the trip home by train and bus, read them dutifully, as if paying a debt. Ludi's killer was dead. It was necessary that she pay close attention to the details.

But there weren't many details. The *Globe* made reference to a police presence at the fundraiser, but did not venture an opinion as to what the cops were doing there. The *Star* concentrated on the scrambling campaign and the implications for the imminent election. Both the *Sun* and *National Post* hinted at conspiracies and smear tactics, but ultimately failed to connect any dots. Tomorrow's editions would be much juicier, albeit a full news cycle behind events. Anya entertained a fleeting thought that she should save the items in some kind of scrapbook, some sort of testament to justice, but in the end she decided that was pointless and recycled the papers in the appropriate bin.

As she headed north on the final leg of the trip, watching the farms and fields roll by, she found herself gnawing on her knuckles, generating a familiar pain, something she hadn't done in a while. Long ago it was her way of holding herself together offstage while awaiting her cue, or in rehearsal, enduring a harsh critique, and sometimes simply to confuse her mind into forgetting other more serious agonies in legs and knees and feet. This morning it seemed that she had other pains to forget, deep-seated aches of heart and mind.

Some would say Dylan had taken the coward's way out, some might say he had done the honourable thing, but to Anya it seemed only logical for him to skip out that way. What did he have to live for? His career was destroyed, his future was bleak, all his debts had come due, it was over for him. And she was the one who had pushed him into the corner, cut off his escapes, exposed him for all to see. It was what she wanted, wasn't it? Now she could live some kind of life, get some rest and perhaps, in time, sleep without dreams full of shadows. So why was there no sense of relief? Why was she still unfulfilled? Why was she biting her thumb hard enough to draw blood? Did she want to kick his dead body? Would that be enough? No. Not enough. Never enough. Was it because he escaped exposure, would never be forced to admit that he murdered Ludi? Perhaps. That was part of it, surely. To convict him of Ludi's death would have brought satisfaction, but she knew it would have been unlikely. More conceivable that Viktor's murder was the one they could prove. Or Louie's. Or could they have proven any of them? With a good lawyer playing up the murky string of events and the dubious backgrounds of the victims, he might have walked out of a courtroom free as a bird. A ruined career to be sure, but no guarantee of a life behind bars. He could have escaped. But his pride could not handle it. In the end it was probably vanity that killed him. How sad that was.

And unsatisfying.

As it turned out, and notwithstanding his energetic romp across the fields, Orwell's breakfast had been something of a disappointment. It was becoming obvious that his wife was cutting back on certain of the morning staples he considered mandatory: bacon, sausages, waffles, unlimited toast and jam, fried eggs basted in butter, the *basics*. Instead, for the past few days he'd been confronted by such items as fruit cups, oatmeal (with 2% milk for Pete's sake), grapefruit juice, a single scrambled egg — it was punitive, no other word for it. Worse, she had begun saddling him with a brown bag for his lunch, a bag containing *raw* vegetables! And a hard-boiled egg! And an apple. He had nothing against apples, they were nature's vitamin pills, but they were far tastier surrounded by pastry and scented with cinnamon or allspice. This of course wasn't the first time Erika had kept such a close watch on her husband's caloric intake, but in the past she had eased up after a while, or relented entirely during traditionally tasty cycles such as Christmas, Thanksgiving, Easter. Well, at least Easter was on the horizon, and there had better be some decent grub *that* weekend or people would hear about it.

He was in a mood, no doubt about it, Dorrie could tell by the way he was clumping up the stairs — it was a dead giveaway to her boss's morning disposition. On good days he charged up filled with energy and bonhomie, on preoccupied days he climbed slowly with pauses for thought and on days when he was in a black mood he clumped. Today he was clumping.

"Morning, Chief."

"Dr. Lorna Ruth," he barked, without greeting. "See if you can get her on the phone." He stomped into his office and reappeared almost immediately, aware that he'd been brusque. "Would you, Dorrie? Please?"

"Of course."

"And good morning," he added.

As she handled the phone calls she could hear him banging around inside his office. "Dang it all!" She heard the distinct sound of a filing cabinet drawer being slammed. "It's a bloody conspiracy!" He was hungry. That's all it was. "Dr. Ruth isn't answering, at her house or office," she said.

"Where the heck is everyone? This is a workday, isn't it?"

"Yes, sir. It's Friday."

"I *know* what day it is. The question was rhetorical. Why aren't people where they're supposed to be on a Friday was the gist of it. Try the Zubrovskaya woman."

"No luck with Ms. Zubrovskaya either."

"Keep trying. *Please.*"

"Yes, sir."

"What's going on?" Stacy whispered.

Dorrie looked up at the new arrival. "The Chief's wife has him on a diet again."

"What's going on out there? I hear whispering."

"Stacy's back, Chief."

"Well, get her in here. I'll have no conspiracies."

Dorrie put a finger to her lips.

Stacy found her boss standing by the window, staring out at the street.

"I'll have my report ready for you in ten minutes, Chief. Just have to print it up."

"Fine, fine, no rush. Sit down."

"Yes, sir. Something come up?"

"There's a man in town, from the Russian Ministry of Culture wants to talk to you. And to Ms. Zubrovskaya of course. She on her way back?"

"I think she took an early train. I can pick her up."

"If she's around I want to talk to her. And Dr. Ruth, too. I want both of them, separately or side by each, I don't care, see what you can do, will you?"

"Right away."

"Good." He turned his head. Dorrie had the Chief's coffee and newspaper and a jelly donut on a paper napkin. "What's this?" he asked suspiciously.

"We took up a collection," she said with a straight face.

He pointed at Stacy. "Both of them. As soon as."

"On it," she said. As she left she caught a glimpse of him wiping a drop of raspberry jelly off his bottom lip.

Adele had no such constraints on what she was allowed to eat for breakfast, or lunch, but she had no appetite this morning. Her last substantial intake had been a handful of macaroons followed by most of a bottle of Spanish red and she was experiencing a certain level of internal discomfort. She might also be carrying the plague judging by the wide berth her colleagues were giving her this morning. Or maybe she needed to change her deodorant. Or it could have something to do with the black cloud hanging over her head. She could feel it pressing down, almost see its dark shadow as she walked. Her mother would have said the Angel of Death was hovering near. That was how she talked: angels of death, ends of days, wages of sin, she loved saying the words, her mouth would curl into a mean smile as she pronounced upon Adele's head the swift and sure retribution of a vengeful . . . fuck, long after the hag was dead and buried and her preaching silenced, those images continued to plague her. Out of my head, you old witch. I'm doing my job.

"Moen, get in here!"

"Captain?"

"We've got a situation."

"What's up?"

Rosebart had the drawn look of a man who had spent far too many hours parrying blows and some of the shots were getting through his weary defences. "Goddamn! O'Grady has two bullet holes."

Adele's stomach lurched and she sat down heavily. "I'm gonna take a wild guess that he didn't shoot himself twice."

"Or even once. The ME says he's got a big hole going in, two holes coming out. Looks like somebody shot him, put the gun in his hand and pulled the trigger over the same hole. Only they didn't line it up just right. Second shot came out half an inch higher than the first one."

"Holy Jesus!"

"You got that right."

"His gun?"

"Oh yeah. His service piece. Looks like he checked it out as soon as he checked it in. I'll be wanting some answers from whoever screwed up down there."

"Where do you want me?"

"Good question, Detective." Rosebart rubbed his face. He hadn't shaved very well, probably used the crummy electric he kept in his desk. His sigh sounded a trifle melodramatic, but the pain in his eyes was genuine. "Goo-ood question. If I had half a brain I'd chain you to your desk so you couldn't bring me any more grief."

"But."

"Yeah, right, *but*. But maybe you should get your ass back up to Dockerville . . ."

"Dockerty."

"Whatever . . . and find out what that loopy dancer lady was up to last night, because as I have it in one of your reports," he waved a stack of papers at her, "which I'm reading far too frickin' many of these days, she likes to sneak out of her hotel room in the middle of the night."

"She was in plain sight when Dilly took off."

"Was she in plain sight at 03:00 when, according to the ME, he popped his clogs?"

"I don't see it."

"I don't give a crap. According to you, she was on O'Grady's case all day yesterday." He swivelled his chair around to show her his back. His shirt had a dark sweat stain down the spine. "And that other Russkie. Serge? Track that asshole down, too. Find out if he can account for his actions all night. Do that forthwith."

"Yes, sir, forthwith."

He waved the back of his hand at her. "With any luck it'll get you out of my sight for the day, and that's not a small thing."

"Yes, sir."

"And don't talk to any goddamn reporters, hear me?"

"Yes, sir."

"Bugger off."

"Yes, sir."

Stacy had no luck at either Anya's apartment or her studio. Likewise with Dr. Ruth, whose office was locked and house empty. She checked the bus schedule. The first bus from Whitby had pulled in an hour ago. She checked the Timmies at the mini-mall on Vankleek and took a slow cruise from the bus stop and back to the apartment building, then made a return trip to Dr. Ruth's locations as well. Nothing.

On her way back to the station the complexion of the day changed significantly. Adele called from the city with the news that Dylan O'Grady hadn't departed this life without help. Adele said she was coming up. She needed to talk to Anya Zubrovskaya. She also wanted to know where the fuck "Serge" was since as far as she could determine, he too had left the city. Citizen Grenkov had no idea where Sergei might have gone, and as far as he was concerned it was immaterial as long as Sergei stayed far away from him.

"He says Serge came by in the middle of the night and packed his stuff, so who knows, he might be on the run."

"Dang. And our little dancer's gone missing, too."

"Be there about two o'clock, give or take. I'll call when I hit town."

Dorrie directed her to go right in. Stacy found the Chief in a meeting with a very small man whose eyes lit up when he caught sight of her. When the man got up to shake her hand, it had the odd effect of making him shorter than when he was seated, but it was a courtesy he would have insisted upon under any circumstance. "Detective Crean," he pronounced perfectly, "it is a pleasure." When he shook her hand she noted that his hand was almost as big as the Chief's. "I am Mikhael Tomashevsky," he said. "Chief Brennan has been singing your praises for the past fifteen minutes."

"How do you do, sir," she said.

"Grab a seat, Stacy," Orwell said. "Any luck?"

Tomashevsky waited until she was seated before he took his chair again. The smile he gave her confirmed that his size had no bearing on his capacity to appreciate an attractive woman.

"I just got a call from Detective Moen," she began. "Dylan O'Grady didn't kill himself. Someone shot him and tried to make it look like a suicide."

"Good Lord," said Orwell. He shook his head.

"And the other parties can't be accounted for. Anya Zubrovskaya and Sergei Siziva are also missing."

"Siziva," said Mikhael. "He has been seen?"

"Yes, sir," said Stacy. "We've interviewed him a number of times."

"That is most interesting."

"You know the man?" Orwell asked.

"Oh yes. I'd very much like a chance to talk to him myself."

"What about Dr. Ruth?" Orwell asked.

"She's nowhere in town," Stacy said. "Her house looks empty."

Mikhael gripped the arm of his chair and leaned forward. "Dr. Ruth, did you say?"

"Ruth," Orwell said. "Dr. Lorna Ruth."

"She is a medical doctor?"

"I'm not sure. She's either a psychiatrist, or a psychologist."

"And what is her connection?"

"Anya Zubrovskaya was her patient."

"Really? You wouldn't have a photograph of her anywhere, would you?"

"Sorry," said Orwell.

"Yes we do, Chief," Stacy said. "We've got her on tape. The security tape from the liquor store. If it's still around."

It took Roy Rawluck all of ten minutes to locate the old VCR machine and monitor, find the tape and cue it up. Mikhael Tomashevsky stared at the frozen image of Dr. Lorna Ruth for a long moment, all the while shaking his big head slowly from side to side. "That is her," he said at last. "Lorena Wisneski. Dr. Lorena Wisneski."

Stupid, stupid, stupid. Lower your guard for just a moment and the world will bite you on the ass. What was it her grandfather used to say? "It is not only the shadows you need to be wary of, sunlight too can blind you." Today the sun was shining, birds were singing, Lorna Ruth wore a bright smile when she slowed her car as Anya came out of the bus station. "Anya, can I give you a ride?" So easy. Never a second thought. A bit weary, heavy suitcase, legs a little tired from two days taking care of business in the city.

"Why not?" And in the car, and buckle up, and away they went. But not in the direction of home. And the seatbelt was jammed so it would not unlatch. And Lorna was not alone, Sergei was lying down on the back seat under a blanket and they were on the highway heading to the end of the earth. Stupid, stupid, stupid.

"You have to talk to me, Anya. We're running out of time."

"You perhaps. *I* have all the time in the world."

"We have to take care of this. Too many things have happened."

"Yes, and too many people have been killed. I do not wish to join their number."

"You won't. I promise. Just give me what I want. It's no good to you. It doesn't belong to you."

"Why not? Who *does* it belong to?"

"Everyone. No one. How do you think the Tsar got it? Legitimately, you think? The poor man in Mandalay who found it two centuries ago. Did he hold on to it for long? The Mogul who held it for a year. And then there was a Persian, and a Turk, and two brothers from India stole it, one killed the other, then another thief killed him, and a bigger thief killed that one, and then one of the biggest thieves of all took it to the Metropolitan of Moscow who pronounced it holy and declared it sacred and from there it went to St. Petersburg to be part of the great Romanov treasure. So, Anya Ivanova Zubrovskaya, who do you think it belongs to now?"

"Whoever is holding it, I suppose."

"Exactly. Where is it?"

"You searched my studio, you searched my home. Did it look like I was holding the biggest treasure in the world?"

"It's a process of elimination. Vassili didn't have it, Viktor didn't have it. The last person who is known to have held it is you. So. Where is it?"

"I am so sorry for you, Doctor. You have been terribly misled all these years. Do you not know? It is not real. It is a big fake. Years ago I took that ugly red thing to a man who showed me, most conclusively, that it was just a piece of glass. Nice red Venetian glass, blown, cut and polished by a fine glassmaker and made to look quite legitimate. But only glass."

"So where is the glass?"

"It is in ten thousand red pieces. I used a hammer. It is no more. It was the only way to be rid of it. If you are looking for the real ruby, I would start with Uncle Joe. That little devil Vissarionovich Dzhugashvili, known as Stalin, was quite the thief. He robbed banks before he started robbing royalty. I hear he got a hundred thousand rubles from that bank in Tbilisi. I hope he got more for the Ember. We poor gypsy smugglers got a piece of glass. It is tragic, is it not? So many lives wasted over a fake. And laughable, too. If not for so many deaths it might be the funniest joke in the world."

"I don't believe you," said Sergei from behind her. "You are too good a liar."

According to Mikhael Tomashevsky, Dr. Lorena Wisneski did have a doctorate in psychiatric medicine from Vienna, although since psychiatry was still held in low regard by many bureaucrats in Moscow, it was not listed as part of her credentials at the Ministry of Culture. Dr. Wisneski explained that an understanding of the criminal mind was a useful weapon in her arsenal, along with her doctorates in art history, archeology, certificates in gemology, restoration and her command of six languages. Until 2003 she had been one of the most respected reclamation operatives in the field, responsible for the return of hundreds of items looted during the Second World War. And then she disappeared.

"She appears to have done it again."

"So it would seem, Chief Brennan."

"And at the time she disappeared she was on the trail of this ruby specifically?"

"Well, initially of course she was searching for the missing cross of the Empress Feodorovna. Among its most valuable components were the four large Kashmiri sapphires, three of which I believe have been accounted for, a large number of diamonds, most of them sold or lost over the years and, of course, a ninety-seven-carat stone worth as much as anyone who lusts after such things would be willing to pay. Ten million, twenty, thirty, it doesn't matter. It would be worth it to a government that believed it had a justifiable claim to the ruby."

"Who would that be?"

"I can think of at least three. India, Pakistan, Iran. But one might get bids from Myanmar, China, who knows? Perhaps even England, although I'm not sure they'd care to spend that much money. The stone has passed through so many hands in its travels, and since it was usually stolen before it made its next stop, a claim could be made and even substantiated by a number of governments. And they wouldn't have to hide it. They could proudly declare that one of their great treasures had been successfully recovered."

"And the person who recovered it?"

"Would have done a great service, would be handsomely rewarded and no doubt set for life in a very comfortable sanctuary."

Adele drove into Dockerty from the east end, just for the hell of it, and because she wanted the extra ten minutes that avoiding 35 and coming up 11 added to the trip. Not that the extra time was going to answer any questions about O'Grady's murder, but it did give her a chance to finish the sack of Twizzlers she had in her glove compartment before showing up in "Dockerville." Hey, what d'ya know, there's the 7-Eleven. How lame is that? I'm visiting this burg so much I'm starting to know my way around. Fuck gas and mileage, cheaper to just move here. Her cellphone started jangling. She swallowed the last wad of red rubbery goodness before answering. "Yeah, what? I'm here, Stace, I'm turning the corner right now."

Stacy was waiting outside the station. She waved Adele to the curb and climbed in. "Make a U-turn. Got a break and enter."

"Oh yeah? Who got robbed?"

"Nobody, yet. *We're* doing the B&E. The shrink's office."

"We are? Cool." Adele got them headed in the right direction. "Horrible thing? I actually know how to get there." Stacy was picking a Twizzler off the floor mat. "Darn! Missed one. Well, it's no good now. Stick it in the glove compartment." She made a left onto Evangeline. "I'll wipe it off later." The glove compartment held an assortment of traveller's rations: Cheetos, beer nuts, half a Snickers bar. Stacy laid the red whip on top of the Cheetos bag and closed the lid. "Hey, you never know," Adele said, "a person could get caught in a blizzard and then where'd you be?"

"Up the creek, definitely."

"So? Wanna give me a hint? We looking for anything in particular?"

"We're looking for her. Where she went, what she's driving, where she took our dancer."

"She scooped her?"

"Or she went willingly. Don't know. One of our constables spotted Zubrovskaya getting into a car near the bus station. Don't have a plate number, don't have a positive ID on the driver except our guy says she had a bandage on her head. Car was a dark blue GM product. Unfortunately the doctor drives a Honda."

"What about her hubby?"

"Ford pickup. He's moved out of the marital house. Could be anywhere."

Adele pulled into the parking lot beside the two-storey Evangeline Medical Centre. "We got a warrant or anything?"

"I've got a credit card. You got anything better than that?"

"Check under the beer nuts. Lockpicks. Black zipper bag. Not kosher, but I'm always losing my house keys."

She was in a barn. She knew it was a barn. She could smell straw, she could hear the echo of pigeons cooing high above. She hoped they'd aim their droppings at the scarf tied over her head. The Hermès scarf. She should have picked up on that right away when Lorna came into the studio wearing it. She had seen it once before. It belonged to Sergei. He will be furious if it's ruined by bird shit. It would serve him right. And to think she almost had warm feelings for him the previous evening. Well, if not *warm* feelings, at least she hadn't been filled with loathing when the two policewomen brought him in. Her own fault. So sure that she was finally in control of events, directing the situation, driving things to a conclusion of her own choosing. She had forgotten the most important rules: never let your guard down. Trust no one.

And she was paying for her stupidity. The crows had won.

"I always thought they would send a man."

"I am not a killer." Lorna's voice was the same as it used to be in her office, calm rational, dispassionate, understanding.

"And yet here you are, prepared to kill me. Who are you? Who employs you?"

"Does it really matter?"

"Moscow?"

"At one time."

"And now?"

"And now we don't have a lot of time, Anya. I tried to do this the soft way. The others who came after you over the years were crude, and ultimately unsuccessful. I hoped that I could gain your trust."

"Ha. You did. I got into your car without a second thought. I think it was when you cried in my studio. And then that wicked cat sat in your lap. I should have known better."

"Just give it back and it will all be over."

"You guarantee that, do you?"

"Of course. I don't want to kill you, I never wanted to kill anyone."

"Is it necessary for me to wear this thing over my head? I do not know where I am, and I already know who you are. What point does it serve?" She heard a hollow clumping noise. Someone was leaving. Then, after a silent moment, the scarf was untied and lifted from her eyes. She was in a small room inside a big room, a space like a stall, or a storage area. There was straw on the floor and rusted things hanging from rusted nails along one wall. The barn boards were loosely fitted and thin shafts of light entered from behind and above. She was tied to a wooden chair. Lorna was standing in front of her. "Why did Sergei have to leave? I already know what he looks like." Lorna didn't answer. "Oh, of course. How silly of me. It *wasn't* Sergei."

It took Adele just a few seconds to pop the lock. "Smooth," Stacy said.

"Shit, I could open one of these with a dirty look. Can't be much worth stealing." The door swung open. The place was bare. "Or much of anything."

Stacy stepped into the place. "Definitely cleared out."

They split up, made a search of outer office, inner office, washroom, closet, and came together in the middle of the main room. "Gonzo," said Adele. "Totally. Last time *I* moved I left enough crap behind the Three Stooges could've tracked me down. What's next?"

"House."

"I'll need directions."

It was Constable Charles Maitland who had spotted Anya Zubrovskaya getting into a car outside the bus station. He had waved to her but she hadn't seen him, and as he was busy writing a ticket for a car with one wheel on the curb in a well-marked no-parking zone, he hadn't waved a second time. When he learned that the Chief was concerned about Anya's whereabouts, he reported in that he'd spotted her driving away but was unable to furnish a plate number. These facts nagged at him all through his lunch break until he remembered the couple whose car he'd cited for the lousy and illegal parking job crossed the street to yell at him for sticking the ticket under their wiper blade. They claimed that they'd only been there for a few minutes while seeing the wife's parents off. By that time Maitland had already written the ticket and couldn't do anything about it. He did say that they had the option of appealing the citation in traffic court, a suggestion that was met with overt hostility. It was while mulling over these events that it occurred to him that the couple in question, a Mr. and Mrs. Amos Wallace, had been taking pictures of Mrs. Wallace's parents prior to their departure and that the parents were posed with their backs to the street. Constable Maitland further remembered that at the same moment the pictures were being taken, Anya Zubrovskaya was getting into a dark blue Chevy Malibu and driving away. There was a chance, a slim chance to be sure, but a chance nonetheless that the Wallaces had a picture of the car in question.

They left her alone for a while. What did they expect her to do? Lose heart? If she had any hope of getting out of this, it rested on her ability to hold fast. She had no doubt they would kill her when they were finished with her. What else could they do? She knew their faces, some of them anyway, they would need to get away somehow, to somewhere. They couldn't afford to keep her alive. They must be desperate. Something must have happened to force this. Well, of course, *I* forced it, did I not? But they forced it, too. Maybe none of us had a choice in the matter. No choice from the time Viktor bought his suitcase of silk shirts and expensive cologne. From that moment on, the die was cast, and all the players were pawns pushed around a board. Vysotsky, Romanenko, Kolmogorov, Kapitsa — they all paid for knowing Chernenko and what he had stolen. It is quite possible they would have died anyway, even if they had not lost his treasure. Just knowing about it might have sealed their fates. Men like

Konstantin Chernenko did not value any lives but their own. So who would care about the little lives of gypsy smugglers caught in a misadventure? Not him. And after he was dead? Not anyone who followed him. How many people had been on the trail over the years? Whoever Lorna Ruth was, she was just the last in a long line of corrupt officials, outright thieves, opportunists. And for what? Was it really worth so much?

How did it happen? How did she let Lorna get so close?

Another rainy night. I only drink when it rains. Not precisely true, but true enough, rain had a way of making her feel more acutely all that she had lost — homeland, career, family, friends — all gone. She was not a person to wallow in self-pity, she was stronger than that, but always, deep within, a secret ache like the ghost of a missing limb kept her company. And on rainy nights it called to her more insistently. The only way to dull the pain was ... well, what else?

The Rose, a lounge attached to the big family restaurant in the West Mall, not far from the hospital. It was almost exactly six months ago. That afternoon, while showing her students a *tour en l'air*, a girl dropped her three-ring binder and in a desperate attempt to pick it up, the unfortunate child kicked it with her toe, sending it sliding across the wood floor. It came to rest exactly in the wrong place. Anya twisted her ankle so badly upon landing that she was forced to cancel the rest of the class. The student whose binder had caused the accident sobbed and hid behind the piano. Anya laughed and told her not to worry, ballet dancers were always getting sprains, she would be fine in a day or two. One of the students was dispatched to the store for a bag of frozen peas, and then Anya sent them all home.

For two hours she huddled in her corner filled with dread, the bag of frozen peas wrapped in a towel, wrapped around her ankle. Pain she could put up with, but being unable to dance, to even walk, made her quite crazy. It brought back such bad memories.

It took them three hours to get around to her in the emergency ward, but in the end they pronounced it a very bad sprain, nothing more, try to stay off it as much as she could for a few weeks. She knew how to look after sprains, she didn't need the lecture, just the reassurance that she hadn't ruptured something, broken something or torn a ligament. A sprain she could deal with. They bandaged her ankle, gave her a few painkillers and an ugly metal walking stick to lean on.

When she stepped outside the rain had begun to fall, a steady, heavy rain. The taxi company said it would be half an hour at least before they could get to her. She told them not to bother. The little shop in the hospital lobby sold her a cheap umbrella and a magazine and she limped the two blocks to the Rose to drink some vodka and ease her various aches and worries.

And that's when Lorna Ruth came in to sit at the next table, or perhaps she had been there all along, Anya couldn't quite remember.

"What are you drinking? Vodka? Brandy for me, on a night like this, warms my blood. I worry about getting a chill. I'm Lorna Ruth. I'm a doctor. Your leg all right?"

"Just a sprained ankle. I will be fine." She hadn't wanted conversation.

Just a few drinks. Perhaps the rain would slow down and she could limp the three blocks to her apartment without getting soaked. But the woman had kept talking to her. Not asking questions, not prying, just making pleasant conversation about weather, and life in a small town, and how the world was changing, and Anya only half listening, half responding, and somewhere along the way the woman bought her another drink without offering, it just appeared, and perhaps one more, and sometime after that she found herself in her own apartment being put to bed. Maybe it was the painkillers, or the painkillers in combination with the vodka, or there might have been something else in her drink, but whatever the case the woman had, for an hour or two at least, taken control of her life. When she woke up she didn't remember much. It didn't look as though her apartment had been disturbed.

The doctor had left a card beside her telephone.

The next day Lorna Ruth called, just to see how she was doing, she said. She suggested that the combination of painkillers and perhaps one too many vodkas had caused her to pass out. She mentioned that when she was being put to bed she appeared to be having a nightmare. She said she was a psychiatrist, and that if Anya ever felt that she needed someone to talk to, she shouldn't hesitate to call.

And then the dream started coming back, and after a few bad nights she called the only doctor she knew. All she wanted was some sleeping pills. Maybe they would kill the night terrors. Dr. Ruth didn't expect pills to help but she suggested, gently, that perhaps a few sessions talking about what was at the root of her anxieties would do some good.

And so, almost without a conscious decision on her part, Anya began twice-a-week sessions with a psychiatrist who, as it turned out, had been searching for answers of her own.

Breaking into Dr. Ruth's house wasn't as easy. There were double locks front and back and the ground floor windows had burglar-proof latches. Adele was getting ready to kick in the back door, but Stacy told her to hold off for a minute.

"Upstairs. Looks like the bedroom window's open a crack."

"Oh sure. Got your rocket pack handy?"

"Standard equipment." In three easy moves Stacy went from the deck to the railing to the roof of the sunroom, and slid open the bedroom window while hanging by one hand.

"You're in the wrong business," Adele called up from the back lawn. "Could have been a cat burglar."

"It's on my resumé," Stacy said, and disappeared inside. Thirty seconds later she opened the back door. "It's harder to clean out a three-bedroom house in a hurry," Stacy said. "Maybe they left stuff behind."

"I'll flip you for who gets the basement."

"You want it?"

"Hell no. That's where my mother used to stick me when I said 'fuck.'"

"No problem. You get the attic."

"Oh fuck, it's got an attic, *too*?"

Stacy grinned. "Meet you back here."

Adele was happy to find out there was no attic. Attics weren't quite as creepy as cellars, but they did hold a few shitty memories. The upstairs had three bedrooms, two baths. The master bedroom was at the front of the house, overlooking a tree-lined street. The trees were still bare of leaves and the curtains were pulled on all windows on the opposite side. The broadloom bore the imprints of a queen-size bed, two side tables, a loveseat close to the window. The carpet had been recently vacuumed. The closet was bare except for a tangle of discarded wire hangers. They must have had a truck, or one hell of a garbage pickup. The ensuite bathroom was clean. The wastebasket held an empty plastic package for a disposable razor, the medicine cabinet had one bent Q-Tip and a dusting of powder on the bottom shelf. That was it for the happy couple. Didn't look like much action had been going on in there for a while.

The other two bedrooms were small and didn't contain beds. In one of them was an Ikea computer workstation, partially disassembled. Maybe they lost the Allen wrench, I was always doing that. Damn Ikea, anyway. Never could figure out the stupid instructions. Left one behind at my last residence too. The computer cable was neatly coiled on the bottom shelf of the empty bookcase.

The small bathroom was almost as clean as the big one except that they'd left behind the terrycloth toilet seat cover and the medicine cabinet held an empty Dristan squeeze bottle. Adele did a final check. On one of the coat hangers she found a torn piece of what looked to be a baggage claim ticket. That was it for the upstairs.

Stacy called up from the main floor. "Anything?"

"Nada. You?"

"Doesn't look like they were really living here. Not long anyway."

"Okay, I get the kitchen, maybe they left some peanut butter or something."

Kitchens are harder to strip bare; upper and lower cabinets, cutlery drawers, refrigerator, oven, nooks and crannies everywhere. Even better, things fall behind refrigerators and stoves and are never seen again unless someone feels like pulling them away from the wall.

"What the hell are you doing?" The man at the back door was loaded down with a lawn sign, a pail filled with cleaning supplies, a broom, a sponge mop and a vacuum cleaner. He wasn't sure if he wanted to confront Adele or yell for help. "You're not supposed to be in here."

"Are *you* supposed to be in here?"

"Yes, of course I am."

"And who are you?"

"What does it matter who *I* am, who are you?"

Adele showed him her badge. "Adele Moen, Metro Homicide Unit. Hey Stace," she called, "you want to come in here? We've got a visitor." She smiled at the man. "Come on in, stranger. State your business."

"Homicide? Oh Christ. Is there a dead body in here?"

"Haven't found one so far. How about you, Detective Crean?"

Stacy shook her head. "Care to show us some ID, sir?"

"I'm Ben Chiklis. I'm the rental agent. This place was supposed to be vacant."

"Oh, it's vacant all right," Adele said.

"This was a rental?" Stacy gave that some thought. "Explains the lack of a personal touch. How long were the tenants here, sir?"

"They had a year's lease. It's up next month but the woman said she'd be leaving early. I'm just here to check it out, make sure it's in shape to show it. Nothing broken is there?"

"Wish my place was this clean," Adele said. "I was just going to check behind the major appliances when you came in, Ben. Why don't you and Detective Crean have a look around and you can tell her all about the tenants."

Stacy led Mr. Chiklis out of the kitchen and Adele went back to muscling the stove away from the wall. Behind it she found a packet of soy sauce, a crushed fortune cookie and paper-wrapped chopsticks from Long Wok. The fortune said, "You will find true happiness." The refrigerator held one limp leaf of iceberg lettuce draped over the bottom rack. There was no peanut butter. So much for fortune cookies.

"Let me help you with that stuff," said Stacy. She relieved him of the vacuum cleaner, the mop and broom and leaned them against the wall. Chiklis laid the sign on the floor. It read, "For Lease Pilon Realty." Stacy had a look inside the pail. It held Windex, Mr. Clean, Febreeze, a sponge and a wad of cleaning rags. "They made it easy for you Mr. Chiklis. The place is clean."

"That's good," he said. "You never know what you're going to find, y'know?"

"So far we haven't found much of anything. So. What can you tell me about the people who leased the house?"

"Not that much," he said. "She was a medical professional, I believe; the gentleman was in the construction business."

"Did he have his own company?"

"I wasn't the rental agent when they took the place. But I can get you a copy of the rental agreement if you want it. They must have had references. It's an executive-level home, all the amenities, fireplace, hardwood floors . . ."

"Yeah, it's a nice house. But it doesn't look like anyone actually lived here."

"I understand the husband had some problems with the police, but I thought that had been straightened out."

"It was."

"According to his wife, he moved out last Monday or Tuesday. That's when she said she'd be leaving as well."

"You're here pretty quick. She can't have been gone long, either. Did they leave together?"

"I don't know. I got the impression they were separating."

"So how do you come to arrive here so fast? I mean, they've only just cleared out. Here it is Friday and already you're putting a sign out, vacuuming the stairs . . ."

"I came by yesterday morning and saw the moving truck here. It looked like everything was going."

"Were either of them still here?"

"No, just the moving men."

"Do you remember which moving company it was?"

"Oh sure, Dorians. Couple of guys with a big truck. Here in town."

"Did you talk to them?"

"Yeah, for a minute. I talked to John. He's the older brother. Just to make sure they were both gone. I wasn't sure of the situation."

"Right. Did you ask them where the stuff was going?"

"Storage. They have their own lockers."

"Hey, Stace," Adele was calling from the kitchen. "A minute?"

"Right there." She turned back to Mr. Chiklis. "You go ahead Ben, you can start upstairs." She handed him her card. "You find anything at all, you let me know, okay? Crean. Rhymes with brain."

Stacy left Mr. Chiklis to struggle up the stairs with his cleaning supplies and headed for the kitchen. Adele was wedged behind the refrigerator. She was holding up something that looked like a boarding pass. "Bingo," she said.

"What have you got?"

"Not a hundred percent sure. Looks like a Via Rail ticket invoice. Montreal–Oshawa."

"She's gone to Montreal?"

"Looks like . . ." She peered at it closely. "Looks like somebody came *from* Montreal. Yesterday."

Lorna was back.

"I am losing circulation in my hands. Can you not loosen the ropes just a little?"

"Maybe, in a while, if you help me."

"And pretty soon I will have to pee."

"Just give it back and it will all be over."

"Really? Over for *me*, surely. If I help you, you will kill me."

"No one wants to kill you, Anya."

"Well, you may not *want* to, but it seems to me you will have no choice."

"Here is how it could work. You tell me where it is, and then when I have it, and I'm safely on my way, I will phone someone to release you."

"My my, that sounds most unappetizing. You phone someone, whom I have not yet seen, and they will free me? Why would they not just shoot me and be done with it?"

"We are not killers."

"Really. And yet so many have died for that silly thing."

"It's nothing but a burden."

"At this moment it is the only thing keeping me alive."

"I'm trying to keep you from being hurt. I am not the only one in this. There are others who want to use harsher methods."

"Who can blame them? Six months of prying into my brains and you got nowhere. They must be most frustrated."

"You won't like it if they take over."

"Are you not breaking some important doctor's oath? Threatening torture?"

"I don't have any more time for this."

At some point, someone, maybe the doctor herself, gave her a shot of something, presumably something that would make her talk. Truth serum? Is there such a thing? Whatever it was, it filled her head with clouds and hazy images of people long dead or missing. She saw Yuri in her dream. For one brief, perfect moment she saw him, as he was so many years ago, saw him in flight, hanging in the air like a great bird of prey, his head flung back, his long arms spread like wings, immortal. Is that *all* immortality is?, she wondered. Someone's fleeting memory of you, there for just a heartbeat, and then gone forever. And what if any memory would serve as *her* legacy? Who alive could even recall how she was, what she once was capable of?

And the rest? An image of Ludi in a dressing room, bouncing on her long bare toes. How we laughed about her feet sometimes, just the two of us. Mine, so hard and cramped and sore. And hers, so white, so unblemished, so plain and *normal*. How odd, that in this drugged state the clearest image is of someone's bare feet bouncing on a cheap blue rug somewhere. Where? A dressing room. Some small theatre. What does it matter? There's your immortality, Ludi dear, I remember your toes.

Eventually they got tired of her meandering babble and they left her alone for a very long while, left her alone to pee where she sat, they didn't care, left her to grind her wrists raw against the ropes and to rock the wooden chair back and forth. It was evening by now, the shafts of light through the barn wall had slipped lower and lower and then died, leaving her to sit in the gloom.

"You got any frickin' idea what's going on here, partner? I mean, any idea at all?"

"It's complicated, isn't it?"

"*Complicated?* It's a ball of snakes. And just when you think you've got one by the tail the whole thing twists around on you." She was rummaging in Stacy's glove compartment. "Should've taken my car."

"We can stop somewhere."

"No, I don't want to stop somewhere. I want to grab some people by the neck and shake some straight stories out of them. I mean, come *on!* Dilly's the bad guy. His fingerprints are all over this thing. Maybe not his *actual* fingerprints, but you get my drift. So we've got him just about backed into a corner and pow! Some new asshole we aren't even looking at blows him away. Now where's that at?"

Stacy concentrated on her driving for a while. "You sure you don't want to stop for a burger or something?"

"You hungry?"

"I'm confused is what I am. Same as you. I wouldn't mind a minute to talk about things."

"Good. Fine. Anything coming up?" Stacy made a quick right turn into the West Mall shopping centre. They had a choice of an A&W, a Taco Bell, a Pizza Pizza and a Subway. Adele clapped her hands. "Fuck. It's the motherlode."

"Knock yourself out. I'm going into Foodland to get something my body can actually use."

"Whatever."

Adele decided on a Mama Burger, onion rings and a root beer. Stacy came back to the car with two bananas, a bag of almonds and a small carton of orange juice with pulp. They sat in the parking lot with the doors ajar and concentrated on chewing and slurping for a while. After polishing off the first banana and a few almonds, Stacy spoke. "What *don't* we know?"

"For starters, we don't know who shot Dilly O'Grady in the fucking head."

"Has to be someone he knew. Sitting beside him in the car. Somebody he trusted."

"Got a list? Wife? His assistant, Chris, Cam, whatshisname?"

"Cam."

"Him? Why? Fucked his career? What does he care?"

"This was his shot at the big time." Stacy finished the second banana and left the car to find a garbage can.

"Yeah. Drastic though," Adele said. "I'm leaning more to somebody close to the jewel business." She followed Stacy across the lot and tossed her garbage as well. They both stood beside the trash bin. "Yeah, gotta be somebody involved in the Nimchuk thing, or those other Russkies, can't keep them straight. The guy in the park, the beaky one in Montreal, and let's not forget Louie."

"And Louie's kid, Darryl."

"I don't see him getting his act together enough to pull it off."

"Me neither," said Stacy, "but if we're making a list we should put everybody on it we can think of."

"Who else is there?"

"We're back to the doctor."

"But no connection."

"Well, no connection to O'Grady that we know of, but we've got a big connection to the jewels. According to Mr. Toma-shevsky . . ."

"Wow. Are we dealing with some odd ducks on this or what?"

"He says the doctor was sent to Canada to find that big rock. She drops off their radar, winds up in my town where she's been hiding out for at least six months."

"Hiding out and working on our dancer."

"And getting married, too?" Stacy asked.

"Hunh?"

"She shows up in Dockerty, a small town in the middle of nowhere, ostensibly to get close to Anya and, what, she meets this guy, falls in love, gets married? Does that sound plausible?"

"Right, who *is* this guy?"

Stacy had three almonds in the palm of her hand. She held them out to her friend. "Have one. Good for you." Adele took one, Stacy ate the second one, and then without hesitation whipped the last one across the parking lot to bounce with a distinct ping against the side of a dumpster. "That's what *I'd* like to know. Who's this Harold Ruth? The poor guy in the wrong place with the wrong gun in his hand who was treated like crap by the cops and set free because he didn't do anything."

"So after that nobody looks at him again because he's just a poor shmuck who got some crappy treatment." She burped and tossed her root beer cup into the trash can. "Let's get back to the station. I want to talk to Hong and Siffert."

When Constable Maitland inquired of Mr. and Mrs. Wallace if he might look at the pictures they'd taken with their new Sony Cyber-shot that morning, they asked him, more or less politely, to get off their porch. When he explained that it was possible that they had captured an image that could help the police locate a missing woman, they relented, but not until Mr. Wallace had secured Maitland's promise to tear up the parking ticket. There was of course no guarantee that they had anything useful in their little camera, and Maitland knew that he might be stuck paying the ticket out of his own pocket, but he agreed to the bargain provided he could borrow the camera for a few minutes.

Mr. Wallace followed Maitland to his cruiser and watched him transfer the images to his cellphone, and when he gave back the camera, Mr. Wallace (rather smugly Maitland thought) tore the ticket in half and handed it back with a facetious "Have a nice day."

Adele pulled her chair over to Stacy's desk. "Wayne Hong's unavailable. Don't know if he's unavailable to me or to the world, but I caught up to Dick Siffert at his mother-in-law's place. I think they were just sitting down to dinner. He was happy to have an excuse. Says she makes the worst pot roast in the universe."

"Was he okay to talk about Harold?"

"Yeah, says he doesn't give a shit. Nothing's going to happen. Be back on the job Monday. They didn't do anything to the guy. I don't buy it a hundred percent, probably tuned him up a bit, but nobody's heard any talk about a civil suit. In fact nobody's heard anything from the guy since his case got tossed. Says the only reason they held on to him was because he dummied up, said he wanted a lawyer and they could go fuck themselves. That's why they were sure he was good for it."

"They didn't look into him? Background check? Talk to the wife? Like that?"

"Nope. Scooped him, locked him up. Figured he'd give it up if he sat in a room for a while. Then your boss started making noises and they had to send him back here."

"Too bad," Stacy said. "They might have found out a few things."

"Such as?"

"Such as, there's no such person. Harold Ruth, H&R Construction, the marriage, all BS." Stacy, as usual, had copious notes. "He doesn't show up anywhere before last September when he rented that house. Buys a truck, has somebody paint H&R Construction on the doors, but aside from renting some equipment at the Rent-All, I can't find any record that he did any construction work anywhere. No building permits, no tax returns, nothing. The doctor arrives a few weeks after he shows up, sometime in October, rents space in the medical building, but she didn't have much of a practice, either. Their marriage doesn't show up anywhere. She wasn't listed with OHIP, Physicians and Surgeons, nada. Both of them totally bogus."

"Mystery couple."

"And no picture of him to show your tiny admirer."

Orwell spotted them as he came out of his office. He was heading home for an early supper and a theatre date with the entire family, if reports of Diana's visit were accurate. As the two detectives across the room seemed entirely absorbed in what they were doing, he decided to leave them alone. Roy Rawluck gave him a smart salute as Orwell headed for the door.

"Anything pressing that needs my attention, Staff?"

"Everything's under control, Chief," Roy said. "Big night tonight, is it? Her debut?" (He pronounced it *day-boo*.) "I'm a Gilbert and Sullivan man myself. *Pirates of Penzance* and all that."

"Yes," Orwell said. "I hear you've got quite the singing voice when the mood strikes you."

"Back in my school days, of course."

"Sorry I missed it. All right, I'm off."

"Wish her *merde* for me, Chief." He leaned closer, as if imparting a secret. "That's what they say in the theatre."

Orwell was almost at the door when he spotted Constable Maitland climbing in a hurry. "What's up, Charles?" he asked.

"Might have a lead on the car that picked up your ballet dancer, Chief," Maitland said. "Got to check a few things first."

"Things you need me for?"

"I don't know for sure if I've got anything. Might take a while."

"Okay. Crean and Moen are up there. Work with them."

"Yes, sir."

"Keep me in the loop."

"Yes, sir."

Maitland was obviously in a hurry to get moving. Orwell slapped him on the back. "Off you go then." He watched his constable take the rest of the stairs two at a time. Darn. He was tempted to linger a while longer, but he'd probably just get in the way. He reminded himself that he should set his phone to vibrate or whatever it did. Wouldn't want Marvin Gaye going off in the middle of his daughter's big scene. That would be disastrous. He clumped down the stairs, feeling somewhat left out.

"All *right*, Charlie," said Stacy. Three heads were close together peering at the computer screen. "You got it all." The shot of the dark blue Chevy pulling away was beautifully framed between the bright faces of the Wallaces' smiling parents, and at over 1,600 x 1,200 pixels, the resolution was more than high enough to enlarge the small portion they were interested in and get a clear image of the license plate. One of the numbers was partially obscured behind the woman's hand raised in farewell.

"What is that, a two?" Stacy asked.

"Definitely a two," said Maitland.

"I'm with Charlie," Adele said. "That's a two."

Stacy asked, "You want to stay with it, or are you clocking off?"

"I'd like to track it down, if you don't mind."

"Go get 'em, cowboy," Adele said. "We'll be right here scratching our heads and looking stupid."

She was sitting in the near dark, it was after sundown, her eyes had become accustomed to the gloom and she could just make out the post beside the door. There was something jutting out of the post that she wanted to get closer to. Shifting the chair was a slow process, side to side, a centimetre at a time, and how much time did she have to work with? Someone would be back before long, and perhaps not the silky-voiced doctor this time, maybe now they would try harsher persuasion. She had a high tolerance for pain, but there were different sorts of pain and she did not want to be around when they decided that they could not waste any more time.

The chair was old and the glue in the cross members was dry and cracked and whoever tied her up did not know how strong her legs were. By working her knees side to side, back and forth, she was loosening the joints and the front chair legs were splayed, on the point of pulling apart. Not just yet, she cautioned herself — if it collapses now I will be tangled in the middle of the floor far away from where I want to be. Where she wanted to be was closer to the post. In the darkness she could just make it out, a big rusty nail holding an ancient license plate, someone's first car probably.

A centimetre at a time and try not to break the chair before you get there. Now, this part will be critical: tilt back until the front legs are off the floor and your back reaches the post, now pull your legs apart, hard. The snap of splintering wood was louder than she thought it would be, but there was no stopping now. First the cross brace popped loose, and then the front legs fell out. She rocked forward, her ankles were still bound, but the chair legs were lying on the floor and she was standing. She bent her knees and slid the back of the chair up the post until it caught under the nail, then she pushed as hard as she could, thighs burning, shoulders twisting, back and forth, working her hands up the splines until, finally, it slipped out from between her arms. She was free of the chair. Her hands were still tied behind her back, but that was no trick. Lie on her back, roll onto her shoulders, arms under her buttocks and feet. Still a mess with the broken chair legs and ropes around her ankles and her fingers swollen and numb. But those were just details, just a matter of working the knots, one at a time, until her legs were completely free and her hands were in front now where she could work on the knot with the nail head, pushing and pulling. She knew her wrists were bleeding, she could feel the blood running down her forearms inside her sleeves. Not too much of that please, she was weak enough. But the knot finally gave up its last secret and she was free.

Now for a weapon. One of the chair legs, rock hard maple, a hundred years seasoning in a farm kitchen, a good weight, still with a jagged piece of the cross member sticking out of the middle. They would feel it.

She edged out of the small room and into a much larger space. There were soft echoes all around, birds fretting and settling high above, her feet sliding across the rough wood planks. Through a high window in the hayloft above her she could see a star.

"Can't be a two," said Constable Maitland. He looked worried and baffled. "I've tried everything else, but nothing pops up with that make and model Chevy."

"What did you get if it *is* a two?" Adele asked.

"A '98 Honda Civic."

"Where?"

"RR2 Janetville."

"That's just down the road," Stacy said. "Maybe somebody's missing a license plate."

"Worth a shot." Adele turned to Maitland. "You wanna come with, cowboy? Or you gotta get home for supper?"

"I'm in."

"Good man," she said. "I knew you were a go-getter. Let's go get 'em."

The Honda was owned by a Mrs. Brewster who told them her car had been in Crater's Body Shop on Highway 35 for two weeks after some idiot had rear-ended her at a stoplight in Port Perry. The body shop claimed they were waiting on a rear bumper and trunk lid and she was getting fed up with the delay. She didn't think Crater was taking the job seriously.

Crater's Body Shop was three klicks north of Highway 7A on 35. The place was definitely not a hive of activity. Three men were sitting around a hoist discussing the hockey playoffs and how much the Leafs sucked. The man in charge, Les Crater, was slow to heave his bulk vertical. It probably had to do with the extra forty kilos he was packing, mostly around his middle. When he saw Maitland's uniform he tried to suck in his gut.

"What's up?"

Stacy took the lead. "You've got a Honda Civic here belonging to a Mrs. Brewster of Janetville, is that right?"

"Look, if she's got any more complaints you can tell her to take 'em up with her insurance company. They're the ones sitting on their asses."

"That's not our concern, sir. Is the blue Honda outside, the vehicle in question?"

"Yeah, that's it. What about it?"

"Were you aware that it's missing its license plates?"

"Well yeah, so? I had to take the plates off, didn't I? Thing's got crumpled bumpers back and front."

"And do you know where those plates are now?"

"Oh hell, over on the workbench."

"I don't think that's where they are," Stacy said. "Would you mind having a look?"

While Crater checked the workbench and the other two men kept their voices low and their eyes averted, Maitland and Moen took slow strolls around the shop.

"Well, I don't know where the hell they are," Crater said. "They're supposed to be in this drawer."

"Who would have access to the drawer, sir?"

"It isn't locked. Hell, *anybody*. I don't know."

"Hey, Stace?" Adele was waving at her from the far side of the shop. She was standing near a plate glass window looking in at a dust-free room where a Ford pickup was getting a new paint job.

Stacy opened the door and stepped inside.

"Hey, that's dust-free in there," Crater yelled. "Don't go tracking shit in."

"Relax," said Adele. "My partner's been sterilized." She followed Stacy into the room. "*I'm* a bit of a slob though."

The two women walked around the truck. Maitland stayed in the doorway, watching closely. "What are you seeing?" he wanted to know.

"Shitty paintjob, for one thing. I can still make out the letters on the door panel."

"H&R," said Stacy. "That mess on the bottom could say 'Construction.'"

Adele looked toward the door where Crater was trying to see past Constable Maitland. "How much you charge for a shitty paint job these days?" she asked.

"Rush job," Crater said. "Guy's business went tits-up."

"You got the guy's address handy?"

Orwell liked seeing his wife in a dress, not least because she had quite nice legs, but also because she didn't wear a pretty frock that often. (Sundays didn't count; the outfits she wore to her obligatory Lutheran church service might as well have been God's righteous armour.) Being a practical woman who spent a great deal of her time digging holes and repotting seedlings, Erika was most often found in wellingtons and garden gloves. Likewise his daughter Patty, who spent most of her free time mucking out stalls and exercising horses. It was therefore a treat for him to see them both wearing heels and earrings and makeup.

"Lovely, lovely, the pair of you," he said.

"What am I, chopped liver?" Diana wanted to know.

"Forgive me, my dear, I meant the *three* of you."

Diana was leaving earlier than the others to deliver Leda to the theatre. She was standing at the front door, waiting for the star of the evening to make her descent. "Let's move it along, Ms. Bernhardt," she called, "the curtain's going up."

Leda came downstairs looking deeply troubled. "I'm going to lay a big egg," she said.

The four family members in the front hall all chirped reassuring noises — "You'll be fine," "This is your big night," "You'll knock 'em dead," "Don't be silly," or words to that effect since it was hard to separate the various encouragements.

Leda paused two steps from the bottom and gave them all a cheeky grin. "See? Act-*ing*!"

Her audience applauded dutifully. Orwell's pocket sang out.

"Da-ad," Leda pointed at him. "Give me that!"

"It's work," he said.

"I'm setting it to vibrate. If it goes off in the middle of my big scene I'll just die a hideous death right there in front of everybody."

Orwell handed it over and Leda pressed the necessary buttons before handing it back. "Brennan," he said. "Stacy? Where are you?"

"They're at the front gate," Diana said. "Three of them."

Stacy, Adele and Constable Maitland were standing by Stacy's car with the four-ways flashing. Orwell looked them over. "Good evening, Detectives, Constable, what brings you this far south? Nothing dire, I hope."

"We may have located Dr. Ruth-Wisneski or whoever she is," Stacy said.

"Go on."

"She may be in a farmhouse in Yelverton."

"And?"

Adele stepped forward. "And she isn't who she says she is, and her husband isn't who *he* says he is, and they may or may not have kidnapped one of your citizens and we were going to pay them a visit, but we figured we should check with you in case you wanted to call in the OPP."

It was a question worthy of some thought and Orwell took his time thinking it through. "Do we have any evidence of a crime?"

"Got a helluva lot of circumstance," Adele said.

"Nothing that would get Dockerty PD, or OPP, or Metro a warrant?"

"Probably not."

"Nothing that would justify us charging in with lights flashing and weapons drawn?"

"No, Chief," said Stacy.

"So we could characterize this as a 'friendly visit' to satisfy your curiosity, right? One of our citizens is missing and we're mildly concerned about her. If she's been invited out for dinner and an evening of Scrabble or charades then fine, no harm done. Certainly no need to raid the place."

"It'll be a friendly visit, Chief," Stacy said.

"Good. Good. Then you have my blessing. Although I'm not certain it's mine to give, but under the circumstances, and considering that there may be a time factor, I think it will be okay if you should drop by. Politely."

"Wanna come, Chief?" Adele asked.

"As much as I might enjoy the visit I don't think it's appropriate in this situation. You will of course call me forthwith should the status change."

"Of course, Chief," Stacy said.

"Tread lightly now," Orwell said.

Diana and Leda were driving up the lane toward the gate as the police car pulled away. Orwell swung the gate wide for them. He leaned into the passenger side window to give Leda a kiss. "Roy Rawluck says *merde*," he said.

Leda was pumped, all she could do was nod.

The cruiser went in one direction, his two daughters in the other, and Orwell stood by the gate, feeling conflicted about his plans for the evening.

Frogs were singing behind the barn. Hundreds of them. Deep-throated croaking and high-pitched warbling. A night chorus, non-stop, unmusical, but somehow comforting. Life was all around her.

She crept along the side of the barn and crouched in the darkness behind a concrete silo. She was out. Free, or as free as she could be in the middle of nowhere without transportation, or any idea of exactly where in the middle of nowhere she was. The farmhouse was twenty metres or so across a gravel lane. Most of the lights were concentrated in a room at the back. People were moving about inside. A few hundred metres to the left, she could make out lights speeding by left and right. The rate they were travelling in both directions told her it was a highway. The moon was rising. That would be east, or a bit southeast this time of year, that meant the highway was running east-west. That was a start. It meant she was on the south side of the highway, but whether she was north or south of Dockerty she did not know. The bigger question was, how was she going to get there?

What did it matter? Getting away from here was the only important part. So why was she not running? Why was she not taking off across that field, straight for the highway? Flag down a car, get a lift to somewhere, anywhere, phone police, that was the only sensible plan. Why was she still crouching in the shadows looking at the farmhouse? Well, there was the matter of her suitcase in the back of that car, the one with the two nice Chanel suits and the little black Dior and Louie Grova's $5,000 stuck in the toe of a shoe. It would be a shame to leave that behind. But much more than that, there was a deep and inescapable conviction that she had to know who they were. All the years of running and hiding, first from this one, then a different one — if it was ever going to end, she would need to know who was chasing her. The black detective was dead, but it did not end there. That meant that someone had been in control of him, someone who knew what he had done, someone blackmailing him. And they had been doing it for a long time. Perhaps from the beginning. Sergei? She didn't think Sergei had the guts for that. Lorna? Perhaps, but there had been someone else in the room with them, someone who did not speak and did not want to be recognized.

She was still clutching the chair leg with the jagged stub sticking out of the middle. It felt good in her hand. She knew she could use it. She would not hesitate. No more inattention, no more blind trust.

She had not heard any barking all afternoon. That was good. They did not have a dog. People with dogs are rooted. These people were transient, they would not linger. Once they had what they wanted, once she was out of the picture, they would be gone. And she would most likely be buried in the wetland behind the barn with a chorus of frogs to sing her death song.

Someone was coming out of the house. A man with a flashlight. He was striding to the barn door and he was not bringing water or food, he was carrying a rifle. Have they decided to end it, finally?

The man went inside, lights were turned on. She heard the man moving around, cursing, heading for the door. There was almost enough time for him to yell that she was gone before she hit him, hard, behind his head, where the neck meets the skull. He fell like dead weight. She poked him in the kidney, twice. He did not move.

Dead weight is hard to move so she did not drag him far, just back inside the door. She found the ropes they had used on her and she tied his hands behind his back and his ankles tightly together. She checked to make sure he was breathing and then pulled off a shoe and stuffed his mouth with one of his own socks. The rifle was close to where he had fallen. It was tempting to think she could shoot people with it, but she did not know how it worked and the idea was offensive. Better to just bury it under the straw, douse the barn lights, pick up her trusty chair leg and return to her hiding place behind the silo to plan her next move.

They pulled up in front of the gate and looked at the farmhouse. Lights were on in what was likely the kitchen at the rear and in one upstairs window. There were two cars parked outside, one of them was the dark blue Chevy with Mrs. Brewster's license plates, the other was an older model Ford that looked like it had seen better days.

"Drive in? Walk in?" Adele asked.

"Let's leave it parked right here," Stacy said. "Then nobody drives out without the password."

They got out and started down the lane.

"Hey cowboy," Adele said. "Around the other side of the house, cover the back."

"Yo."

Adele's head swung around. "Yo?"

"Sorry. I mean, yes, Detective."

"No, fuck, 'yo' was cool, just wasn't expecting it. Go."

Maitland angled away from them. Stacy and Adele continued past the front of the house. There were lights at the back. They put distance between each other, kept their eyes open. Stacy had a quick look into the Chevy as she walked. Adele signalled her to stop. Someone was coming out of the kitchen. They heard a woman's voice, "Haro! What are you doing?! Haro! Bring her in here!" The woman walked into a patch of light.

"Dr. Ruth!" Stacy called out. "Hi there. Detective Stacy Crean, Dockerty PD. Like to talk to you for a minute."

Lorna Ruth froze for a second, tried to smile. "Oh, hello. What are you doing here?"

"We're looking for Anya Zubrovskaya. We understand the two of you took a drive this afternoon."

"Oh. Yes. We did. She needed a lift." She looked over her shoulder to see Adele behind her, looking into the kitchen.

"Excuse me. What's going on?"

Stacy kept moving forward carefully. "That's what we're trying to find out. Who were you calling to? Who's in the barn? Who is it you wanted them to 'bring out'?"

"This is private property, you know. And you are nowhere near Dockerty, Detective."

"These are simple questions, Dr. Ruth. Or is it Dr. Wisneski?"

"Goodness gracious, Stace. Look who's here! It's my old friend Serge. How you doing, pal?"

Stacy said, "Why don't you take the doctor inside with Mr. Siziva while I check on who might be in the barn?"

"Sure thing, partner. Toss me your cuffs. I only brought one set."

Stacy handed her cuffs to Adele, then crossed the lane, heading for the barn. Halfway there a figure emerged from the shadows carrying something that looked dangerous. Stacy's hand immediately went to the butt of her weapon. Then Anya came into the light.

"Anya, you all right?"

"My favourite detective. Yes, thank you. I am fine. My wrists are bloody and I do not smell very nice, but I am otherwise all right. There is a man tied up inside the barn. I hit him with this."

"Would you mind putting it down now, Anya, please?"

"Oh, of course, I have been clutching it so tight. My hands are not working very well." She needed to use her free hand to pry the chair leg loose. She dropped it on the ground. "The man inside had a rifle. I pushed it under some straw."

"Good. Why don't you come and sit in our car? We'll take care of things from here."

"Yes. That's a good idea. I am a little weary." She began to fall and Stacy caught her before she hit the ground.

Stacy carried Anya into the kitchen and got her seated, got her a glass of water, had a look at her bleeding wrists. Adele was keeping her eyes on Dr. Ruth and Sergei who were sitting with their backs to each other. Whenever either one opened their mouth to speak, Adele told them, "Shut the fuck up!"

"There's a man tied up in the barn I should check on," Stacy said. "And a rifle somewhere."

"Go ahead, partner," said Adele. "We're all just going to sit here quietly and wait for a bus to take all these assholes to the slammer."

"Detectives!" Constable Maitland was coming through the door holding a man by the arm. "This guy was trying to slip out the back. He wasn't running very fast."

"Way to go, cowboy," Adele said. "Who have we here?" Charlie pushed the man into the room and Adele slapped both hands to her face in complete surprise. "Holy fuck!" she said. "Marty!" She shook her head. "In a bazillion years I wasn't expecting you, and that's a fucking fact."

Martin Grova shrugged. "I have nothing to do with these people."

"That's okay Marty. I'll make sure you get your own cell."

When it came to theatre, Orwell tended to favour sung drama such as *Madame Butterfly* or *The Music Man*, but he granted that Thornton Wilder's old chestnut *Our Town* was a relatively painless theatrical affair, folksy, mildly amusing, and proceeding without flubs, miscues or undue coughing from the audience. When the curtain fell and the applause died down, the crowd heading for the lobby appeared to be in a uniformly good mood.

Orwell and family spent the first few minutes fielding compliments about the impressive stage presence of the youngest member of the Brennan clan.

"She's great, isn't she?" Diana was proud of her kid sister.

"Her voice carries very well," said Erika.

Sam Abrams was easing his way in their direction through the crowded lobby. "Mrs. Brennan," he said, nodding politely. "Chief. And ..." he did an elegant quarter turn, "... the new law partner of the redoubtable Georgie Rhem, Diana Daily." His bow was courtly.

"Hello, Sam," she said. "It's been a while."

"Not a bad show, don't you think? Leda's very good."

"I hear they might take it to Peterborough in a couple of weeks," Sam said.

"Leda on tour," Diana laughed. "Watch out, world."

"I need some air," Orwell said.

Erika looked over her shoulder as she and Orwell made their way to the exit. Sam and Diana were chatting comfortably. "He's married?" she asked.

"Sam? To the paper, maybe."

"She likes him."

"He's a nice fellow."

There were small groups of people on the sidewalk, a few clouds of smoke. Mayor Donna Lee Bricknell was coming toward them.

"Good evening, Chief. Mrs. Brennan. How nice to see you." She motioned Orwell to stand a bit closer. "By the way," she said. "I was speaking with a friend of mine on the Newry Township Acreage Preservation Assembly. Your petition for a severance should go through without any problem."

"Well now," Orwell said. "That is good news, Madam Mayor. I was sure I'd be going there hat in hand."

"These things can usually be accomplished smoothly, when we all work together." The *Register*'s ace photographer, Kathy somebody, was pointing a camera in their direction. "One hand washes the other, as they say," said Donna Lee. "Now, let's have one of those big Orwell Brennan smiles."

Orwell bent his knees slightly and smiled at his friend, the Mayor of Dockerty.

Sam and Diana passed by. "We're going across the street for a quick coffee," she said.

Orwell watched them cross the street, Diana in her high heels, Sam holding her elbow. "She giggled," he said. "I distinctly heard a giggle."

"Don't you interfere," Erika said.

"Wouldn't think of it," he said. His pocket began to vibrate.

Thirteen

April

Orwell Brennan was not by nature a whimsical man, but April 1st was for him a High Holiday. He considered April Fool's Day an appropriate date on which to begin a baseball season, since it was the one day a year that fans could be sure their team had a legitimate shot at winning the World Series. In most cases this hope would either be dashed or severely pummelled before the month was out, but for this brief moment at least, universal optimism was in the air.

The date was also a gentle reminder that however carefully he dealt with life, and with whatever attention to detail, the ultimate resolution of events would forever be outside his forecast or control. A clear case in point was the matter of the missing Russian ruby, a situation so complicated that the Blue Jays would be nicely settling into their yearly battle for third place in the tough American League East before even the first of the principal players made a court appearance.

Orwell was sincerely grateful that most, if not all, of the various crimes, had taken place far outside his purview, and that his personal involvement in the laborious untangling of personalities and circumstances was minimal. Stacy Crean was making frequent trips into the city for identifications, interviews, statements, depositions and discoveries and she provided him with regular reports, which occasionally made sense of what was going on, but, he had to admit, often confused the hell out of him.

First there was the question of exactly how many crimes Dylan O'Grady had been personally responsible for. Since the accused was conveniently (or *inconveniently*, depending on one's point of view) dead, the Crown was having a tough time assigning blame and framing charges to bring against the still-living participants. It appeared that O'Grady was the most *likely* murderer of one Ludmilla Dolgushin in Montreal some twenty-nine years previous, the *probable* murderer of one Vassili Abramov, eight years in the past, the *presumable* killer of one Viktor Nimchuk, in March, and at least *partly* responsible for the demise of one Louis Grova, some days later. The allocation of responsibility in these separate but obviously connected deaths was of serious concern. If a strong case could be made by a defence team that O'Grady was in all instances the *lone* culprit, then pending cases concerning Lorena Wisneski (a.k.a. Lorna Ruth), Haro Ruta (a.k.a. Harold Ruth), Sergei Siziva, Yevgeni Grenkov and Martin Grova would be greatly simplified. There was, alas, the matter of Dylan O'Grady's own death, for which he quite obviously was *not* guilty. While the Crown had a wealth of circumstantial evidence and theory, placing any *one* of the suspects definitively inside O'Grady's car on the night he sustained *two* gunshot wounds to the head, was proving to be very difficult. They were convinced that it had to be one of the principal players, but which one?

Framing conspiracy charges against the six was also going to be hard, since it appeared that in many cases they had acted independently and often at cross purposes. It seemed likely that Martin Grova, in concert with his brother Louis, had been blackmailing Dylan O'Grady by threatening to release proof that he had murdered Ludmilla Dolgushin long ago. Martin Grova was refusing to release whatever proof he was holding until he had secured a deal from the Crown that he would not be charged with anything at all. Lorena Wisneski maintained that she had never even *heard* of Martin Grova until he had contacted her following his brother's death. The Crown believed their connection went further back than that, but were still trying to piece together when, and how, they were introduced. It was possible that Sergei Siziva had brought them together, but Sergei maintained that he had been acting alone and perfectly within the law for many years on behalf of the Soviet (and eventually Russian) government to effect the return of a national treasure known to have been in the possession of members of a ballet company who defected in 1981.

The eventual allocation of blame and disposition of the various cases being cobbled together by the Crown in Toronto would, in the fullness of time, reach some kind of resolution, he knew, perhaps in six months, or longer, it didn't much matter. The only case that had directly impacted the town and its citizens was the odd and coincidental (and no doubt for all miscreants involved, *inconvenient*) murder of Toronto Homicide Detective Paul Delisle, and in that instance Orwell Brennan could point with a measure of pride to how well his force had resolved the matter. Edwin Kewell was convicted of second-degree murder in the death of Paul Delisle. He was sentenced to life, which would likely mean he'd be out in fifteen years. Doreen informed Mr. Kewell that under no circumstances would she be waiting for him.

That his daughter, Diana, had rather efficiently effected the freedom of a man who turned out at a later date to be part of an international and highly publicized (alleged) criminal conspiracy, was a topic of much entertainment value around the Brennan dinner table for much of April. Through it all, Diana maintained her sense of humour and bore the various japes and gibes with good grace. She wasn't in the least abashed, but she was a bit testy on the matter of Harold Ruth's bill, which might go unpaid for some time.

Anya Zubrovskaya, the only one of the alleged smugglers still alive, was initially considered by the Crown to be an invaluable asset in building their cases, but ultimately it became clear that she would be no help at all. Her sole concern, it seemed, was that Dylan O'Grady be posthumously convicted of the murder of her dear friend Ludmilla Dolgushin. Beyond that she had no interest. She maintained that since the disappearance of her friend, she had been on the run from people who were trying to kill her. People who were trying to obliterate any trace of the initial theft of Empress Feodorovna's priceless crucifix, since it pointed directly to still-living persons high up in the Russian government. As to the centrepiece of the crucifix, the fabled "Sacred Ember," Ms. Zubrovskaya maintained (an opinion supported by many in the gemstone world) that the ruby was a fake all along, and that the real one had disappeared long ago when the freshly triumphant Communists sold off a fortune in treasures looted from the assassinated Tsar Nicolas and family. Sotheby's was still going through their records and so far hadn't turned up a specific reference to the Ember, but it was quite clear that Stalin and friends had sold enough treasure to finance their Revolution and provide them with a few good meals besides.

A positive development was the complete exoneration of Detective Paul Delisle and a posthumous commendation for his invaluable contribution to the investigation. It was determined that his revolver had been stolen by Dr. Ruth on the night he was killed, and that the gun in question had been subsequently stolen by someone, probably Yevgeni Grenkov during a break-in of the doctor's offices and returned to Detective Adele Moen by Sergei Siziva. The doctor denied having anything to do with the theft of Delisle's gun. Nonetheless, any question that Detective Delisle was involved in a crime was dismissed, his pension and insurance were secure and his picture went up on a number of walls of Fallen Heroes.

This made Adele Moen very happy. On Orwell's recommendation she had secured the services of Rhem & Dailey to establish a trust fund and expense account for Danielle Delisle, which would be solid, protected and probably enough to put her through university and give her a solid start in life. While it was also necessary to maintain regular support payments to the ex–Mrs. Delisle, these would cease upon Danielle's eighteenth birthday.

Rather than go through the horror of moving, selling or disposing of everything in Paul Delisle's apartment, Adele, with Danielle's total blessing, simply sold off or gave away the contents of her own sparse and underfurnished apartment and moved into the place. She felt comfortable there, surrounded by Paul's stuff, the record collection, sound system, furniture, memories. It wasn't bad. Some nights it was a little sad when the music and the wine got to her, but mostly it was a comfort.

It was clear that the trials would be lengthy, and in some cases at least, avoided entirely by the possible deportations of Siziva, Wisneski and Ruta, although it had yet to be determined exactly to what country Haro Ruta belonged. Grova and Grenkov were both Canadian citizens and, in all probability, not involved with each other. Grenkov was free, pending developments. It was doubtful that he would be charged with anything. He was still considering a civil suit against Stacy Crean for grievous assault, but it was highly doubtful that would even be considered. He was advised to leave the matter alone and to be more careful in his choice of associates.

Martin Grova, on the other hand, was believed by many to have been the driving force behind subsequent developments, but as yet there was nothing substantial they could pin on him. His contention that the "old diamonds" in the crucifix were more trouble than they were worth and that he had refused to touch them was dubious to say the least. According to Sergei Siziva, Martin Grova had taken possession of, and sold at great profit, over one hundred and fifty carats of high quality stones. This information, however, was entirely hearsay, since it was supposedly passed on to Sergei by the dead Louie Grova and as such, worthless as evidence. Martin Grova maintained that he had never touched the diamonds, had encouraged (nothing more) Dylan O'Grady to search hard for the four Kashmiri sapphires, but that he had never been presented with even one. He, too, believed that the ruby everyone was interested in was a fake and of no interest to him whatsoever. And he still refused to help the police in their investigation of Ludmilla's murder until he was given a complete discharge. It seemed likely that he would get his wish.

Mikhael Tomashevsky became quite a familiar figure in the Toronto courts. As a recognized expert in all matters pertaining to missing treasures and specifically the crucifix once in the possession of the Dowager Empress Feodorovna, he gave testimony on many occasions. He also expended a great deal of effort lobbying for the return of the three Kashmiri sapphires known to exist, one of which had to be somewhat forcibly removed from the finger of Dylan O'Grady's wife, an event that was recorded by some enterprising teen on a cellphone camera and subsequently went viral on YouTube.

The fourth sapphire was still missing. Darryl Kamen, heir to Louie Grova's pawnshop and collectibles, was (with the help of law enforcement and Canada Revenue Agency) still searching for it. Hopes were not high.

Closer to home, Donna Lee Bricknell was reelected Mayor of Dockerty. The vote wasn't even close. Gregg Lyman and his lovely wife, Cheryl, moved back to Port Colborne to reassess their plans for his political future. Orwell and Erika secured, without difficulty, the severance of ten acres of the "Brennan Estate" to give to his daughter and son-in-law as a wedding

present. Patty Brennan and Gary Blomquist loosely set a date
for their wedding, sometime in June, and were now discussing,
at length, the details of the service. Gary, a Quaker, explained
to the Brennans that weddings were entirely simple affairs at
the Meeting House, with no rings exchanged, no ministers
involved and merely a public declaration of their desire to
be married. Erika was hoping to persuade Patty to at least
participate in a second, more celebratory service with cake and
perhaps some music. Negotiations were ongoing. Diana took
an apartment in Dockerty. She seemed to be happy working
alongside Georgie Rhem and seeing Sam Abrams socially. Leda
Brennan was considering a career in the theatre. She was also
considering careers in art and literature, and was determined
to save the planet. Her budding romance with the young man
named Peter dissipated when he moved to Toronto to try his
luck as a standup comic.

RandyVogt turned in his papers and retired from the Dockerty
PD to take a private security job in Toronto. This left Emmett
Paynter with an odd number of investigators. For the foreseeable
future, Stacy Crean would be able to resume her role as utility
detective, a situation she embraced happily. Any thoughts she
might be harbouring about moving to Toronto to become a big
city detective were, at least for the time being, placed on hold. Joe
Greenway, her wandering fishing-guide boyfriend returned from
a lengthy sojourn in B.C., to find the rowan trees in Stacy's front
yard well established, and the woman herself happy to see him.

Stacey Crean, dedicated investigator that she was, dropped in on
Anya Zubrovskaya often. There were many questions that she felt
needed answers. But while Anya contributed what she could to
unravelling the story, all she really cared about was the sad fate of
her friend Ludmilla. She had some sympathy for Vassili Abramov,
whom she believed had been so in love with Ludmilla that he
kept poking and snooping until he tracked down the identity of

the mysterious "big black musician." It was too bad for him the musician turned out to be a murderous policeman.

Anya was also visited, at least once, by Mikhael Tomashevsky, who told her, "The government of Russia would be prepared to pay a reward, a finder's fee if you like, to the person who could help with the return of the Ember. No questions asked."

Anya found that an interesting idea. "Really? Yes, I suppose, considering how it wound up lost in the first place. They might not care to have the full story come out."

"The finder's fee would be quite substantial."

"And discreet?"

"Of course," he said. "A person could perhaps have enough money to start a new life. Without always looking over their shoulder."

"There is that."

He gave her his card. "If you should hear of anyone . . ."

"Yes, if I should hear of anyone."

It was possible that Mikhael wasn't convinced that the ruby in question was a fake at all.

Anya Zubrovskaya had no intention of returning the ruby. She had no need for riches. She did not need much to live. A little school, a small apartment, a promising student now and then. What else was there for her now? Mrs. Lytton had offered her a teaching position in the new arts centre, if it ever got built, or maybe she could go back to Russia, they might welcome her, it would be nice to speak her own language again. Who knows? The rest of Louie Grova's money might make a good start to a travel fund. But for now she was content to live her quiet life in her quiet town without too much fear, and with fewer and fewer nightmares as time went by.

She would keep the ruby. It was safe, hanging in plain sight on the wall of her little studio, surrounded by a few framed photographs, safe inside the toe of a battered pink dancing shoe, protected by the scrawled signature of Yuri Soloviev, the greatest dancer she had ever known.

The cat was on the fire escape. At his feet was the black-feathered carcass of a crow.

"A gift? I am honoured. You have outdone yourself. Crows are not easy to catch. He was either very stupid, or you are very smart. Which is it? I will go with the latter. Are you coming in? The dead thing can stay outside. If that is all right with you."

She opened the window to let the cat inside. Crows were cawing above her, but she didn't care. They were just birds, and she had an assassin of her own.

Author's Note

For those who care about such things:

Although certain organizations familiar to Canadian readers are referred to in the story, the people mentioned are fictional and their involvement in those organizations is imaginary.